PRAISE FOR DIANNE EMLEY
AND HER NOVELS

THE DEEPEST CUT

"Emley's solid police procedural offers intriguing insights into a killer's mind, with a few unexpected plot twists."
—*Lansing State Journal*

"Emley saves the best for last in this chilling conclusion to her trilogy. Relentless suspense, compelling characters, and vivid descriptions of Emley's native Pasadena make this a supremely satisfying read."
—*Booklist*

"[Dianne Emley] captures the unpredictable alchemy of human relationships. . . . A fascinating look at the bizarre bond between a serial killer and one of his intended victims."
—*The Oak Ridge Observer*

"A thriller that will keep you reading far into the night."
—BookLoons

"[Captivates] from the first scene and [doesn't] let go."

"Filled with . . . ne sequel that stands alon . . . thriller."

"The tone and pacing is just right in this dark novel."
—*Library Journal*

CUT TO THE QUICK

"*Cut to the Quick*'s razor-sharp plot and lightning-fast pace kept me on the edge of my chair from the first page to the last. Add Dianne Emley to your list of must-reads—this is one not-to-be-missed thriller writer."
—MARIAH STEWART

"Dianne Emley sets a cracking pace in this crime thriller, a follow-up novel to her blistering debut, *The First Cut*."
—*The Sunday Mail*

"Compelling . . . Readers will look forward to seeing more of this edgy, unpredictable heroine."
—*Publishers Weekly*

"A taut, suspenseful thriller that will leave readers eager for more."
—Fresh Fiction

"This pulse-pounding sequel to *The First Cut* is packed with even more relentless suspense and vivid characterizations."
—*Northern Daily Leader*

THE FIRST CUT

"A great read . . . *The First Cut* should immediately establish Dianne Emley in the front ranks of thriller writers."
—MICHAEL CONNELLY

"Stunningly good! Hurtles the reader down a razor's edge of suspense to the final, shattering end."
—LISA GARDNER

"Emley is a writer to watch."
—*Tucson Citizen*

"Gritty, intense, and hard-edged, *The First Cut* is first rate."
—TESS GERRITSEN

"Action-packed, with plenty of suspense and enough twists and turns to keep the reader guessing long into the night."
—LISA JACKSON

"An edge-of-your-seat plot . . . nicely developed characters and genuine suspense elevate this impressive crime debut."
—*Kirkus Reviews*

"Emley's thrilling debut novel has all the makings of what promises to be a captivating and enduring series. Filled with a hearty dose of the police procedural, a slight teasing of possible romance, and characters that appeal, Emley has created a solid foundation for what's to come, and one that will leave readers eager for its arrival."
—New Mystery Reader

BY DIANNE EMLEY

The First Cut
Cut to the Quick
Love Kills

DIANNE EMLEY

THE DEEPEST CUT

A NOVEL

BALLANTINE BOOKS • NEW YORK

The Deepest Cut is a work of fiction. Names, characters, places, and incidents are the products of the author's imagination or are used fictitiously. Any resemblance to actual events, locales, or persons, living or dead, is entirely coincidental.

2010 Ballantine Books Mass Market Edition

Published in the United States by Ballantine Books, an imprint of The Random House Publishing Group, a division of Random House, Inc., New York.

BALLANTINE and colophon are registered trademarks of Random House, Inc.

Originally published in hardcover in the United States by Ballantine Books, an imprint of The Random House Publishing Group, a division of Random House, Inc., in 2009.

This book contains an excerpt from the forthcoming book *Love Kills* by Dianne Emley. This excerpt has been set for this edition only and may not reflect the final content of the forthcoming edition.

ISBN 978-0-345-49953-0

Cover design: Jem Buthcher

Printed in the United States of America

www.ballantinebooks.com

9 8 7 6 5 4 3 2 1

For
Linda Marrow
and Dana Isaacson
My brilliant editors who light the path

ACKNOWLEDGMENTS

Thank you, Linda Marrow and Dana Isaacson. I'm awed by your superb editorial instincts. Special thanks to Junessa Viloria for her valuable comments about the manuscript and assistance with so many things. Kate Collins also made important contributions to the book.

I'm grateful for the continued support and enthusiasm of the Ballantine team: Gina Centrello, Elizabeth McGuire, Kim Hovey, Scott Shannon, Rachel Kind, and Lisa Barnes.

My agent, Robin Rue at Writer's House, provided much-appreciated wisdom and hand-holding. Thanks also to Beth Miller.

While I write about many actual locations (used fictitiously), some are the products of my imagination. You won't find the city of Colina Vista among the San Gabriel Valley foothill cities. Its police department is fictional. I've also made up several streets in Pasadena, California, and neighboring cities where evil acts take place.

Although this is a work of fiction, the book has benefited from the kind assistance of law-and-order professionals. Any errors in policy or procedure are mine.

Thanks always to the Pasadena Police Department. I'm especially grateful to Lieutenant Lisa Perrine for being so generous with her time and to Officer Kim Smith for her help.

Retired police captain Steve Davidson was again immensely helpful.

Karla Kerlin, judge, Los Angeles Superior Court, and Colleen Crommett, deputy district attorney, Orange County, gave advice about criminal law.

Gerald Petievich, author, pal, and former Secret Service agent, helpfully batted around plot points.

Author and pal Eric Stone and book club buddy Roseanne Wong offered insight into Chinese culture.

My cousin Bill Tata of Imagine Design does a fantastic job of designing and maintaining my website: dianneemley.com.

My cousin Robin Hayhurst gave me a local's perspective of Montaña de Oro, one of the most exquisite places on earth.

I'm blessed with terrific friends. Some contributed to the manuscript. All endured bouts of writer craziness. Thank you: Jayne Anderson, Rosemary Durant, Ann Escue, Mary Goss, Katherine Johnson, Toni Johnston, Dottie Lopez, Leslie Pape, and Debra Shatford.

And last but never least, thanks to my wonderful husband, Charlie, my safety net, my love, who can now fully embrace what it means to be married to a crime novelist.

They were separate people with separate destinies. Why should they seek to each lay violent hand of claim on the other?

—D. H. LAWRENCE, *The Rainbow*

ONE

This was his chance to get it right. He was nervous but confident. This was good. No . . . great. Perfect. A fresh start. A new day. The first time had been a bloody mess. Of course, it counted. It had been *everything*—which was part of the problem. He'd been careless. He wouldn't do that again. Because he'd learned that killing is never as easy as you hope, but it's sooo worth taking the time and trouble to do it with style. Practice makes perfect. Here he was and here she was. Take two.

Looking up at California State Park Ranger Marilu Feathers, he let a smile tickle his lips and said, "Where there's smoke, there's fire."

He pulled one corner of his mouth higher than the other, crafting what was intended to be a rakish grin. She'd know that he knew it was a corny old saying, and that would show his mastery of the situation. While he was at it, he arched an eyebrow, aiming to look clever, disarming, maybe even handsome. He was rewarded. She smiled. She was flirting with him.

In no mood, Feathers smirked. It was Christmas Eve and this clown was about to make her late to dinner at her parents' house with her brother and his family. Her young niece and nephew wouldn't care, but her sister-in-law would find it an opportunity to remind single, childless, thirty-something Feathers about the importance of schedules for children.

She'd taken her horse instead of the Jeep to do one last patrol of the nearly deserted sandspit, ringing in the holiday and a well-earned break with a sunset gallop. And now this.

The stranger looked Feathers over with a measure of scrutiny and delight, as if examining a long-sought-after rare book found by chance at a yard sale. He had watched in awe from the moment she'd appeared with Gypsy, her big roan mare, from the pass-through between the dunes and had begun galloping across the sand. She scattered spindly-legged sandpipers and inky black cormorants feeding in the surf while brown pelicans and Western gulls circled above, the gulls calling, "*Kuk, kuk, kuk.*"

He had known she'd take Gypsy from the stable behind the dunes, would go down the Jeep path onto the spit, and would turn right, toward the Rock. He had known exactly where to position himself. She often rode at sunset, when the sandspit was quiet, but not always. He'd spent disappointing hours, primed, waiting, only to return home unfulfilled. While frustrating, waiting taught him discipline, which he knew he sorely needed. Now, at last, his *reward*. His heart had thrilled with each beat of the horse's hooves upon the sand.

He felt his emotions running away with him and— just as Feathers had reined in her horse—he seized command of himself. His reward was near. His memories of this moment would keep it alive and fresh forever. All he had to do was hold on. *Hold on.*

Feathers pulled up her horse beside the makeshift barrier and managed an insincere "Good evening, sir," and then the admonishment. "You're in the snowy plover restricted habitat. You can't be here, let alone have a campfire."

He knew that. Who could miss the miles of yellow nylon rope on four-foot metal stakes marked with signs, some drawn by schoolchildren, "Share the beach!" "We love the snowy plover!" He thought the stupid bird deserved to go extinct, but he knew that if she could Ranger Feathers would sit on their nests—mere shallows in the sand, the lazy birds. He'd not only purposefully gone into the restricted habitat, he'd built a fire with driftwood. Brilliant. Did he know how to push her buttons, or what?

Near him now, she was a sight to behold, tall in the saddle, her dun-colored uniform fitting loosely on her big-boned, lean frame. He was beguiled by her uniform, her round, flat-brimmed Ranger Stetson hat, her gun, and her badge. Her plain face so easily adopted that no-nonsense bearing. He'd seen her laugh, but soon after, her face would reassume that stern countenance, that *command presence* coveted by cops. It came naturally to Feathers. She had been born for the job.

He'd told her, "Where there's smoke, there's fire." Rakish grin. Arched eyebrow.

He returned his attention to the marshmallow he was roasting on the end of an opened wire hanger. The next move was hers. He was so excited, he could hardly stand it. *Get a grip, buddy!*

Feathers thought, *What's he doing? Trying to flirt with me?* She guessed he was one of the college kids that abounded in Morro Bay and Los Osos, the relaxed beach cities adjacent to the sprawling state park. A state university was nearby, and students frequented the park to hike in the jagged coastal mountains or to surf and raise hell on the long stretch of secluded sandy beach reached by foot or horseback via twisting, steep trails that traversed the dunes. Only rangers were allowed to drive there.

She had invested a lot of time over her years at the

park reprimanding, citing, and sometimes arresting the drunken, the loaded, and the pugnacious of all ages. In addition to providing the public information about hiking trails, campsites, local flora and fauna, and the locations of public restrooms, her job was to enforce the law in the park. Those who did not revere this sacred space would feel her iron hand. She was protective of these eight thousand acres. Her corner of paradise. Her mountain of gold.

The young adult visitors were usually in packs, or at least pairs. This jackass was alone, sitting on a cheap, webbed-nylon folding chair. He wore a heavy plaid wool jacket, buttoned to the top, blue jeans, and sand-caked athletic shoes. A wool watchman's cap was pulled low over his ears. She saw no belongings other than the chair, the open bag of marshmallows on the sand near his feet, and the wire hanger. The jacket, though, had deep pockets.

The park was nearly empty. Only a few campsites were occupied. The sandspit was deserted except for this guy. He was burning driftwood, an additional insult to the park. Her park.

"Sir, you're going to have to put out that fire and move out of the restricted area. Now."

"I know, Ranger Feathers." He pulled the golden, softly melting marshmallow from the flames and swung the wire toward Feathers. "Toasted marshmallow?"

The sudden motion startled the horse, and she pranced backward. Gypsy was Feathers's personal horse and unaccustomed to aggressive movements.

"Watch it, pal." Feathers steadied Gypsy, the horse moving so that Morro Rock was behind them. The giant, crown-shaped, long-extinct volcano at the mouth of the bay was silhouetted by the fading winter sun.

She was wearing a brass name tag, but his vision had to be extraordinary if he could read it at that distance in the dim light. She leaned forward and gave the horse a couple of firm pats while eyeballing the stranger.

The watch cap covered his hair and part of his eyebrows. He was seated, but his legs and arms were long. She guessed that standing he would be at least six feet. His clothes were bulky, but his build looked average. His face was ordinary. Not handsome or ugly. No distinguishing scars or marks. It was a blank canvas, brightened only by the way he looked at her: adoring and consuming. It put her in mind of the way her brother played with her infant niece, slobbering kisses over the baby while taunting, "I'm gonna eat you up. *Eat you up.*"

"Didn't mean to scare Gypsy." Tossing off the horse's name was good. He was golden. He could almost see the wheels turning as she sized him up, wondering, "Do I know this guy?" It was all this nondescript, young Caucasian male could do to keep from grinning. He knew how the world saw him. He had learned to use it to his advantage.

His adoring gaze made her wary. It aroused her instincts of danger. He hoped it also appealed to another part of her. She would be unaccustomed to such attention from men. She was a rawboned woman with a lantern jaw, a squat nose, and thin lips framing a gash of a mouth. Calling her handsome would be generous. She wasn't the type of woman who inspired sonnets. But *he* loved her. He could hardly wait to show her how much. He caught his breath, feeling overwhelmed.

Control, he told himself. *Control.*

Christmas always made him emotional.

She asked, "Do I know you?" She searched her mind, grabbing at a memory that stubbornly slipped back into the shadows. "Where have I seen you?"

He pulled the sticky marshmallow from the end of the hanger with his fingers and blew on it before tossing it into his mouth. He chewed with obvious pleasure, letting out a little moan. He stood and stabbed the wire into the sand, where it wobbled back and forth.

He struggled to calm his breath. "Nowhere. Everywhere."

"What's your name?"

He retrieved the wire hanger and intentionally held it by his side in his left hand, farthest from her, in a nonthreatening manner. He ducked beneath the yellow rope and walked a few feet toward the surf. He wrote in the wet, smooth sand.

Feathers cocked her head and squinted at the scrawling. "What does that say?"

He shrugged, chucking the wire away. "Doesn't matter."

"Okay, pal . . ." Feathers reached behind her and pulled a small spade from a loop on the saddle bag. "You're gonna put out that fire and I'm gonna escort you out of the park. Being Christmas Eve, if you cooperate, I won't cite you. If you don't, I'll arrest you and you'll spend the night in jail. Got it?"

"Ranger Feathers, you know about death."

He was standing a few feet away from her and the horse, his hands by his sides. He didn't want to breathe through his mouth, but he couldn't help it. He'd never been more rock hard. He was afraid that the slightest movement would make him explode, which would be awkward.

Control.

"Tell me what you know about death, Ranger Feathers. I want to know. I want to know everything."

She shifted the spade to her left hand and pulled out her two-way.

The call would go to Ranger Dispatch. Budget cuts had made staffing thin. They would probably reach out to the San Luis Obispo County Sheriff's Department. Backup would arrive, but not in enough time.

"Do you wear the pearl necklace?"

The question caught her off guard. She released the radio button.

"Yes, Marilu. *That* necklace. Do you like it?"

"So you're the one who gave it to me."

"That's right."

"Why?"

"You earned it. The heroism you showed the day you brought down Bud Lilly . . . You were judge, jury, and executioner, ridding the world of a worthless creep. That should be honored in a special way."

Finally, she raised Dispatch.

He detected relief in her eyes. A crack in the armor.

She announced her location into the two-way and asked for an assist with a nine-eighteen—a psycho/insane person.

Now.

In a flash, his hand was in and out of his pocket. He aimed the snub-nose .38 at a spot between her eyes as if it were something he did every day, even though it was the first time he'd aimed a gun at a human being, other than at his own reflection in the mirror.

She reacted quickly, but not quickly enough. He fired.

He couldn't believe he'd missed. He looked at his gun as if it had betrayed him.

At the sound of the gun blast, the horse had reared. With one hand, Feathers tried to rein in Gypsy while pulling out her gun with the other. Struggling with the frantic horse, she got off a shot. The horse reeled.

His hand flew to his neck, which stung like crazy. He drew back bloody fingers. He stared at the blood. She'd grazed him. He started to giggle. She'd only grazed him. But the blood . . . And the heat radiating from the long fissure across his skin. It thrilled and calmed him. His hand was steady. It was like magic. He aimed again.

Feathers did too, but this time, his aim was true.

Gypsy took off at full gallop. After fifty yards, mortally wounded Feathers fell from the horse into the surf, scattering the sandpipers and cormorants. The calls from the soaring birds grew more frantic.

Overwhelmed, he dropped to his knees. He tried to keep his eyes open, but the pleasure of release was so sublime, he had to close them as he cried out, his hands clutching the sand.

Still panting and fuzzy-headed with bliss, he pulled himself together to finish his mission. He picked up his beach chair and bag of marshmallows and walked to retrieve Feathers's Ranger Stetson from where it had fallen just within reach of the foamy fingers of the surf. The mare Gypsy, hovering near her fallen master, galloped off at his approach.

He took a long, final look at his prize, Ranger Marilu Feathers, bleeding into the sand. The young man—whom years later Detective Nan Vining would give the nickname T. B. Mann—then turned and walked into the lengthening shadows. The next phase of his life had begun.

A wave washed away his handwriting in the sand.

TWO

*P*asadena police Detective Nan Vining was in her kitchen looking at a paper shopping bag that stood on the floor. She was in a ready position, hands by her sides, fingers twitching, feet shoulder-distance apart, as if the bag and its contents were about to harm her and her daughter. It was too late for that. Still, Vining's instincts overrode logic.

Fourteen-year-old Emily leaned against a counter, arms folded across her chest, head tilted down, peering at the bag from the corners of her eyes. In contrast to her mother, who was all about action, Em was the more introspective member of the household of two.

"Mom, is that the shirt he was wearing when he attacked you?"

Vining exhaled, relaxing a little. Leave it to Em to cut to the quick of the matter. The bag held a garment: a pale yellow, polo-style knit shirt, size large. On its breast was an embroidered logo of a lamb dangling from a ribbon—the insignia of Brooks Brothers. The shirt alone couldn't hurt them. It was ordinary. Nothing that would draw most people's attention. For Vining, however, it was consistent with her memory of the man who had been wearing it when he'd ambushed, stabbed, and almost murdered her. For just over two minutes, he *had* murdered her. Flatlining, she'd been sent on a journey from which she'd yet fully to return. He was not merely a bad man; he was Vining's and Emily's personal bad man. And so they had given him a name: T. B. Mann. *The* Bad Man.

The only thing that did make the shirt extraordinary was the thickly caked dried blood that had saturated the front and trailed down the back. Vining was sure it was her blood. Testing would prove that T. B. Mann had been wearing that shirt when he'd plunged a knife into her neck after first slicing and disabling her gun hand. The incident had happened in June, the previous year. For nearly a year, she'd been on Injured on Duty leave.

Her scars were still pink. There was a diagonal slash across the back of her right hand and a long garish scar on her neck that started behind her left ear and disappeared beneath her shirt collar. That was the one that garnered stares, and helped strangers place her as the cop who'd let herself get ambushed. That cruel judgment held truth. She *had* hesitated during her confrontation with T. B. Mann, and consequently he'd been able to stab her and flee, leaving her for dead. Her body had complied for two minutes. She often felt her mind was still trying to claw its way back from the other side.

Just as spilled blood had created something horrifying out of a mundane shirt, it had also transformed an outwardly mundane human being. There had been nothing remarkable about T. B. Mann apart from the coldness in his eyes. She'd detected the coldness even through the dark brown contact lenses that she'd later assumed he'd been wearing to complete his disguise.

Even as blood poured from her wounds, Vining had sought to get a good look at him, knowing that if she survived, she'd need an accurate description to track him down. She'd also had little choice. After he'd stabbed her, the knife jutting from her neck, he'd tightly held her, like a lover. She'd felt his moist, mint-scented breath on her face as he gazed into her eyes. He was panting, his face flushed, as if they'd been engaged in a sexual act. She could have looked away, but Vining hadn't, thinking those cold eyes might be the last thing she'd ever see.

She knew that he wouldn't take his eyes off her until he was forced to. He had *lived* for that moment, watching the life drain from her. He'd released her when he'd heard her backup arrive, gently letting her slip to the floor, she thought with great regret at not being around to observe her stepping away from this life. Then he'd successfully executed a well-planned escape and was gone.

She had many memories of that day—some clear, some hazy. One that was decidedly clear and as unsubtle as a baseball bat was his erection pressing against her belly. Of course he would get off on his triumph of having ensnared her. That was what defined him. That was what made this ice-eyed nobody into *somebody*. The sick fuck.

Vining vowed to take that from him and more.

She answered her daughter with a fib. "It might be the shirt he was wearing. Testing will show whether that's my blood."

Emily had found the shirt among dirty sheets and towels in a basket on top of the washing machine in the garage. It was nine o'clock on a school night, and she had gone to fold the clothes that she had left in the dryer. Deciding to empty the basket, she saw the shirt when loading the washer.

Vining had cleared the garage, house, and yard, service revolver in hand. Instinct told her this was a low-risk operation. Whoever had left the shirt was long gone. The shirt was a boast. A power play. T. B. Mann didn't *want* to get caught. That was the stuff of fiction. Killers like him loved their craft and planned to keep at it as long as they could.

He was playing with her, inciting fear, keeping her off-kilter, like a terrorist. He couldn't leave her be. Vining was both T. B. Mann's greatest failure and achievement.

Pinching a small corner of the shirt between her thumb and index finger, she'd carried it into the kitchen and deposited it in a paper grocery bag. It was important evidence—the best piece she'd had in a long time. Even though it repulsed her, she had to handle it with respect. Beyond its evidentiary value, its appearance in her garage was important for another reason. It revealed a flaw. It showed that he was as obsessed with her as she was with him. Flaws in a nemesis were good. They could be fatal.

It didn't take a genius to figure out the best ways to get to her. Her home. Her daughter. Just a few days ago, he'd made a veiled threat against Emily. He'd left a note for Vining at L.A. County General Hospital, where she'd put a goofball she was convinced was T. B. Mann's minion, under psychiatric evaluation. The goofball wouldn't speak. Even though he had a talent for drawing, the Pasadena Police couldn't get him to write his name, so they nicknamed him Nitro. T. B. Mann had known she'd return to Nitro at the Big G, again taking advantage of his bland appearance to slip in and out without anyone taking notice. The note he'd left her had been written on a panel card in his usual fountain pen. The jerk favored fine inks and papers. The note read:

Vining, your daughter looks just like you.

She didn't want to admit how well his strategy had worked. It had taken massive self-control for her to quiet her trembling heart and hands and to remain focused. She couldn't afford to let her rage get out of control, to let him goad her into making mistakes, to let him lead her into yet another ambush. She had to steel herself and stay the course, making slow and steady progress, tracking him via a trail of dead female cops and pearl necklaces.

Skein by skein, she wove a tapestry, built a web, one thread leading to another. Some she'd found via solid investigative techniques. Some had been thrown into her lap. She wondered why. Some, she'd broken the law to get, knowingly and with forethought. She'd even lied to her PPD partner, Jim Kissick, and her supervisor, Sergeant Kendra Early, violating both her sworn oath and her own ethics. She hadn't fully plunged into his murky slime pit, but she'd danced along the edge.

But the world was turning, casting light in his direction, chasing shadows into the corners where he lurked. Every clue she tracked down, every victim of his she located, made the light grow brighter. As she circled him, drawing nearer, pulling the noose tighter, she felt him stirring in the shadows, throwing out his own sticky skeins of spider's silk. He wanted her to know that he was lurking outside her window, watching her dance alone. He wanted to dance, too, with her, ultimately dragging her headlong into his stinking morass.

She saw evil as a parasite on good. Without good, evil would not exist. Without her, what would he be?

She'd had a nice life before he'd burst into it. Once he was dead—his violent death was the only suitable end she'd envisioned for him—she could resume her life. Couldn't she?

She wished Kissick were here right now. Wanted his strong, calm presence near her. They were work partners and, recently, much more. She looked at the clock on the microwave oven and wondered what was taking him so long.

The mother of Emily's school friend was also coming

by, to pick up Emily for the night, giving Em a reprieve from this house of horrors. Giving Vining a reprieve from her daughter's questions, for which she had few good answers.

Emily clutched herself tighter. "So T. B. Mann was here, right?" She was a younger version of Vining, nearly as tall, and shared her lanky form, dark hair, pale skin, and deep-set, green-gray eyes.

"I doubt it, sweet pea." Vining ran her fingers through her straight, nearly black hair, which fell past her shoulders. She dug a rubber band out of the odds-and-ends drawer. Using the glass door of the microwave as a mirror, she fashioned her hair into a ponytail. She gave herself a hard look. She was only thirty-four, but she thought she'd aged considerably over the past year. She rubbed the back of her long neck, which was moist with perspiration.

The windows were open, the air-conditioning was off, and the night air was cool. She and Em had been enjoying a quiet evening at home before T. B. Mann had again upended their lives.

"I don't think he would take such a risk, showing up here." Vining was fibbing again. She thought it was exactly the sort of thing he'd do. If T. B. Mann himself hadn't brought the shirt onto her property, maybe he'd sent Nitro, the silent, mysterious, pale, gangly young creep who had literally streaked into their lives a few weeks ago. Vining had temporarily ensnared him in the Big G's psych ward, but he had slipped away and disappeared.

"Why now?"

Vining raised a shoulder and shook her head.

"Mom, something's happening and you're not telling me." Emily's eyes welled with tears. Lately, she was quick to become emotional. A surge of hormones was stealing away Vining's sweet baby girl.

Vining reached toward her daughter. "Em—"

"You've been acting strange, Mom. I know you're hiding something. You used to tell me everything."

"Yes, and that was a mistake." After she'd been injured, Vining had confided in her daughter about her hopes and fears, and her theories about T. B. Mann. She'd been weak to latch on to Em, who was not only the person closest to her, but also the purest soul. While she would never do anything to put her daughter in danger, she'd since put Emily on a need-to-know basis.

"If everything's okay, why do you want me to stay at Aubrey's house tonight?" Emily's gaze burned with indignation. "You always said that T. B. Mann wouldn't come around here. Now everything's changed. I have a right to know, Mom."

Vining closed her eyes. "Em, please . . ."

They heard a car pull up in front, followed by a toot of its horn.

After Vining had loaded Emily into the car and exchanged pleasantries with Aubrey and her mom, she returned to the kitchen.

The house was silent.

She took out tongs from a drawer and used them to take the shirt from the bag. She held it in front of her. There was a lot of blood on it, but she'd left much more on the floor of the kitchen in the house at 835 El Alisal Road.

She had deconstructed the events of her ambush until it was robbed of nearly all its emotional power. One component, the diamond core of rage, had resisted the hammer and chisel. Some things refused to be pounded into oblivion by sheer will.

The veneer of control she'd clung to while Emily was there dropped away. Throwing down the tongs, she grabbed a knife with a six-inch blade—the same size as the one he'd used to stab her. Her rage gained speed, like a runaway train. She grabbed the shirt and marched from the kitchen, through the TV room, and into the living room. Adrenaline made her legs tremble. She flung open the sliding glass door with a bang, sending it shaking in its frame.

Her better angel warned her to calm down. Giving in to her rage was not productive. She was being careless with important evidence. Plus, revealing herself to him like this only played into his sick fantasies. The Magic Eight Ball of her conscience warned: *If you're not careful, he'll win.*

Her dark angel did not heed the warning. This scenario was being played out with greater frequency. Part of her felt she was on the road to ruin. Part of her didn't care.

From her hillside home, the twinkling lights of the hindquarters of Los Angeles were splayed out off her right shoulder, stretching like a giant river to the distant ocean. Wind chimes hanging from a rod above the sliding glass door began to ring vigorously in the still air.

She didn't turn to see what was disturbing them. She knew she was being sent a message from the friendly ghost of murdered LAPD vice officer Frances "Frankie" Lynde. Vining had more than just solved Frankie's murder, she'd meted out justice, yet Frankie's spirit still did not rest. Vining interpreted the pealing wind chimes as a warning. She ignored it.

Grabbing the shirt, she held it in front of her and struggled to stab the fabric with the knife. She couldn't do it. She set the shirt on the railing, pulled the fabric tight with one hand, and stabbed it with the other. She pulled up the shirt, pierced by the knife, and held it like a flag, putting it on display for the illuminated city.

"Do you see me?" she yelled.

Her mind felt bubbly, like her brains had been replaced with champagne.

"Do you hear me?"

Dogs started barking. Lights went on in nearby houses.

She raged on. "See me *now*. Hear me *now*. You're going down. *You are going down!*"

She stabbed the knife with the shirt attached into the wooden railing. The knife wobbled with the force.

Giving a final, fierce look at the nearby dark hills and the lights of the metropolis in the distance, she went inside.

The silence was broken by the tinkling of the terrace wind chimes. The air was still, yet the chimes vigorously rang.

THREE

*J*im Kissick held up the bloody shirt by the shoulders. His expression was grim as he fingered the hole in it. "This goes all the way through, like someone stabbed it or something."

"I did." Vining realized she'd left the knife on the terrace. "Well, I put a knife through it."

He looked at her with those steady hazel eyes and nodded as if it all made perfectly good sense. After a moment, he asked, "Are you okay?"

"Why wouldn't I be?"

She saw him let out a breath, measuring his next comment.

He changed the subject. "You keep your garage door closed, right?"

"Yes," she said. "I watch when it opens and closes to make sure no one comes in. Something I started after the incident." She and Emily had taken to calling T. B. Mann's assault an "incident." Other words were fraught with emotion. "He's good at getting in and out of places without being seen. Em and I were gone for a couple of hours, running errands. I asked the neighbors if anyone saw anything. No one did. He could have worn a uniform, like from the gas company, or even posed as a cop. He wore a disguise at the El Alisal house to look like Dale David, the realtor who was selling the house. He had on a black wig and I'm convinced he wore brown contact lenses. His Brooks Brothers polo shirt was even the same kind that Dale David often wears."

Kissick dropped the gruesome shirt into a brown paper evidence bag he'd brought with him. "Forensics can send it to the county crime lab tomorrow." Setting the bag on a kitchen counter, he walked to the door that led into the garage and went out, clicking on the light switch.

Vining pulled a chair from the dinette set, dropped onto it, and held her head in her hands. She was embarrassed by her outburst on the terrace. She prayed none of her neighbors had heard her. What had gotten into her? Was she losing her mind?

She listened to Kissick's familiar footsteps in his favorite well-worn loafers as his long legs made quick work of the two-car garage. He opened and closed the door of her ten-year-old Jeep Cherokee.

When she heard him return, she wiped away tears of anger and frustration. She tried to calm down, but couldn't grab hold of her emotions. "He was here, Jim. Either him or his buddy, Nitro."

He stood near, not saying anything. She liked his

quiet strength, the way his eyes spoke volumes while he remained silent. His thick, wavy, sandy brown hair was mussed on one side, revealing a shadow of the boy obscured by the man.

She had made it on her own for a long time, needing no one, especially a man. Particularly a man. But now *this* man was in her life. He had been in her work life for several years as her partner. They had been lovers for a brief period two years ago, and now, very recently, were again. She felt she wanted him wholesale, but could not allow herself to give in. She kept him at arm's length for his own protection. She had to protect him from her.

She raised clenched fists. Her rage took flight, like a kite catching the wind. "Jim, he was *here*, on my property. First, he sent Nitro to torment me, but that wasn't enough. He had to get closer. He came *here*, close to Emily. Letting her find that . . . *thing*. He saved that shirt, the asshole. Who knows what else he did with it. And that note he wrote about Emily . . . If he wants to come after me, then come after me. Leave Em out of it. If his goal is to scare me, he's doing a good job, I'll give him that."

"Let's put a patrol car on your house."

"Yeah, maybe, though I don't think he's stupid enough to come back. He wanted to make a point and he made it."

"He was stupid enough to put that shirt in your garage." Kissick squatted down in front of her.

She looked at his good, strong face, which she had only lately allowed herself to love again. "You know what the worst part is? The lying. I tell lies because of him. I lied to Emily about the shirt. She doesn't even know about Nitro, finding him in Old Pasadena with his disgusting drawings. And I've lied to you . . ."

She reached to smooth his errant patch of hair. "It's like he's split me into two people: the old Nan, and someone else whose morals are compromised. Someone like him."

Her face grew pinched with the confession. Kissick had discovered one of her lies by accident, but there was more he didn't know and that she didn't want him to know. Revealing all her secrets would transfer the blackness onto him. She could be fired from the Pasadena Police Department for the things she'd done. Nan didn't want to put Kissick in the position of having to choose between her and the career that he loved so much. Since they'd resumed their relationship, he'd not mentioned pursuing a promotion to sergeant, something he used to talk about a lot. She was already standing in his way.

She went on. "I try to keep my life compartmentalized. I just want to protect the people I love from this monster that's shadowing me, that's changing me in ways I don't like."

She took in a shuddering breath. "I've changed, Jim. I don't like what I'm becoming." Tears again welled in her eyes. She blinked, frowning at the floor.

He raised her chin with his hand. "We'll get through this."

A tear snaked from the corner of her eye. "I can get pumped up and believe that, but there are times when I'm not so sure. I don't know if I'm sure about anything anymore."

He wiped her tear with his fingertip.

She saw the love and concern in his eyes. She had to kiss him. She cupped his cheeks between her palms and he leaned in to meet her. They kissed tenderly. They drew apart, but not completely. He stroked her nose with his.

Anger and despair had already quickened the pace of her breath. Now a different kind of passion roiled her, and him. Their lips again found each other, their kiss more urgent. He moved to his knees. Still sitting in the chair, she let her thighs drop open to accommodate him.

As they kissed, he rubbed his hands down her neck and across her shoulders, easily pulling away the spaghetti straps of the summer dress she'd thrown on. She shrugged her arms from the straps and he pulled the dress to her waist. As he took her breasts into his hands and mouth, she worked the buttons of his shirt. The clothing quickly morphed from a tease to an impediment. She gave up on his shirt and stood, yanking the dress over her head and tossing it aside while he did the same with his shirt, not bothering with the rest of the buttons.

His mouth tore at her silky bikini panties and he started to get to his feet when she pushed him back down.

"Don't you want to go to the bedroom?" he panted.

"No. Here." She hooked her thumbs into the panties' waistband. They were soon off and tossed away.

"Here?" he asked.

She worked at his belt buckle and he didn't protest further.

He kicked off his shoes, struggled out of his khaki pants, and lowered himself to the floor. She followed him there, her hands on his shoulders. She was nude and he wore only brown socks. She straddled him, letting loose a gasp of pleasure, then moans of ecstasy, which were supplanted by a yelp of pain when her knees could no longer take the linoleum floor.

Keeping her astride him, he moved until he was sitting. She wrapped her legs around his back.

Through her slit eyes, she saw the evidence bag with its grisly artifact. She closed her eyes. Arching her back, she became aware only of herself and Kissick and their rising passion.

She heard a phone ringing somewhere, maybe through the open window of a neighbor's house. He gave no indication he heard or cared about a ringing phone. Her excitement mounted. Everything was erased from her mind except the moment. She'd wanted something to restore her concentration. She'd found it. The sublime present that seemed to go on forever reached a brilliant, exhilarating high point, then melted into a rosy glow.

She leaned away from him, supporting herself with her hands on the floor, blinking as the world came back into harsh focus. She tipped back her head and closed her eyes, keeping the world at bay for a few more seconds. She licked her lips and lazily drew her hand down the perspiration on her chest.

He slid to lean against a cabinet, carrying her with him. He looked at her dreamily. "Wow."

She raised her eyebrows to concur.

He pulled her forward to lie against him. "Ow." Rolling onto one hip, he reached his hand beneath his butt and pulled out a broken piece of dried penne pasta. He lobbed it into the sink and tried to brush off the fragments.

She rested her head against his chest and sighed.

They were jostled from their afterglow by a sharp, electronic beep.

"That's my cell phone," he said. "There's a new message. Can you reach my pants?"

As she slowly crawled toward them on her hands and knees, her phone on the counter started to ring.

They looked at each other.

She didn't answer it.

After four rings, the answering machine played her outgoing message. Then they heard Sergeant Kendra Early's voice. "Vining, you there? Pick up. We've got a one-eight-seven—"

Vining scrambled to her feet. She snatched her panties from where they'd landed on top of the phone. She cleared her throat before picking up. "Hi, Sarge. I'm here. What's up?"

"Good evening, Nan. Sorry to disturb you, but we've got a homicide at South DeLacey and Jacaranda. The old Hollenbeck Paper Company building. Homeless guy looking for a place to sleep in a construction site there found a man who was shot to death. The deceased's name is Abel Espinoza. He's covered with NLK ink."

The Northside Latin Kings gang was a well-established presence in gang-infested Northwest Pasadena. Violence there between Latino and African American gangs had spiked in the past few weeks, along with the temperature in the waning days of summer. The city was in the siege of a black-versus-brown gang war.

The Hollenbeck building was farther south, in the popular area of restaurants, movie theaters, and shops in restored historic buildings that was officially called Old Pasadena. Locals called it Old Town.

"Scrappy Espinoza." Vining picked a strand of Kissick's chest hair off her breast.

"You know him?" Early asked.

"He was one of my confidential informants when I worked gangs. Nice guy. Almost beat his pregnant girl-friend to death. Scrappy must be in his thirties. Ripe old age for a gangbanger."

"Caspers and Ruiz are on their way, but I need you or Kissick there, too."

Early didn't have to add that Caspers was too green and Ruiz brought too much attitude to be trusted to handle the scene without adult supervision. Early was slow to anger, but Vining could tell she was ticked off. "I couldn't get ahold of Kissick at home or on his cell. I called your cell and got no answer. Glad I got you on your land line. Thought I was going to have to tell the watch commander, 'Sorry, Lieutenant I've got two senior detectives on call, but I can't reach either one.'"

Vining remembered that her cell phone was in her bedroom.

"That's part of the reason I like being the boss, so I don't have to go out to homicide scenes in the middle of the night."

Vining knew better than to offer a lame explanation.

Early spoke loud enough for Kissick to hear. "Do you know where Kissick is?"

He winced.

"No, Sarge, I don't." Vining dropped the tone of her voice with the last syllable so she wouldn't sound hesitant.

There was a long pause, which Vining and Kissick both interpreted as Sergeant Early weighing whether Vining was telling the truth. They had been careful to keep their private lives private, but there were rumors.

"Get in touch with him, if you can . . ." The sergeant layered in another pregnant pause. "This might be retaliation for the murder of Titus Clifford on East Colorado, which was retaliation for the drive-by shooting at the Carrillo family party. Which was retaliation for the one before that and the one before that . . . Now it's spread to Old Town. We have to get control before this gang war blows up the city."

FOUR

Claiming that her bathroom in the master suite was a mess, Vining brought Kissick towels and a disposable razor so he could shave his stubble and take a shower in the guest bathroom. He didn't want to take the time to go to his house in Altadena to change, so he had to put on the khakis and rumpled shirt he'd been wearing when he'd come over. He always kept a spare sport jacket and tie in the car. Vining couldn't help him in the wardrobe department, as she'd long ago carted to the Dumpster any personal items her ex-husband, Wes, had left behind when he'd walked out on her and Emily twelve years ago.

Kissick set off on the eight-mile drive to Pasadena from Vining's home in the hilly Mt. Washington neighborhood of Los Angeles. It was best to arrive separately at the crime scene. While romance between PPD officers was not forbidden, neither of them wanted to be targets of smarmy gossip. Vining in particular was leery, having had her fill of low remarks, ostensibly said in jest, and with cutting nicknames, called out with a playful wink.

She quickly showered and put on slacks, a tailored blouse, and comfortable, thick-soled shoes. From its nightly resting place beneath her pillow, she retrieved her friend, her Walther PPK. Sitting on the straight-backed chair at her desk, she secured the Velcro strap of the ankle holster onto her right leg, and tucked in the Walther.

Standing, she took her badge from the desk and hooked it onto the front of her belt. While she did so, she looked at the artifacts she'd arrayed across her bed-spread earlier that evening, before Em had found the bloody shirt and all hell had broken loose.

She indulged in her obsession behind her closed bed-room door. She'd taken out the oddball collection from where she kept them hidden, like contraband, in the back of a dresser drawer. Each was a gift from T. B. Mann, each either fashioned or procured by him for them—his women.

For us, Vining thought.

An elite sorority of which no woman wanted to be a member.

Fortunately, she'd remembered the artifacts were dis-played in her bedroom when Kissick had suggested they move their tryst there. He and the PPD knew about some of the items. Others belonged to that growing part of her life that Vining kept secret.

On the bedspread were three pearl necklaces. Each had a pendant set with a different semiprecious gem-stone surrounded by small fake diamonds. There were two notes, handwritten in fountain pen on panel cards. And there were photocopies of four charcoal drawings. Both notes and one of the necklaces, the one with a large pearl in the pendant, had been personally and mysteriously delivered to Vining.

The pearl-on-pearl necklace she'd worn publicly, but no one besides Emily knew that it was a gift from T. B. Mann. It had shown up in her mailbox six years ago with a panel card attached to it with a ribbon. On the card, neat handwriting said:

Congratulations,
Officer Vining

At that time, she had just been vindicated in the on-duty shooting death of Lonny Veltwandter, a has-been rock star, in an incident that brought her considerable notoriety. She became hero to some, a villain to many. She received gifts—and hate mail—but the pearl-on-pearl necklace with its simple yet ominous message was the most lavish and curious offering.

Only years later would she realize that the necklace had been from T. B. Mann. Vining's high-profile shooting had drawn his twisted attention. By the gift of the necklace, he was anointing her, welcoming her into his elite circle, in which the rules—and the endgame—were defined by him. She had certainly not known then that he would spend the next several years carefully, methodically preparing another prize for her: death by his hand.

The second note on a panel card had been left for her at L.A. County General Hospital's psych ward after the puzzling, silent waif Nitro had slipped into the wind. The message on this card was more ominous:

Officer Vining, your daughter looks just like you.

Kissick had been with her when she'd received that one, so it was not a secret.

The other two necklaces were secrets. Big ones. She had stolen them and had told lies to many people, including Sergeant Early and Kissick, in her fervor to possess them. One necklace had belonged to the only other victim of T. B. Mann whom Vining had yet identified: Tucson P.D. detective Johnna Alwin. Its pendant had a garnet surrounded by a circle of small cubic zirconias. Alwin had been wearing the necklace when she'd been murdered. It was still splattered with her dried blood.

The third necklace had been Nitro's. It was shabby, with peeling fake pearls and a scratched fake sapphire surrounded by tarnished and missing rhinestones. This necklace intrigued Vining the most. Its age and condition made her wonder whether this was where it had all started. She surmised that if she could crack the secret of this necklace, she would crack the secret of T. B. Mann.

The four drawings had been in Nitro's possession when he'd been apprehended by the Pasadena P.D. in Old Town. The originals were in a spiral pad locked away in the PPD's Evidence Section. The drawings were skilled. The artist, talented.

One accurately depicted in loving detail the Johnna Alwin murder scene. Alwin had been stabbed to death in a storage closet in an office building. Another showed Vining after T. B. Mann had plunged the knife into her neck. The third showed an unidentified woman in uniform, a Ranger Stetson on her head. Silhouetted in the foreground was a man aiming a gun at her. A giant rock with a distinctive domed shape was in the background.

The fourth was the most grisly. A nude woman was tied by her ankles from the rafters of what looked like a tumbledown barn. Blood dripped over her face and onto the ground from a gash in her neck.

Each piece of Vining's collection evoked terror, blood, and death. Yet, she indulged in this secret habit of taking them from the dresser drawer, removing them from their bags and boxes, and displaying them. Sometimes, she'd pick one up and hold it between her hands with her eyes closed, as if, given the chance and a safe, quiet place, the object might reveal its secrets.

Vining's artifacts filled her with both heartache and sweet longing, like the cremated remains of a loved one kept on a shelf in the house, shrink-wrapped and locked inside a cedar keepsake box. If she just got rid of them, she'd be free of the constant reminder of what they represented. She should take the necklaces and notes to the Pasadena P.D. and book them into evidence. But then she would no longer have them, these paltry traces of T. B. Mann. They were just pathetic crumbs, robbed of flesh, blood, and soul, but at least they were hers to keep. Tangible links to him.

Revealing her collection would be the same as scattering her loved one's ashes into the ocean. She'd have to do it eventually, but she wanted to hold on to them a little longer, until she had crept yet closer to him. She was breaking the rules, but felt deep in her gut she was doing the right thing. Shining a light too brightly into his lair would send him scampering through a hole, again escaping her. She knew what she was doing. She was drawing him out. He was getting closer. While there was a limit to what she would do to get him, she didn't exactly know where the line was. She trusted her instincts to pull her back before she plunged over the edge.

She didn't ask herself the follow-up question: When her instincts warned her to go no further, would she listen?

She gathered the necklaces, cards, and drawings. She lingered when slipping her own pearl necklace into its satinette bag.

Instead of storing it, she unfastened the clasp and put it on. Until a few months ago, she hadn't touched it for years, keeping it buried in the back of the dresser drawer. But lately, she'd felt compelled to wear it, and had on occasion.

Outside, the wind chimes on the terrace jangled again. Vining resisted believing in ghosts, but had to believe in this one, as she'd seen her with her own eyes.

Vining interpreted Frankie's message. She took off the necklace and put it away.

Her cell phone pinged. Kissick's text message said: Whr R U?

She responded: On my way.

In the kitchen, she retrieved her Glock .40 service revolver from where she put it to bed at night in an empty box of Count Chocula cereal in a cabinet. Magazines were in a kitchen drawer behind tea towels. She loaded the gun and slipped it into her belt holster.

Her cell phone pinged again, signaling another text message. She groaned with irritation.

On her way to the garage, she childishly kicked the paper bag that had held the bloody shirt. Kissick had taken the shirt with him.

She got in the department-assigned navy blue Crown Victoria she'd parked in front of her house, and headed off to investigate yet another pointless murder.

FIVE

By the time Vining arrived at the scene in Old Pasadena, it was nearly midnight.

The neighborhood straddling Colorado Boulevard from Pasadena Avenue to Marengo had been the city's first commercial district. The city was established in 1886, but the buildings in Old Town mostly dated from the twenties and thirties. By the seventies, the area had gone to seed and the grand buildings were home to cheap bars, flophouses, and pawnshops. A community revitalization effort restored the historic buildings. Old Pasadena became a model for other cities with decaying urban cores. The formula had worked almost too well. High rents were forcing out the eclectic shops and quirky restaurants that had been the first to move in, taking much of the charm of the area with them as luxury retailers and trendy chain restaurants took their place.

Construction of condos and apartments wasn't far

behind, as well-heeled yuppies sought to live in the newly chic area. Historic buildings were gutted, only their distinctive shells left intact as new construction melded original design elements with cutting-edge architecture.

What weren't melding well were the new, pampered residents enjoying their nouveau urban lifestyle, walking their fashionable rat-size dogs, and the established street gangs previously engaged in a decades-long turf battle.

The Hollenbeck Paper building was near the corner of Jacaranda and DeLacey. The incident commander had set a wide outside perimeter for the crime scene, cordoning off the entire block and stopping traffic on DeLacey in both directions. It was a weeknight. The shops were closed and the last diners were straggling from restaurants, but the police activity had still created a traffic jam and had lured gawking pedestrians. People gathered outside the yellow crime-scene tape were badgering the uniformed officers posted there for information about what had happened. A rumor that the shooting was gang-related sent a chill through the good citizens who had flocked to Old Pasadena for good, clean fun.

The public generally saw murder discordant with Pasadena's genteel image of stately homes on tree-canopied streets, with croquet on the lawn and Tom Collins cocktails on the patio. Pasadena was home to the Rose Parade on New Year's Day, to Caltech, to pricey, private grade schools, to old money, to Greene and Greene-designed Craftsman houses, to exclusive private clubs and golf courses. It hosted the occasional murder as well.

The twenty-three-square-mile city of about 150,000 residents shared its western border with Los Angeles. The Southland's car culture guaranteed that there was no immunity from that megalopolis's problems. The Pasadena Police Department's 240 sworn officers worked in the shadow of two behemoth law-enforcement agencies: the LAPD and the L.A. County Sheriff's Department.

Elected officials worked to preserve the uniqueness of Pasadena, its small-town feel with big city features. The PPD borrowed the best tactics from the big guys, and scuttled the worst—the corruption, secrecy, and adversarial relationships with citizens. The PPD operated under the "Pasadena Way," a philosophy of proactiveness, transparency, community involvement, and being fair but firm.

After many years of relative calm, incidents of gang-related violence had skyrocketed over the past twelve months, showing that the giant was merely sleeping. The dozen or so active gangs in Pasadena were either African American or Hispanic. Other race-based gangs had never taken hold. Historically, gang violence had been black-on-black or brown-on-brown. This new incarnation was race versus race. Evidence suggested that former rival gangs were joining forces along racial lines.

An increase in graffiti and new and unusual graffiti characteristics supported this. The PPD didn't have a handle on why the gangs were shifting. Could be a turf war over narcotics trafficking ordered by "shot callers" in prison. Maybe the mayhem had been kicked off because a gangbanger thought a banger from another neighborhood had disrespected him. Or the increased violence might be a symptom of a deeper issue based in the changing demographics of Northwest Pasadena, which thirty years ago was predominantly African American and now had a Latino majority.

This new street battle started with a flurry of attacks on older Latino immigrants. The men had been assaulted by groups of young African-Americans when walking alone late at night, going home from work. The police learned this was a gang initiation ritual called SOM, for

"Sock on Mexicans." The victims, fearing retribution against their families, had been reluctant to report the incidents to the police.

One night, an assault turned deadly. A young Latino immigrant tried to intervene in an attack against an older man and had been shot in the face and killed. Retribution followed. Two black gang members were shot dead in a liquor-store parking lot in the neighboring city of Altadena.

A month later, a group of Latinos standing on the front lawn at a house in Northwest Pasadena during a party were sprayed with bullets from a passing car, hitting six people from the same family. Four escaped with minor injuries. One boy was paralyzed; another died in his father's arms.

Within a week, Titus Clifford, a long-retired member of the Crooked Lane Crips, was shot in the head while leaving a convenience store on East Colorado Boulevard after buying a gallon of milk and a wild cherry Slurpee. Witnesses saw a Latino man shooting from the passenger window of a black Toyota Camry. Darkly tinted windows prevented witnesses from seeing the driver. The shooter and driver were later arrested. The shooter said he and his homey had been driving around looking for a black gang member, any gang member, to kill in retribution for the shooting at the front-lawn party.

And so it went.

The PPD implemented Operation Safe Streets, focusing resources and maintaining a highly visible police presence with black-and-whites and uniforms on the streets in Northwest Pasadena. The chief's goal was simple: Keep the streets safe so that citizens can go to the store or to work without the threat of violence. The message was clear: This kind of violent activity will not be tolerated in Pasadena. The community rallied to support the police.

Arrests came swiftly. The shootings abated. Tense weeks passed without incident. The PPD did not release its iron grip on the streets and the gangs. The citizens of Northwest Pasadena did not exhale. They avoided the streets at night, kept their children inside, and kept their eyes averted when they saw a crime, lest they become targets.

The majority of Pasadena's residents, especially in the affluent neighborhoods in the southwest and western sections, were not affected by the violence beyond uttering a disheartened "tsk-tsk" when reading about the latest gang-related shooting in the *Pasadena Star News*.

They could keep their distance no longer. Gang violence had landed smack in Old Pasadena, at a construction site where condominiums that would sell for over a million dollars were being built.

Vining nudged the Crown Vic through the crowd, the light bar inside flashing. She drove past the officer who was directing traffic away from the area and parked near Kissick's pickup truck, close to the ribbon of yellow barrier tape. On the other side was the black Chevy Tahoe where the command post was set up. Lieutenant Karen Garner was the incident commander and was working out of the back of the Tahoe, which opened to create a desk.

Vining grabbed her flashlight and a pair of latex gloves and pressed through the crowd. She eyeballed the bystanders as she made her way, wondering if T. B. Mann would show up, guessing that she would be here. She walked with purpose, head high, movements sharp. If he was here, she wanted him to know that she was out in the open, not cowering at home.

A young man in the crowd shouted, "Detective Vining, show us your tits!"

She didn't turn, but out of the corner of her eye, she spotted a couple of guys laughing and high-fiving. She recognized one as a particularly belligerent witness she'd interviewed in relation to the Titus Clifford shooting.

Two uniformed officers, young guys whom Vining knew only by sight, were maintaining the perimeter. They didn't openly smile, but both gave in to a break in the façade, a tiny twitch at the corners of their mouths combined with a quick exchange of glances as Vining ducked beneath the tape.

Vining was not amused, nor was she surprised that her fellow officers were condoning her humiliation. She'd made enemies at the PPD. Many on the force thought she was aloof and ambitious. She had climbed the ladder, but only because she'd focused on doing a good job. When an opportunity presented itself, she took it. Promotions meant more money in her and Em's pockets. Working as a detective gave her more autonomy. Sure, she was distant. She didn't hang out with a clique or join the gang at happy hour to gossip. She was a single mom. When she wasn't working, she had other responsibilities. Still, seeing her subordinates smirk at her didn't give her a warm feeling. If they didn't like her, would they be less likely to go through a door with her?

Out of nowhere, Kissick sprinted down the street, plunged under the yellow barrier tape, and dodged into the crowd. Still wearing the latex gloves he'd donned to examine the crime scene, he grabbed by the collar the guy who had insulted Vining.

"What the fuck, asshole?" the stellar citizen complained.

Kissick clinched the guy's collar tighter and got close to his face. "You talk to your mother that way?"

"You can't put your hands on me like that."

Kissick released the guy with a shove, sending him colliding into his friends. "I just did."

Vining slowed as she continued toward the command

post. Beyond it, floodlights run by generators illuminated the street and interior of the hollowed-out building.

Behind her she heard Kissick reprimand the two officers who had smirked. "You find that funny, Brewer? What about you, Kling?"

Chastened, they both muttered, "No, Corporal."

Kissick caught up with Vining.

Out of the corner of her mouth, she chided him. "My knight in shining armor."

"You can't let that stand, Nan."

She felt the hair at the back of her neck bristle. She stopped and peered into his face. The yearning she'd felt a few hours ago for his strong, comforting presence had dissipated as quickly as the last spasms of their sexual encounter. She chafed at him trying to manage her affairs. She'd given up control once before when she'd married Wes, her high school sweetheart, and that had turned out miserably, except for having had Emily, of course.

"I appreciate your effort and the sentiment behind it, Jim, but I'll pick my battles."

He reared his head back as if he'd been slapped. "Okay. I'll keep that in mind in the future."

"Not to mention the rumors we're confirming for everyone with you running out there like that. Your little show of force. Not exactly subtle."

"One, my actions were not inappropriate. Two, I don't care."

The officer who was acting as the scribe, maintaining the log sheet of who entered and left the crime scene, moved toward them. He thought better of it and returned to where the incident commander was using an oil pen to update the status on "the board," a glass-topped counter on the open rear of the Tahoe.

Vining and Kissick walked a few feet away. She lowered her voice further. "Well, *I* care. I told you, relationships between cops on the force always make the woman look like she's sleeping around. Like she has bad character and judgment." She responded to his eye-rolling. "That Victorian crap still exists, whether you believe it or not. What if we're found out or we go public, do you think Sarge will let us continue to be partners?"

"As long as it doesn't interfere with our job performance—"

"Bull. One of us will be transferred out and I can tell you right now, it won't be you. I'm the damaged one, remember?"

His jaw became rigid.

She went on. "Could work to your advantage. Then you'd feel free to take the sergeant's test. I know you've set that aside because of me."

"Nan, not everything's gloom and doom. It wouldn't hurt you to lighten up a little."

"*Lighten up?*" She gaped at him, unable to think of a rejoinder.

He placed his hand against the back of her arm and began walking. "Come on. I know you've got a lot on your mind."

She stepped out of his grasp. "Please don't be so familiar with me in public."

He gave her a sour look. "I'm just guiding you down the street, like I would my grandmother."

She let out an exasperated sigh. "Would you put your hand on Sergeant Early like this? Think about it. I can feel eyes on us."

He quickly looked around. Turning back, he said, "Nobody's watching us. The ell-tee's busy and Brewer and Kling are flirting with a couple of girls."

"Okay, I'm paranoid. But still . . ."

He raised his hands and stepped away from her. "Whatever you want, Nan."

She moved toward the command post. "Let me check in and see what's on the board."

She and the lieutenant greeted each other. Vining said, "I understand that Scrappy Espinoza's ticket got punched."

"Shot execution-style through the back of the head apparently while he was tagging a wall." Lieutenant Garner was a trim and youthful-looking forty-five. She wore her sandy hair in a short bob favored by most of the female officers because they didn't want the hassle of tightly pinning up their hair so that bad guys couldn't grab ahold of it.

She continued. "There's a security guard posted at the construction site at night, but during questioning, he confessed that he was asleep in his car parked on the street behind the building. Didn't hear anything until we rolled up. Homeless guy by the name of Kevin found the body and called it in. Patrol officers are canvassing the Old Town clubs and restaurants with mug shots of known Crooked Lane Crips."

Kissick added, "The Lane Crips were bound to respond to the Titus Clifford murder. Vario Pasadena Rifa might be good for it, too. They've been at war with NLK for years. But this isn't anywhere near NLK territory. Why was Scrappy tagging here? Why was a thirty-something gangbanger tagging at all, making noise on the street? Guys Scrappy's age usually aren't even active anymore."

Vining examined the board. "Cameron Lam from the Gangs Unit is on-scene."

"I called him in," Lieutenant Garner said. "Corporal Lam has the latest intel on what's doing on the street. Scrappy just got out of prison after a drug-sale rap. Corporal Lam says the word is that he was trying to go straight."

Vining looked toward the brightly lit shell of the building. It was circled by yellow barrier tape, marking the interior perimeter of the crime scene. "If Scrappy was out of the life, why was he shot while tagging a wall in Old Town? What did the tag say?"

"That's another puzzle," Kissick replied. "Says 'China Dog, one-eight-seven.' "

The California Penal Code number for murder is 187.

"Death to China Dog," Vining said. "Who's China Dog?"

"No one knows," the lieutenant said. "Corporal Lam asked his guys on the street and no one has a clue."

"Is it a death threat against a Chinese gangbanger?" Vining looked at Kissick. "Chinese gangs have never gotten a foothold in Pasadena."

He returned her grim gaze. "Looks like they might be moving in."

SIX

A county coroner sedan and vehicles from PPD's Forensic Services Unit were in the street in front of the gaping entrance to the partially demolished building. The façade, portico, and exterior walls of the original 1964 structure were intact while the guts were being scooped out. The cement portico was shaped like a large zigzag and was supported by austere square pillars. The walls were of polished cement with small, smooth pebbles pressed into them. The adult trees on the property were being preserved, encircled with wire mesh to protect them from the construction equipment.

Vining and Kissick walked through an open gate in

the chain-link fence that surrounded the site. A sign on the fence announced: 60 LUXURY CONDOS AND STREET LEVEL RETAIL. DEVELOPED BY RED PEARL ENTERPRISES, LLC. There was an artist's rendering of the finished building. It showed angular towers of steel and glass that incorporated the building's original design elements and expanded on them in the greenest way possible. Yuppies would be able to have Midcentury Modern chic but without the icky small rooms, low ceilings, and devil-may-care attitude about the environment.

Inside the shell, standing among half-destroyed offices that had been carved away around it, was a solitary wall that was fifteen feet high. It and the surrounding area were illuminated by floodlights that made it bright as day, but that faded to shadows and darkness beyond the lights' reach. A clutch of people were gathered at the base of the wall where the corpse lay. PPD Forensic Services specialists were searching the ruins of offices beyond the halo of light, the darkness nearly sucking up their flashlight beams, which flitted like shooting stars. The quarter moon cast scant light through the openings where large picture windows once were, from which the glass had been removed.

Floodlights lighting their path, Vining and Kissick walked past heavy machinery and huge piles of debris—broken sheets of dry wall, blocks of concrete, and splintered lumber. The flooring had been pulled out and the subfloor was marked with tire tracks from construction equipment.

From a dark room to their right, Vining and Kissick saw Detective Tony Ruiz approaching with a flashlight. Shuffling ahead of him was a thin, tall man whom Ruiz occasionally nudged to move along faster. The lanky man, who appeared to be barely in his twenties, made forty-seven-year-old Ruiz look even shorter and rounder. Kissick turned his flashlight beam on the man, revealing filthy clothes and long, matted hair. He was Caucasian and his skin was deeply tanned. He clutched a bundle wrapped inside a dirty blanket against his chest.

"Must be Kevin," Kissick said. "The homeless guy who found the body."

The man squinted as he stepped into the bright light, peering at Vining and Kissick with apprehension. He looked wide-eyed and skittish.

Vining had seen that feral look before and guessed that he suffered from a mental illness, as was the case with most of the full-time homeless. She had seen him around. He was among Pasadena's steady homeless population, which hovered near one thousand in number. The city wasn't a bad place to land on the skids, with mild climate and services offered by the many churches and shelters.

After giving the guy another shove, Ruiz dropped back, maintaining his distance. Vining guessed why, and as they drew close, her suspicions were confirmed. The stench emanating from the young man was overpowering.

"This is Kevin Conker," Ruiz said. "He found the body. I'm gonna get one of the uniformed guys to take him to the station. He stinks too much to get in my car."

Ruiz directed his comments to Kissick, not bothering to acknowledge Vining's presence, as was his habit of late. He and Vining had a lengthy history. Their more recent interactions hadn't improved matters. When Vining had returned from her extensive Injured on Duty leave, Sergeant Early bumped Ruiz from his long-sought-after desk in Homicide to return it to Vining. Some of Ruiz's venom was no doubt due to a falling-out he'd had years ago with Vining's longtime mentor.

Ruiz worked assaults, under Sergeant Early's command, and had been brought onto the task force working the spate of gang-related incidents.

"Don't take me to jail." Kevin more tightly squeezed the blanket-wrapped bundle. "I can stay here. I won't bother anything."

Ruiz's irritation showed. He looked ragged. His fringe of hair and his face were oily and he needed a shave. "I'm not arresting you, but I will if you keep giving me crap."

Kevin's knuckles were turning white from where he held the bundle. Breathing through his mouth, he shuffled backward a few steps. "I want to be outside."

"We're going to the station to get your statement. Got it?"

Ruiz was being a bully for no reason that Vining could fathom, other than the fact that he could. He had no legal grounds to force Kevin to go to the station. He was handling Kevin all wrong. A better strategy would have been to build a rapport with him.

"I already told him everything," Kevin appealed to Vining. In such situations, people often did, believing a female officer would be more compassionate, which was not always the case.

Kevin said, "I went to look for aluminum cans. When I came back, I saw that clown. He was on the ground, dead. I went to the cigar store down the street and told them to call the police. That's all I know. I don't have anything else to say." He hunched over as he spoke, as if to ward off a blow.

Clown? Vining thought that was a harsh way to refer to a murder victim.

Ruiz reached behind his back, beneath his jacket, and brought out his handcuffs. He stepped toward Kevin, who stumbled on a broken block of cement. "Are you coming with me voluntarily, or do I have to arrest you for trespassing?"

Vining knew that was another lie. The property owner would have to be there to press charges.

"Tony . . ." Kissick put out his hand.

"I called the police." Kevin's protests became frantic. "I did the right thing. Don't arrest me."

"Ruiz, come on." Vining knew all the detectives were running on fumes after working day and night sorting out the gang-war carnage, but Ruiz's behavior was unnecessarily callous. She'd watched longtime cops grow bitter. Ruiz had never been a ray of sunshine to begin with. He should retire before someone got hurt.

Ruiz nearly shouted at Vining. "*Come on?* He's our witness. I want a good statement. I don't want to be sitting in court with the defense attorney poking holes in it."

"Did you see it happen, Kevin?" Kissick asked. "Did you see anyone?"

Kevin stared at the ground and rapidly shook his head.

"I have my own methods," Ruiz said. "They've worked for me for many years."

"So much for values-based policing," Vining shot back. The PPD emphasized not just getting the job done, but how the job is done.

Ruiz pointed at Kevin. "Don't move." He looked at Kissick. "Can I have a word?"

Kissick followed Ruiz, who walked a few feet away.

Ruiz spoke in a stage whisper that Vining clearly heard. She turned to the homeless man. "Look, Kevin, if I take you to McDonald's for some food, will you tell me what you saw, and let me tape record it?"

"You need to teach her not to second-guess a fellow detective in front of the public," Ruiz said.

"Tony, all due respect, but you're handling that kid all wrong. We need to earn his trust so we can find him if there's a trial, not scare him to the point that he'll flee the city and disappear."

Ruiz drew his eyebrows together. He was nearly bald,

which made his eyebrows seem even more bushy and unruly.

"Tony, look," Kissick said. "Nan and I will take it from here. We've all been burning the candle at both ends. Go home and get some sleep."

The pink tip of his tongue stuck out from the corner of his mouth as Ruiz gave Kissick a sarcastic look. "Poison Ivy's got *you* under her spell."

Poison Ivy was one of the two monikers Vining had been anointed with at the station. The other was Quick Draw, which she'd earned after she'd shot the rock star to death. She hated both nicknames and Ruiz knew it. She didn't respond, but instead continued talking with Kevin. "Where do you usually hang out?"

Kissick moved close to Ruiz. He kept his voice low, but there was no mistaking the tone. "Tony, I'm in charge of this investigation. You're either on this team and enthusiastic about being on this team, or I'll ask Sergeant Early to reassign you."

"No problem, Jim. I'll talk to Sarge myself first thing tomorrow. I just might tell her that I don't think it's smart to have two detectives who are fucking each other working on the same investigation. I apologize for being so blunt, but I feel compelled to speak my mind."

"Do whatever your conscience dictates, Tony," Kissick replied. "For now, take Kevin to the command post and have him wait there. Tell the lieutenant I'll be out in a minute. You can go home."

"Fine by me."

Kissick walked back. "Kevin, Detective Ruiz is going to take you outside. I'll come get you in a minute and we'll go get some food, okay? Or maybe you want to go to Union Station." He spoke of the local homeless shelter.

When Ruiz left with Kevin, Vining pulled on her latex gloves. "What happened?"

"I'm telling Sarge I want him off this case. I can't work with him."

Vining nodded. "I never could work with him." She added, "I heard what he said about talking to Sarge about us."

He met her eyes. "Nan, Early has certainly heard the rumors. If she's got a problem with it, she'll bring it up. Would it make you sleep better at night if we go in and come clean with her?"

She thought about it. "Yes." After a pause, "No . . . Well, maybe, but not right now."

"Okay."

They walked toward the wall that had been peeled away from the rest of the building. It had been bolstered by a wooden frame.

The wall looked majestic, standing like a giant tombstone, eerily shimmering beneath the spotlights. Drawing near, they saw the reason for the visual effect. The wall was covered with a vast mosaic composed of thousands of tiny squares of colored tile that had an iridescent glaze. The mosaic depicted the Colorado Street Bridge, a Pasadena icon and favorite subject of local artists. Instead of the typical 1920s romantic picture-postcard treatment, the style reflected the Space Age influence of the early 1960s. The bridge was rendered with sparse details and was surrounded with a border of boomerangs and atoms in a jarring contraposition. Blood splatter on the wall couldn't have jibed with the artist's vision.

"How about that?" Kissick said admiringly.

"Who knew that was in here all this time?" Vining said.

"Looks like they were making a path, hoping to get that mosaic out of here in one piece."

The wall was partially shielded by plastic sheeting that appeared to have been carefully taped into place at one time. Part of it had been pulled off and lay crumpled on the ground. At the base, they could see the corpse's tennis shoes and legs between the people gathered there. Maybe it was the effect of the artificial light, but Vining thought he looked as if he was wearing striped pajamas.

Vining spied some of the graffiti between two of the Pasadena Police's own, Detective Alex Caspers and Corporal Cameron Lam, who appeared to be doing little besides watching a comely, young female coroner's investigator crouched on the ground, working on the corpse.

Vining had worked with this coroner's investigator before and knew her name was Bambi. Her parents had bestowed their sweet baby girl with a stripper's name. It didn't help matters when Bambi developed a stripper's figure. No one could have predicted that Bambi would pursue a career that called her out in the middle of the night to creep beneath freeway underpasses and around mean streets, analyzing corpses.

Caspers and Lam gave Kissick and Vining a perfunctory greeting. They were absorbed in observing not the corpse but Bambi as she supported the victim's head and probed the single gunshot wound in the back of his skull. Both men were in their twenties, handsome, cocky, and attractive to women. Caspers especially was preoccupied with sex—having it, pursuing it, or thinking about it his every waking hour, and probably while he slept, too. Vining guessed he wasn't different from other guys his age, or even much older, but most were more restrained in vocalizing their obsession, at least during working hours. She'd tried to curb him while on the job. While she hadn't completely housebroken him, at least she'd trained him to go on the newspaper.

When Kissick saw the corpse, he released a perverse

laugh. "Guess the homeless guy, Kevin, was right. The deceased *is* a clown."

Scrappy was wearing a clown costume. Voluminous, shiny fabric with orange, red, and purple stripes was gathered in ruffles at his wrists and ankles. Pompoms in primary colors were sewn down the front. Askew on his nose was a big, red plastic honker attached by an elastic band around his head. An oversize Afro wig, striped pink, green, and yellow, was on the ground nearby.

"A clown suit?" Vining looked at the others for an explanation.

Caspers held up both hands in an elaborate shrug.

Vining looked at Lam as if he might have an answer. All he offered was "You got me."

"Maybe he was dressed up for a kids' party," Kissick said.

"What kind of parent would hire him to entertain kids with those gang tats on his face," Vining mused.

"The gangbangers' Teddy Bears' Picnic." Kissick began taking photos of the victim and scene with his personal digital camera.

Vining added, "The kids bring their teddy bears dressed in gang colors."

"Little do-rags on their heads," Caspers joked.

The detectives laughed.

Absorbed with different concerns, Bambi pointed at the blood splatter. "He wasn't facing the wall when he was shot. I think he was standing sideways. See this pattern here?"

Vining moved in for a closer look. Scrappy was on his back. His right hand still clutched a can of black spray paint that had stained his fingers. His eyes were wide open. He had a long, narrow mustache that was just a line of hair extending around both sides of his mouth to his chin. He had been a good-looking guy. The mustache accentuated well-shaped lips and a strong chin.

The bullet wound was easy to see through closely shorn hair that looked like velvet. His gang affiliation, NLK, was tattooed across the back of his scalp in ornate letters, three inches tall, inside a crown that signified "Latin Kings." Three dots tattooed down his cheek meant *Mi Vida Loca*. Ironically, a clown face was tattooed on his neck. In street gang lingo, it meant "Smile Now, Cry Later."

Vining knew they would find more tattoos across his abdomen, done in blue "prison ink" culled from Bic pens. The tattoos were a map of his life.

She turned her attention to the fresh graffiti marring the beautiful mosaic.

Kissick asked, "Nan, did you say that this guy used to be your informant?" When she didn't acknowledge him, he called her again. "Nan . . ."

Vining was gawking at the graffiti. The bold, three-foot-tall black letters spelled:

CHINA Dog
187

Now everyone except Bambi was looking at her.

"Nan, what's up?" Kissick asked.

The blood pulsed in her head while at the same time she felt she was being drained of blood. "He was here. He murdered Scrappy and he painted that tag."

She looked at Kissick. "T. B. Mann painted that tag."

SEVEN

Caspers scrunched his face. "T. B. *Who*?" Vining stared off and briefly closed her eyes, not believing she'd uttered that name in front of everyone. "It's what I call the man who attacked me." She added defensively, "I have to call him something."

Bambi didn't look up from her work, but straightened a little while leaning over the body, reacting to the moniker T. B. Mann as if someone had lobbed a pebble at her.

Lam remained silent.

Kissick was direct. "Nan, what makes you think he was here?"

She pointed her latex-clad hand at the graffiti. "Look at the C and the O. Those curlicues . . . They're identical to the notes he wrote me."

"He wrote you notes?" Caspers's flippant facial expression alone bordered on insubordination.

Kissick silenced him with a raised hand. "You're confident about that?"

"I'll never get that handwriting out of my head." She darted her index finger at the writing. "It's all right there. The C and the O."

Caspers was undeterred. "So Nan, you're saying that the guy who stabbed you also shot this homeboy execution-style, then spray-painted this tag, then put the paint can in Scrappy's hand, and then pressed Scrappy's finger on the nozzle to make it look like he painted it."

Vining conceded, "I know it sounds nutty."

Lam asked, "Why China Dog? Why not 'Vining one-eight-seven'?"

Caspers walked to the wall and pointed. "This thing. Is this what you call a curlicue?"

Bambi protested. "Watch where you're putting your clodhoppers in my crime scene."

Lam sagely rubbed his chin, but Vining could tell he thought she was cracked.

She threw up her hands. "It *is* nutty." She thought it best to confirm what they were thinking and what she logically felt, even though the little hairs still standing up on the back of her neck told her otherwise. Battling intuition, she told herself that her obsession with T. B. Mann was like being in love—everything reminded her of him.

She offered a terse "Forget it. Just a crazy idea that flew into my head."

Without further comment, she asked, "Bambi, may I have a look?" After getting the go-ahead, she walked to the corpse and leaned over to look into his dead eyes. "Old Scrappy. I was first on-scene after his girlfriend called nine-one-one when he'd beat the crap out of her. Broke her nose and nearly put her eye out when she was five months pregnant with his son. He was high on meth and didn't like the way she was talking to one of his homeys.

"He went away for that, but not long enough. After he got out on parole, I caught him with a joint and I flipped him. He gave me a good tip about an old drive-by shooting murder up on El Sereno. Gave me decent information for a few years. For twenty bucks to buy drugs, he would have sold out his best friend. He was a player in NLK once, but his drug use got out of control and they sidelined him."

She drew her gloved index finger across the three tat-tooed dots on his cheek. "They didn't give him the moniker Scrappy for nothing. Can't say I'm surprised to find him with a bullet in his head, but what was he doing here?"

"And why tag that wall?" Lam asked.

"That mosaic is probably valuable," Kissick said. "Looks like they were getting ready to move it out of here."

"Tara, how's it goin'?" Vining called out to the supervisor of the PPD's Forensic Services Unit, who was walking from the darkened, partially demolished offices, making her way with a high-powered flashlight.

Tara Khorsandi's blue jumpsuit made her look even more petite. Walking over to the detectives, she was carrying a clipboard and was accompanied by a portly Latino, who was also in a jumpsuit and had a camera around his neck.

"No blood or weapons," Tara said. "There are footprints everywhere from the workmen. This is going to be a bear to measure and sketch. There's a bunch of offices still intact. We'll have to go through everything again once it's daylight."

"Let's do a videotape," Kissick said.

"That's what I was thinking," she said.

"Anyone else camping here other than that one homeless guy?" Kissick asked.

Tara shrugged. "Don't think so, but it's hard to tell. There's refuse in the offices. I'm going to talk to the lieutenant and see if we can't get more floodlights in here. We'll be back." She and her companion left.

Bambi began unbuttoning Scrappy's clown suit. Beneath it, he wore a white, sleeveless T-shirt and baggy jeans. A gold Saint Christopher's medallion was on a chain around his neck. On his feet were expensive Air Jordans.

She went through his jeans pockets, handing Scrappy's cell phone to Kissick. Vining looked over his shoulder as he scrolled through the recent calls and contacts list.

From a case on the ground, Bambi took out scissors and cut open the front of the T-shirt. Then she took out something that looked like a meat thermometer. Without hesitation, she stabbed it into Scrappy's chest beneath his left pectoral, taking the temperature of his liver to determine the time of death.

Caspers involuntarily grunted and looked away.

Bambi gave him an impish grin. "Haven't seen that before, Detective?"

Kissick patted Caspers on the shoulder as the younger detective shuffled a few feet away. "He's never been first on-scene at a homicide before."

"You ought to ride along with me one night." Bambi smiled.

Caspers leaned against a bulldozer. "That would be great," he muttered. His complexion suggested otherwise.

Bambi watched the thermometer. "I estimate he's been dead about two to four hours."

Kissick looked at his watch. "That puts the TOD between eight and ten o'clock tonight. Plenty of people in Old Town then, but this area is off the main drag. People park on the streets here, though. Maybe someone walking to their car saw something."

Lam helped Bambi roll the body over. She found a wallet in Scrappy's rear jeans pocket and turned it over to Kissick.

He took Scrappy's driver's license from it and gave it to Caspers. "Alex, run that license number through DMV. Find out if any of the cars parked around here are registered to Scrappy."

"Got it." Caspers eagerly accepted the job and the change of scenery.

Vining looked at a photo that Kissick had taken from the wallet. It was of a young Latina and a small boy. "That's Scrappy's girlfriend. The one he beat up. The baby would be about five now." She found a photo of Scrappy with a different woman, who was holding an infant.

"Word on the street was that Scrappy was trying to get out of the life since his last stint in prison for selling drugs. He's got a new baby momma," Lam said, using street jargon. "Trying to make the world a better place."

Kissick examined a business card he'd found. "Aaron's Aarrows. Human Directionals. Marvin Li, Owner. Address is on Las Tunas Boulevard in San Gabriel."

Vining threw up her hand when the solution to the mystery hit her. "That explains the clown suit. Scrappy was one of those guys with the arrows. You know, the ones that stand on street corners with the big arrows that advertise new apartments or store openings."

"That's right," Lam said. "They wear stupid hats and costumes and twirl the arrows around, distracting drivers. I saw a guy advertising Liberty Insurance dressed as the Statue of Liberty."

"It seems like a complete waste," Kissick said. "But every weekend, there's an army of those guys all over the city. Someone must figure it's worth it."

Vining said, "The Scrappy I knew wouldn't have been caught dead standing on a street corner in the hot sun, wearing a clown uniform, dancing with a plastic arrow."

"There's talk that some of those guys are lookouts for drug dealers," Lam said.

Bambi got to her feet. "I'm done with him." She packed her equipment into her case. "I'll call again for the meat wagon. We're busy tonight. From here, I go to El Monte. Homicide and suicide."

"These hot nights," Kissick said. "Brings out the gremlins."

"Unless you need me for anything else, I'm taking off," Lam said. "Talk to my guys. See what's going down on the street."

"I'll walk you out," Kissick said. "I need to deal with that homeless guy." He turned to Vining. "You coming?"

"No." She didn't offer further explanation about why she wanted to remain with the corpse.

Kissick didn't ask, and left the area.

Vining heard the voices of the forensics team coming from other parts of the building, but she was alone with Scrappy. She walked to the mosaic wall and studied the graffiti. She examined the C and O and the other letters that had appeared in T. B. Mann's notes. It was completely illogical to think that T. B. Mann had been there, had murdered this gangbanger and painted that tag. It did not fit his M.O.

She squatted beside Scrappy and thought of the photo of his sweet-faced son. She hoped the little boy would escape the lure of street gangs, but if tradition held, it was unlikely.

She picked up the multicolored Afro wig from the ground. "Shit!" she exclaimed when something flew out from beneath. It startled her so much that she reached for her Glock and fell backward onto her butt at the same time, landing on Scrappy's upturned hand, and facing the floodlight, which blinded her.

The creature that had flown out brushed her face with its wings. She swatted madly at the air while trying to blink away the whiteout. Her vision returned and she saw fluttering near the floodlight. She heaved a sigh. It was only a yellow butterfly with black spots. As she got to her feet, it fluttered into the darkness beyond the floodlights.

While dusting off her slacks, she heard a commotion on the street outside the building. One voice was especially strident, and female. She heard Kissick's voice, remaining calm, yet forceful. There was more arguing, this time in a foreign language that sounded Asian.

As Vining strode toward the entrance, the drama outside moved in. Silhouetted by the streetlights, she saw Kissick, Lam, an unidentified, tall young man, and a petite woman. The woman was speaking agitatedly, gesturing dramatically with long, slender arms.

Lam, fluent in several Chinese dialects, was doing his best to keep up with the angry, well-dressed Asian woman.

She might have been in her forties but possessed the type of ageless beauty that made it hard to tell. She was slim and elegantly dressed in a black suit with a lilac-colored blouse. The fabrics were understated but draped her body in a way that whispered "expensive." Her hair was slicked back into a tight bun, revealing huge diamond drop earrings. A large, round diamond in a simple setting on a chain was nestled into the hollow at the base of her neck. She wore little makeup but indulged in dark red lipstick on sharply outlined lips. She wore no rings. Her nails were short and painted the same bloodred as her lips.

When Vining approached, Kissick handed her a business card. It was printed in English with Chinese characters in a smaller font below. The English said: Red Pearl Enterprises, LLC. Pearl Zhang. President and CEO.

Vining recalled the sign posted on the chain-link fence outside the construction site.

Lam introduced Vining to Pearl Zhang.

Zhang glanced at the badge attached to Vining's belt with a hint of scorn and said in perfect but accented English, "How do you do, Detective Vining? I own this property. This is my son, Lincoln Kennedy."

"How do you do?" Bowing slightly toward Vining, the boy was handsome, with Asian and Caucasian features. He was probably in his late teens and was definitely uncomfortable with the commotion his mother was causing. Sidling back near the entrance as if hoping to make an escape, he looked at the ground.

Vining said, "Nice to meet you both. What seems to be the prob—"

Peering past Vining, Zhang gasped. Her hand with its perfectly lacquered nails flew to her perfectly painted lips.

Vining could tell by the direction of her gaze that she wasn't looking at the corpse on the ground, but at the graffiti.

Wordlessly, the detectives parted to let Zhang get a better view, exchanging glances among themselves.

She moved several steps closer, the high, narrow heels of her black patent-leather pumps clacking on the bare cement. "Look what they did . . ."

Lam put his hand on her arm to stop her. "Ma'am, a murder was committed here. This is a crime scene."

She glared at his hand. "I saw worse during the Cultural Revolution."

Lam released her, letting his hand hang in the air as if to suggest that he was happy not to touch her.

Now free, Zhang did not attempt to get closer. She leaned forward as she took in the graffiti. "What does that mean? That number?"

"One hundred eighty-seven is the California Penal Code number for homicide," Kissick said. "When it appears in gang graffiti, it's a death threat. It means, 'Death to China Dog.' "

Zhang's arched eyebrows moved higher on her forehead and her red lips formed an O.

Kissick went on. "Mrs. Zhang, do you know who China Dog is?"

The boy began, "Isn't—"

A hiss from his mother silenced him. He again dropped back and looked at the ground.

EIGHT

Kissick pressed her. "Mrs. Zhang, do you know anyone who goes by the nickname China Dog?"

She didn't correct him for calling her "missus." "I know a lot of people who go by a lot of names. I would have to check and get back to you."

Vining said, "You seemed upset when you saw the graffiti."

"Of course I'm upset. Look at the damage to the mosaic. It's the work of renowned artist Woodrow McKenna, the largest mosaic ever done by him. It was appraised at a half million dollars and now it's ruined. A collector put a down payment on it. I pay for security to watch the site all night. I don't know where the guy is. Have you seen him?"

She and her son turned to look as two coroner techs pushed a gurney into the building. Both were young men, one black, and the other white.

Lam directed them to the body.

Kissick replied to Zhang's question. "The security guard said he was asleep in his car and didn't see anything."

Zhang's eyes burned. "They are paying for this. My insurance is not paying for this."

Vining faced Zhang's son. "What about you? You were about to say something about China Dog."

The young man had been watching the coroner techs move the body. He looked at Vining and rapidly blinked, as if surprised.

"Do not talk to my son," Zhang said. "He's a minor child. He's only seventeen."

"I'll talk to him and you and whoever else I think might have information about this murder," Vining said. "Lincoln Kennedy, is there something you're not telling us?"

His lips parted and he took in a breath. When his mother shot a comment to him in Chinese, instead of looking at the ground as he had done before, he stood tall, squared his jaw, and returned Vining's direct gaze. "People call me Ken."

"Okay, Ken. What do you know about China Dog?"

Zhang interrupted, raising her chin to look at the taller Vining. "Do I need my attorney?"

Vining was glib. "Have you committed a crime?"

Her bloodred lips barely moved when Zhang said, "Of course not. But where I come from, one needs to protect oneself from people like you." She said it with a straight face, adding, "From the police."

The group made room as Tara, the Forensic Services supervisor, and her assistant returned with video equipment. They were accompanied by Lieutenant Garner, who was leading three uniformed officers carrying floodlights and portable generators.

Meanwhile, Zhang had started a heated conversation with Lam in Chinese. He mentioned Sergeant Kendra Early, who was Vining and Kissick's boss, and Lieutenant George Beltran, who was Early's boss.

Vining expected Zhang to voice the tired remarks that moneyed people who were having confrontations with cops often whipped out of their designer satchels: "I pay your salary" and "I know your boss."

When Zhang and Lam had concluded their discussion, Vining said, "Mrs. Zhang, you may have an attorney present if you want to pay one to observe our friendly conversation." She matched Zhang's steely demeanor and intentionally stood straighter, emphasizing the half foot in height she had over her. "I find it curious that a man was murdered on your property and you're more concerned about your damaged mosaic and your absent security guard."

"Of course I care about the dead man," Zhang retorted. "Who is he?"

As if on cue, the coroner techs moved toward them, pushing the gurney.

Ken gaped at the mound encased in a body bag on top.

Kissick took the clipboard one of the techs handed him.

Vining unzipped the top of the body bag and pulled it open to reveal Scrappy's face.

Mrs. Zhang stoically observed the corpse, while her son, disturbed by the sight, took a step backward.

"Do you recognize this man?" Vining asked Zhang.

Zhang arched an eyebrow. "I don't know him, but I don't know everyone on the construction crew. Maybe my project manager, Joey Pai, knows who he is."

"What about you?" Vining asked Ken.

He pressed his lips together and shook his head. "No, ma'am."

"His name is Abel Espinoza." Vining added, "He goes by the nickname Scrappy. Are those names familiar to you?"

The Zhangs again denied knowing Scrappy.

Vining rezipped the body bag and signaled the techs that they could leave.

"Mrs. Zhang . . ." Kissick began. "Do you know anybody who has a grudge against you, who might want to hurt you by defacing your property like this?"

"I am a businesswoman, Detective. I've lived in the United States for eighteen years. I've run my own property development company for ten years. When you're in business, especially when you're a woman, especially when you're a minority, you have to be tough. Of course I've made enemies."

"I understand." Kissick was deferential. He spoke softly, trying to defuse the tension that Vining had whipped up. "Mrs. Zhang, would you come to the station with us so we can better discuss this and you can look over photos of people who might be responsible?"

"It's late," Zhang said. "My son has to go to school tomorrow and I have a busy day. I've already told you what I know. You have my business card. Should you wish to speak with me again, I am easy to find. My crew starts work at eight in the morning. Mr. Pai, my project manager, will be in his office in that trailer across the street. I need to see what's to be done about that mosaic."

"I can't guarantee that we'll be able to release the crime scene by then," Kissick said.

Zhang slid her cuff up her arm and looked at a thin gold watch set with diamonds. "It's nearly two in the morning. Certainly you'll be finished by eight o'clock."

Lam shifted his feet, sensing the brewing confrontation.

Vining felt smug as she saw Kissick slowly losing his cool.

He held up his hand to indicate Tara Khorsandi, who was directing the officers setting up the additional lights.

"Mrs. Zhang, we haven't even begun to search yet. We have to completely measure, sketch, and photograph the scene. Then we'll divide the area into a grid and then we'll start to search. It's going to take a long time. I'm keeping control of the scene until I'm confident it has nothing further to tell us."

Zhang frowned as she looked around the partially destroyed building, as if the magnitude of the task was sinking in. She looked back at him and demanded, "When will that be?"

An edge crept into Kissick's voice. "When we're finished. It could take a few days. It could take weeks."

"Eight this morning, work starts again. I pay the crew if they work or not. Who's going to pay me for money I spend on workers who don't work?"

"I'm in charge of this murder investigation and this crime scene is released when I say it's released."

"You are an employee of the city of Pasadena. I do business in Pasadena. I pay city taxes. I pay your salary. I support charitable organizations in Pasadena. I know your boss, Chief Haglund. I know him very well."

Vining snickered and shook her head as Zhang fulfilled her expectations.

Zhang's eyes shot daggers at her, but Vining kept the closed-lipped smirk on her face.

Lam silently watched, staying out of it.

Zhang's son had moved a few feet closer to the entrance.

Kissick was irritated, but kept his cool. "Mrs. Zhang, I might be just a civil servant, but I can arrest you for interfering with the duties of a police officer."

Vining couldn't resist adding, "After you're settled into your cell, we'll notify the chief that you're there."

Vining was prepared for Zhang's retort, but saw her distracted by something. Vining turned to see the yellow-and-black butterfly that had flown up from beneath Scrappy's wig. It now flitted above her right shoulder. She ducked, but it landed on her anyway.

She blew at it. It leaned away from the wind on its slender legs and folded its wings.

Kissick was surprised by the visitor.

Lam said, "You're lucky, Detective. In the Chinese culture, butterflies symbolize happiness and young love."

Zhang shifted her gaze from the butterfly to look intently at Vining, as if only now becoming aware of a characteristic that had been there all along, but that she had overlooked.

Vining gave her a wry smile and said, "See. I really am a sweet person."

Zhang turned to her son. "Ken, let's go. It's late." On her way out, she shot over her shoulder, "My crew starts work at eight in the morning."

Kissick walked after her. "Officers will be posted here around the clock. They're instructed to arrest anyone who comes onto my crime scene."

Vining trailed behind with Lam, asking him, "How much do you think she knows?"

He replied, "More than she's going to tell us."

"How did she get inside the perimeter?" Vining watched Ken accompany his mother, his long legs taking one step for every two of hers.

"She parked on the street below and cut between two buildings where no one was posted."

Caspers was standing in the street, flirting with a young female officer.

Kissick called to him. "Caspers, did you find Scrappy's car?"

The female officer sped away toward the command post, leaving Caspers in midsentence.

Vining told Kissick, "I'll escort them out."

Lam joined Kissick with Caspers.

"I did find Scrappy's car," Caspers said energetically. "It's a pimped-out Honda Civic, lowered to the ground, wide rims, parked over on Dayton. There's a big, plastic arrow on the seat. I called for a tow."

"So Scrappy was one of those arrow guys, like we thought," Kissick said. "Why aren't you with the vehicle?"

"I told an officer to wait there."

Kissick regarded him dubiously. Caspers was working in Detectives, but he was new to the unit and held the rank of officer himself. It had been noticed that he was enjoying his new status a little too much.

"It's cool, Corporal. I cleared it with the ell-tee."

Kissick gave him a slap on the arm. "Good work." He turned to watch as Vining lit the way for Zhang and her son with her flashlight and the three disappeared between two buildings.

"Who are they?" Caspers asked Kissick.

"Pearl Zhang and her son Lincoln Kennedy, known as Ken. Her property development company owns this building. They know who China Dog is, but they're not talking. Cam, what was the big discussion you and Pearl were having in Chinese?"

"She wanted to know who my family is. How long we'd been here. She's from a province in Mainland China that's notorious for organized crime triads. My family background isn't as exotic. Both my parents are from Taiwan. My father is a dentist in San Gabriel. She knows of him. She asked if my father is proud of his son, the police officer. I told her that he's very proud."

"Why would she ask that?" Caspers wanted to know.

"In the Chinese culture, being a police officer is not a respected occupation," Lam said. "She wondered why the son of a dentist would carry a gun for gwailos."

"Gwhy-lows?" Kissick repeated.

"That's Cantonese slang for Caucasians, but it's used to refer to anyone who's not Chinese. It means 'ghost people.' "

"So even an African American is a ghost person," Kissick said.

"That's right."

"She sounds like a dragon lady," Caspers said.

Lam added, "In Armani."

* * *

Walking in silence, Vining followed Pearl Zhang through a narrow, trash-strewn breezeway between a closed florist shop and a small brick apartment building. They exited onto a quiet, narrow street lined with small businesses that were closed.

Taking keys from his pocket, Ken clicked the attached remote control. A shiny, new black Mercedes S-class sedan parked down the street flashed its lights.

As they moved closer to the car, Vining saw a shadow of someone sitting in the backseat. "Who's that?"

Zhang responded, "My mother."

The car's back door opened and a small, older Chinese woman dressed in a trim light blue pantsuit stepped onto the street. Her silver hair was peppered with black and neatly coiffed in a simple short style. She spoke to her daughter in Chinese.

Zhang responded in a tone considerably more respectful than the one she'd used with the PPD. Zhang introduced Vining. "This is my mother, Wan Li."

Li bowed to Vining. "A pleasure to meet you, Detective Vining."

Vining returned the bow, though the gesture did not come naturally. "Nice to meet you, Mrs. Li."

The older woman gave her a stare, surprising Vining with its intensity. Mrs. Li pointed at Vining's shoulder and smiled.

Vining looked at her shoulder and saw that the butterfly was still there. She raised her hand to brush it away, but before she could, it took flight on its own.

Mrs. Li watched it flutter away into the darkness and said, "A ghost follows you, Detective Vining."

"A ghost?" Vining said with surprise.

Still smiling, Mrs. Li nodded, clasping her hands in

front of her chest. "You have not made this ghost happy, so it follows you."

Zhang spoke to her mother in Chinese.

Mrs. Li turned back toward the car, but then watched as the butterfly again flew near and lit on Vining's shoulder. She bowed to Vining. "I hope to meet you again, Detective." She bowed again, lower, in the direction of the butterfly. She got inside the car and Ken closed the door.

Vining tried to ignore the butterfly, which she could see out of the corner of her eye. She felt embarrassed and exposed, in a way that recalled a recurring dream of hers. In the dream, she's going about her day and everything is fine, but everyone is treating her strangely. Then she suddenly realizes that she's dressed only in her underwear.

Zhang said, "I hope my mother didn't offend you. We Chinese take our ghosts seriously. They need to be attended to. Appeased, so that they don't trouble us, the living."

"No offense taken. What about you, Mrs. Zhang? Do you see a ghost following me?" Vining's question came out sounding harsher than intended. She was still embarrassed by the stupid butterfly that had drawn this unwanted attention to her.

"I don't have that talent." Zhang's response matched the tone of Vining's question. "But I do not discount my mother's capabilities."

Ken opened the passenger door for his mother and she got inside.

Vining handed her a business card. "I'll be in touch, Mrs. Zhang."

Zhang set the card on the console without looking at it.

As Ken was closing the door, he asked Vining, "Are you Emily's mother?"

The question surprised Vining. "Yes, I am."

The question also surprised Zhang, who put her hand against the door, stopping Ken from shutting it.

"She's in my photography class."

"You go to the Coopersmith School?"

"Yes. I'm a senior. Actually, Emily and I are working on a school project together."

"A project . . . Are you?" Vining detected a spark in his eyes when he said Emily's name. Judging from the way Zhang was looking at her son, she discerned the same thing.

Neither mother was pleased.

"In our digital photography class." He was beaming, more lively than he'd been all night.

Zhang snapped, "Lincoln Kennedy, time to go." She slammed the car door.

Vining walked the young man to the driver's door. "Ken, do your mother a favor and make sure she doesn't come back here in the morning."

"I'll remind her." He didn't sound hopeful.

Finally finding a private moment with him, Vining asked, "Do you know who China Dog is?"

His eyes darted away and he didn't answer.

"We'll eventually find out the truth, Ken. It will be easier on your mother and you in the long run if you tell us what you know now."

They were startled when the Mercedes's horn blared.

Through the window, Vining saw Zhang leaning onto the driver's seat, watching them, her red lips frozen. Zhang again pressed the car horn.

Vining had a long list of human peccadilloes she despised. Near the top, perhaps only slightly below homicide, was having a car horn honked at her.

"I apologize, Mrs. Vining . . . Detective . . . But I have to leave." Ken got inside the car, turned over the ignition, and sped off.

Vining stood in the street. Through the rear window,

she saw Zhang's elderly mother turn around, watching her, until the car turned the corner and disappeared.

When they were gone, Vining angrily stared at the butterfly on her shoulder. She raised her hand to swat it, but lost her nerve. Instead, she growled through clenched teeth, "Leave me alone."

The butterfly lifted off, fluttered in front of Vining's eyes, and spiraled away.

NINE

At almost seven o'clock the next morning, Vining drove into the PPD garage off Ramona Street. A young female officer, about to be late for the Day Watch briefing, tailgated Vining's Crown Victoria past the gas pumps until she had room to swerve around and speed on.

Vining found a parking place next to Kissick's car. When she got out, she saw the woman running toward the back door, her uniform in dry cleaner's plastic slung over one shoulder and a new handbag in the latest style slung over the other. Even though Vining was just thirty-four, she envied the young officer's youth and energy, meanly reveling in the knowledge that there was no way she'd be on time.

Vining had gotten only a couple of hours' sleep. She was tired, physically and mentally. Tired of having her life directed by forces outside her control. By gang-bangers and their generations-long blood feuds. By peers with not-so-hidden agendas. By her primary harbinger of ill will—T. B. Mann. By her personal hobgoblins, which felt out of her control, which had arrived on the heels of T. B. Mann's perforation of her life. Sometimes she wondered whether they'd been there all along and T. B. Mann had simply shoveled the first mound of dirt to uncover them.

That was fatalistic, sad thinking, and she forced herself to stop. Move on. A good night's sleep, a weekend without spilled blood, and she'd be good as new.

She could have grabbed a little more shut-eye in the sleep room off the PPD's women's locker room. She kept a blanket and pillowcase in her locker for that purpose, not caring to use the communal bedding, but she'd had her fill of nights like that during this murder wave and needed her own bed. At home earlier, she'd put on a navy blue suit with subtle pink pinstripes that she'd worn only once, to a school event of Emily's. She paired it with a pale pink cotton shirt fresh from the cleaners. She'd finally given in to sending her shirts out. She no longer had time to wash and iron them—even the "no iron" ones needed pressing—and they never turned out as nice when she did them at home.

Around three o'clock that morning, she and Kissick had left the Hollenbeck Paper building and had gone to the home of Scrappy's mother, Renalda, in the Kings Court housing project in Northwest Pasadena. They weren't the first to break the bad news. Word had spread fast through the NLK network. The detectives had arrived at the upstairs apartment to find it filled with Scrappy's relatives and homeys. Renalda's face was tear-stained, but she was stoic. Scrappy was her second son lost to gang violence. Scrappy's girlfriend, Monica, was inconsolable, wailing as she carried their infant son, Abel, whom the family had already doomed to the gang lifestyle by giving him the moniker Li'l Scrappy.

Renalda insisted that after Scrappy's last stint in

prison, he was clean, off drugs and living a legit life. His parole officer had gotten him a job with a Chinese man named Marvin, standing on street corners, holding advertising signs. It paid minimum wage, but it was the first real job Scrappy had ever had. With pride, she'd given them one of Scrappy's Aaron's Aarrows pay stubs.

When Vining asked Renalda if Scrappy had ever referred to Marvin Li as China Dog, the woman suddenly didn't know anything. She also didn't know anything about anyone who might have threatened Scrappy. She didn't know anyone who was in a gang, even though her apartment was filled with men, boys, women, and girls who were covered with gang tattoos. Many of the people there were known by the PPD. Vining and Kissick had interviewed some in relation to other crimes.

Elsewhere in the city, Alex Caspers, Cameron Lam, and officers in Lam's gang unit were questioning members of the NLK's longtime rivals, Vario Pasadena Rifa, and the black gang that was most likely to seek retribution for the Titus Clifford murder, the Crooked Lane Crips.

Predictably, on the record, no one knew anything. Officers were surprised when, off the record, the most reliable confidential informants had no information about who was good for Scrappy's murder. Gangbangers always bragged about their exploits to their homeboys. After thoroughly jacking up the familiar suspects and coming up with nothing, the PPD began to think that Scrappy's murder was not part of the recent cycle of gang violence. They needed to expand their horizons.

Even as she began the new day, Vining felt worn down. With each homicide she worked, she sacrificed a small part of herself. She still cared for the victims and their families. She was still on fire to see justice done. But she felt less. Each murder touched her heart, but didn't resonate quite as loudly. She'd seen this among veteran cops. Even after twelve years with the PPD, she'd never thought it would happen to her. But it was happening. She recognized its vital importance: She'd never survive otherwise. She only hoped that, like an oyster producing a pearl in response to the intrusion of a grain of sand, something good would come of the slow callus growing over her heart. She knew her experience brought heightened instincts and focus to her Job—so important it always had a capital J in her mind. She prayed she wasn't on the way to becoming Jaded.

Gang murders were especially draining. The endless cycle of violence. The perpetuation of the lifestyle across generations. The gangs' fierce stranglehold on entire neighborhoods and terrorization of its honest, hard-working citizens. The police tried to break the backs of gangs using every legal tool possible—injunctions, RICO, and going after them where they lived by filing code-enforcement violations. The PPD also tried to be proactive, involving community and clergy, creating healthy ways for kids to spend their time. Sometimes they busted heads and took names.

The PPD's efforts to hammer the gangs would eventually force down the recent spike in violence. Inevitably, it would then pop up in a neighboring city.

Officers just getting off Morning Watch, the graveyard shift, were spilling out the station's back door, jogging down the short set of cement steps.

Vining went up the steps and past the normally locked back door that was held open by the officers who were leaving. She walked up a flight of bare cement steps to the second floor, carrying her soft-sided briefcase. In her purse was the satinette bag with the pearl-on-pearl necklace that T. B. Mann had given her. She had almost put it on last night. Again, this morning, she'd felt drawn to wear it. Instead, she'd put it in her purse. Sometimes she carried it that way, a weird talisman.

The note that T. B. Mann had written on the panel card was also in the satinette bag:

Congratulations, Officer Vining

She'd scrutinized it, comparing it to her memory of the China Dog 187 tag, looking for the similarities in the handwriting that last night had seemed blatant to her. She could compare the note on the panel card to Kissick's photos of the China Dog tag, but decided it was pointless. In the cool light of day, she saw that her obsession with T. B. Mann was getting the best of her. Worse, it was starting to show. She regretted having shot off her mouth about her harebrained handwriting analysis at the crime scene.

The public entrance of the 1989 Mission Revival–style police department was off Garfield Avenue. The polished wood and glass-paned doors opened into the lobby, which had a soaring three-story atrium and an open staircase and catwalk. The floor and stairs were paved in brick-colored fired tile with a sprinkling of colorful patterned tiles. Simple Mission-style wood benches lined the walls. Morning sun streamed in through tall arched windows.

Vining liked to walk down the open staircase and across the lobby. It was a calming environment. Still, much more potent magic was needed to soothe the souls of the people she saw sitting on the benches waiting to speak to a detective.

Now walking down the second-floor corridor, she passed cases that held antique badges and toy police cars donated by a retired lieutenant. At the end of the hall was the Detectives Section. She opened the door and passed through the small waiting area furnished with a plain, slightly worn couch. A pay phone was on the wall. Behind a counter were the desks of the two staff assistants who had not yet arrived for work.

Beside the locked door that led to the back office, Vining moved a magnetic tag on the In/Out board next to her name to show she was in. She saw that Kissick was already there. She checked the cubbyhole for her mail, then unlocked the door and entered a large space honeycombed with gray cubicles. She passed the coffee room and the conference room. Whiteboards lining the wall there and large pads on easels were covered with details about the recent spate of gang-related murders and assaults.

They needed more whiteboards.

In her cubicle, she stashed her purse inside her desk drawer and wedged her briefcase on the floor between her desk and a low filing cabinet. Taking off her jacket, she draped it over a hanger on a plastic hook attached to the cubicle wall. Another hook held a hanger with her Kevlar vest, marked with a bright yellow badge on the breast and POLICE in prominent yellow across the back. She wore this when serving warrants or engaged in other high-risk operations.

Without sitting, she grabbed a coffee mug decorated with a photo of her, Emily, and "I Love You Mom."

In the coffee room, she was glad to see that someone had made a fresh pot. For once, she didn't find just burned dregs in the bottom of the carafe. She filled her mug and dumped in powdered creamer and a scant teaspoon of sugar.

On the counter was a box from Winchell's doughnuts. All she'd had to eat that morning was a banana in the car. The assortment in the box had been picked over, but someone had left half of a chocolate doughnut with chocolate sprinkles. Even though her GI tract would make her pay later, the fried dough beckoned.

Nibbling the doughnut, she circled back to her desk, taking the long way past the two offices for the lieutenants and the large corner office shared by the four detective sergeants in charge of the different detective units. A large window there overlooked the suite. The exterior windows gave a view of Garfield Avenue to the east and Walnut Street to the north. The windows on Walnut faced the Spanish Renaissance-style Central Library, built in 1927. Across Garfield was the somber Superior Courthouse. Farther south was City Hall. The huge wedding cake had also been built in 1927. Its landmark Spanish Baroque dome glistened after a years-long renovation and retrofitting.

Vining's boss, Sergeant Kendra Early, in charge of the Homicide-Assault Unit, was already at her desk. Vining wasn't surprised. Everyone involved in the recent gang war violence had been working long hours. The strain was showing.

While Sergeant Early possessed a wickedly dry sense of humor, her typical demeanor was solemn, an effect enhanced by permanent dark circles beneath her large eyes. Vining saw how Early intentionally injected levity into meetings with the people under her command, cracking jokes, knowing their jobs were hard enough as it was.

African-American, petite, round, and in her forties, Early wore her hair in a short Afro and had been lately applying a reddish rinse to cover gray. It was her sole cosmetic enhancement. She wore no makeup. She had a habit of rubbing her eyes, digging in the pads of her fingers with such force it was surprising she didn't hurt herself. Right now, she sat stock-still as she listened with rapt attention to Jim Kissick, who was sitting in a chair in her office.

They appeared to be discussing documents arrayed

on her desk. He was leaning over them, pointing, and speaking animatedly.

The office door was closed, which was unusual. None of the other three detective sergeants were there.

When neither Early nor Kissick looked up as she passed, not raising a finger or an eyebrow to acknowledge her, Vining's suspicions were piqued. Nothing had transpired with the Scrappy Espinoza murder to merit an intense and confidential discussion. Kissick couldn't be coming clean about their romantic relationship, could he? Wouldn't Early pull them both in? Was he talking about her harebrained "curlicue" theory and how she'd seen T. B. Mann's handprint on the Scrappy murder? She decided it wasn't that. It wasn't Kissick's style to tell tales.

Holding her mug of coffee, she kept walking, deciding she was letting her mind run away with her. She passed Tony Ruiz's cubicle.

"Morning, Tony."

No response.

And women are accused of being on the rag.

Most other days, she would have let it go. But today . . . She leaned to look into his cubicle, which was catercorner to hers.

"What's up, Tony?"

"You oughta know."

"Why should I know?"

"Oh, pillow talk." He gave her a simpering smile.

"What's that supposed to mean?"

"Again, you oughta know."

Alex Caspers shuffled past, nursing a grande Starbucks coffee.

Ruiz said to him, "Look what the cat dragged in. That's one thing I'm not gonna miss. Dealing with Casanova's morning-afters."

Caspers croaked in a thick voice, "Morning."

Vining gave him a piercing stare, to which he responded, "What?"

The whites of his eyes were unnaturally bright, suggesting a liberal application of Visine. His complexion was sallow and he'd cut himself shaving.

"Did you stay out all night?" Her tone was more statement than question.

"Not all night. None of us got much sleep, right?"

"Nice . . ." She lowered herself onto her chair, disappearing behind the walls of her cubicle. She had plenty of work and little time for personal dramas.

"Caspers . . ." She knew he'd hear her through the cubicles' fabric walls.

He uttered a drowsy "Yo."

"I have a lead for you to follow up." She picked up a sheet of paper on which she'd photocopied the Aaron's Aarrows business card and Scrappy's paycheck stub. Without standing, she dangled it over the top of the cubicle into Caspers's area. When she felt him take it from her fingers, she added, "Find out what you can about that business and Marvin Li, the owner. Tony . . ."

"Yes, ma'am." He managed to make sarcasm drip from even that brief utterance.

"Did you write up your interview with our witness, Kevin?"

"Kissick took that over, remember?"

"You were the first to question him. Your report needs to be in the file."

"You'd better touch base with Kissick about that."

She frowned at the cubicle wall in the direction of his desk. "Oh-kay . . ."

Her eyes trailed to a bulletin board above her desk on which she'd displayed mementos and photos. She'd recently installed a couple of new ones, including a nice shot of her entire family during a recent dinner at

Mijares, a favorite family-style Mexican restaurant in Pasadena. She and Em were there, as was Granny. Her mother, Patsy, was there with her current beau and prospective fifth husband. Her younger sister Stephanie was with her husband and their two young boys. Looking at the photo anew, Vining was struck by how mature Em looked. She seemed to have grown up overnight.

Beside that was a photo that Emily had taken for her photography class. Her teacher had heaped praise on it and was going to submit it for inclusion in a city-wide exhibit. In the background were the imposing gates of the Pacific Asia Museum in Pasadena. The 1924 two-story structure, with a courtyard garden and pond, was originally a custom-built home designed to look like a Chinese palace, complete with a teal-green pagoda roof. The iron gates were painted brick red and decorated with serpentine dragons. The gates were rounded at the top and set inside a cream-colored arched entryway that was decorated with an elaborate bas-relief frieze. A pair of Chinese-style stone lions guarded the entrance.

The photo was in color, but the primary hues were shades of cream, gray, and red. On the sidewalk in front of the closed gates, a young man, dressed in a long black coat, was bent over, picking up a red hibiscus flower from the sidewalk.

Emily's teacher had praised the intense detail in the shot, the effective use of red, and the contraposition of the formal gates and lions with the casual act of the youth reaching for a flower that was incongruously on the sidewalk.

Vining had often looked at this photo, but today it commanded new interest. The boy's face was in profile, a shock of pale skin visible between his black hair and the high collar of the coat. She took a magnifying glass from her desk and rose from her chair to examine it more closely. She realized it was Ken Zhang.

"Nan, do—"

She wheeled around at Kissick's voice, clasping the magnifying glass to her chest. "Jeez . . ."

"Sorry." He gave the magnifying glass a questioning look. "Do you have a minute?"

"Sure." She returned the glass to her desk drawer.

"Early wants to have a brief meeting."

"Okay."

She walked ahead of him down the row of cubicles.

"Nice suit," he said.

"Thanks."

"New?"

"Sort of." Under her breath, she asked, "Does this have something to do with what you and Sarge were talking about behind closed doors?"

"Yes," he replied, not offering a further explanation. "By the way, I turned over that bloody shirt to Forensics. Tara's taking care of it personally."

She dubiously pulled her mouth to the side. "It's evidence in an old case. The Crime Lab won't get to it for months."

"It's become a high priority. Tara's going to have it expedited."

"Why is it now a high priority?"

As they rounded a corner, passing Ruiz's area, Vining saw him packing items from his desk into a box. "What's going on here?"

Kissick only said, "A lot." He let her enter Early's office ahead of him and closed the door.

The sergeant stood and extended her hand to Vining. "Good morning, Nan. Have a seat."

Vining pulled a chair over. Kissick sat in a chair beside her. The papers on Early's desk that she and Kissick had been discussing were gone.

Early didn't begin speaking right away, but silently studied her. Only a few seconds passed, but it was sufficient to make Vining uneasy. She recalled Ruiz's comment about "pillow talk." That was it, she decided. Her and Kissick's affair had been exposed. They'd been discreet, but his behavior had become more casual. Their work hadn't been compromised, but maybe their relationship was creating a distraction for others or . . . Who knows? She'd warned him. She would take the fall for it. He had more seniority and less controversy. Early was going to transfer her out.

"Nan," Early began.

Vining's palms grew clammy.

"You'll be taking the lead on the Scrappy Espinoza homicide. I'm assigning Jim to a special project."

TEN

Vining blinked, not certain she'd heard correctly. She was relieved, yet not. She looked at Kissick. What did he know and when did he know it? And why hadn't he told her?

He was the master of the dead stare. She was unable to read him.

Early did little to answer Vining's unasked questions. "Jim's going to be working another investigation. I'll tell you more about that in a minute."

Vining was certainly capable of spearheading the Scrappy Espinoza investigation, another round-up-the-usual-suspects gang murder. Even with the possible

Chinese connection, it was all the same—taking names, asking questions, getting answers. But the thought of not having Kissick to back her up made her a bit uneasy. She hated to admit how much she'd come to rely on him. They were a *team*. Their alliance, that had at first been only professional, had become personal, too. She also had to admit a twinge of jealousy. He was off to do something interesting while she was left to sweep up. What gives?

"There's another change." Early languidly blinked. Some had mistaken her low-key persona for sluggishness. They had also felt her swift reprisal. "Ruiz is transferring out of detectives. He'll be working on a multiagency task force in conjunction with the DEA."

Privately delighted with this news, Vining just nodded. So that's what Ruiz's venom toward her had been about. When he'd had to work with her, he'd been civil. Now the veil had been pulled away and she was surprised to see the depth of his animosity.

The transfer sounded like a lateral move, although some would perceive it as a demotion, even if the job classification was the same and there was no pay change.

Transferring a problematic cop to a different job was a strategy sometimes used to juice his enthusiasm and improve his performance. Often, the transfer was to an area where there was less risk to the public and other officers. She didn't know if that was part of the strategy with Ruiz. She didn't care. Glancing toward the suite, she saw Ruiz leaving with his box. She tried not to gloat.

Early continued. "Alex Caspers will be working with you until Jim completes his project, which we figure might take a week. With any luck, we'll have this Scrappy Espinoza case wrapped up before then. Use

Sproul and Jones as much as you need. In terms of Jim's special project . . ."

She paused. "He's going to be following up new leads in your attempted murder."

Vining couldn't hide her surprise. Unlike Kissick, she hadn't mastered the dead stare. What new leads? She couldn't be talking about the bloody shirt. If it concealed a hair, fiber, or bodily fluid that led them to a name or location, then their work would begin.

"Jim, why don't you explain?" Early picked up a manila file folder from her desk and handed it to him.

From it, he removed four sheets of photocopy paper.

Vining knew the images on them well. They all did. They were copies of the four grisly drawings found on the pad of art paper in the mute transient Nitro's backpack.

The mysterious stranger the PPD had nicknamed Nitro had entered their lives a few weeks ago. They guessed that he was in his early twenties. His skin was pasty white; his spiky hair was also nearly white, with dark roots. His eyes were an innocent cornflower blue. He had been well-dressed with some cash on him. What he didn't have was ID. No one could explain his behavior that day. Nitro, if he could, wouldn't. He would not speak. Not one word.

In the middle of the Labor Day holiday, in the middle of Old Pasadena, Nitro had stripped down until he was nude except for penny loafers, socks, and a beat-up pearl necklace. He then ran through the streets, eluding a horde of PPD officers until one finally managed to tackle him. They would have considered him just another nut, perhaps more colorful than most, except for that spiral-bound drawing pad in his backpack that hinted at something sinister.

Among Disney-like drawings of cute animals and flowers were four charcoals of women either being attacked or threatened with violence. Not just any women. The details were sparse but evocative.

One depicted Vining's stabbing. She was drawn from the shoulders up, a knife deeply embedded into her neck. A shiny, black trail of blood flowed from her wound. Her lips were parted in what could be horror or ecstasy. Her attacker was standing close to her. As close as he'd stood in real life. The drawing showed only the back of his head, but in her wide eyes, his shadowy image was reflected.

One depicted the upper body of a woman in uniform wearing a round-brimmed Ranger Stetson. On her long-sleeved shirt, a badge and insignia were sketchily outlined. In her left hand, she held two leather straps that disappeared off the edge of the paper. She looked afraid. In the distance, off her right shoulder, was a distinctive, domed mountain. Kissick had said the mountain looked like Morro Rock in the Central California coast city of Morro Bay, a favorite getaway spot for him and his two sons.

One depicted a woman lying on the floor of what appeared to be a storage closet. Her white blouse was covered with dark stains. She looked dead. Around her neck, on top of her blouse, was a pearl necklace with a pendant.

Through Vining's surreptitious investigation, she'd learned that this drawing portrayed another victim of T. B. Mann—Tucson Police detective Johnna Alwin. Only the killer, the cops, and Alwin's husband knew she'd been given a pearl-and-pendant necklace and was wearing it the day of her murder.

Vining had secretly traveled to Tucson and met with the lead investigator, Lieutenant Owen Donahue. She'd planned on stealing Alwin's pearl necklace and had succeeded.

Then there was the fourth drawing. It was by far the

most gruesome. The setting was a ramshackle barnlike structure. A nude woman was tied by her ankles and hanging from the rafters. A great pool of blood had spilled from a gash across her neck onto the dirt floor. A cloud of fluffy, dark hair obscured most of her face and kept the necklace around her neck from slipping off. The necklace was drawn with loving details. Dozens of tiny circles depicted pearls. From the middle dangled a pendant.

Some at the PPD had made good arguments that Nitro was a crime groupie. The assault upon Vining had been well publicized. The other women in the drawings could be creations from Nitro's twisted imagination or he could have gleaned inspiration from media reports of real crimes.

While the necklace the silent streaker Nitro was wearing when the PPD had apprehended him had been a source of amusement for the officers involved, Vining knew better. He was not T. B. Mann. She detected something eerily reminiscent of T. B. Mann in Nitro, but *he was not him*. He was his messenger. To Vining, T. B. Mann's message was this: *My evil acts have a long and complex history, and I'm not finished. Watch what happens next.*

Nitro's necklace—a sorry, beat-up thing—was also in her collection. She'd confiscated it with aplomb. Unfortunately, her other scheme for Nitro had gone to hell. She'd planned to wait for him after his release from the seventy-two-hour psychiatric hold at L.A. County General Hospital, where the PPD had sent him. But Nitro had eluded her. He was gone.

After quickly leafing through the drawings that she knew only too well, she looked from Kissick to Early. "We have new leads?"

Kissick began, "I followed up on my hunch about that one drawing, that the mountain in the background is Morro Rock. The woman in it is wearing a Ranger Stetson and there are a couple of state parks in that area. I sent an inquiry to the California State Park Service headquarters. Last night, they faxed a response." He took stapled papers from the folder and handed them to Vining.

She silently skimmed them, stopping to reread this line: "In response to your inquiry, the woman in your drawing might be California Park Ranger Marilu Feathers."

Vining repeated the name. *Marilu Feathers*. It glowed for her. It was as if she'd found a long-lost sister. She continued reading.

"Ranger Feathers was stationed at Montaña de Oro State Park. While patrolling the sandspit on Christmas Eve eight years ago, she exchanged gunfire with an unknown suspect and was shot to death. Her murder is unsolved. After an exhaustive investigation by the California Park Service and the San Luis Obispo County Sheriff's Department, the case went cold. We would be happy to share our information with you in the hope of bringing the perpetrator to justice, and delivering closure to Ranger Feathers's family and to her fellow rangers."

Closure, Vining thought. *Feel-good bull*.

With the letter was a copy of Feathers's official Park Service photograph, in uniform. In the background were the U.S. flag and the California state flag with the now-extinct California grizzly on a white background. Feathers's thin lips were closed, the edges barely upturned. Her features were plain and square. Her lank, dark hair, cut in a blunt, utilitarian style that reached her large jaw, looked plastered to her head. Her appearance was severe, yet there was something open, honest, and kind about her face.

Vining silently asked her: *What did you do to attract his attention?*

Kissick said, "I've had a telephone conversation with the assistant director. He says a park ranger, named

Zeke Denver, who was stationed at Montaña de Oro at the time of Feathers's murder and who participated in the investigation, is still there. I'm driving up to meet him as soon as we're finished here."

Vining wondered why Early said that it would take Kissick a week to work the new leads. It shouldn't take more than a day or two at most. He'd found Marilu Feathers. Good for him. She desperately wanted to go to Montaña de Oro. Kissick was a great investigator, but this case was different. She knew the right rocks to turn over. She knew the right questions to ask, such as: Had Feathers been involved in an incident on duty that had propelled her into the limelight? Had she subsequently been given a pearl necklace with a gemstone pendant that foretold the month of her murder?

Of course, Kissick could ask these same questions if she turned over all the information she'd gathered. She'd have to someday. Maybe that day was here. Her dilemma was how to do it while omitting the companion piece to the tale, that she had lied, cheated, and stolen to get the evidence. Still, only she could bring her unique perspective to the investigation. Only she and T. B. Mann had breathed the same air, charged with violence and sex.

She set the fax on her lap, on top of the drawings, not daring to hand the materials back to Kissick lest he see her trembling hands. She folded her hands on top of the papers.

Kissick continued. "Since I got a hit on my hunch about Morro Rock, Sarge and I decided to examine the last two drawings for clues about who the women might be."

He held out his hand for the papers that Vining held.

She quickly passed them on, again clasping her hands in her lap as the trembling hadn't completely subsided.

He found the drawing of the woman hanging by her

ankles and held it up. "Sarge remembered a murder like this."

Early spoke up. "After we'd dismissed Nitro as a nutcase, I didn't give those drawings another thought and hadn't looked at them too closely to begin with. Our star investigator here, with his tremendous instincts, felt there was more than what met the eye. He wouldn't let it go and thank goodness, because we finally have some new leads."

Vining knew that Kissick was embarrassed by Sarge's praise. He allowed himself a modest smile. Meanwhile, she, who had taken great personal and professional risks in pursuing T. B. Mann and had collected critical evidence, was forced to suck in her pride and sit quietly.

Early held out her hand for the drawing of the dangling woman, which Kissick gave her. "So while Jim and I were looking at this sketch, a murder that happened in Colina Vista popped into my head."

Colina Vista was one among the string of what locals called the foothill cities. They numbered about a dozen, and the northern border of each abutted Angeles National Forest in the San Gabriel Mountains. Pasadena was one of the largest. Several of the foothill cities were little more than villages, throwbacks to a gentler era tucked away from the hustle-bustle of their larger neighbors and blissfully free of most of their big-city problems. Their well-heeled, well-educated, and mostly Caucasian residents shared other traits—disdain of urban sprawl and chain retailers, fear of wildfires, and a fierce protectiveness of their lifestyle.

The twin cities of Colina Vista and its neighbor, Sierra Madre, the jewels in the crown, had both been mountain resort towns in the late 1800s. Both shared a deep connection with the Pasadena P.D. Each had a female police chief who had come up through the ranks of the PPD. Colina Vista was the smaller of the two towns, with a population of barely 7,500 and a police department of eleven sworn officers, plus the chief.

"I called the Colina Vista P.D. earlier this morning," the sergeant said. "Of course, my friend Betsy Gilroy was already at her desk. Do you know Chief Gilroy, Nan?"

"Not personally," Vining replied. "I'm familiar with her reputation."

"She was deputy chief at the time of the murder I was recalling. It happened ten years ago. The victim was a young female police officer named Clarissa Silva. Her nickname was Cookie."

Cookie Silva, Vining thought. *My sister.*

"Chief Gilroy was the lead investigator. She's more than happy to discuss the case with Jim, though she says they got their man. He's on death row in San Quentin."

That information meant nothing to Vining. The lieutenant in Tucson had also been certain they'd nailed Johnna Alwin's murderer. He was wrong.

Early said, "We've tentatively identified with some confidence the women in three of the four drawings. One is you, Nan. One is Ranger Marilu Feathers, and one is Officer Cookie Silva."

Kissick held up the drawing that depicted Johnna Alwin on the floor of the storage closet. "This is the only one we haven't identified. Still, we have nothing to link these women to your attacker."

Two of them are wearing identical pearl necklaces, Vining thought. *It's right in front of you.*

She just nodded. She knew that Early's assigning Kissick to work the leads full-time was a boon to the investigation, especially now. T. B. Mann was stirring in his hole, darting out, taking risks. It was a good time to ramp up the chase, yet she again had her hands tied with a new homicide investigation. Kissick could spend all the time he needed and openly travel to follow up leads, whereas she'd had to sneak around and pay expenses out of her own pocket. But without giving him the information she had, she could see these new leads being squandered, turning into dead ends or worse.

Get too close, too soon and everything could disappear. Revealing the evidence she had could keep the investigation on course, but how could she tell all without hanging herself?

Kissick had found out about one of her infractions. He knew she'd stolen Nitro's necklace. He'd kept her secret. She didn't want to risk revealing more to him. If he told her secrets, her career would be dust. If he kept them, he'd put his career at risk. She cared about him too much to do that. Her motives were not completely altruistic. She also didn't want him to learn about the dark part of herself that she'd discovered. How she'd found herself capable of things that she would have never dreamed possible *before*. She used to feel that she knew the lengths she would go to to solve a case, the boundaries she absolutely would not cross. That was before one particular homicide case had landed in her lap: hers.

He fixed her with a look that made her wonder if he suspected what she'd been thinking. "Nan, I know you have theories about the man who attacked you. You told me that while you were on leave, you'd done research on murders of female police officers."

Vining felt a slow flush starting beneath her breastbone and moving up her neck. She had never told him that. He was guessing, and guessing correctly. He had inadvertently found out that she had stolen Nitro's necklace. He'd been shocked by her audacity. She'd demonstrated the brio of a practiced thief and liar, which suggested there was more where that had come from.

His eyes on hers didn't waver. "Before I get started, I'd like you to give me any information you've found, even if it's speculation. How about over a cup of coffee?"

Vining knew her neck was pink and hoped it hadn't traveled into her cheeks. "Okay. Great. We can do that right now." She rose to leave.

"Nan." Early stopped her. "I've called a briefing on the Scrappy Espinoza murder at four o'clock. Lieutenant Beltran will be there."

"Four o'clock. I'll be ready, Sarge."

On her way to get her purse, she stuck her head into Caspers's cubicle. On his desk was a DMV report on Pearl Zhang. Caspers was leaning on both elbows, his head propped up by his hands, looking as if he were reading it. Vining could tell by his deep breathing that he was asleep.

She knocked one of his arms out from under him.

His head nearly hit the desk before he recovered. He glared at her. "Wha the . . . ?"

His annoyance was no match for her seething anger. She snarled into his ear. "You're working the Espinoza case with me. Kissick's been assigned to a special project. Ruiz isn't working on this floor anymore. I'm going to be gone for an hour. Take a nap in the sleep room. Have another coffee or a Red Bull. I'll cover for you this time, but next time, I'm nailing your ass to the wall."

For a minute, he didn't know what to say. Finally, he got out, "Yes, ma'am."

She grabbed the DMV report. Beneath Pearl Zhang's was the report for her son, Lincoln Kennedy.

She stomped after Kissick.

Before they had left the floor, Sergeant Early came out after them. "Pearl Zhang's in the lobby with her attorney. She wants the crime scene released so her crew can start working. You two finish your business. I'll handle her."

Early turned to head toward the lobby staircase. Vining and Kissick went out the back.

ELEVEN

*K*issick got in the passenger side of the Crown Vic after tossing his suit jacket across the backseat. Vining had left her jacket at her desk, since she'd be returning to the office while he'd be taking off.

While she drove, he read Pearl Zhang's DMV report. "She's forty-five years old. She mentioned being around during the Cultural Revolution. She would have been a child. What a nightmare that must have been."

Kissick was a history buff and read voraciously. He had a bachelor's degree while Vining had barely skated through high school. She had the smarts to do better, but a college education had been the furthest thing from her mind then. All she'd wanted to do was marry Wes, her high school sweetheart, flee her mother's home and lifestyle, raise a family, and build a *different* life than the one in which she'd been raised. She'd accomplished that. It had been great for nearly four years, until it all went to hell when Wes abandoned her and Emily when the girl was just two.

Kissick said, "I wonder when Pearl left the mainland. The Chinese have eased their emigration policies, but years ago, it was tough to get out of the country. You had to pay somebody to smuggle you out, like the coyotes that bring people across the border from Mexico into the U.S. She or her family would have had to pay plenty."

"She told us she's lived in the U.S. for eighteen years."

Kissick looked at Lincoln Kennedy's DMV report. "The son is seventeen, like she said. I wonder if Pearl was pregnant when she came to the States. She married?"

"I haven't searched all the databases yet, but she wasn't wearing a ring last night." Vining hiked a shoulder. "Guess I could just ask her."

She gave him a wry smile. "See what you're going to miss by heading off to Montaña de Oro? I'm sure Madame Zhang would much prefer talking to you than me, but you've gotta do what you've gotta do."

"We both have a bad guy to track down."

"True, but you get to pursue a cagey, smart, serial killer of female police officers who's eluded capture for years and I get to find out who put a bullet in the head of a lifelong, gang-banging, drug-dealing, girlfriend-beating ex-con who finally got what was coming to him."

It came out sounding more vitriolic than she'd intended.

After leaving the police garage, she turned left onto Ramona and stopped at the intersection with Garfield. "You want to go to Conrad's?" When he didn't respond, she turned to see him studying her. "What?"

"Nothing."

She thought she detected pity in his eyes and it enraged her even more. "Don't get all high-and-mighty on me. You think the same thing about Scrappy Espinoza, whether you'll admit it or not."

"Nan, relax."

"Easy for you to say." She grabbed her sunglasses from the sun visor. "Conrad's." She turned left.

"You're right, Nan. It is easy for me to say. This saga is taking a toll on you."

"Saga? You mean my life?"

"Come on, Nan. We're friends. I don't like seeing you so upset." He put his hand on her knee.

She pinched the bridge of her nose beneath her sunglasses. She was getting a headache.

"Everything that's happened . . . It's changed you, Nan."

"Ya think?" She waved at a passing patrol car, smiling stiffly at the two officers inside. "Can't you see the way people look at me? I feel eyes on me all the time."

By his expression, Vining knew she was proving his point. She *was* losing it. At the end of the block, Walnut Street, she turned the vehicle right.

"Nan, what's happened to you would make the best of us—"

She cut him off. "What, Jim? Unhinged? Is that what this little talk is about?"

He sighed. "If you would let me finish. It would be a challenge for anyone to overcome."

She entered the diner's large parking lot. Big office buildings had sprung up all around it. Pasadena's old-style restaurants with their sprawling parking lots were being gobbled up by land-lusting developers. With the graying of the restaurants' clientele, the owners were reluctantly selling out. So far, Conrad's had held on to its corner.

She cut the engine, and had started to get out of the car when he stopped her with a hand on her arm. She looked at his hand as though affronted, but he didn't release her.

"Jim . . . I don't know what you want from me. No, that's not correct. I *do* know what you want from me. You want to know why I stole Nitro's necklace. Why it was so important for me to possess that I took a huge risk to get it. You want to know all the evidence I've gathered and all my theories about T. B. Mann and his victims. You know what? I'm going to tell you."

She knew it would come to this and had already sorted out what she would tell him and what she would hold back. He might be the lead investigator on record, but she would stay in charge. Her blood had been spilled. It was her right to distribute the results of her hard work any way she saw fit.

She tried to pull from his grasp, but he wouldn't let go. She tensed the muscles in her arm and pressed her lips together. She pulled harder. He held tighter.

"Nan . . ." The look in his eyes made her catch her breath. He had something to say and she sensed he was struggling to find the right words.

She couldn't. Not now. Not there. "Jim, please . . ."

He released her and she bolted from the car. He grabbed his manila file folder and followed her into the rear entrance, where a sign over the door said LOUNGE ENTRANCE. They walked through what used to be a dark cocktail lounge, lined with tufted semicircular booths, built in the days when businessmen had a snort before heading home to the little woman, battle-ax, ball-and-chain, or better half. Now the room was used for general dining, with not a cocktail in sight.

The former lounge was separated from the main restaurant by a panel that shielded an open doorway. They went around it and entered a large, sunny room where the walls were decorated with framed prints of sailing ships done in watercolor.

Vining asked the hostess, who looked the same vintage as the diner, for a booth in the back. Even though the police station was a few blocks away and officers often ate there, other diners looked at them, especially her. The focus of their attention was always the same. First they looked at her face, and then their eyes dropped to the gun and badge on her belt, then back to her face, with a decidedly different attitude.

When they had barely sat, a young waitress appeared to take their drink order. The servers all wore white shirts tucked into black pants, and red neckties.

Kissick glanced up from perusing the menu to order coffee.

Vining didn't pick up her menu. "I'm just having coffee."

When the waitress had left, Kissick said, "Why don't you order something? You're going to have a long day."

"I ate before I came in." She'd only had a banana and that half doughnut, but she'd lost her appetite.

"Did you? Emily spent the night at her friend's house. I know you don't bother to fix food when she's not around."

"Jim, I've taken care of myself and Emily for many years."

He gave her that same look that had set her off before. This time she let it go.

The waitress returned with the coffees.

Kissick said, "I'll have an egg-white omelet with vegetables and no cheese, fruit instead of hash browns, and whole-wheat toast, dry." He closed his menu, picked up Vining's from the table, and handed both of them to the waitress. "The lady will have a Denver omelet with fruit and whole-wheat toast."

Vining looked up from stirring her coffee and saw the concern in his face. She couldn't stay mad. "Thanks. An omelet does sound good after all. You remembered that Denver omelets are my favorite."

He folded his hands on the table and leaned toward her. "Of course I remembered. Nan, I think about you all the time."

It was a sweet thing to say. Her head knew it was terrific that he was devoting his full energies to the T. B.

Mann case. Her heart was having a hard time getting with the program. He *was* her friend. She managed a smile over the top of her coffee cup.

In response, he further softened his tone and began to unload things that had been troubling him. "I'm worried about you. You've lost weight. I bet you've lost ten pounds and you didn't have it to lose."

She shrugged. "I never weigh myself." She had noticed that her clothes were fitting looser.

He leaned closer. His lanky frame was now more than halfway across the table. She reflected that if they were a normal couple, he would have taken her hands, but there was little normal about them.

"Nan, you've always brought intensity and focus to your work, but lately you seem . . . haunted. The recent big cases we've worked are enough to take a toll on anyone. I've felt the strain. On top of that, you've had all this other stuff to deal with. Nitro and his drawings. The psycho bastard who attacked you and his notes and bloody shirt. I'm only telling you this because I'm worried about you."

Everything he'd said was true. Lately, she didn't like what she saw when she looked in the mirror. Dark circles beneath her eyes. Sallow complexion. To compensate, she put on extra makeup and avoided mirrors.

"Nan, something is weighing on you so heavily. You're never completely present. Even when it's just us, in our private moments, I feel like there's an elephant in the room."

She was not immune to his genuine concern about her. She let her guard down a little. She took in a deep breath and slowly let it out, feeling her shoulders relax and her back ease from its rigid pose and melt into the booth.

"Nan, it's keeping us from being truly together. From fulfilling what I know is tremendous promise for a life together. When I found out that you stole Nitro's necklace, it was an eye-opener. I thought, my God, she values her pursuit of the creep who attacked her, her obsession—whatever you want to call it—more than she values me."

He's right. It was no surprise to her. *Until death do we part.*

He slid his right hand toward her, palm-up, shoving out of the way the chrome napkin holder, salt and pepper shakers, and a steel basket stacked with packages of jam.

She set the coffee cup she'd been clutching between both hands on the saucer and placed her palm atop his. He closed his fingers around it.

"Nan, I love you."

That was the second time he'd uttered those three little words. The first time had been when they'd dated two years ago. Her response had been to end the relationship. He'd just put his heart on the table again.

Before she was aware of it, a tear sprang into the corner of her eye and slid down her face. It was soon followed by another and another. She pulled her hand from his, snatched paper napkins from the holder, and held them against her eyes.

The waitress appeared, plates lining an outstretched arm. She didn't seem to notice the drama being played out at the table as she recited the orders while setting down the plates. "Can I get anything else for you? I'll come back with some coffee."

Nan had stanched the flow of tears. She looked at his good, strong face. They were right for each other. She'd known it two years ago. She'd known it during the lonely years in between. It was time to come clean, about everything.

"I love you, too, Jim. I really do." After she said the words, she felt something inside her snap. A chip might have even fallen out, a tiny porcelain sliver. She had put a crack in T. B. Mann's stranglehold on her life.

His eyes brightened. He flashed a broad smile, then brought it under control. "I just . . . I didn't know what to think. I tell you I love you and you start to cry."

"Just a lot of stuff bottled up."

A realization hit her with the force of a sunbeam. Her crafty plan to tell him barely half the truth of what she'd learned about T. B. Mann was so wrong. She would tell him everything she'd done. She'd reveal everything she was. It was time for the secrets to end.

"Jim, I felt I had to do certain things to learn about his victims and to get closer to him. To T. B. Mann. Things I couldn't tell you because if I did, you'd be complicit, too. Yes, I'm obsessed with him. I think about him all the time. About trapping him. Killing him."

"Nan, I won't let anything happen to you or Emily. You're not alone anymore."

"Thank you for putting up with this. With me."

"Just doing my job, ma'am." He jokingly saluted.

The aroma of the food made her realize that she was hungry. The food looked great. She picked up her fork and dug in.

TWELVE

After the waitress had cleared their plates and topped off their coffee cups, Vining began her confession.

"Jim, you've got to promise me two things. One: No judgment."

He considered that, and then replied, "Okay."

"Two: Whatever I tell you has to stay with you."

He didn't need to think that over. "I can't make a blanket promise like that. I could care less that you stole that Froot Loop Nitro's necklace, but what else did you do? How bad does it get?"

"Not that bad." She became defensive and fibbed. "I just . . . *bent* the rules. I couldn't take the chance of evidence disappearing. I was afraid that T. B. Mann would retrace his steps and do a better job of covering his tracks. That look on your face . . ."

He rubbed his hand across his mouth, as if subconsciously forcing an attitude change.

She took a breath. "All I did was this. I told a white lie to you and Sarge so I could make a quick trip to Tucson."

"Tucson?"

"A quick turnaround, one afternoon coming back that evening. We were working that double homicide and you went to the desert by yourself."

He nodded, remembering. "Why Tucson?"

"Well, before I get to that . . ." It was time to drop the other shoe. "While I was in Tucson, I came into possession of another necklace."

"Came into possession." A dimple formed between his cheekbone and jaw.

"Yes." There was no need for him to know the tawdry details.

"What is the significance of these necklaces? Does your bad guy give his victims necklaces?" He frowned as a realization dawned on him. "They look like the one Nitro had. That's why you think Nitro is connected to your bad guy. His drawings weren't what made you so worked up, it was his necklace. That's why you took it."

"Yes to everything."

"So what's the Tucson connection?"

"Can I see Nitro's drawings?"

From the file folder, he took them out and handed them to her.

She found the one of the woman on the floor of the storage closet, her blouse stained with blood.

"This is an accurate drawing of an actual murder that happened three years ago. The victim is Tucson Police detective Johnna Alwin. I learned Alwin's name when I was on leave and doing my own investigation into murdered policewomen. Her last assignment was vice. She was killed on a Sunday evening. She was off-duty, dressed to meet her husband for dinner at the hotel where he worked. On her way there, she received a surprise call from her informant, Jesse Cuba, a recovering heroin addict. He asked her to stop by the medical building where he had a job as a janitor. Alwin relayed this to the watch commander and assured him that Cuba wasn't dangerous. He probably just wanted money.

"Alwin's body was found the next day. She'd been stabbed seventeen times. Cuba's body was later found in a fleabag motel where he was living. He was dead from an overdose of high-grade heroin. Alwin's purse and blood were in his room. Case closed.

"Whoever made this drawing had inside information

about that crime scene. The media knew Alwin was found in a storage closet in that building, but photos were never released. The person who drew this knew she had been wearing that particular necklace. It's a string of pearls with a pendant made of a garnet surrounded by fake diamonds. I have it at home."

Kissick's eyes didn't waver as he listened. He seemed to be peering into her soul. She understood how unnerving it would be to be interrogated by him.

"I own a nearly identical necklace." From her purse, she took out the satinette bag. She pulled open the drawstring closure and dumped her necklace onto the table.

Kissick picked it up. "Haven't I seen you wearing this?"

"I wore it just once to work, right after I came back from my leave. Months later, when Nitro showed up wearing his similar necklace, I was afraid someone might remember mine, but no one did."

"Everyone was wrapped up in that double homicide we were working. You were the only one who cared about Nitro. Now I understand why. Nan, if you'd only come forward about how important Nitro was, we could have put somebody on him to make sure he didn't just walk out of that psych ward and disappear."

"I agree." She knew it had been a stupid decision on her part.

He compared Vining's necklace with the necklaces in the drawings of Johnna Alwin and Cookie Silva. "A big clue right in front of me, and I missed it." He picked up her necklace and dangled it from his fingers. "If you'd worn only this and a pair of high heels, I might have remembered it." He playfully wiggled his eyebrows.

He was trying to cheer her up and she appreciated it. She smiled crookedly. "Or maybe not."

"Maybe not," he agreed. With a grin, he sat back in the booth. "So what do you know about these necklaces?"

"Mine and Johnna Alwin's are high-quality costume jewelry. I had mine appraised. The jeweler said it was well made and worth about five hundred dollars. Five years ago, someone dropped it into my home mailbox. It wasn't wrapped. It had this card attached to it."

She fished inside the satinette bag and pulled out the small panel card with its message in fountain pen: Congratulations, Officer Vining. A red ribbon was threaded through a hole punched into the corner.

"Five years ago," he said. "That was around the time of the Lonny Veltwandter incident."

Lonny Veltwandter, better known to legions of 1980s heavy-metal fans as Lonny Velcro, was the man Vining had shot to death in a controversial incident. Velcro had pulled a gun on Vining after she'd responded to his call claiming that a young actress-model had committed suicide with a gun at his home. The shooting had been found to be in policy, but the media and angry Lonny Velcro fans had dogged Vining for ages.

"The Veltwandter shooting gave you your fifteen minutes of fame," Kissick said. "Do you think that's what drew your bad guy's attention to you?"

"Absolutely. I received tons of cards and gifts after that, but everything was sent in care of the Pasadena Police Department. All except the necklace."

"Why didn't you turn it in?"

Vining shrugged. "I don't know. Partially because it came to my house and no one knew about it. Partially because I didn't know what it meant. If I had a stalker on my hands, I wanted to keep everything. A nice piece of jewelry like this . . . Things have disappeared from evidence. Years went by and no stalker surfaced. I put the necklace away in the back of my dresser drawer and there it sat for years. I've only recently taken it out and I wore it just that once to work."

Kissick asked, "How did Alwin come by her necklace?"

"Similar to me. Her husband said it had shown up in their mailbox about a year before Johnna's murder, with a panel card attached. He thought the note had said, 'Congratulations, Officer Alwin,' but he wasn't sure. He didn't keep the note. Alwin had also been involved in a high-profile shooting. She killed a local mob associate. The media couldn't get enough of her girl-goes-up-against-the-mob story."

The waitress came by with a coffeepot in each hand. Seeing the necklace on the table, she commented, "Isn't that pretty!"

Vining nearly said, "Thank you," but felt the impulse was twisted. Not wanting to ignore her, she said, "It's unusual, isn't it?"

They turned down more coffee and Kissick asked for the check.

Holding both coffeepots by their handles in one hand, she yanked checks from her back pants pocket, shuffled through them, and set one in front of him.

"How does Nitro's necklace fit into this scheme?" he asked, after the waitress had left. "As I recall, it was pretty beat-up."

"It's older and more cheaply made than mine or Alwin's. I wonder if it has something to do with where it all started. Based on what we found out today, Cookie Silva might be T. B. Mann's first victim."

Vining took the drawing of Cookie Silva strung up by her ankles and moved it to the left on the table. "Cookie was murdered ten years ago. Next is Marilu Feathers, eight years ago." She moved the drawing of the park ranger to the right of Cookie's.

"Then Johnna Alwin, three years ago. And me, a year

and three months ago." She put those two drawings in order.

"You said that Alwin's necklace had a garnet in the pendant. Yours has a pearl. I don't remember Nitro's that clearly."

"His has what looks like a fake sapphire," Vining said. "They're all birthstones. Garnet is the stone for January. Sapphire is September. Pearl is June."

"But pearl isn't your birthstone. Your birthday's in April."

"True. But T. B. Mann attacked me in June."

He thought about that. "What month was Johnna Alwin murdered?"

She felt herself getting worked up, excited by talking about her hypotheses. "January. See, these aren't birthstones, they're *death* stones."

She could tell he wasn't as enthused.

"Jim, don't you see the connection?"

"I see the connection, but I think we need to take a step back."

She didn't like the sound of that. "What do you mean?"

"I don't buy criminal mastermind theories. Sure, there are serial killers who target a certain type of victim, who stalk them and execute a planned attack, but what you're proposing takes this to a whole other level. Frankly, to an absurd level, in my opinion."

"Absurd?" She was shocked.

"Think about it, Nan. According to your theory, your psycho carefully picked his victims, perhaps from news reports, had jewelry made for them with gems that foretold the month in which he was going to kill them, and then expertly pulled it off. Not killing streetwalkers or runaways or housewives, but *policewomen*, trained to do battle with bad guys."

Vining glowered at him.

"Nan, the impulse to murder for these guys is an itch they have to scratch. They're not spending years planning, tracking, having jewelry made." He poked at the necklace.

She remained silent.

"I'm sorry, Nan, but I have to be honest with you."

"What about the profile of T. B. Mann we've developed? There's not a single piece of evidence that goes contrary to it. He appears to have a law-enforcement connection. He could be a cop. He could be a clerk, a technician, or even a police volunteer. We found a police scanner in the house on El Alisal Road where I was attacked. Street gangs use scanners to keep track of who's on patrol, so we can't assume he's on the inside. He could be a clever police groupie. He's methodical and patient. He carefully plans before he acts. He planned everything when he ambushed me, even an escape route.

"He's definitely hunting female cops, but not just any female cop. Johnna Alwin and I both killed a man in the line of duty. Most cops never even fire their gun in the field, but Alwin and I both killed a man. We don't just have the aura of being dangerous and fearless, we've proved it. What's Marilu Feathers's and Cookie Silva's history? Further, the four women in these drawings aren't just cops, but we're also wives, sisters, mothers, girlfriends. Who is he killing over and over? We have to get inside his head."

"I'll track down leads and follow the evidence."

"But we *have* evidence and it all points to a serial killer of policewomen."

He tapped the drawing of Johnna Alwin. "Tucson P.D. told you she was murdered by her informant."

"The informant was conveniently found dead of a drug overdose. I say he was framed."

He tapped the drawing of the woman strung up in the barn. "Cookie Silva's murderer is on death row."

She narrowed her eyes. "Wasn't a guy released last week after serving twenty years for a murder he didn't commit because of testimony from a jailhouse snitch who later confessed that he'd lied?"

"Nan," Kissick said softly. "I'll get your bad guy. I'm one hundred percent committed to this. Just because I don't share your methodology doesn't mean I'm going to let him slip away."

"Are you mad because I turned up more leads in your investigation in my spare time and when I was on leave without access to the criminal databases than you did while working on it full-time?"

She saw the dimple again.

She'd resisted spitting out the cruel truth, but she'd had enough of being grilled and having her theories questioned by him.

"What about those leads?" he shot back. "You should have immediately come forward. Why didn't you?"

"I had to go after T. B. Mann my way and without Sergeant Early, Lieutenant Beltran, or anybody looking over my shoulder. You have to admit, it worked. Think about it. If I'd gone to Sarge right after I learned about Johnna Alwin, the investigation would have been ripped out of my hands and yours, too. Beltran would have beat the drum like he always does about a break in a big case. He lives to stand in the spotlight. He might have called in the FBI, who would have stomped through our business with their polished wingtips. Do you think Nitro would have shown up then? Think T. B. Mann would have left that note for me or put the bloody shirt in my garage? You agreed at the beginning of this conversation, no judgment."

"That cuts both ways, doesn't it?"

She took a deep breath, trying to calm down. In the space of a few minutes, they'd gone from expressing their love for each other to this. She didn't think of herself as a fatalist, but had to wonder if they were doomed as a couple. The atmosphere between them had changed as if a noxious gas had seeped into the room.

A shadow crossed his face. He felt the change, too. He looked at his watch and began gathering the photocopies of the drawings. "We'd better get going."

She grabbed her necklace and put it inside the satinette bag with the panel card.

He held out his palm. "Can I have that, please? I can use it when I go to Montaña de Oro and Colina Vista. Where are the other two necklaces—Johnna Alwin's and Nitro's?"

"At my house."

"Leave them there for now. This is the only one Sarge might have seen you with."

He responded to her grave expression. "Don't worry. I'll figure out a way to legitimize all the evidence you've found. Try my best, anyway."

His last comment didn't fill her with warmth.

She handed him the bag. As she did so, she felt a strand of the spider's silk that bound her and T. B. Mann being stretched to the breaking point. Given the psychic toll he'd taken on her, she should have felt relieved to shift the burden onto someone else, particularly onto Kissick's capable shoulders. She was coming to the sad realization about the extent to which the relationship, even though toxic, had defined her recent life. Who was she now?

THIRTEEN

*I*n the PPD garage, Kissick and Vining both got out of her car.

"I'm gonna take off," he said. "You're rolling with Caspers, right? Let me know how things go, okay? I'll see you."

He lingered for a telling second. In that second, she was sorry. Sorry about everything she'd done to contribute to sending her life sideways. Sorry she'd argued with him at the diner. Sorry she'd ended their first relationship two years before. Sorry she'd not called for backup sooner when she'd answered the suspicious circumstances call at 835 El Alisal Road. Sorry she'd worked overtime that day instead of just relaxing at home.

She of all people should understand how a person's life could change on a dime. How it could change from being fine to being crap in a nanosecond. Still, the utter fragility of life never ceased to amaze her. But after the flesh, blood, and bone were long gone, love remained. And hate.

She had a feeling deep inside that all was not lost between her and Kissick. She had to back off a little. Soften a little. It did not come naturally to her in her relationships with men. She'd had poor models growing up. Her biological father had abandoned her when she was a toddler. Her mother had remarried, giving birth to Stephanie with her second husband, whom she'd later ditched for husband number three. Thankfully,

Vining was out of the house by the time number four had entered the scene.

She couldn't continue to blame the sins of her mother for her own failings. Everything was her own doing now.

She managed a tentative but sincere smile. Typical lovers would have hugged and kissed. All Vining could offer was her hand. "Good luck, Jim."

He brightened with that small gesture. "Good luck to you, too. I'll keep you informed."

"Thanks. Stay safe."

"You, too."

She walked toward the station's back door, not looking back.

Upstairs, Sergeant Early told her that Lieutenant Beltran had had a conversation with Pearl Zhang and she'd agreed to stop work on the Hollenbeck building until the PPD investigators were satisfied they'd completed their investigation.

"Wonder how much of a fight she put up." Vining surveyed the cubicles. "Jones and Sproul take off?"

"I took the liberty of sending them to do knock-and-talks in Old Town. I figured you wanted to interview Marvin Li, Scrappy's employer, yourself."

"That's correct."

"While you were gone, we found out that Li's moniker is China Dog."

"Really?"

"Yolanda pulled Li's criminal history." Early was referring to one of the staff assistants. "His rap sheet's a mile long. Been getting in trouble since he was a teenager in San Francisco. The usual bad guy stuff. Barroom brawls. Assault. Narcotics possession and sale. Most notable was a twenty-year stint he did at Pelican Bay for second-degree murder. Li participated in a big shoot-out at the Golden Lotus restaurant in San Francisco's Chinatown between Li's gang, Wah Ching, and the Chinatown Boys."

Early showed her Li's mug shot and a current driver's-license photo. His upper body was heavily tattooed, his head was shaved, and he had a long Fu Manchu mustache.

Vining asked, "Was the tag that Scrappy painted an outburst from a disgruntled employee or a sign that Asian gangs are moving into Pasadena?"

"We need to know more about Asian street gangs. Corporal Lam's gone to meet with the Sheriff's Asian Gang Specialist at the Temple City station. He'll tell us what he learns at the briefing this afternoon."

"So Marvin Li is out of prison and running a business in San Gabriel," Vining said. "Word is that Scrappy was out of the life. Is Li presumably legit?"

"After completing parole for the murder rap, he moved down here from the Bay Area. Owns a house in San Gabriel. Outwardly, he's an upstanding citizen. He's founded an organization called Guns Gone. He consults with cities and law-enforcement agencies to help them get gangs and guns off the street. Recruits former gang members to try to knock some sense into current gangbangers. Caspers found Li's name in several newspaper articles. Guns Gone was awarded a six-figure contract from Los Angeles and smaller contracts from other cities, including a couple in the San Gabriel Valley. Li works with the local parole office, giving jobs to gangbangers in this Aaron's Aarrows company he has."

Vining took the packet of information that Early handed her. "Should be an interesting conversation with Mr. Li. I'll get Caspers and we'll be on our way."

"Caspers looks ragged today. Haven't seen him in a while."

Vining knew he was getting forty winks in the sleep room. "We're all working long hours."

"That we are, but we don't want anyone getting hurt because they're overtired."

Vining read between Early's words. Sarge was aware that Caspers's off-duty shenanigans were impacting his job. Caspers was a favorite in the unit. His sense of humor and energy brought a much-needed bright spot, but that would only carry him so far if he continued to shoot himself in the foot.

"Agreed, Sarge. I'll make sure he understands that."

"Kissick get everything he needed from you?"

Vining answered truthfully. "Yes."

Traffic had been released on the street in front of the Hollenbeck Paper building, but yellow barrier tape was still attached to the chain-link fence surrounding the construction site. Arriving workmen carrying lunchboxes were being intercepted by a tall Latino in a white polo shirt embroidered with a Pai Builders logo. They weren't happy to be told to go home until further notice. PPD vehicles were parked along the curb. A uniformed officer with a clipboard was standing at the building entrance, keeping track of who entered and left the scene.

Vining parked near two PPD sedans marked "Forensics."

Standing outside the barrier tape, looking more cheerful than Vining would have expected, was Pearl Zhang. She was with Lieutenant George Beltran. Homicide-Assault was one of the detective units under his command. They were standing between two tall steel-protected Canary Island date palms in front of the building.

From the way Zhang and Beltran were leaning toward each other and talking animatedly, it appeared they were flirting.

"Looks like Beltran's trying to get some tail." Caspers

was more alert than when Vining had first encountered him that morning, but he was somewhat less than his usual effervescent self. This was okay with Vining, who wasn't up to dealing with full-strength Caspers.

"His magic seems to be working on the Dragon Lady," Vining said. "At least she's not in *her friend* the chief's office, complaining how much the work stoppage is costing her."

Beltran reached to grab Zhang's forearm to punctuate a point he was making. She did not retract but leaned even closer. They both broke into laughter.

"Go George," Caspers remarked with admiration.

Beltran's glee caused him to twist away and spot Vining and Caspers. He regally waved them over.

Passing the entrance to the building, Vining glanced inside. Sunlight streamed inside the debris-filled hull. Wooden stakes and twine divided the area into a grid. PPD forensics specialists and a half-dozen uniformed officers were sifting through the rubble.

"Good morning, Detectives." Beltran's cheery greeting was more fitting for a surprise encounter across a ballroom at a charity event than standing on the periphery of a murder scene. Rumors about Beltran's affairs had been grist for the gossip mill for years. Now that he had recently separated from his wife, his much-ballyhooed reputation as a ladies' man was on open display.

Beltran wasn't Vining's type, but she could see why women found him attractive. He was Latino and had a square jaw, strong cheekbones, and thick black hair that was just starting to show silver at the temples, as if by master plan. He likely tweaked it. It was known that he bleached his teeth, so they would stand out better against his perennially tanned olive skin. He was athletic and outdoorsy. He wore clothes well.

Cameras loved him and he loved cameras. He enjoyed being the public face of the PPD at press conferences and had garnered female fans who'd sent him e-mails, gushing about how hot he looked in his uniform. He liked to hobnob with the rich and famous. Pasadena had attracted the rich and merely affluent since the early 1900s. Hollywood celebrities were now discovering its small-town charms with big-city features, to the dismay of longtime residents who resented the glitzy influx. But Beltran liked the glitterati just fine. The better to shop around his screenplay *Death in a Blue Uniform*. Rumor had it that his Hollywood ambitions had derailed his upward mobility in the PPD, which had once been his overarching passion.

"Good morning, Lieutenant." Vining shook his hand and then greeted Pearl Zhang without a handshake. "Mrs. Zhang. You remember Detective Caspers."

Zhang nodded in greeting. "Good morning, Detectives." She wore a slim dress with a patent-leather belt around her tiny waist. The style was understated, but the fabric was rich: lustrous royal blue silk. Her hair was still tightly pulled back. Today she was wearing big diamond stud earrings so heavy they bent her earlobes. Around her neck was a round disk of carved apple-green jade set inside gold with a large diamond at the top. She wore no makeup on her flawless face other than mascara and her trademark deep-red lipstick.

In the sunlight, Vining could detect Zhang's age in the fine lines around her eyes and mouth.

She carried what Vining guessed was a pricey designer handbag. It was a study in understated elegance, with black leather quilted in a distinctive pattern and three dangling gold charms. The handbag didn't shout its pedigree by having the designer name plastered all over it. It was like a secret handshake between society ladies, as much of an insider symbol as the hand signs thrown up by street-gang members.

Vining couldn't care less about such status symbols, except when it came to firearms. Then she coveted the very best. Her only exposure to luxury clothing and accessories had rubbed off from Emily who had become alarmingly aware of such through the influence of her stepmother, *arriviste* Kaitlyn.

Vining knew that Zhang might well have a dramatic and inspiring up-by-her-bootstraps story. She could have arrived in the States with ten dollars in her pocket, worked hard, saved every penny she'd earned, taken calculated risks, and built an empire. She might think that put her on a pedestal above a lowly cop like Vining, and that she hovered above any requirement to tell all she knew about Scrappy Espinoza's murder. Vining privately relished the thought of yanking her off that pedestal and making her understand that no matter who she was or how much money she had, if she didn't talk, she was an accessory to murder. And one more thing—Vining didn't want her son around Emily.

Beltran was cheerful. "Excuse me, Mrs. Zhang, while I talk to my investigators."

"Of course. I have to be on my way. Thank you very much, Lieutenant, for your time. And please call me Pearl."

"Pearl, I'll let you know the minute we release the scene. I've committed maximum resources to processing it as quickly as possible, to not only give us the information we need but to put your crew back to work. You have my cell-phone number if you have any questions or concerns."

"Yes, I do. Thank you, Lieutenant."

"George." He extended his hand.

"George," she replied, returning his handshake with a smile and a bow.

He bowed as well.

Vining had to admit that Beltran excelled at spreading the royal jelly.

He was still smiling when he turned to Vining and Caspers.

Vining was waiting for the right time to tell him that Zhang was holding back on what she knew about China Dog when he beat her to the punch.

"China Dog is the street moniker of Marvin Li." Beltran watched Zhang getting into her spotlessly polished Mercedes. "Li owns a business in San Gabriel that employed Scrappy Espinoza and has been in and out of jail most of his life."

Vining already knew this and was about to voice her concerns about Pearl Zhang's integrity when Beltran added, "Marvin Li is Pearl Zhang's cousin on her mother's side. Pearl was forthcoming about Li's criminal history. She insists he's stepped into the light and is one of the good guys now. He's dedicated his life to keeping gangbangers employed and out of the life. Pearl apologized for not revealing this when you spoke last night. She was upset about the murder and afraid that her cousin's former life was splashing onto her business and reputation, a fear she's had since Li moved into her part of town. Pearl contacted Li early this morning and told him about the murder. She said he was shocked and knows nothing about it. Pearl believes him."

He took a business card from his pocket and handed it to Vining. It was for Aaron's Aarrows and had a handwritten cell-phone number on it. "Li will be at his place of business all day and looks forward to talking with you."

Beltran's success with Pearl Zhang brought home a truth that Vining's grandmother often reminded her about and that Vining often forgot: You can catch more flies with honey than vinegar.

"Thank you, Lieutenant." Vining slipped the card

into her jacket pocket. "You got a lot more from her than I did last night."

He looked at the large placard on the chain-link fence with the rendering of the completed condominium and retail complex, developed by Red Pearl Enterprises.

Vining looked at it, too, and privately conceded that the finished project would be impressive. She glanced at Caspers, who was listening attentively, respectfully silent.

Beltran added, "Pearl confessed that not many people in her professional life know that Marvin Li is her cousin. He was once a very bad guy."

Vining nodded. "I saw his criminal history. We found out that he was Scrappy's employer last night."

"You have to appreciate her concerns about maintaining her reputation with the many civic and charitable organizations she's involved with and all the citizens who have a certain image of her. People who trusted her enough to invest money in her business."

Vining was familiar with the destructiveness of a hidden life. One could try to bury it, yank it out by the roots, douse it with poison, but, like a pernicious weed, it kept sending shoots to the surface, often in a different place, where one would least expect it. She and Pearl Zhang had that much in common.

FOURTEEN

Vining and Caspers walked to a white modular building in the adjacent parking lot where Pai Builders had their on-site office. On their way, Detective Louis Jones called Vining on her cell phone. He and Detective Doug Sproul had learned that the brother and cousin of Titus Clifford, who had been murdered in a shooting attributed to the NLK, had been seen at the Volcano restaurant in Old Town around the time Scrappy was murdered. Jones had issued a BOLO—Be On the Look-Out for—the brother and cousin who were sought for questioning.

Vining led the way up the steps to the Pai Builders office, opened the flimsy door, and stepped onto thin indoor-outdoor carpeting that was tracked with dirt. Desks and filing cabinets were arranged along the walls. A plump young woman with chin-length two-toned hair—platinum on top and raven-black beneath—sat at the desk closest to the door. Both ears were lined with pierced earrings, including a small gold squiggle through the cartilage at the top of her right ear. Cleavage overflowed her snug and partially unbuttoned blouse. Her face was reminiscent of a Kewpie doll.

She asked, "Can I help you?"

"Detectives Nan Vining and Alex Caspers to speak with Joey Pai." She moved her jacket to show her shield.

Caspers was behind her, but she could tell by the look

in the woman's eyes that he was showing her more than professional interest and she was not immune to it.

At the rear of the trailer, a large Asian man stood from behind a cluttered desk. He appeared to be in his forties and wore a white polo shirt with a Pai Builders logo on its breast. He was tall, broad, and deeply tanned, looking as if he'd once been an athlete but had since filled out. "Find any more bodies?" he jokingly shouted to them.

Vining approached. "I'm Detective Vining."

He held out a big palm to shake. "Joey Pai. How can I help you?"

Instead of taking his hand, she gave him her card. "This is Detective Alex Caspers. We'd like to ask you some questions about the murder on your construction site last night."

"So, Detective . . ." He glanced at her card. "Vining. Have a seat. How can I help you?"

She sat across from Pai. Caspers remained standing, looking out a small window. She took out Scrappy's most recent mug shot. "This is the dead man. His name is Abel Espinoza. Nicknamed Scrappy. Do you recognize him?"

Pai took the photograph and studied it. "Can't say that I do." He handed it back to her. "That guy's got gang tattoos. I don't hire gangbangers. I wouldn't let him set foot on my construction site."

He was either born or raised locally. He had that breezy, almost too-familiar manner of Southern Californians born after the Kennedy administration, as if life was just a dream, dude.

"Excuse me a minute." He picked up a two-way radio from his desk, keyed it, and spoke into it using adept Spanish.

Vining looked at a calendar from a heavy-equipment supply company on the wall. It had a photograph of a model wearing a bikini and high heels. She had mile-long legs, huge breasts, tiny waist, and hips that would be appropriate for a ten-year-old boy. She was suggestively climbing astride a backhoe.

The photo had already attracted Caspers's attention.

Vining commented, "She looks like a Barbie doll."

With complete sincerity, he said, "I like Barbie dolls."

"Real women don't look like that."

He turned up his hand and shook his head, as if nonplussed by her comment.

Pai set down the two-way. He rested his hands on the arms of his desk chair. Like the other office furniture in the room, it was utilitarian and far from top-of-the-line.

"I wish I could be of more help, Detective. That murder was terrible, of course, but did they have to deface the mosaic, too? It had been commissioned by Mr. Hollenbeck years ago and had been on a wall in his office. Now I have to hire a specialist to restore it, if possible, and get the security company that was supposed to be watching the site to pay for it. Mrs. Zhang is displeased, to put it mildly. She's worried that the murder will put a chill on condo sales once the complex is finished."

"The dead man had two little kids, a mother, and a couple of siblings. It's put a chill on their lives, too."

"For sure. I mean, that goes without saying." Pai became flustered as he attempted damage control. While citizens condemned gang violence, the flower of their fervor was still reserved for NIMBY—Not In My Back Yard.

"Mr. Pai, do you know of anyone who has a grudge against you or your company?"

He made a dismissive sound. "Where do I begin? Burning the place down or destroying equipment would be more their style. Some in the community see property developers as the enemy. We tear down notable buildings, use up open space. But Pearl Zhang is known for her adaptive reuse of historic buildings. She won't settle for anything less than top-of-the-line work. That's why she hires us."

"How long have you known Mrs. Zhang?"

"About five years. This is my third job with her, and the biggest. She's becoming a giant in the San Gabriel Valley. She's tough, but reasonable. She's a good businesswoman. We work together fine."

"Who's backing her financially?"

"I don't know specifics. She has investors. She'll bring by men in suits to the site. I get paid on time. That's all I care about." Pai had second thoughts about what he'd said. "She's totally legit. Everything's aboveboard. I don't work that way."

"Do you know anyone who has a grudge against her?"

"You don't make friends in this business. The local preservationists get mad, the residents in the area get mad, the businesses nearby get mad, at least while construction is going on. Then they're happy when people move into the apartments and condos and the street-level retail draws foot traffic. But there are projects in Pasadena that have been tied up in lawsuits for decades."

"Do you know Pearl Zhang personally, beyond your business relationship?"

"Not really. I've been to her office in San Marino. She's come in here with her son and mother, but I don't go out drinking with her, if that's what you're getting at. It's all business."

Vining handed him the recent DMV photo of Marvin Li. "Have you ever seen this man around here?"

Pai took his time, finally shaking his head. "No. I would have remembered that guy, all inked up and with that long Fu Manchu mustache."

"Does the name Marvin Li ring a bell?"

"No."

"How about Aaron's Aarrows?"

He laughed. "Aaron's Aarrows? What's that?"

"Those guys who stand on the street corners with the big arrows advertising apartments or new shops."

"Right. I've seen them, but not around here."

"Does Pearl Zhang ever talk about her extended family? Aunts, uncles, cousins . . . ?"

"You think she's mixed up in this?"

"I'm just asking questions, Mr. Pai."

"I don't know anything about her family, other than her mother and son."

"Are any of your employees Chinese?"

"No."

"You don't employ anyone who's Chinese?"

He became serious. "I'm of Korean descent, Detective."

Behind him, she saw Caspers quickly face the wall, as if to hide his grin.

"I know. All Asians look alike, don't they, Detective?" Pai was grim.

Vining felt her cheeks grow hot.

Pai laughed. "I'm just messing with you. People take me for Chinese all the time. Your face . . ." He laughed some more. "My brother's a deputy sheriff out of the Altadena station. I love to give him crap. I'm sorry. I shouldn't mess with you."

"No problem," Vining said.

"My parents emigrated from South Korea during the war. I was born and raised in Northeast L.A. I graduated from Wilson High School. There are so many Chinese immigrants in the San Gabriel Valley these days. People come up to me and assume I don't even speak English. I'm always like, 'Hey, I'm a native American.' But to answer your earlier question, my crew is nearly all Latino. That's the business now."

"Thank you for your time, Mr. Pai." Vining stood.

"You're welcome. If I find out anything, I'll call you right away. Hey, did you hear about the Chinese couple that had a blond baby? They named him Sum Ting Wong."

"Joey, you're so bad," the receptionist said to him over her shoulder.

Caspers spared her until they were back on the street. "I'm not Chinese, I'm Korean, he says. You think we all look alike." He began cackling.

"Shaddup," she said, provoking more laughter from Caspers.

She unlocked the Crown Vic and he opened the passenger door.

"I'm surprised he works for the Dragon Lady," Caspers said when he was inside the car. "The Chinese and the Koreans don't like each other."

"I think it's the Japanese and the Koreans."

"Really? It's not the Chinese?"

Vining cranked the ignition. "In the immortal words of the great philosopher Rodney King, 'Can't we all get along?' "

"One word," Caspers replied. "No."

At the corner of Colorado Boulevard and Lake, they saw a guy wearing a gorilla costume with a full-head mask doing a choreographed dance with a large arrow that said: Archstone Apartments Now Leasing.

FIFTEEN

They took the local streets the five miles to San Gabriel, heading south through Pasadena and its well-heeled neighbor, San Marino. Driving curvy, tree-lined streets, they passed stately mansions set back on manicured lawns. The small city's affluent residents tried hard to hang on to old traditions, which came to feel like wrapping one's arms around a palm tree in a hurricane. The area had experienced a huge demographic shift over the past thirty years as wealthy Chinese immigrants bought large homes there, prompting wags to label the city "Chan" Marino.

After they crossed Huntington Drive, they were still within San Marino's city limits, but left the mansions behind as the homes and lawns grew more modest. Entering the city of Alhambra, houses and front yards became more modest yet, apartment buildings appeared, and the Chinese influence was more pronounced. The signage on virtually all the commercial buildings was in Chinese and English, and often only in Chinese. Many of the quaint single-story brick-and-masonry buildings along the main thoroughfares had been razed and replaced with multistory minimalls that housed Chinese video stores, specialists in foot massage, and scads of Chinese restaurants.

The San Gabriel Valley is home to the best and most authentic Chinese food outside of Hong Kong. Among the more commonly available Taiwanese, Shanghaiese,

Hunan, Sichuan, and Cantonese cuisines were restaurants specializing in Chiu Chow, Macanese, Shenyang, Hakka, and Yunnan. There was always great controversy among the S.G. Valley Chinese food aficionados over where to find the best Xiao Long Bao—juicy pork dumplings.

Reaching Main Street, they turned left, heading east.

At the city limits of San Gabriel, Main Street becomes Las Tunas Drive. The shape and color of the street signs change to incorporate a Spanish adobe design as one of the twenty-one California missions is here, dating from 1771. The Mission San Gabriel Arcángel's greatest legacy was set in motion in 1781 when a party of two padres and several families left it to hike nine miles west to found El Pueblo de Nuestra la Reina de Los Angeles.

As Vining and Caspers continued down Las Tunas, the street narrowed and became dotted with small storefront businesses. They observed another phenomenon in the constantly evolving culture of the region— tucked between camera shops, nail salons, dumpling restaurants, escrow offices, tae kwon do studios, and karaoke bars were dozens of large and tiny bridal shops. The unique mixture of retail businesses extended beyond the San Gabriel city limits into its neighbor, Temple City.

The bridal shops catered to brides of all stripes, but had a Chinese bent; alongside traditional white wedding gowns and colorful bridesmaid's dresses were floor-length, formfitting silk sheaths with Mandarin collars and deep side slits. The dresses were in vibrant tones of red, gold, or emerald green and were lavishly embroidered or sequined with designs of dragons, phoenixes, lotus flowers, or butterflies.

Caspers looked for Aaron's Aarrows while Vining drove.

"What's with all the bridal shops?" he asked.

"They took hold here some years ago. They have good prices, and sell cocktail dresses and evening gowns too. Makes it easy if you have to buy a dress because you can park once and go door-to-door."

"Sounds like you've shopped here before."

"I have a relative who insists upon a wedding each time she gets married." Vining was thinking of her mother. "I've heard that some of these bridal salons are fronts for Chinese organized crime. Escrow offices are another common front. No customers ever come in. Then one day, the shop just closes up. Gets emptied out in the middle of the night."

"Slow down." Caspers pointed. "That's the address for Aaron's Aarrows."

It was a small bridal shop. A large sign above the front display windows said: LOVE POTION BRIDAL.

Vining made an illegal U-turn and had no problem finding street parking right in front. It was eleven o'clock on a weekday morning. No shoppers were around, but all the shops had "Open" signs in their windows.

Love Potion's two front windows were crammed with mannequins dressed in frilly wedding gowns festooned with shimmering sequins, beads, and crystals sewn onto yards of poofy white satin and lace. Some of the gowns had been in the window so long, the fabric had yellowed from the sun. Open parasols were stacked in the corners. Strips of silver-and-gold metallic stars hung from the ceiling.

The mannequins had hourglass figures and bullet breasts and appeared to have been rescued from a mannequin graveyard in downtown L.A.'s garment district. The eyes and lips on their Caucasian faces were heavily painted. They were all brunettes, wearing stiff synthetic wigs that would have been at home in an Annette Funicello and Frankie Avalon beach-blanket movie. Their plaster arms and hands were poised as if they were jockeying for position at the front of the window.

The centerpiece, standing alone, was a mannequin in a tasteful white strapless wedding gown. In her hands, posed primly in front of her, she held a bouquet of red silk roses. The upward tilt of her head was dignified and distant, her face solemn. Her red lips were parted slightly, the lower one pouting. Her dark, painted eyes were cast downward and to the side.

Vining and Caspers got out of the car and gaped at the display. She took photos of the shop with her digital camera and returned it to her pocket.

Caspers cracked, "Instead of Love Potion, this looks more like love poison."

Vining stared at the mannequin in the middle. "That has to be the saddest bride in the world."

Caspers joined her in examining the bride's joyless face. "Maybe she just found out that the groom's banging her maid of honor."

"Or he's having an affair with his much younger hair stylist at SuperCuts." As soon as the comment was out of her mouth, Vining regretted it. What had possessed her to say such a thing? That was her and her ex-husband Wes's story, although he'd waited until four years after their modest wedding to break the news of his affair.

It went over Caspers's head. He chuckled and reached for the door to pull it open.

When it didn't budge, Vining pointed out a sign above the handle that said: Push. The lower half of the door was covered with a dented steel plate.

When he pushed it open for her, a loud buzzer sounded.

Heavy metal music played, originating from the back of the store.

Caspers bobbed his head to the beat.

A desk at the rear of the shop was empty.

"Hello," Vining called. "Anyone here?" She again opened and closed the door, sounding the buzzer.

"We're interested in looking at a wedding dress," Caspers joked.

The long and narrow shop was floored with large black-and-white linoleum squares. Tiered garment racks bolted side by side along the walls were crammed with gowns filled with plastic bust forms. Two chairs, upholstered in pale pink, were near the entrance. A round coffee table between them was strewn with well-thumbed bridal magazines and *Sports Illustrated*. A crystal ashtray was free of butts, but was coated with ash.

A spiraling freestanding rack was loaded with puffy veils. Two dressing rooms on one wall had their pink velvet privacy curtains pulled open. Between them were three-way full-length mirrors set atop a carpeted platform.

Boxes of shoes were stacked on the ground with samples on display. A glass case held gloves, lacy garters, strapless, long-line bras, and beaded headpieces. On top of the glass case was a fish bowl with blue glass pebbles at the bottom. Swimming in it were eight goldfish and a single black one.

Large framed posters of Asian brides lined the walls. All of them wore demure expressions even if the gowns they modeled were not. Also in a frame on the wall was a long, red silk robe. The full sleeves and hem were spread. It was covered in embroidery depicting a man and a woman wearing traditional Chinese dress, kneeling facing each other. Above them, two brilliantly hued butterflies soared.

"Hello . . ." Vining called. "Anyone here?" She felt that something was not right. She took out her gun. She had well earned her moniker "Quick Draw," but didn't care. She'd rather err on the side of caution and live to tell about it.

As for Caspers, he needed no encouragement to ramp up the force level. He quickly had his gun in front.

"This is Detective Vining and Detective Caspers of the Pasadena Police. We're looking for Marvin Li." They stayed still, looking and listening, hearing only the heavy metal music.

She pointed for him to head down one side of the shop, while she took the other.

A flash of light drew her eye to a corner where a square mirror was attached to the wall near the ceiling. She thought it was there to watch for potential shoplifters.

They searched through the racks of densely packed gowns, moving down each side of the long store, heading toward an open doorway at the back that appeared to lead to a storeroom.

The desk at the back had an old cash register and an old-fashioned heavy, twelve-ring ledger book. On the wall next to it was a big calendar with a photo of an Asian bride in a frothy dress gazing dreamily at a white orchid she held in her hands. The calendar was in Chinese and English. Also on the wall was a glass and wood display case with two sets of small swords that were about six inches long and three inches wide. One set had a dragon motif etched into the blade. The other had a flower and scroll pattern.

On the floor behind the desk was an old boom box broadcasting the heavy metal music. She reached down to turn off the radio just as an announcer was saying, "This is KROQ, the rock of Los Angeles."

A large wooden screen, covered with a swarm of hand-painted butterflies, partially obscured an extra-wide doorway that led to the back room. As Vining approached it, the little hairs on the back of her neck raised up.

She was startled when a phone on the desk began

ringing. Given the abundance of old office equipment, she was surprised that the phone was modern. After five rings, it fell silent.

Caspers hit the doorway to the storeroom first and spun inside, with more bravado than necessary.

Vining slipped around the screen, kicking open a partially closed door with a sign that said RESTROOM.

Caspers made his way around the storeroom, which was a third the size of the front room, looking behind rolling racks crammed with an odd mixture of wedding dresses and outlandish costumes. Some of the costumes were made of brightly colored shiny nylon; others were fake fur or soft plush fabric.

Leaning against a wall were giant, plastic arrows with bold lettering in primary colors. Shelves were stacked with arrows, boxes of shopping bags, and full-head masks—gorilla, rooster, Frankenstein—and multicolored Afro wigs, like the one Scrappy had been wearing when he'd been shot.

A door at the rear was fortified with heavy bolt locks that were all engaged.

A safe tall enough to hold long weapons was against a wall.

There was a second desk in the back room, the same vintage as the one in the front, but this one had an open laptop computer on it. A narrow table against the wall held a stoneware teapot atop a base with a tea light candle beneath. Four straight-sided cups were turned down on top of paper doilies. A red On light glowed on an electric kettle. There was a square metal tin with a lid.

Vining moved through the room in the opposite direction from Caspers. Seeing movement, she swung her gun up only to spot her own reflection in another mirror affixed to a corner of the ceiling.

After they had cleared the back room, Vining gestured to Caspers to position himself on the other side of the outside door. She unlatched the bolt locks and flung the door open. After not hearing anything, she ducked her head out. Signaling "all clear" to Caspers, she holstered her gun and walked outside.

An alley ran behind the block of small businesses. Parked outside Love Potion's back door was a restored 1960s panel van. Its lustrous maroon paint had a metallic undercoat that glistened in the sun. Across the hood and down the sides were flames painted in lavender and silver. The effect was subtle; the design almost invisible. The van sat on oversize tires that had chrome "spinner" wheel rims in which a round face inside the rim would keep turning even while the car was stopped, creating an illusion that the car was still moving.

"Sweet," Caspers said.

Vining looked inside the van's tinted windows.

Attached to the rear was a hydraulic ramp.

"Somebody here use a wheelchair?" she asked at the same time they heard a bang at the front door coincident with the brash buzz emitted when the door was opened.

Caspers quickly had his gun out and strode back inside the store. "Police! Hands where we can see 'em!"

The abrupt entrance had startled Vining, too. She'd drawn her gun, but when she went back inside the store, she soon holstered it and took in the man who had rolled through the door in a manual wheelchair.

He had his fingers laced across his shaved head, as if he was well familiar with this drill. Tattoos covered his entire upper body, on display in a loose tank top that looked like a handkerchief against his massive chest and shoulders. Illustrations caressed his arms like sleeves, covering every inch of flesh up to his hands and to his collarbones, where the illustrations circled but did not creep up his thick neck. Inset into each earlobe was a half-inch cylinder of steel that was open in the middle.

Sunlight from the shop windows shone through the round openings. A silver ring with a ball pierced his right eyebrow. A Fu Manchu mustache trailed down his cheeks and extended past his chin onto his chest. The ends were braided with narrow red ribbons.

His lower body was in stark contrast with the top. Jeans were draped loosely on withered legs. His feet on the footrests of the manual wheelchair were clad in spotlessly white, high-end athletic shoes. His thighs supported a large Styrofoam drink cup. A brown paper bag was on his lap.

Vining had never seen someone react so coolly to having a police officer hold a gun on him.

Marvin Li grinned as he took in Caspers, his eyes twinkling with amusement. "Ease up, man. Don't shoot the crippled guy."

SIXTEEN

Caspers holstered his gun and began searching him. "Are you Marvin Li?"

"You have no legal right to pat me down. All I've done is enter my place of business. I have not behaved in a threatening manner toward you or broken any laws. You don't have a warrant. But go right ahead. Knock yourself out. The Pasadena Police actually lets you have a loaded gun, young Turk?"

"Are you Marvin Li?" Caspers angrily repeated.

"Yes, I am." Li passively endured the young officer's

vigorous patting down, while not-so-passively giving Vining a prolonged once-over.

Vining hadn't seen someone in an old-fashioned manual wheelchair outside a hospital in ages. Nowadays, the motorized ones seemed the norm. She now understood why the shop had wide doorways.

Caspers felt Li's jeans pockets. "You have anything on you that's going to stick me or hurt me?"

"Look at you, Pasadena," he said to Caspers. The edges of Li's mustache rose when he smiled, revealing straight, white teeth. The planes of his face were strong yet refined, giving him an aristocratic look. It was underscored by the way he held his head and the fluidity with which he moved, in spite of his muscle-bound physique. His voice was mild and calm, belying his intimidating persona. He had a slight accent, clipping some words while drawing out others.

Caspers repeated, "Do you have anything that's going to stick me or hurt me?"

"My needle days are long over and I'm not carrying a weapon." Li caught Vining's eye and arched an eyebrow. "You're gonna get yourself a bad guy one day, aren't you, Pasadena?"

The only people Vining knew who would behave so glibly in such a situation were career cops and career criminals.

"That wouldn't be you, would it?" Caspers took Li's wallet from his pocket. "What's in the bag?"

Li said to Vining, "You should tell him to identify himself and explain why he's searching me in my place of business without a warrant."

Vining hadn't reined in Caspers because she was happy he was searching Li. Since Caspers had naturally stepped into the role of bad cop, she'd assume the counterpart. Yet she was surprised by Caspers's behavior toward Li. It went beyond the young detective's innate disdain for criminals. Caspers had only recently been pulled inside from the streets into detectives and Vining hadn't worked with him long, but she'd never seen this side of him.

"I'm Detective Nan Vining and this is Detective Alex Caspers from the Pasadena Police. We'd like to ask you some questions about your employee Abel Espinoza."

"Detective Nan Vining," Li said. "A pleasure."

Caspers handed Li's wallet to Vining and picked up the bag from Li's lap. He took out a white clamshell container and opened it.

That annoyed the tattooed man more than being searched. "As for you, Pasadena, you're testing my patience. That's an egg-white frittata with sautéed spinach and feta cheese. The container stuck between my legs is full of coffee. Are you finished, because there's one thing I hate—cold food. Two things . . . and cold coffee."

Vining went through Li's wallet. It contained the usual: driver's license, credit cards, and reward cards from Staples, Vons supermarket, and BevMo. He also had nearly six hundred dollars in cash. With the cash, she was surprised to find her business card. She wondered if this was the card she'd given Pearl Zhang last night.

Li started to lower his arms.

Caspers snapped. "I didn't tell you to relax."

Li ignored him and put his hands on the arms of his chair. "I'm telling *you* to relax. I'm happy to answer all your questions, but you need to take a chill pill, my man."

His comment riled Caspers. Vining could almost see the adrenaline begin racing through his veins as his movements grew more brisk and his face flushed. Li seemed to have keyed into some deep-seated issue with Caspers. She had seen this before when cops had encountered someone—a suspect, witness, or even during a routine traffic stop—who reminded them of an ex who'd dumped them or an abusive parent. Perhaps Caspers's lack of sleep was making his emotions raw. She was annoyed with him. Personally, she couldn't care less about Marvin Li, who was too slick and glib for her by half, but they needed him to cooperate.

Vining shot Caspers a warning look.

They heard music. Vining recognized the tune as Led Zeppelin's "Whole Lotta Love." Her ex-husband had worshipped the group. The music was coming from the cell phone attached to Li's belt.

"I'm going to answer my phone, all right?"

Vining said, "Go ahead." She put her card back inside the wallet and folded it closed.

Li picked up his phone, looked at the display, pressed a button to connect the call, and began speaking in Chinese.

Vining handed Li his wallet. While he was on the phone, she sneaked glances at Li's tattoos. The illustrations weren't coarse like common prison tattoos. They were colorful and delicate: of animals, flowers, lush forests, and butterflies. They momentarily distracted her, their artistry and complexity drawing her in.

She caught Li watching her, a wry smile on his lips. She moved away, feeling as if she was a tiny fish that had barely escaped the paralyzing yet beautiful tentacles of a sea anemone that had lured it close.

Caspers remained ready to pounce, standing with his hands away from his sides.

Vining slipped beside him. "Alex, back off. It's not helping. Guy like him, he's been around the system for so long, intimidation won't work and will likely backfire."

"The bigger they are, the harder they fall." Caspers looked at Li as if he could eviscerate him with his eyes.

Li ended his call and put his phone away. "See how easy that was, Pasadena? I thought the Pasadena Police had it together better than this."

Caspers said with complete seriousness, "Just following procedure when dealing with convicted murderers."

"That was twenty-five years ago, Pasadena. I did my time. I sit before you a reformed man."

"My name is Detective Caspers." Using his index finger, he poked Li in his beefy bicep with each word.

"Pasadena, don't tell me you're gonna rough up a guy in a chair."

When Vining saw Caspers tense further, she put a hand on his arm.

"You'd better keep that mad dog on a short leash." Li rolled his wheelchair forward.

Vining slapped her hand on his shoulder. "You! Don't move until I tell you."

Li looked at her with admiration. "Whatever you say, Detective."

Vining and Caspers were startled and quickly had guns in their hands when they heard the back door open. The painted screen prevented them from seeing the door.

Li called, "Auntie Wan?"

An older female voice called back in Chinese.

Vining holstered her gun and shot Caspers a look, telling him to do the same.

Li explained. "This is my aunt's shop. She lets me use the back room to run my business."

Soon, Auntie Wan appeared, nearly hidden behind a large vase of giant white chrysanthemums. She continued speaking in Chinese as she carried the vase toward them, apparently heading for the round table in the front.

Vining saw that she was Pearl Zhang's mother, the older woman she'd met the night before.

Through the stems, Wan Li spotted Vining and Caspers.

"Hello. Good morning." Auntie Wan tried to move the magazines on the table out of the way while still holding the vase. She was dressed in a red knit suit that had gold buttons on the jacket. Around her neck was a double strand of choker-length pearls.

"Let me help you." Vining took the vase from her.

Marvin Li rolled his chair to the display case where Caspers had set his breakfast. He picked it up and began heading toward the back. He turned to look at Vining and especially at Caspers, who was still scowling.

"Detectives, I'm going into the back to eat. If you'll come with me, I'll be happy to answer all your questions." He continued moving. "I'll make you a cup of tea."

Caspers bolted toward the front door. He slammed into it, forgetting it opened in and not out. He jerked it open, sounding the harsh buzzer, and left.

After Auntie Wan had cleared the table and Vining had deposited the flowers there, she went outside after Caspers. She couldn't figure out what had gotten into him. He had taken a simple situation and had made it untenable. She found him at the end of the block. "What's going on with you?"

He looked around, flicking his fingers, as if trying to conjure a good answer. "Nothing's going on."

She kept her voice low and steady, but left no doubt about her anger. "Alex, you're bringing some sort of personal history to this. I don't know what it is, but I don't need it getting in the way of this investigation. So tuck it back inside your little bag of personal garbage and save it for your shrink. Got it?" She thought, who was she to condemn?

Caspers's body language conveyed that he was still deeply agitated. The harsh look in his brown eyes softened. For a second, the brash cop, the guy who was always first on-scene, throwing them down, hauling them in, looked boyish. "I don't know, Nan. Guys like that . . . I have a problem with them."

They watched as a Lexus SUV pulled to the curb and parked in front of the Crown Vic. Two Asian women, one in her twenties and the other perhaps her mother, were ebullient as they exited the car. They went inside Love Potion.

"I'm sorry, Nan. I was out of line. It won't happen again. I won't let you down. I'm a professional."

He raised his eyebrows and uttered a warning sound in anticipation of the smart-aleck retort for which he'd left an opening.

She said it anyway, wanting to make a joke to soften the mood. "A professional what?"

She patted him on the shoulder. "Sit in the car."

As she unlocked the door for Caspers, she felt a wave of emotion about Kissick and how much she missed having him by her side. She missed the way they worked together and communicated nonverbally, like hand-in-glove. She despised this pain-in-the-ass investigation and was jealous when she thought of the case he was working on. Vining followed the blushing bride and her mother inside Love Potion.

SEVENTEEN

When Vining came back inside the store, the bride's mother was helping her daughter try on a long veil that had many layers of voile fabric.

Auntie Wan was walking from the back with a wedding dress draped across her arms. The dress was so voluminous, it nearly engulfed her.

She smiled at Vining and said, "Marvin in back." She hung the dress on a brass stand and began fluffing the skirt to peals of delight from the bride and her mother.

The bride pointedly caught Vining's eye, wanting to share her foaming joy with all the females there.

Vining gamely gave her what she sought: "Very pretty," accompanied by a big smile. She thought that just because her husband had been a philandering jerk and her marriage had gone to hell, didn't mean that everyone's would.

In the storeroom, she found Li finishing the last of his coffee. The takeout container that had held the frittata was in the trash. The ends of his mustache were looped together, perhaps to avoid dragging them into his food.

He drew them apart with his fingers. "Can I offer you some tea, Detective?"

He pointed to the narrow table with the electric kettle, teapot, and straight-sided cups.

"I have special tea that a friend brings from China. It's delicious. You won't find it here. It has a hint of licorice with an undertone of hibiscus."

"I'm not much of a tea drinker. Just herbal tea, when I can't sleep."

"Are you often sleepless?"

She didn't know why she'd revealed personal information to him. From his interaction with Caspers, he'd shown himself to be the type of person who would leap on any hint of weakness. She didn't respond.

Auntie Wan entered the storeroom and poured tea from the pot into one of the stoneware cups. Attached to her wrist by an elastic band was a pincushion shaped like a tomato that was stuck with straight pins.

"See, Detective?" Li smiled. "The tea is safe. My aunt's not going to poison her customers."

He rolled his chair close to the teapot. He turned over two of the cups, and filled them with hot tea.

While he was looking away, her eyes were again drawn to his tattoos. A leopard crawled from his back over his right shoulder. One of the eyes hidden behind the strap of his tank top was revealed when he stretched forward. The leopard seemed to fix her in its gaze. A flock of bluebirds sprang from beneath the leopard's claws and spiraled around Li's right arm. Beneath the birds was a meadow from which tiny yellow butterflies poured. There were layers upon layers of images. The effect was three-dimensional. The illustrations seemed to tell stories. She'd follow one thread, and then was distracted by another, frustrated when an image was hidden by his top. She felt stymied by Li's clothing. With no sexual impulse behind it, she wondered what he looked like nude.

He turned back, holding a cup out for her.

She walked to take it. Her fingers accidentally brushed his.

"Where's your partner?"

"He had to make some phone calls." Holding the cup by the base was burning her fingers. He had filled it to an inch from the top. She held it by the rim between the fingertips of both hands, as he was doing.

"Junior taking a time out?" Li swirled the tea in his cup. He breathed in the aroma before taking a small sip. "Please sit, Detective. Give the tea respect."

She backed up to an old upholstered chair and sat. The tea was delicious, and it made her feel calmer. She didn't know if it was due to the tea or just because she was drinking something hot. As the tension ever so slightly loosened its grubby clutches on her, she realized how tightly wound she was. How desperately she needed to rest, yet couldn't. Every night, she'd lay down her head, exhausted, but her mind wouldn't shut off. It was as if she sensed T. B. Mann out there, also awake, thinking of her, equally restless and anxious for resolution.

She stared into the depths of the small cup and watched the tea leaves settle at the bottom. Was her fate written there among the tea leaves? If she looked deeply enough, would she see T. B. Mann?

Marvin Li was watching her, holding his cup in one hand and twirling both tendrils of his braided mustache with his index finger. "Trying to read your tea leaves, Detective?"

"Can you?"

"A little, but I know people who are experts."

"Do you believe in that?"

"Some people are in tune with such things. My aunt, for example, says she sees ghosts. She's very superstitious. See those mirrors?" He pointed to a small mirror in the corner near the ceiling. "They're supposed to reflect the bad luck. In the front of the shop, you might have seen a fish bowl. Its black fish is supposed to absorb the bad luck and die before the gold ones in the bowl. Clever shopkeepers sell black fish that don't live as long."

Vining smiled. "So you don't believe in magic."

"I didn't say that. There's powerful magic in the world. Just because I can't see it, doesn't mean it's not there. Certainly, you've been in love, Detective."

She didn't respond and he didn't wait.

"We can't see love, but there's no doubt that it exists and that it's a source of considerable magic."

She didn't like the way he was watching her, as if he was savoring her like he savored the tea. He was strange and she didn't trust him, but she felt he'd be more cooperative if she went at his speed. Flirting would advance her cause. She knew female detectives who unabashedly manipulated a male interviewee's attraction to them—be it sexual, sisterly, or motherly—to get what they wanted, which was always honest answers to their questions. Vining had attempted such before, but it always felt awkward to her, being a more what-you-see-is-what-you-get kinda girl. This looked like fertile ground for such a technique. Right now, Li had requested that she give the tea respect. She could do that.

Truthfully, it was the first time she'd stopped to take a breath since she'd gotten out of bed that morning and it felt good. She gave in to Li's one characteristic that she found compelling and somewhat magical. She let herself be drawn into that butterfly-strewn meadow on his body.

He noticed where she was looking. His skin seemed to shiver beneath the light of her gaze. His voice was low and soothing. "How are you enjoying the tea?"

"I'm enjoying it very much."

"The tea ceremony is an art in China. They have authentic Chinese teahouses here in San Gabriel. Maybe you'll let me take you to one some day. Of course, when all this sad business is over."

The front door buzzed. It sounded as if the two

women were leaving with as much liveliness as they'd entered. The store became quiet.

Vining didn't know if Auntie Wan was still there or not.

As Li twirled his mustache, his muscles undulated, making the swarm of tattooed butterflies appear to come alive.

"You have a butterfly theme." She quickly amended her comment so that he wouldn't think she'd been studying his body, even though she had. "In front, there's that silk robe in a frame on the wall. There's a painted screen."

"The embroidery on the robe depicts the Chinese Romeo and Juliet story called the 'Butterfly Lovers.' It's the legend of two fourth-century lovers who could not get married in their lifetime due to different family backgrounds. After their deaths, they turned into a butterfly couple, flying together for eternity. In the Chinese culture, two butterflies flying together are a symbol of love."

He hooked his finger in his tank top and pulled it down to reveal a perfectly-formed, muscular pectoral. On it were tattooed two entwined butterflies. They were spiraling, frenzied, as if engaged in a sexual act, if butterflies even did that. He seductively drew his fingers across the image. His hand was masculine, but his fingers were long and tapered.

"I like butterflies because they symbolize a beautiful and free spirit."

"I'm not a fan of tattoos, but I have to admit yours are beautiful. They're works of art."

His eyes met hers. "They're not finished. They will never be finished. They evolve as I evolve. The story only grows more complex with each passing year."

Their encounter crackled with sexual energy. She was not immune to it. She felt as if his tattoos had taken her unawares, like a stranger stepping from behind a tree into the path of a schoolgirl on her way home, a bag of candy in his sweaty fist. Just as he'd drawn out the worst in Caspers, he seemed to have keyed into a hidden aspect of her and drawn it out. But she was no schoolgirl and his tattoos were only skin deep. She wondered if everything else he was reputed to be—the reformed bad guy who now dedicated his life to good works—went deeper than that ink.

"You have beautiful eyes, Detective. They're very deep. Full of pain."

She huffed out a dismissive laugh while lowering her eyes, as if flattered.

"You have a long scar on your neck. Do you mind if I ask what happened?"

"I was ambushed while I was on patrol. A man stabbed me and got away." She stopped short of saying that that probably explained a lot about her.

"I have scars, too, from the gunshot wounds that paralyzed me. We're both warriors, but in different wars."

"But we're on the same side now."

"True." He smiled, twirling both ends of his ribbon-braided mustache around his finger.

"Is there a man in your life, Detective?"

"That's not pertinent to our discussion."

"I would like to take you out to dinner."

"That's flattering, but—"

"Don't underestimate guys in chairs, Detective. Because of our physical limitations, we're very tuned in to women, their needs, and desires."

Did she see his tongue dart from between his lips or did she imagine it? Standing, she walked to set the cup on the table. She'd gotten him to warm up to her, all right. Now she wished she had a garden hose to turn on him.

"Marvin, why was my business card in your wallet?"

"My cousin Pearl gave it to me. She came by my house early this morning after having met you at the Hollenbeck building."

Li's cell phone rang. He looked at the display and didn't answer. "Pearl is obviously concerned about how that murder on her property, and a suggestion that I'm somehow involved, will affect her business and reputation. She doesn't know anything about Scrappy's murder. I don't either."

Vining took a small audio recorder from her pocket and turned it on. "I'm going to record our conversation if that's okay." She recorded the date, time, and people present and set the device on Li's desk.

He grinned. "Back to business."

"Marvin, tell me what you know about the murder of Abel Espinoza, aka Scrappy."

"I know nothing about it."

"Why did Scrappy paint a death threat to you in your cousin's building?"

"I honestly wish I knew, Detective. I'm disturbed by that. I used to be China Dog, once upon a time. I don't allow people to call me that anymore, but people won't let you forget your past. All I can figure is that Scrappy had a beef with me."

"Like what?"

"I don't know. To my knowledge, everything was fine. Yesterday was a normal work day."

"Where was Scrappy last working?"

"He was promoting a new apartment building at the corner of Orange Grove and Newcastle."

"What were his hours?"

"Evening into night."

"Can you be more specific?"

"He started at seven and went on from there."

"What time did he go home?"

"Midnight, usually."

"Midnight? He was advertising apartments. Who rents apartments at midnight?"

Li shrugged. "If that's what the customer wants, I'm happy to provide it."

"When's the last time you saw Scrappy?"

"Last night, around seven-thirty."

"How long did he work for you?"

"Just over a month, I think."

"How many other employees do you have?"

"Six."

"All ex-cons?"

"That's correct. I'm committed to giving these guys something to do with their time other than gang-banging. There should be a twelve-step program for gangbangers trying to get out of the life. The lifestyle is just as hard to leave behind as an addiction to drugs or alcohol."

"You're telling me that these guys who used to have a lot of money in their pockets from selling drugs and had earned street cred from their homeys are happy to wear a clown suit and stand on a street corner holding a big arrow for minimum wage."

"They earn more than minimum wage. In the industry, they're known as 'human directionals.' It requires more skill than you think. My employees attend H.D. University, where they learn the acrobatics of spinning the arrows over their heads, around their backs, jumping over them. Plus they're salesmen, like carnival hucksters. They need to know how to interact with people on the street, kids and such."

"I want to talk to your other employees."

"I'll give you a list."

"Where were you last night between eight and ten?"

"I was shooting pool at the social club I frequent, the China Orchid. I saw several friends there, including the owner, who will vouch for my whereabouts."

"You were in prison for murder. Tell me about that."

"I was a tough guy as a kid in San Francisco. When I was nineteen, I was involved in a gang-related shooting at the Golden Lotus restaurant in Chinatown. Six people were murdered: four gang members and a man and his young daughter who were having dinner. Five other people were injured, two seriously, including myself. I got twenty years' hard time. I was damn lucky that was all I got. When I was released, I was a changed man, and I don't mean just physically. I'm reformed, and have committed the rest of my life to keeping kids out of gangs, and guns off the street."

He recited his story with braggadocio. Vining had learned that criminals, similar to fishermen or hunters, never tired of telling about their exploits—the ones who put up a battle, the ones they bagged, the ones that got away.

"Anybody want you dead?"

"I have a lot of enemies with long memories. I can't count them all. I can't even remember them all. It's possible that someone paid Scrappy to paint that tag."

"What about your cousin Pearl? Does she have any enemies?"

"Probably. She's in a tough business for a woman and she's a tough woman. I can't name any."

"What's her background?"

"She grew up on Mainland China. Had a hard life. Worked in a factory. She made her way to Hong Kong. She had to stay there and work for years until she'd paid back the people who'd smuggled her off of the mainland."

"Doing what?"

"She was a cocktail waitress in a big restaurant there."

"Was she involved in any sort of criminal activity?"

"No. Not her style."

"Where did she get money to start her business?"

"She's very entrepreneurial."

"Meaning?"

"She worked. She saved. She got wealthy people to invest. She built it, brick by brick."

"Was she married?"

"No."

"What about your nephew, Ken? Has he ever been in any sort of trouble?"

"Not to my knowledge. He's the light of Pearl's life. He's a good kid, good student, respectful . . ."

"Who's his father?"

"An American businessman living in Hong Kong."

"Does he have a relationship with Ken?"

"Why are you asking these questions? What does this have to do with Scrappy getting murdered in my cousin's building?"

It had nothing to do with it, but Vining remembered the bright spark in Ken Zhang's eyes when he mentioned that he and Emily were schoolmates. She let it go.

"Marvin, is there anything else you can remember about Scrappy or his friends or associates that might help us?"

"No, but I'll call you if I think of anything." He smiled lasciviously. "I promise."

Vining recorded a date and time to mark the end of the interview. "Thank you, Marvin."

"The pleasure was mine."

"You were going to give me a list of your employees."

"I have their information in the desk outside."

In the front part of the store, while Li got the information, Vining saw Auntie Wan tapping flakes into the fish bowl while soothingly talking to the fish.

Vining walked over to her and looked through the glass at the fish.

Auntie Wan said, "Goldfish good luck."

Vining nodded. She'd had a goldfish when she was a kid. She'd won it at a carnival. It hadn't lasted too long.

"You know what your problem is?" Auntie Wan put the cap back onto the fish flakes.

Vining was surprised by her boldness. "Uh . . . No."

The older woman darted her finger at Vining. "The ghost is hungry. You do not take care of the ghost."

"Excuse me?"

"You do not feed the ghost. Have you made a place for the ghost in your house?" Auntie Wan tried to paint a picture with her hands. "A place."

When Vining wasn't getting what she was trying to convey, Auntie Wan spoke to Li in Chinese.

He translated. "She wants to know if you have a shrine in your house for the ghost. Chinese families often have shrines at home to make sure that those in the family who have passed on are well taken care of and don't come around to give the living grief."

Vining did not discount Auntie Wan's assessment. "How do I feed a ghost?"

"Find out what the ghost wants," Auntie Wan said. "And do it."

Gathering papers from the desk, Li set them on his lap and rolled his chair to Vining. He handed her the information. "A ghost. That explains a lot."

Vining looked from Li to his aunt. They were both looking at her earnestly.

"Thank you for your time. I'll be in touch." She left.

EIGHTEEN

After leaving Vining at the PPD garage, Kissick got on the 210 at Walnut Street. From there, he took the 118 west to the 101 north, which would take him nearly all the two hundred miles to Los Osos, the small bayside town that abutted Montaña de Oro State Park. Even though it was past morning drive-time, he had designed his route to circumvent the leg of the 101 through the San Fernando Valley that was always congested, no matter what time of day.

He drove as if on autopilot, his mind replaying the night and morning with Nan. He stirred with the recollection of their urgent and very hot sex on her kitchen floor. Now, only hours later, there was another apparently gang-related murder in Pasadena and he was heading out of town to work a different case without her. *Her* case, as she so strongly argued. He had suspected that she would not warm to Sergeant Early sending him to work the new leads, but had been surprised by both her vitriol and vulnerability.

He thought about the evidence Nan had stolen, the necklaces belonging to Johnna Alwin and Nitro. A small part of him admired her determination and ability to pull it off, just as he had to admire the skill of the better criminals he'd come across. A larger part was appalled that with calm forethought, she'd broken not only the law, but her sworn oath as a police officer.

He slipped his hand inside the pocket of his jacket

that was on the passenger seat and took out the satinette bag that held Vining's own pearl necklace. He slid it from the bag onto his lap and fingered the pearls as if they were worry beads. Funny how she could have worn that necklace to work, suspecting that the man who had attacked her had given it to her, and not have told a soul. Was she hoping the psycho would see her wearing it? What weird neurosis was that?

He tried to put himself into her shoes, to try to understand why she had acted dishonorably in her quest to track down her attacker. He knew that what had happened to her had been life-altering. He knew she'd flatlined for two minutes. He'd never asked her about it, but had always wondered if she'd had a near-death experience. The whole moving toward the white light thing, seeing dead friends and relatives, seemed clichéd, but still he wondered. He'd given her openings to talk about it, but she'd never taken him up on it, so he hadn't pried. Funny that they could share hopes and fears, secrets and dreams, and open up to each other sexually with abandon, but asking her what had happened when she'd died felt too personal.

When she'd returned to work after the ambush, she'd seemed more tightly wound, more easily hitting both high and low notes. Their recently renewed sexual relationship was more intense than when they had first been a couple two years ago, as if she was grabbing for all the gusto she could. Not that he was complaining. Nan *was* different. Only time would tell if the change was permanent.

It was good that he was working on her attempted murder case without her, but it put him in a difficult spot. He decided to be circumspect in what he told her. He'd dole out enough information to satisfy her, but nothing that would prompt her to roar off on her own. To lie, cheat, and steal.

His heart was heavy.

More than an hour had passed before he realized it and he was already passing through Ventura and breathing the cool ocean air. The sight of the Pacific never failed to cheer him.

Today, the ocean was calm, its color a deep blue. The hue changed with the weather, season, and time of day. The ocean was alive. The sky was clear and the horizon was sharp. Seeing that straight line where ocean met sky always cleared the clutter from his head. It assured him that there were straight lines in life, unambiguous and true. The city was all noise, crowds, asphalt, and exhaust, and it was only getting worse. While he knew that the ocean was changing too, the variations were not visible to his eye and so it seemed eternal. A refuge for his soul.

The land however was changing at an ever-increasing rate as real estate development and people pushed farther across the remaining farms and ranches and into the rolling hillsides.

Nature still did a fine job reminding people of the transience of material possessions and of life itself. South of Santa Barbara, he passed the tiny community of La Conchita nestled at the base of a giant bluff across the freeway from the ocean. It was nothing more than a couple of streets with a few dozen pastel-colored houses decorated with abalone-shell garlands and wood carvings of pelicans. In 2005, after weeks of heavy rains, ten residents of the three hundred died when tons of water-soaked earth slid down the hill and buried them. Beyond a deep ravine in the face of the bluff, little physical evidence of the tragedy remained.

Nothing about California stayed in one place. Nothing stayed the same. Human emotions included. Fickleness was not exclusive to the Golden State, yet perhaps something about the ever-changing landscape here gave it permission to roam free.

At Gaviota, a town just north of Santa Barbara, the freeway entered a picturesque stone tunnel cut into a rocky hillside. After that, the road turned inland and he witnessed another recent intrusion upon the gently rolling hills: acres of wine grapevines. Grapes were better than shopping malls, he supposed, but he missed the natural, golden hills. Some of the hillsides were scraped bare in preparation for installation of irrigation systems and planting. The bare earth looked as jarring as a teenager's white scalp after having fallen victim to a frat party prank involving barber's shears.

He looked at his watch and saw he was early for his meeting with California State Park Ranger Zeke Denver, who had worked with Marilu Feathers. He happily realized he had time for lunch at a joint he loved. He drove past the exit to Los Osos and continued on to San Luis Obispo, passing more mission bells on rook-shaped poles that marked the historic El Camino Real.

In San Luis Obispo, he cut off onto the Morro Bay exit and Highway 1 and entered his favorite stretch of the drive. Cattle still grazed the hills. West of the highway was a picturesque chain of volcanic plug domes, outcrops created by lava flows from now-extinct volcanoes that dramatically jutted from the chaparral. More than thirty-five of them stretched in a relatively straight line from San Luis Obispo to Morro Bay. The seven most prominent ones are called the Seven Sisters and each has a name. Morro Rock, the "Gibraltar of the West," a 577-foot-tall, crown-shaped dome at the end of a sandspit, is the most famous. When Spanish explorer Juan Cabrillo discovered it in 1542, he named it "Morro" because it resembled a Moorish turban.

He entered Morro Bay, the working man's Carmel, and stayed on the highway.

The city of 11,000 had not yet fallen victim to the gentrification that was running rampant through Pasadena, gobbling up asphalt parking lots and low-level buildings in a rush to maximize population per square foot. The streets of Morro Bay's commercial district were still lined with modest storefront businesses and free public parking lots. The power plant blighted the view. Built in the 1950s, before the existence of the California Coastal Commission, the three 450-foot cement stacks north of the pier were usually cropped out of publicity photos.

He pulled off the highway and followed the frontage road to the outskirts of town, turning into the parking lot of Taco Temple. Several motorcycles were parked in front. Starving and stiff after making the four-hour drive without stopping, he unfolded himself from the Crown Vic, laced his hands over his head, and stretched, breathing deeply of the ocean-kissed air. It was free of the ash that still lingered in the air down south from the horrible round of brush fires that had been barely extinguished. It was sunny, but the temperature was mild. It was perfect. It had been a hard summer for the Southland, the Pasadena P.D., and for him and Vining. It would end eventually. These things always did. There was no guarantee that the ending would be happy.

Inside the plain, white wood-frame building, he was delighted to see that soft-shell crab tacos were among the specials listed on the handwritten whiteboard. He placed his order and eschewed the indoor dining area for the picnic tables outside.

A few young men and women, probably students from nearby Cal Poly San Luis Obispo, were sitting on top of the wooden tables, with their dirty tennis shoes or flip-flops on the benches. They were smoking and discussing some "he said, she said" story with such fervor, they had to be on the cusp of solving the world's problems. They had long, shaggy hair, nouveau hippie clothing, and were trying hard to look alienated. They seemed oblivious of the perfect weather. Different day, same gorgeous environs.

A server brought Kissick his food and a glass-and-chrome condiment dispenser that held four different types of salsa. He dug in, unable to avoid overhearing the college kids. They made him think of his own boys, Cal and Jimmy, thirteen and sixteen. *James*, he mentally corrected himself, hearing his older son's admonition that he wanted to drop the nickname of his youth.

He knew that in a blink of his eye, they would both be through college and on their own. Nan's Emily would be grown, too. As he ate, he thought of the future. He envisioned a time not far away when he and Nan would both have more than twenty years with the PPD. They could cash out the equity in their homes and buy something out of L.A. Even up here. He'd always loved the Central Coast. He could work part-time for the Morro Bay P.D. or for the Cal Poly Campus Police. He couldn't see giving up entirely the profession he loved so dearly, not until he was much older. Maybe in his spare time he'd build a sailboat or buy a neglected jewel and restore her to her former glory. As for Nan, he couldn't imagine another career for her either. She never spoke of wanting to get out. Not yet, anyway. Still, what wasn't there to like about moving to someplace with a slower pace and clean ocean air?

Nan and he would both be free to pursue the rest of their lives. Their second act. A clear horizon.

He took the plastic lid off his Coke, stabbed the ice with the straw, and drank the last of it. He closed his eyes and tilted back his head to soak up the sun.

The brightness against his closed eyes dimmed as if a shadowy figure had stepped into the path of his happily ever after. Letting his eyes drift open, he saw a white, puffy cloud had appeared out of nowhere and had nearly blocked the sun. A chilly breeze whipped through the air, bringing more and darker clouds that had been hanging back in the sky but were now moving quickly.

The college girls in their thin tops complained and the group broke up, cramming into an old Volkswagen hatchback with surfboards in a rack on top.

Kissick gathered his garbage and stood. He again looked at the sky. The sun was completely obscured by clouds.

NINETEEN

Kissick took a detour through the bay front touristy stores and did a little shopping before heading to Montaña de Oro State Park. On the way, he passed the estuary, hearing through his open car windows a cacophony of bird songs from the cormorants, herons, and egrets. The eucalyptus tree branches were clogged with nests. Farther off, through clutches of trees, he glimpsed the bay where birds soared and moored boats rocked.

Passing through Los Osos, he entered the state park. The road meandered across the bluffs above the dunes, giving a vista of the miles-long, wide unspoiled beach. The road then ducked inland, and he drove in speckled sunlight beneath the canopy of a dense eucalyptus grove. His tires crunched the brittle acorns that had rolled onto the road. Through the open car windows, he drank in the eucalyptus's dusty pungent odor.

At Spooner's Cove, waves crashed against the rocks

that sheltered the small beach there. He turned onto a path between Monterey pines that led to the white clapboard Spooner Ranch House, circa 1892, where the visitor's center and Park Service headquarters were located.

Kissick parked beneath a sprawling Monterey cypress. A Park Service Jeep was the only other vehicle in the packed-dirt lot. The wind had whipped up a dust devil. He grabbed his manila folder and headed for the house's wooden wraparound porch. A sign posted beside the screen door said the visitor's center was closed. Pamphlets about the park were stuck inside the screen door's frame.

He tried the screen door and found it unlocked, as was the heavy wooden door behind it. When he stepped inside onto a wood-plank floor, he was surprised by a sharp, loud sound. He jerked his head around to see that he'd startled a ruddy-faced older man.

"Zeke Denver?"

He'd apparently been catching a nap in a rocking chair in front of a stone fireplace. The loud retort had come from a hardcover book that had slid from his lap onto the floor when Kissick had jolted him awake.

"Yessir." He pushed himself up with the assistance of the chair arms. He was tall. "You must be Detective Kissick."

Kissick took the gnarled hand he offered. "Call me, Jim, please."

"Everyone here calls me Zeke. Nice to meet you. Welcome." His big head was crowned by a mass of wavy silver hair that he wore parted on one side and combed back. A well-trimmed mustache was the same burnished silver as his hair. Bright blue eyes stood out dramatically. His barrel chest and round belly tested the shirt buttons of his moss green uniform. His long legs were slender in comparison. His eyelids were still at half-mast. He blinked as he struggled to wake up all the way.

Kissick would never have matched Denver's soft telephone voice with a man of this stature. The ranger was also older than Kissick had anticipated. Judging by his crow's feet and the texture of his skin, Kissick guessed he was at least sixty.

"Nice to meet you, too. Thanks for taking the time to talk to me, Zeke."

"Anything for Marilu. We still haven't gotten over what happened to her. Can I offer you some coffee? I've got a fresh pot. Sorta fresh."

"That would be great. Thank you."

"I'll be back in two shakes." The clomp-clomp of his footsteps drew Kissick's eyes to the ranger's ornately tooled cowboy boots. At a doorway into another room, he turned back and asked, "How do you take it?"

"A little sugar and cream."

Kissick set his file folder on top of a small counter in the corner. He wandered around looking at the historic photos on the walls, and then meandered into the back room where Denver had gone. He didn't see the ranger, but heard him rustling in yet another room in the far back. The middle room had displays about the local flora and fauna, with taxidermic specimens of a mountain lion, lynx, raccoon, rattlesnake, and sea otter on display in glass cases decorated to mimic their natural habitat. A stuffed hawk was suspended from the ceiling, wings spread. Windows on the two outside walls were furnished with aged Venetian blinds.

"How much sugar?" Denver stepped into the doorway, holding a cardboard box of sugar.

"About a teaspoon." Kissick walked over to him and observed as Denver poured sugar into a dark green mug of coffee.

"That's good. Thanks."

As Denver stirred the two coffees, Kissick looked around the room that was crammed with old furniture and office equipment. Above the table with the coffeemaker were two framed photos of Marilu Feathers. One was her official photo. The Park Service headquarters had faxed this to the PPD. The second photo was new to Kissick. It showed Marilu from the waist up, wearing a short-sleeved uniform shirt. An official patch on her shirt had a California grizzly bear on it. Binoculars hung from a strap around her neck and she was wearing a heavy backpack. The sun was harsh as her Ranger Stetson cast a shadow across half her face and she was still squinting. Her right arm was raised and bent, her forearm protected by a leather sleeve on which a falcon was perched. Her mouth was open as if caught in mid-sentence. She was turned slightly away from the camera, showing her sharp jaw and square chin.

On the table beneath the photos was a glass vase of blue wildflowers and sprigs of woody stalks with small grayish leaves. They looked freshly cut.

Denver handed Kissick a mug. "Marilu loved the park's wildflowers. Loved everything about it, but especially the flowers. The park was named Montaña de Oro because of the poppies and wild mustard that turn the hills golden during springtime. Marilu used to say that being here was like living inside a potpourri bag."

He pinched a few leaves from the woody stalks, rolled them between his thumb and fingers, held them to his nose and sniffed. He held the crushed leaves up for Kissick. "That's sage."

Denver led the way to the front room. He set his mug on the fireplace mantel, rolled over a wooden desk chair from behind the counter, and placed it in front of the unlit fireplace.

"Take a load off, Jim."

Denver bent over to pick up the book that had slid from his lap. It was a well-worn hardcover edition of *Lonesome Dove*. He also picked up a bookmark printed with a photo of California golden poppies, found his page, about a quarter of the way in, and slipped in the marker. He set the book on the mantel.

Kissick inclined his head to indicate the book. "You a McMurtry fan?"

"Oh, yes. I must have read *Lonesome Dove* ten times by now." Denver retrieved his coffee mug and slowly lowered himself onto the rocker that released an almost welcoming creak beneath his weight. "How about you?"

"It's possibly my favorite book. That and *Moby-Dick*."

As Denver rocked the chair, it sent forth a different chorus of creaks. He plunked his boots on top of a crate that was standing on its end. "Of course. Ahab and the white whale. Another tale of an obsessive quest that eventually destroys the hero even though, at the end, he achieves his heart's desire."

Kissick got the file folder from the counter and sat on the desk chair. He sipped the coffee. The brew was much better than he'd expected.

"This is a theme that perhaps resonates with you, Detective."

Kissick nodded. "I like the epic aspects of those two books. The male bonding. They're classic buddy stories."

"They are that, but we can't discount their larger themes."

"Absolutely, but being a bit narrow-minded myself, I like to focus on the journey and not the end."

The ranger's eyes brightened. "I suspect you're anything but narrow-minded, Jim."

"My ex-wife would probably disagree with you on that last point."

Denver chuckled heartily.

Kissick changed the subject. "What can you tell me about Ranger Feathers?"

His boots on the crate, Denver rocked the chair, tipping the crate as well. He held the mug between both hands against his belly and gazed out a dirty window. His mood grew heavy. The room was silent other than the creaking of his chair.

Kissick didn't even hear a car pass outside.

"Marilu ... Where do I begin? Horsewoman. Nature lover. No. Stronger than that. She *revered* nature. Markswoman. Loved children. Loved animals. Loved to laugh. Loved everything that was simple and pure. She was simple and pure. The purest soul on God's green earth that I've had the pleasure of knowing. That's a peregrine falcon perched on her hand in that picture in there. Morro Rock is a protected falcon reserve."

"I didn't know that. I used to climb it years ago."

"No more. Now it belongs to the falcons. Marilu loved those falcons."

His blue eyes that had sparkled with amusement a minute before grew dark. He stopped rocking.

Outside, Kissick heard the screech of a bird.

"I'll never get over it," Denver began. "It happened on Christmas Eve, you know. The timing was what made me think he'd planned it. He knew the park would be empty. He knew a campfire on the beach would draw a ranger's attention, especially in the snowy plover habitat. I've always wondered. Did he target her or was he gunning for any ranger who showed up? Guess we'll never know.

"That Christmas Eve, I was home with my wife. My kids and the grandkids were over. Marilu lived in the ranger residence in the park. Ten years ago, ranger staffing was thin. It's even worse now, with the budget cuts, but don't get me started. We usually patrol the sandspit by Jeep, but when it was quiet, Marilu liked to take out her horse Gypsy. The most she'd expect on an evening like that was to cite someone for walking their dogs on the beach."

"Horses are allowed but dogs aren't?"

"That's right. Again, don't get me started. So, Marilu was planning on spending Christmas Eve with her parents, brother, and his family. Nice people. Her father's dead now. Must be six years. I think what happened to Marilu killed him. Mother still lives up in Cambria. She's a retired professor. Taught sociology over at Cal Poly."

While Denver talked, Kissick slipped his hand inside his jacket pocket and felt for Vining's necklace. He rolled the pearls between his thumb and index finger.

"Round about six-thirty that evening, the gal that runs the private stable where Marilu kept her horse called me and said that Gypsy had come back, but without Marilu. This is a small community. We all know each other. The hairs on the back of my neck prickled. I knew something was wrong. I called Ranger Dispatch and Marilu hadn't reported that she was off-duty. Course I thought Gypsy had thrown her someplace. I checked with her parents. They hadn't seen her. Then I called the county sheriff's. They offered to put their bird in the air and start looking for her. I came out. Thought I'd take the Jeep along Marilu's usual route across the dunes and onto the spit.

"Didn't take the sheriff's helicopter long to find her. One sweep down the beach did it. The tide was coming in and had nearly lifted her into the surf. If we'd waited any longer, we might not have found her body. There were footprints and hoofprints in soft sand, but nothing distinct enough to recover. Never found her Stetson. I think about that hat sometimes. Wonder if someone in Australia picked it up out of the ocean."

Denver slowly pulled one foot then the other off

the crate, rocking the chair upright. "We didn't have any experience investigating that sort of crime, so the sheriff's took over. They've got the files on it. I kept close to it, though. They did a hell of a job, but didn't turn up a thing. No one saw anything. No one heard anything. Just like that. Marilu was gone. Twenty-seven years old."

He gulped his coffee and stretched to set the mug on top of the mantel, beyond his easy grasp, as if he was finished with it.

Kissick downed the last of his. It had gone cold. "What was Marilu's background? How long had she been a ranger and what had she done before?"

"Marilu was born and raised in Santa Maria, about forty-five miles south of here. She told me she always loved the outdoors, ever since she was a little girl. She was a tomboy. Her father would take Marilu and her brother hunting and fishing. They'd go camping right here in this park. One summer vacation when she was in college, she went to the Yosemite Rock Climbing School. That's when she decided she wanted to be a park ranger. She followed her dream."

"How long have you been here, Zeke?"

"Feels like I've always been here. Twenty-nine years. I could retire, but my wife won't let me. Doesn't want me underfoot at home." The ranger chuckled, and then fixed Kissick with a steady gaze. "What sort of lead are you following that brought you here, if I may ask?"

Kissick felt the lawman's heart that beat beneath Denver's grandfatherly surface. He rose to set the empty mug on the counter, and then returned to open the file folder. He pulled out the photocopies of Nitro's four violent drawings, and handed them to Denver.

Finding the one of Feathers, Denver said, "Lord have mercy. That's Morro Rock and that's Marilu. Looks just like her." He looked at the others. "Who drew these?"

Kissick took out a snapshot of Nitro. "They were found in the possession of this man. We believe he drew them. Do you recognize him?"

Denver drew his fingers down his silver mustache as he scrutinized the photo. "Can't say that I do."

"How about this guy?" Kissick took out the composite drawing done based upon Vining's description of her attacker.

Denver shook his head. "You think one or both of them had something to do with Marilu's murder?"

"Possibly. Was Marilu ever involved in an incident on duty that was in the news?"

Kissick elaborated while Denver thought it over. "Something that would have put her in the public eye, like a shooting on duty, arresting a celebrity, or—"

"There was something like that." Denver stood and went behind the counter where he began looking through a low bookcase beneath a window. "I know it's here somewhere." His boots scuffed against the wooden floor as he shuffled to maneuver his large frame around the small area. He grunted as he pulled something from a bottom shelf. He rose with an old scrapbook and blew the dust from it as he carried it to the fireplace. He dragged the rocker closer to Kissick and sat with the book on his lap.

He smiled as he turned the pages. He pointed at a photo of a group of rangers in uniform in front of the ranch house. "That's Marilu when she first came here." The pages were of cardboard covered with semi-adhesive cellophane that held the items in place. The cellophane had grown cloudy with age.

Kissick tried to nudge him along. "You said that Marilu was involved in a newsworthy incident."

Denver sped up, moving to the back of the book. "Here we go." He read the headline from an old newspaper clipping. " 'Park Ranger Kills Child Molester. Montaña de Oro Ranger Hailed as Hero.' Nine years ago last July. How time flies."

He carefully peeled away the cellophane, removed and unfolded the brittle newspaper clipping, and handed it to Kissick.

As Kissick skimmed it, Denver recounted the events. "Bud Lilly was a local creep. His mother lived in Los Osos and he stayed with her off and on. He was always showing up in the park, hanging around the beach or the campgrounds. There were stories about Bud exposing himself to little girls. All the kids in town knew to stay away from him. Whenever I found him in my park, I chased him out."

Kissick looked at Lilly's mug shot in the clipping. He was Caucasian with a shock of mussed hair. Nondescript, except for dark pop-eyes on a diamond-shaped face that made him look like a bug. Something about him shouted, "Scumbag." The article said he was thirty-two years old.

Denver continued. "The police finally arrested Bud for fondling a twelve-year-old girl in a bathroom in Vegas. He got a wrist slap and was out of jail in no time. He had no place to go, so he came back to his mom's. Of course, he started showing up here again, where all the families and kids are during summer. To make matters worse, he'd bought himself a van.

"One July day, Bud drove his van to a campground and tried to drag a ten-year-old girl into it. The girl started screaming, attracting the attention of some of the adults around. The girl got away, and her parents hopped into their car and started chasing Bud in his van. At a bend up by Hazard Canyon Reef, Bud lost control and crashed his car into a tree. The girl's father pursued him on foot, but Bud was faster and disappeared. Marilu was patrolling on horseback and joined in the chase. Bud headed down the bluff, probably thinking he'd hide in one of the caves there. Marilu cornered him. He pulled a gun on her and she shot him.

"No one around here shed a tear for Bud Lilly, but that shooting was investigated every which way. Marilu was vindicated. The incident was considered 'suicide by cop.' The TV stations and newspapers were all over Marilu. She hated the attention, of course, and was glad when it finally died down."

Kissick reflected on the similarities between the on-duty shooting that had catapulted Marilu Feathers into the public eye and the incidents involving Vining and Johnna Alwin. Still, he resisted the notion of a criminal mastermind.

"Zeke, may I have a photocopy of this article please?"

"Most certainly. There's a machine in the back."

"One last thing . . ." Kissick took Vining's pearl necklace with the pearl pendant from his pocket and handed it to the ranger.

"Do you know if Marilu ever received a pearl necklace similar to this one as a gift? It would have been given to her after the Bud Lilly incident had landed her in the news. It might have had a card with it that looked something like this."

He handed Denver the panel card with the handwritten note: "Congratulations, Officer Vining."

Denver scrutinized the necklace and shook his head. "People sent Marilu all sorts of stuff. Invited her to their homes to dinner. I don't remember her mentioning having received a gift like this. You might ask her mother."

"Zeke, thank you for your time. You said that Marilu's mother lives in Cambria."

"Be happy to call her for you."

TWENTY

In the observation room outside the Detectives Section interview room, Vining held one earphone from a pair to her ear as she watched through the two-way glass. Detectives Louis Jones and Doug Sproul were interviewing yet another in a series of street gang members they'd pulled in. They were working their way through the players in the Crooked Lane Crips, Pepper Street Bloods, and the Gangster Kings—African American gangs—and the Villa Boys Pasadena, Northside 18th Street, Latin Boyz, and Vario Pasadena Rifa—Latino gangs. Another team of detectives were grilling a gangbanger in an adjacent room.

Many more bangers were in the basement-level jail, hauled in during an early-morning sweep. Members of rival gangs were segregated into different cell pods. Some had been arrested for drug possession, carrying concealed weapons, or parole violations. Most were still on the street, lucky enough not to have been breaking the law when the cops rained down. They were disinclined to come voluntarily to the PPD to be interviewed. The patrol cops let them know that they were watching and if they so much as jaywalked or threw a gum wrapper in the street, they'd be pulled in.

Vining and Caspers had interviewed three of Marvin Li's six employees: Daniel "Dan B" Boone Shin, age twenty-four, Victor "Kicker" Chang, age eighteen, and Ernesto "Chuckles" Ronquillo, age twenty-eight.

They were nicely dressed and polite and had shown up on time. Shin and Ronquillo had long arrest records and were on parole. Their parole officers sang Marvin Li's praises for the skill with which he wielded an iron fist in a velvet glove to keep former career criminals off the street and on the straight and narrow.

Victor Chang's sheet was clean, but he had been seen with members of a local set of a long-established Chinese gang, Wah Ching. The local set's name was Hell Side Wah Ching. Marvin Li was a family friend and had taken Chang under his wing ostensibly to steer him from gang influences.

All three knew Scrappy Espinoza through working with him at Aaron's Aarrows, but none had socialized with him. Victor Chang said he thought that Scrappy was back on drugs, which was news to Scrappy's parole officer.

Daniel Boone Shin said that Scrappy had cryptically told him that he "wasn't going to be working that piece of shit job much longer" as he had "something big" coming down.

Vining had checked out Li's Guns Gone public-service organization. The commendations on the Guns Gone website from the mayors of Los Angeles and other Southland cities praising Li's work in helping to stem gang violence were legitimate.

On the PPD's third floor, the brass was handling the outraged public and their representatives. Owners of businesses in Old Pasadena, where Scrappy had been shot, were gathered in the lobby, waiting for a meeting with the chief. Neighborhood groups clamored for a stop to the gang violence. That night, a community meeting of citizens, clergy, elected officials, representatives from the local NAACP chapter, El Centro de Acción Social, and the PPD police chief would take place at All Saints Episcopal Church.

Scrappy's murder had been the tipping point. The violence had seeped into Old Pasadena. The public outcry had not only widened, but had deeper pockets. Merchants feared that what had happened in Westwood Village in the eighties would happen to Old Pasadena. Westwood had been a thriving weekend destination of shops, restaurants, and grand old movie palaces until two gang shootings, one claiming the life of a bystander standing in line for a movie, turned the village into a ghost town. It took decades for it to recover and still wasn't what it had once been.

Vining watched and listened as Jones and Sproul pressed an African American male whom she did not recognize. He appeared to be in his early thirties which, if he was a gangbanger, would make him an elder statesman.

From his clothing, Vining determined that he was a member of the Bloods. The Bloods always wore red and their archrivals, the Crips, always wore blue. In years past, these two gangs used to be bolder in flying their colors. With the police cracking down hard on street gangs, they'd found cagier ways to proclaim their gang affiliation. This guy's red shoelaces and red belt gave him away.

The lights reflected off his shaved head. The hems of his ultra-baggy jeans flopped over bright white athletic shoes with the red shoelaces. When he was standing, the crotch of the jeans would reach his knees. The waistband was around his hips, revealing several inches of his print boxer shorts. Woven through the jeans' belt loops was the bright red webbed belt. Tucked into the boxers was a white sleeveless Tee showing off his well-developed upper body and tattoos. Large diamond stud earrings were in both earlobes. A heavy, twisted gold chain was around his neck.

Corporal Cameron Lam entered the observation room. He'd met with the head of the Sheriff's San

Gabriel Valley Asian Gang Task Force and was going to present what he'd learned at the briefing.

"Hey, Cam. Who's that fine citizen?"

"That's Andre Spranger, aka Chinaman. He's new in town. Was recently released from Folsom after serving a sentence for assault, battery, and mayhem."

"Mayhem," Vining repeated.

"Bit off a guy's ear and most of his nose in a fight."

"Nice. His moniker's Chinaman?"

"His homeys think he looks Chinese," Lam said. "Maybe Scrappy meant to threaten Chinaman and wrote China Dog."

"Scrappy wasn't the sharpest knife in the drawer," Vining said.

"Spranger lives with his grandmother in a house around the corner from the apartment where Scrappy lived with his mom.

"Jones and Sproul have been hammering him for over an hour. He's sticking to his story that he was home with his grandma the night of Scrappy's murder, watching *American Idol.* I checked and *Idol* was on then."

Lam looked at Vining. "Maybe Chinaman came upon Scrappy painting the China Dog one-eight-seven tag and he thought Scrappy was threatening *him.*"

Vining gave Lam a deadpan look.

Lam read her thoughts. "I've known these guys to do dumber things."

"Thing is, Scrappy was tagging in such an isolated area. It was off the main action in Old Town, inside a dark construction site. Who knew that Scrappy was even there? And why was he there?"

"It's a mystery," Lam agreed.

"Has your team spotted any other China Dog tags around town?"

"No and we've looked. I've checked with sheriffs in Altadena and Temple City and the Alhambra P.D. and

San Gabriel P.D. However, we did find two one-eight-seven tags with my name and one with yours."

"With my name? Where?"

"On the back wall of a tire store on Orange Grove east of Newcastle."

"Is it recent?"

"One of my guys took a picture of the tags in that alley a week ago and it wasn't there."

"Huh."

"You're just a popular girl, Nan. Making friends wherever you go."

She laughed without amusement and again turned lackluster attention to Chinaman's interrogation.

Lam commented, "That's going nowhere. He's not giving anything up."

"I think he's telling the truth. *American Idol.*" She sighed. "I've got to finish getting ready for the briefing."

Vining had collected, photocopied, and stapled selected documents from the Scrappy investigation. A set was squared on the table in front of each chair in the conference room. She'd straightened the chairs. At the last minute, she snagged Caspers and asked him if he'd put bottles of water at each place.

He gave her a crooked smile. "You're not nervous, are you, Nan?"

"A little." It was obvious, so she might as well admit it.

"You've never been the lead on a homicide before?"

"Not one like this." The PPD homicide detectives investigated all suspicious deaths. The cases she'd worked apart from Kissick had been cut-and-dried. Husband kills wife in front of the kids. Wife kills husband and confesses. Homeboy shoots a rival in front of ten witnesses, who won't talk, and a CCTV camera that will. Depressed man or woman kills himself or herself, leaving a suicide note.

The more complex cases, she'd worked with Kissick. She never considered that he was "in charge." To her, and she knew he would agree, the investigation had been a collaboration, but she'd always let him take charge of the briefings. It would be good for her career if she sometimes held the dry-erase pen and fielded the pointed questions. She didn't care. She already had the job she wanted.

"Time for your turn in the spotlight," Caspers said.

That was another common misconception about her, that she had third-floor aspirations because she was focused and aloof. Working at a police station could be like high school, only with guns and badges.

She didn't protest, but simply said, "Time for you to shine too, buddy. Show that you've stepped up."

He gave in to a small smile, clearly flattered.

Being political did not come naturally to her, but she'd learned to appreciate its benefits and to fake it for self-preservation. She wanted to keep Caspers on her side. She ought to have earned that and more after she'd covered for him today with Sergeant Early and Marvin Li. She'd had a chat with Caspers in the car on the way back and had given him some big-sisterly advice, which he'd received well. While he was still capable of annoying her to the core, she'd come to like him. He was a good cop and generally strove to do the right thing. She needed someone to back her up during the briefing. The heat being put on Beltran would filter down to her.

She wondered what Kissick was doing. It was late afternoon and he had certainly met with the park ranger by now. She regretted not having leaped on the Morro Rock connection when Kissick had first mentioned it after seeing Nitro's drawings.

Who was she kidding? When Nitro had shown up, she'd been in the thick of investigating a grisly double homicide. She'd lied to Kissick and Sergeant Early when she'd slipped off to Tucson to investigate Johnna Alwin's murder. She'd barely managed to disappear for a few hours.

Now, the murder of a career gangbanger whose life had ended as if foretold was keeping her from the only murderer she was obsessed about bringing down: T. B. Mann.

Standing in the perfectly set-up conference room, dreading the meeting that was about to begin, she looked at the big clock on the wall and tried to quiet the acid churning in her stomach. She left to get the Maalox tablets in her desk.

TWENTY-ONE

A n hour into the briefing, Vining thought it was going as well as could be expected. Her team had turned over a lot of stones and was aggressively pursuing a couple of solid leads. Yet, judging by Lieutenant Beltran's expression—he was facing her at the opposite end of the table—she felt he thought she'd been watching soap operas and eating bonbons. Certainly, he'd never looked at Kissick that way, or had Kissick just brushed it off? She recognized that while Beltran craved attention, the type of spotlight that was being put on him from upstairs was casting an unflatteringly harsh glare. She guessed he was just sharing the love.

Vining bolstered her confidence by making eye contact with the others there: Detectives Alex Caspers, Louis Jones, Doug Sproul, and Corporal Cameron Lam.

Caspers's contribution had been helpful and smart. She was proud of him. Sergeant Early was seated to her right. While Vining couldn't directly see her, she welcomed Sarge's solid and encouraging presence, as if Early were Kissick's surrogate.

Vining had presented what they had learned so far in their two-pronged investigation. On one hand, they were looking into a possible Chinese gang connection through Marvin Li, aka China Dog. On the other, they were chasing down the usual suspects in the ongoing gang war. She had stood through most of the briefing, making use of the diagrams and photos on poster board that one of the staff assistants had helped her put together.

After she'd concluded, Lieutenant Beltran was the first to speak.

"The business owners are hammering us to solve this, and quickly." His tone was clipped. "They're afraid of people staying away from Old Town because of gang violence. They remember what happened to Westwood Village."

Silence followed his last comment.

Vining's skin prickled with perspiration and she feared wet half-moons were spreading down the armpits of her shirt. She was glad she'd selected a light pink shirt which wouldn't show the perspiration as obviously as one of her medium blue ones. Beltran's disparaging facial expression had fanned her nervousness during her presentation, but with this comment, he'd made her angry. A word of encouragement from him wouldn't have been out of line. He knew gang murders were notoriously hard to solve. Anyone who knew anything wouldn't talk, out of loyalty or fear. Her team was doing everything by the numbers and then some.

She was about to respond when he opened his mouth and raised his index finger, telegraphing that he wasn't finished. "Nan, in my humble opinion, we don't need to waste any more time investigating Pearl Zhang, her family, or her business associates."

Now, he'd really ticked Vining off. She recalled one of Kissick's favorite sayings that went something like, just because you're paranoid, it doesn't mean they're not out to get you.

Early shifted her feet beneath the table, but remained silent. Everyone was waiting for Vining to respond. If she lay down, she'd lose her power and authority.

She stole a phrase from Kissick to preface her comments. "All due respect, ell-tee, but Scrappy's murder doesn't fit the mold of the recent gang-related incidents. None of our informants report the local gangbangers taking responsibility for Scrappy's murder, which is unusual. Usually, we have the opposite—guys claiming to be good for a murder when they weren't anywhere near it. We need to think outside the box."

Sergeant Early finally stopped holding back. "I agree. We need to let the evidence lead the investigation. We start speculating and we could end up being wrong. Scrappy was tagging 'Death to China Dog' on property owned by a family that has connections to a well-established Chinese gang. Asian gangs haven't taken hold in Pasadena. You'll remember a few years ago, when a man connected to a Chinese gang opened a video arcade near Pasadena City College. We found out about it early and were able to chase him out of town before he and his crew got established here. Scrappy's murder may be a wake-up call that there's something going on that we haven't yet caught wind of."

Beltran turned up his palm, conceding. "Point well taken, Sergeant, but you said we need to follow the evidence. Marvin Li says he's retired from the Wah Ching gang and the facts bear this out. He's spent years trying to help gang members get out of the life. Sure, Marvin's newfound respectability could be an elaborate front. I'm not naïve to that possibility. But the question remains: Why would Marvin Li or Pearl Zhang want Scrappy dead? If they were going to eliminate him, why do it on family property? While Pearl Zhang at first denied knowing China Dog's identity, she was simply embarrassed about her cousin's criminal past. She apologized to me and I feel she was sincere."

An image of Beltran and Zhang laughing together popped into Vining's mind.

Beltran continued. "Let's follow this thread through, but do it quickly and move on. It doesn't help our image to harass Pearl Zhang, a fine citizen who's done so much for the community."

Vining saw that Pearl Zhang had Beltran in her pocket, or perhaps in her pants.

Beltran looked at the wall clock. "You'll have to excuse me. As I mentioned, I have a meeting with the chief."

He hadn't mentioned it, but Vining was glad he was leaving. She no longer wondered if perspiration was soaking her shirt. She was certain of it. When he had left the room, Vining glanced at Sergeant Early, who gave her a quick smile.

Caspers's shoulders dropped as he exhaled. Everyone remained sitting stiffly until Sarge leaned back and laced her hands across her broad middle. Only then did the mood become more relaxed. Jones, Caspers, and Lam almost simultaneously leaned back, too. Sproul took a small white cloth from his shirt pocket and began cleaning his glasses.

Vining was the only one with her posture still erect and her hands on the table. "Cameron's done research on Asian gangs. Can you bring us up-to-date, Cam?"

"Be happy to." Lam scanned through handwritten notes. "I met with Sergeant John Velado, who's the head of the Sheriff's San Gabriel Valley Asian Gang Task Force, working out of the Temple City station.

"As everyone here knows, the Asian population in the San Gabriel Valley has skyrocketed over the past twenty years. Asians comprise fifty percent of the population in some cities and in some areas, the numbers are even higher and they're growing. The Department of Justice estimates there could be fifteen thousand Asian gang members in California and as many as five thousand in the S.G. Valley. In Orange County, Asian gangs are principally Vietnamese, Laotian, and Cambodian. In the S.G. Valley, they're generally Chinese and Korean.

"Unlike African-American and Latino gangs, Asian gangs don't claim a turf. They aren't attached to a street or neighborhood. Gang loyalty is not their priority. Their number-one goal is to make money. Gang members fighting one day may later get together to pull off a crime.

"They prey on their own communities, targeting Asian businesses and homes. They specialize in extortion, robberies, especially home invasion robberies, identity theft, illegal immigrant smuggling, prostitution, drug trafficking, and import/export fraud. Using the tried-and-true formula that's worked for all organized crime groups, most of their crimes go unreported because of the victims' fear of revenge.

"Their crimes are conducted with precision, demonstrate organization and planning, and are characterized by extreme violence. The larger gangs operate under a hierarchical structure. Among Chinese gangs, at the top are the 'dai los' or big brothers. At the bottom are the foot soldiers or 'sai los,' little brothers. In between are lieutenants, crew chiefs, and associates. The leaders try to insulate themselves from the gang's activity. Not all Asian gang members are Asian. Some get in because the dai lo likes them or they were sponsored by an Asian girlfriend.

"Investigating Asian gangs is tough. We're up against cultural barriers, a code of silence, and language issues. Being a police officer is not a respected occupation among Chinese and Southeast Asians.

"Another unique aspect of Asian gangs is that members don't admit to being in a gang. They don't get tattoos with their gang name. They don't tag. The kids lead double lives. Many are from affluent families. Honor students. When they're home, they're respectful, dutiful sons and daughters. Their parents have no idea."

Vining again recalled Ken Zhang's eyes flashing that night outside the Hollenbeck Paper building when he said, "Are you Emily's mom? She's in my photography class."

Lam continued. "In the nineties, there was a member of the Asian Boyz who got straight A's in school, volunteered at a hospital, and had a part-time job, all while he was involved in a month-long crime spree that left seven people dead."

He sat back in his chair, finished. There was a period of silence, as if following a sermon.

Vining finally spoke, "Which brings us to our friend Marvin Li."

She held up an 8 x 10 mug shot of a much younger and clean-shaven Li. To her, he looked like any other of the hundreds of young punks she'd encountered, out to subjugate the world, or die trying. A sprinkling of acne in the hollows of his cheeks contraindicated his tough-guy mien. The V of skin visible beneath his open shirt collar was not yet covered with tattoos. His eyes were different from what she'd seen that morning. In the photo, he had the dead eyes of a life-long criminal. The touch of whimsy that she'd observed in person was missing. He was a killer, but he loved butterflies.

"Cameron, did Sergeant Velado have a take on Marvin Li and his transformation since he got out of prison? His Guns Gone organization and alleged other good works?"

"Velado says the sheriff's and the FBI have been watching Li and his allegedly former gang, Wah Ching, for years. Like I said, the gang leaders do a great job of insulating themselves. In Chinese, Wah Ching means 'Chinese Youth.' It originated in San Francisco's China-town in the sixties, formed by immigrants who banded together to protect themselves from other gangs. They eventually developed into a criminal organization that controlled illegal gambling, prostitution, and narcotics trafficking in San Francisco's and L.A.'s Chinese communities. In Southern California, Wah Ching is active throughout the region covered by the six-two-six area code. Recently, Wah Ching has attempted to consolidate its power by aligning with various Asian organized crime groups."

"Marvin Li is charismatic," Vining said. "It would be easy to talk myself into believing that he's being honest. Everything he claims to be checks out. He sent his employees here to be interviewed. They were all cooperative and nice . . ." Her voice trailed off, leaving an opening.

"Makes you wonder what's wrong with this picture," Sproul said.

"Exactly," Vining agreed.

"Some pieces don't fit," Jones said. "Pearl Zhang's company, Red Pearl Enterprises, owns the Love Potion bridal salon. Makes sense to have her mother's shop under her corporate umbrella, but why is Red Pearl incorporated in Curaçao? Maybe that's for tax reasons, but generally anyone who sets up a corporation there is trying to hide the true owners."

Sergeant Early rubbed her eyes, digging in her fingers in a way that looked painful. "I'm a believer in the American dream, but it's a stretch to accept that a woman who supposedly worked as a cocktail waitress in Hong Kong to pay off the men who smuggled her out of China became one of the area's biggest property developers in a few short years."

Caspers added, "Why does Marvin Li have guys wearing costumes standing on street corners all hours of the night? Are they lookouts for drug dealers?"

"Human directionals," Vining joked. "Li informed me that it's a trained profession."

"My apologies to the Union of Professional Human Directionals," Caspers said.

"I guess a fancy job title makes the work more attractive." Early shook her head.

"Scrappy was working on the corner of Orange Grove and Newcastle," Vining said. "Caspers and I drove by earlier today, and Li's got another guy out there. There's also one standing a block north, on Newcastle and Mountain. Apparently, they're there until midnight. We have to check it out. Seems like a strange way to advertise apartments. Cameron, do your guys have any information about drug activity over there?"

"No reports of any drug activity."

"There's a little residential neighborhood tucked in there, above Orange Grove." Sergeant Early squeezed her eyes closed as she visualized the area. In the decades that she'd lived in Pasadena and served in the PPD, she had become familiar with every street and alley of the city. "That stretch of Orange Grove has a lot of small businesses. There's a hubcap place and a brass plating place." She opened her eyes. "My husband took our doorknobs to that brass place."

Caspers said, "There's a tire place and auto repair shops. On the southeast corner, there's that new building that got some cosmetics company in it. What's it called?"

Vining responded, "Terra Cosmetika. It's a line of organic, eco-friendly cosmetics. No animal testing, sustainable, yada yada . . ."

"Groovy," Caspers said.

Sproul asked an obvious question. "Where's the apartment building these human directionals were hired to advertise?"

"Good question," Early added.

Vining said, "Li told me it was on the corner of Newcastle and Orange Grove, but there's no apartment building there. I want to surveil that block of Newcastle between Orange Grove and Mountain. I also want to know who comes and goes in that bridal salon."

"I'll set up the surveillance," Lam said.

Vining concluded the meeting. "I want to believe in redemption and that Li's a changed man. Still . . ." She rifled through the documents she'd prepared and found a crime-scene photo of the Golden Lotus shoot-out twenty-five years ago. It showed the innocent bystanders—a man and his daughter—with plates of food on the table in front of them, their bodies riddled with bullets and slumped in the booth. "We can't forget this."

TWENTY-TWO

Vining returned to her cubicle at nearly seven o'clock. She still had work to do before she went home. She needed to check in with her grandmother, whom she'd asked to pick up Emily from school and stay with until she got home. Em was old enough to stay by herself, and had, and she could have gotten a ride home from a friend's parent, but they hadn't spent much time with Granny lately. Vining wanted Granny to feel useful. Vining's mother and sister rarely called, much less visited the old woman. Vining's attempts to encourage them to do so, even to try and make them feel guilty, fell on deaf ears. Granny still drove and lived in her own home, but Vining saw the handwriting on the wall.

Plus, Vining admitted to another motive. Based upon the photograph of Ken Zhang that Emily had taken, the girl had spent time with Ken outside of school. Vining wanted to keep her daughter on a tighter leash.

The message light on her phone was blinking. She quickly went through her messages, deleting most, saving others, not hearing the one voice she most desired to hear: Kissick's.

She heard a new voice that she didn't immediately recognize. It was Marvin Li, again inviting her out to dinner. While she found an invitation to dine with the illustrated, sexually aggressive murderer and key suspect in her investigation unappealing, there was something alluring in his melodic voice. His tone had a quality that made him sound like a dangerous man. Something in it evoked things she knew well: crime and criminals. And things she didn't: distant lands and foreign flavors. There was a suggestion of things she'd indulged in rarely: sensuality and wild abandon.

The allure was fleeting. She deleted the message.

She phoned home. When Granny answered, Vining could barely hear her warbling voice over the television blaring in the background. Granny's hearing had deteriorated to the point that she should wear her hearing aid all the time, which she stubbornly refused to do. The device was old-fashioned, large, and prone to emitting a high-pitched buzz. She rebuffed Vining's offers to help her with the expense of a new one. This forced everyone to yell if Granny was to hear them.

"Hi Granny, it's Nan. *Nan.*" Vining had Caller ID on her home phone, but Granny wouldn't look at the display. She cupped her hand over the receiver and shouted, "Turn down the TV."

The remaining detectives in their cubicles tittered.

Granny had turned down the television's volume, but Vining still had to speak loudly. "Everything okay?"

Even though Vining's hearing was perfect, Granny shouted in response. "Everything's fine. How are you?"

There were more titters. The detectives enjoyed this mundane family drama, distracting them from whatever bleak task they were engaged in.

"I'm fine. Emily okay?"

"Sure. She's in her room working on a school project."

"Okay. Good. Thanks for picking her up."

"What's that?"

"Thanks for picking her up."

"Don't mention it. Will you be home late?"

"No. I'll bring home takeout for dinner. I'll call you when I'm on my way. Gotta go. Bye."

Granny was in the middle of asking her something

about the case when Vining hung up. She didn't enjoy cutting off her grandmother, but the yelling was getting on her nerves and she didn't like being comic relief for bored detectives.

She was tired and cranky. She was really feeling her lack of sleep. She'd worked other cases where the passion to solve it had propelled her to work days on end without a break, barely feeling the fatigue. She just had to keep at it. Scrappy's family deserved to know what happened. Scrappy deserved justice. The homicide detective's mantra was: We work for God. For murder victims and loved ones, the homicide detective was their last chance to see justice meted out in this life.

Luck played a larger role than detectives liked to admit. She hated depending upon luck, but was now praying it would shine upon her.

She needed to go home. She needed her chenille throw, a box of vanilla wafers, and an old flick on her classic movie TV channel. She needed a hug and a big, wet kiss from her daughter and her grandmother's papery lips on her cheek. She wished she'd given in to Emily's pleas for a dog because she'd take that big, sloppy kiss, too. A memory of spooning with Kissick flitted into her mind, her butt nestled against his thighs and belly, his strong arms enveloping her . . .

She forced the image from her mind.

She stuck her head into the detective sergeants' office and told Sergeant Early that she was thinking about calling it a day after she checked with Cameron Lam about the surveillance of Newcastle Street.

Ron Cho, the large Latino/Korean sergeant who was one of the three that shared the office razzed her, "Working another half day, Vining?"

She was too tapped out to think of a snappy comeback. "Yeah." She managed a feeble laugh.

Sergeant Early, whose piercing gaze had made criminals

quake, showed Vining another side of that intensity. She felt as if Early was looking through her, but the scrutiny felt maternal, laced with concern. Vining didn't recall ever seeing that in her mother's eyes. It touched her and she felt suddenly teary, a sure sign that she was overtired.

An exhausted cop wasn't good for the PPD or the public.

Early didn't see the red that had shot through Vining's eyes because she'd returned her attention to the report she'd been reading. "Any news on that shirt?"

"I'm going to check on my way out." Vining made a move to leave, hesitating in the doorway. "Any word from Kissick?"

"Not since he called to tell me he'd arrived in Morro Bay."

"Thanks for everything, Sarge. See you tomorrow."

Vining left the Detectives Section and walked down the corridor until she reached a door with a window at the top that was stenciled FORENSICS.

Through the glass, she saw her friend Forensics Services supervisor Tara Khorsandi peering into a microscope. Tara looked up when Vining came inside.

"Hey, Nan. What's doin'?"

"That's what I was gonna ask you. Any word on when the Crime Lab will be able to process that shirt?"

"You know how it goes with them. 'We have three agencies ahead of you.'" Tara flashed a broad smile. "But I told them it was a ten." Meaning, high-priority.

The Los Angeles Forensic Science Center processed forensic materials for the LAPD and the LASD and had contracts with smaller law-enforcement agencies. Even after the expanded, state-of-the-art facility opened on the nearby campus of Cal State L.A., backlogs were still long.

"Thanks, Tara."

Khorsandi added, "I've been thinking about that shirt. How he kept it for over a year. Wonder if he has other mementos."

"That's assuming I'm not his only victim."

"I've always assumed that. Haven't you?"

Vining smiled sadly. "Definitely." Tara was her only real friend at the PPD other than Kissick. She hadn't confided in Tara about her surreptitious investigation into T. B. Mann and his victims, even though she knew she could trust her with anything. Hell, Vining hadn't even confided in Kissick until forced to. Her relationship with T. B. Mann *was* like an illicit affair.

"Matter of fact," Vining said, "Jim's in Central California right now, following up on a lead that came about from that mute guy's, Nitro's, drawings. There's evidence my bad guy targets female cops."

Khorsandi looked up in alarm. "Really?" She shook her shoulders. "That just gave me a chill. What kind of weird psychosis is that?"

"Who knows? I'm not big on psychoanalyzing psychos, although some people make careers of it."

Khorsandi looped a lock of her straight, shoulder-length black hair around her ear. She wore simple, small gold loop earrings. "Still, it makes you wonder. I mean, even murderers have mothers, right? Was your bad guy the devil spawn of a prostitute, abused as a child, like Charles Manson? Or did he grow up in an affluent family, educated in private schools, playing tennis at posh members-only clubs, giving no hints about the monster within until the terrible night his fury was unleashed, like the Menendez brothers?"

Vining laughed. "You're watching that true-crime cable station too much."

She smiled. "Maybe so. A person will watch just about anything when up in the middle of the night with a colicky baby."

Nan remembered how fond she was of Tara. They had started with the PPD around the same time, and had helped each other up that high learning curve. Tara was now married with a toddler, but in those early years on the nights that Emily was with her dad, she and Tara had often gone out on the town. Nan had been invited to Tara's house, where she had lived with her Indian parents and U.S.–born younger brother and sister. Life at the Khorsandi house was warm, lively, and loud; its kitchen smelled of wonderfully exotic spices. Nan had liked being there very much.

Vining went on. "I'll leave the analysis to the so-called specialists. I just want to put the creep in prison for as long as possible." That was a white lie. She actually wanted to see T. B. Mann's head on a stake, but some things were best left unsaid.

Khorsandi laughed. "Thatta girl. Hey, I processed your creep's prints through the databases." She frowned. "Zilch."

"You'd think this jackass would at least get picked up for being a Peeping Tom. A DUI would be too much to ask, I guess. Thanks for doing that every single week, Tara. You don't know how much I appreciate it."

"No problem. Happy to contribute something."

Khorsandi segued from the horrible to the social in a way common within their profession. "We should get coffee soon. It's been too long."

"I know," Vining said with regret.

"You've been so busy lately."

Vining thought, *You don't know the half of it.* "We'll make a date soon."

"I'm gonna nail you down now. Next week?"

"Sure."

"I'm holding you to it."

Vining smiled and turned to leave. At the door, she said, "Thanks, Tara."

Her friend wistfully returned the smile. "You're welcome, Nan. Take care."

TWENTY-THREE

Vining drove to the corner of Newcastle Street and Orange Grove Boulevard. She recognized one of the PPD surveillance vehicles, a van painted as a mobile pet shampooing service, parked near the corner.

One of Marvin Li's employees, Victor Chang, stood on the corner, swinging a large plastic arrow that advertised apartments for lease. He was dressed in a black T-shirt and chinos, but wore a King Tut headdress that extended to his shoulders.

She slowed while driving past. Chang spotted her and gave a half-hearted wave. She gave him a nod and continued up Newcastle to Mountain.

There she saw Daniel Shin, another of Li's crew she'd interviewed earlier. He wore a multi-colored Afro, like Scrappy had worn, but no costume. His sign advertised LUXURY CONDOS and he was swinging it to point across Mountain.

Vining continued driving in that direction.

Three blocks north of Mountain, she stopped in front of the first apartment building she saw. A wooden sign on the façade in script letters said: *Bali Hai.* A large tiki head near the entrance was losing a battle with dry rot. It had two stories and was built in a 1960s courtyard style with exterior corridors facing a kidney-shaped pool in the center patio. Vining took a picture of the building.

The managers were an older couple, the Shugarts, who let her inside. They knew nothing about anyone hiring human directionals to promote their apartment building. When they had a vacancy, they always placed an ad in the PennySaver.

Next she drove to the alley behind the tire store where Cameron Lam said his team had found a tagged death threat against her. The words were pure street-gang bravado, but the tag didn't look like any she'd seen before:

VINING 187

It had been done in spray paint, the tagger's typical medium. While many taggers' work was artistic, Vining had never seen this style of lettering. Plus, the tag was huge; the letters were about three feet tall. The edges were clean and precise. After studying the work with her flashlight beam, Vining saw remnants of a pencil sketch that the tagger had done before he began painting. This art wasn't the result of a spur-of-the-moment inspiration. This had been well planned and had to have taken a long time.

The walls on the backs of the buildings along the alley were covered with graffiti. Attempts had been made to cover it up with neutral-colored paint, but that only provided a fresh canvas for new tags.

She looked around and didn't see any security cameras. A wooden plank fence was on the other side of the alley. A couple of planks were broken or missing. Vining directed her flashlight beam inside and saw the backyard of the bungalow that faced the side street. The yard was mostly dirt but had persistent patches of grass. Weathered white resin lawn furniture and toys were scattered around.

She walked the street that was perpendicular to the alley. It was lined with small houses and ramshackle apartment buildings. She went down a cracked cement path that led to the front door of the house that was along the alley. Shifting land had made the three cement steps that led to the porch separate a few inches from it. A beat-up couch and a small table were on the porch.

She pressed the doorbell buzzer, but the button sank beneath her thumb without sounding. After knocking and announcing, "Police," she saw movement from behind the closed drapes. A young Latina opened the door holding a baby boy on her hip. The baby had wide brown eyes and was sucking a pacifier.

Vining asked her in English about the tag, and then exercised her rudimentary Spanish. The young woman said she didn't know anything, which didn't surprise Vining. No one around there would want to be seen talking to the cops.

She returned to the alley and walked down it behind two auto repair shops. Their yards were surrounded by chain-link fences topped with barbed wire. Neither had security cameras. She walked in the other direction, passing the loading dock of the Terra Cosmetika building.

The cosmetics firm might have been on the cutting edge of eco-friendly, but it took an unfriendly stance when it came to intruders. It was all about high-tech security. CCTV cameras were positioned on both corners of the building to observe the loading dock. The one on the western side might have caught the length of the alley behind the tire store.

She walked to the front of the building. The corner diagonally across was where Scrappy had last worked, waving his arrow in his clown suit, and where Victor Chang was still standing, wearing his King Tut headdress.

She thought of Scrappy's tag in the Hollenbeck Paper building: China Dog 187. The style of the "Vining 187" tag was completely different. She thought it unlikely that Scrappy was responsible for both tags. Still it was odd to find a tag with the same verbiage on a wall near where Scrappy had last worked.

There was a CCTV camera over Terra Cosmetika's front entrance. The building's façade was of stamped concrete and bamboo wood. Drought resistant plants spilled from large painted concrete planters. A plaque beside the door stated that the building was built with environmentally friendly materials and largely powered by renewable resources.

Vining looked around at the homely but friendly mom-and-pop businesses on the street—the brass shop, the hubcap shop, the mechanic who specialized in British sports cars—and reflected that the Pasadena that she knew and loved was being crushed under the steam-roller of so-called progress.

She tried Terra Cosmetika's sepia-tinted glass door and, of course, it was locked. There was a smart-card device for employees and a buzzer for visitors. She looked up at the CCTV camera and waved. Guess no one had figured out a way to make criminals eco-friendly.

She'd come back tomorrow.

Back in her car, she called Kissick. He was 13 on her cell phone speed dial. His phone rang several times before going into voicemail. Her name would show up as a "Missed Call" anyway, so she might as well leave a message.

"Jim, just checking in. Hope everything's going good. Bye."

As tired as she was, she felt a little horny.

After a years-long sexual drought, Kissick hadn't just awakened her sensuality, he'd jump-started it. She'd never felt this way before. She'd never craved sex. She'd had few sexual partners. Her ex-husband Wes had been her high school sweetheart and her first. After he'd walked out on her, she'd dated a little, mostly for revenge. She'd soon given it up, not wanting to re-create with her daughter the parade of men that her mother had made her endure. She still took pains to hide from Emily her true relationship with Kissick.

She'd thought that her and Wes's sexual relationship had been good. Now that she knew the difference, she realized it had been warm and comforting, like a bowl of Cream of Wheat. During the short months that she and Kissick were together the first time, she'd thought their sexual relationship was lovely and nice. Now she knew she'd been tentative and restrained.

All that had been before. Before T. B. Mann had bro-ken her down and seized her life, until, at the last sec-ond, she'd seized it back. "Restrained" wouldn't be in the vocabulary of words she'd use to describe her and Kissick now. Only tired clichés came to mind—fireworks, runaway trains, geysers erupting. Still, sometimes clichés were apt.

That brought her up to today. She thought of her strange meeting with the subversive Marvin Li, when he stroked the spiraling butterflies on his pectoral with his fine, long fingers. Was what she was feeling now set in motion by him? Maybe she should be disgusted.

Maybe she should just tell her brain to shut up and relax.

She looked at the cell phone in her palm. She again dialed 13 and pressed the pound sign. Again she got Kissick's voicemail. Her message was plain.

"I need you tonight."

She mashed her thumb on the button to end the call and immediately regretted having left the message.

TWENTY-FOUR

Standing on the sandspit near the yellow nylon rope that marked the snowy plover restricted habitat, Zeke Denver pointed to show Kissick where they'd found Marilu Feathers's body. He also showed him where they'd found the remains of the campfire inside the restricted area.

Even though September was still summertime in California, with long, warm days into which twilight crept slowly, the beach was not crowded. Groups of surfer dudes, the tops of their wetsuits pulled down to reveal toned-and-tanned torsos, gathered on the sand with their girlfriends in bikini bottoms and hoodies. The wind had kicked up as the sun began to set. The ocean was dotted with whitecaps.

After Denver had indicated the spot, he dropped into thoughtful silence. They both watched as the setting sun disappeared behind a fog bank, radiating bright orange. It reappeared beneath the fog a few minutes later.

Out of the blue, Denver said, "There are people who believe this place is magical. Where else can you stand on the beach and be eye-level with the ocean?"

Kissick looked straight-on at the roiling waves.

"Mighty force, that ocean," Denver added. "I believe she wants to kill us. Rogue waves snatch people off this shore a couple of times a year."

As if on cue, a woman on horseback appeared from the passageway between the dunes. After the horse trotted across the softer sand, it eased into a gallop once it hit the waterline, seemingly without urging.

Kissick thought he saw moisture in the corner of Zeke Denver's eye.

After Kissick bid Denver good-bye, he headed to Cambria, to the house where Marilu Feathers had grown up and where her mother, Margaret, still lived. He drove with all the car windows down, traveling north on Highway 1 along one of the most beautiful, unspoiled stretches of coastline in California. He used to drive this route as a college student off to visit friends at U.C. Santa Cruz in his Volkswagen Beetle that he'd modified into a Baja Bug and painted tangerine with a metallic flake.

He reached Cambria, an artsy town that straddled the ocean and a mountainous pine forest. He followed Margaret Feathers's directions into the forested part, winding higher through narrow streets until he found her address.

The small, sturdy wooden cottage was set off the road and nestled among pine trees. Its red paint with brown shutters needed refreshing. Two stone chimneys pierced the pitched roof that was littered with dry pine needles. The modest flower beds were planted only with shade-loving impatiens that had grown leggy. The small front yard was circled by a white picket fence and consisted of sandy dirt and pine needles beneath towering pines.

The house wasn't decrepit, but it looked careworn. Zeke Denver had told Kissick that Margaret Feathers had been a widow for several years and lived in the house by herself. Marilu's brother and his family lived nearby. Denver and his wife checked in on Margaret and helped her with chores and maintenance. Her son was encouraging her to sell the house and move into a senior community in a bigger city that was closer to more services. Margaret, vibrant at age sixty-eight, wasn't ready for that just yet.

Kissick opened the gate in the picket fence and walked down an uneven flagstone path, avoiding stepping on pinecones. The air here was warmer than on the sandspit and smelled of pine forest rather than ocean. The forest side of Cambria gave no hint of the ocean on the other side.

As he approached the cozy, solid-looking house, he understood Margaret Feathers's unwillingness to move. A wreath of silk flowers framed a brass look-through in the door that had a grate of narrow bars on the outside and a knocker beneath. Kissick knew that inside he'd find a small brass door that closed with a latch. He had something similar on his front door.

The front door swung open before Kissick had a chance to sound the knocker.

"Detective Kissick. I'm Margaret Feathers. Please come in."

"Nice to meet you, Dr. Feathers."

"Call me Margaret, please. A doctor of sociology doesn't even get a good dinner reservation."

Kissick smiled appreciatively at her wit as she stepped aside to let him in.

Dr. Feathers was tall, big-boned, and lean like her daughter Marilu, but her face was softer and more feminine. Marilu had inherited the strong features of her accountant father. Margaret was dressed in a white blouse trimmed with lace tucked into gray slacks. Her gray hair still showed a little brown and was styled in soft, close-cropped curls.

The house was as inviting as Kissick had imagined. The front door led directly into the living room, which had a deeply pitched ceiling with exposed knotty-pine beams. The Early American maple furniture covered in plaid fabric was in need of reupholstering. The floor was of random-width knotty-pine planks covered with an oval braided-wool rug. There was a stone fireplace with a raised hearth and a tarnished brass fireplace set. Firewood was stacked in an iron basket and kindling was in a brass bucket. Two easy chairs and a couch were positioned to enjoy the fire. One chair was draped with a throw that was heavily coated with light-colored pet fur. Through an archway beside the fireplace he saw a dining room and a kitchen beyond it. To the left was a comfortable-looking den with an old television on a stand.

The fireplace was clean of ashes. That was reasonable as it was late summer, but Kissick wondered if Margaret ever built a fire just for herself. He thought of his own parents, who were both alive. If his father were dead, would his mother continue the simple routines they enjoyed that made the house a home? Would the traditions bring warm memories or would they feel hollow if not shared? Perhaps a fireplace fire made too big a mess at the end of a life in which much time had been devoted to cleaning up messes.

"Can I offer you tea or coffee, Detective?"

"Whatever you're having would be great."

"I enjoy English Breakfast tea, even in the afternoon." Margaret's voice was evenly modulated and she precisely enunciated her words, reminiscent of the college professor she'd been. "I hope you won't turn down a slice of my banana nut bread."

"I wouldn't consider being so impolite."

"You're a fit young man. I'm sure you can handle a little piece of something sweet. Everyone's so concerned about eating carbohydrates these days. When I grew up, we had dessert after every meal and I did the same in my household. I guess it's all about staying active. People these days spend too much time indoors, looking at computer screens. Please make yourself at home. I'll be right back."

She left for the kitchen. Her footsteps in low-heeled shoes were alternately muffled on the area rugs and resonated softly against the hardwood floor.

The silence in the house was broken only by the ticking of a grandfather clock that Kissick spied in the adjoining den. It emitted a firm "tick" followed by a lower-pitched "tock," and silence in between, like a heartbeat. Kissick found the silence in older homes unique. They didn't so much exclude sounds, but rather were selective about the ones they embraced. The silence felt rich. It wasn't missing anything, but rather was full and complete in itself.

He looked at framed photographs that were arrayed on the mantel, end tables, and built-in bookcases beneath the windows. He'd examined many such collections in the homes of murder victims' families. The photos always made him reflect about that corner turned when murder takes its place at the table, never to leave. For the loved ones left behind, the photographs still provoked happy memories, but the happiness was forever tarnished. No amount of polishing would restore its prior beauty. He sensed that tainted happiness in the silence of this house.

There were rocks and shells placed around the photographs. Kissick absently picked up one of the stones and carried it as he explored. It was gray and marked with fine, darker gray striations. It was lighter than it looked.

An overweight, orange tabby cat sauntered into the room from the den. The large cat moved straight toward Kissick, delicately placing one paw in front of the other, like a gymnast on a balance beam, her gold eyes fixed upon the intruder. She sniffed Kissick's outstretched fingers, but reared her head beyond his reach when he attempted to touch her. She minced to the easy chair that was draped with the fur-covered throw, and leaped onto it with ease that belied her girth.

He continued perusing the photos until he saw one

that pulled him up short. It was a studio photograph of Margaret and her husband, perhaps taken ten years ago. Margaret's hair was worn in the same style, but wasn't as gray. He had on a coat and tie and she was in a pale blue dress. Around her neck was a pearl necklace. It was nearly identical to Vining's—the same length, the same size pearls, the same pendant surrounded by small stones that glittered like diamonds. The only difference was the gem in the pendant. Vining's necklace had a pearl. Kissick couldn't quite make out the stone in the photograph, but it wasn't a pearl.

Margaret returned, carrying a silver tray laden with a china teapot, sugar bowl, cream pitcher, cups, saucers, and small plates, one holding fanned slices of rich-looking banana nut bread. There were also small, crisp linen napkins with embroidered flowers, and silver tea-spoons and dessert forks that looked as if they'd been recently polished.

Kissick returned the photograph to the shelf and realized he was still holding the rock. "I'm sorry. I picked this up and I don't know where it goes."

She had set the tray halfway onto the coffee table and was picking up copies of *National Geographic*, *The Saturday Review*, and *The Economist* with one hand. "Oh, just put it anywhere. Marilu was always giving me rocks and shells. She always brought me shells that were pink and rocks that were heart-shaped."

Kissick looked at the rock and realized that it indeed resembled a heart. He set it on the mantel.

"That photograph you were looking at was taken on our fortieth anniversary." She set down the tray. "Harold died a year later. I see Miss Persimmon has deigned to grace us with her presence." She scratched the cat's ears. The cat heartily rolled her head against Margaret's hand as if in ecstasy, eyes slit, and began purring robustly.

She stroked the cat once more then patted a wing-backed chair beside the sofa. "Please have a seat, Detective."

She perched on the sofa and poured tea into a china cup decorated with hand-painted flowers and a gold band around the rim. "Cream? Sugar?"

"Black, please."

She set a cup and saucer on the coffee table near him and followed with a slice of banana bread on a small plate, tucking a napkin beneath it.

He picked up the delicate napkin. He wouldn't have dared to soil it, but she wanted him to use it, so he opened it at the first crease and draped it across one leg.

"In your anniversary photo, you're wearing a pearl necklace. Does it have a history?"

Something about the way she looked deeply into his eyes made him suspect that she had always had a question about the necklace. "Someone gave it to Marilu. She felt it was an extravagant gift and would have refused it, but she couldn't. It had been left in a bag on the doorknob of the ranger residence where she was living. She asked me if I wanted it."

"When was this?"

"About nine years ago." Her spoon tinkled against the china cup as she stirred in cream and sugar.

"Nine years ago. That was around the time Marilu shot Bud Lilly."

"Yes. Why the interest in the necklace?"

"It's a lead we're following."

"So that's why you came here. I knew you had something personal to discuss beyond what Zeke could tell you about Marilu's murder."

He was about to ask her if she still had the necklace when she took in a breath, as if to speak.

"I believe I was wearing it that Christmas Eve. The one when we waited for Marilu. I wore it to her funeral. It was something beautiful that she'd given to me."

She paused, holding the cup in mid-air. "Are you suggesting that the person who killed Marilu might have given it to her?"

Kissick sensed the pain she'd endured all those years. It started that Christmas Eve with mild anxiety when Marilu, who was never late without calling, had not shown up. Anxiety turned to fear as time dragged on. She'd probably served the Christmas Eve dinner anyway, lest it completely dry out in the oven, but no one had eaten much. Before long, her worst fears would be confirmed.

He felt it was cruel to stand on protocol about not revealing salient details of the investigation. The forkful of banana bread he was chewing turned to mush in his mouth.

She gently pleaded. "I won't tell a soul or do anything to jeopardize your work, Detective. I've waited a long time. My hope is to see Marilu's murderer brought to justice before I die. My fear is that I won't."

He set down the plate and fork and absently blotted his mouth with the linen napkin, forgetting his intention not to soil it. From his jacket pocket, he took out Vining's pearl necklace and handed it to her. "A Pasadena police officer was given that under similar circumstances before she was attacked."

She held it between her hands. "This is the same as Marilu's, except the pendant in hers has a polished turquoise."

"It was left at our officer's home with a handwritten note, congratulating her."

"Congratulating her?"

Kissick indicated that he also found it bizarre. "Near as we can figure, congratulating her for having killed a bad guy in the line of duty. She was front-page news for a while."

"Like Marilu with Bud Lilly."

"Yes."

Margaret handed the necklace back to Kissick. "Marilu's necklace was dropped off before she was attacked. That means he'd been stalking her. Her murder wasn't a random act." She rubbed her hands over her arms. "That gives me chills."

From his jacket pocket, Kissick took out the artist's rendering of Nan's attacker and the photo of Nitro. "Do you recognize either of these men?"

She closely examined the images. She held up the one of Nitro. "This one looks harmless. This one, though . . . Is this drawing based upon that police officer's description of the man who attacked her?"

"Yes."

"He looks so plain, doesn't he? He looks like anyone. The political theorist Hannah Arendt wrote about the banality of evil, the interdependence of thoughtlessness and evil. This fellow's picture certainly brings that phrase to mind." Finally, she shook her head and sighed. "I'm sorry I can't be of more help." She gave him back the photo and drawing.

"You've helped tremendously. Thank you for your time."

"It's the least I can do. I'm so grateful for your effort. I have a good feeling about this. I think you're going to get him. I really do."

"I'll do everything in my power. I'll let you know how things are going."

The grandfather clock chimed the hour. The light in the room had grown dim and the shadows had lengthened.

Margaret was pensive. "If he's murdered two, there are probably more. Is that your theory?"

"We are examining that possibility."

"All females in law enforcement?"

"Perhaps."

"Makes one wonder who he really seeks to kill. Marilu and your officer attracted his attention. By giving them a necklace, he's anointed them. In his mind, he's transformed them into this iconic woman. He murders the stand-in, and for a while, finds release." She made a face, as if she feared she sounded ridiculous. "Forgive the pop psychology."

"I'm intrigued. So does he stop after he kills the prototype?"

"He may not be able to kill her. Perhaps he can't get up his nerve. Perhaps he's not fully cognizant of his motives and doesn't realize that *she's* the one he wants dead. Perhaps she's already dead. When these warrior women appear, he's compelled to knock them down." She shrugged, again dismissing her theory. "But who knows?"

She stood and walked around the room, turning on lamps. "You'll want Marilu's necklace. I'll get it."

While she was gone, Kissick took a small spiral pad from his jacket breast pocket and made a few notes, including: Turquoise = December? He didn't broach the death stone issue with Margaret. There was no need for her to know how well-planned the assassination of her daughter had been.

Nan's attacker was sentimental and romantic, in a twisted way. Thinking of how he'd planned, watched, waited, and then had coolly executed the murders rattled Kissick's bones. The psycho had given Nan the necklace five years before he'd attacked her. *Five years.* He'd had a romantic relationship with Nan during that time. Had that creep been following them? Watching them? The thought made his blood boil. He finally had to concede the possibility of a criminal mastermind.

Shortly, Margaret returned, dangling the necklace from one hand, holding it away from her body, looking at it like she might a friend who had lied to her. She seemed relieved to give it to him.

He turned to a fresh page on his spiral pad. "I'll write you a receipt. You'll likely be able to get it back once things are resolved."

"I don't want it back. I don't want it in my house anymore."

It was another example of a truth that Kissick knew too well. Death changes everything. Death takes something that was beloved and turns it inside out, rendering it into bloody viscera.

He ran his thumb over the polished turquoise oval surrounded by small diamond-like stones. He dropped it inside the jacket pocket with Vining's necklace.

He gave Dr. Feathers a warm good-bye and promised to let her know of any developments.

Back inside his car, he retraced his trip on Highway 1, heading south. He was looking forward to having a cocktail and a nice dinner at Dorn's restaurant in Morro Bay, checking into the modest motel he'd selected, and getting to bed after a long couple of days.

While driving back, thinking of the martini glasses shoved into the vat of chipped ice that he remembered on the bar at Dorn's, and almost tasting that first martini, he affixed his Bluetooth to his ear to check his cell phone messages.

One was from Nan. It was nice of her to call and check in.

The next message was also from her, but had a decidedly different intent.

I need you tonight.

He pondered what she meant by "need." That she missed him and wanted to see him? But wouldn't she have just said that if that was what she'd meant? Her slightly breathy tone suggested another meaning. He played the message again and became convinced that "need" meant *need*. He'd accused her of being tightly wound and not herself, but this sort of craziness he could more than handle.

His martini, seafood dinner, and motel bed lured, yet . . . He nearly called her back, but decided not to. She had left the message impulsively and he responded in kind. He didn't stop in Morro Bay but continued to the 101. Maybe she'd have changed her mind by the time he arrived, but maybe not.

TWENTY-FIVE

*P*arking on Green Street near Tarantino's was always nearly impossible. Vining could have parked in the red, but there had been a rise in complaints about the local cops violating parking and traffic laws. Even though the Crown Vic was unmarked, many citizens recognized it as a cop car. She circled the block, and on her return, nabbed a spot as someone was leaving.

Inside the shoebox-size restaurant, the handful of tables was full and people were lined up along the wall in back, waiting. It was a late dinner hour for the local crowd who patronized this hole-in-the-wall place, but the too-warm September night was a siren call that awakened the continental spirit in the most stalwart soccer moms and overworked dads who broke the school-night rules for their overscheduled children.

At the counter, Vining paid for a large sausage pizza she'd ordered over the phone. She thought she'd surprise

Emily with her favorite. She knew Granny enjoyed a slice of Tarantino's pizza even though she'd been having problems with her dentures lately. Vining thought there was a bag of prewashed spring salad greens in the fridge. Dinner was going to be later than she'd wanted, but she was happy she was going to be able to sit down at a table with her daughter and grandmother. When she was overly tired, she had a tendency to become sentimental and vulnerable. She needed the anchor of the two relatives who were most precious to her. Her grandmother was a tie to her past. Her daughter was her hope for the future.

She adored her younger sister Stephanie, but their bond had weakened over the past years as stay-at-home-mom Stephanie's life became focused on her husband and two little boys. Vining appreciated Steph's commitment to her family, but wondered if she was using it as an excuse to distance herself. Vining felt her attempted murder had damaged a fragile equilibrium and Steph was now circling the wagons around her husband and kids. While Vining was recovering from her injuries, Steph had done and said the right things, but Vining sensed she was doing it more from obligation than from love and a heartfelt desire to help.

Now, over a year later, Steph was often unavailable to meet for shopping and lunch, just the two of them. As their grandmother became frailer, Steph had become nearly invisible. Vining doubted Steph was as busy as she claimed, but had convinced herself she was. Vining felt like telling her that life was hectic, complicated, and it frequently stank, but that was no reason to wash her hands of familial responsibilities. She was going to have that conversation with her sister, once her own life stopped being so hectic and complicated.

Their childhoods had been a sea of upheaval and unsettledness. Products of different marriages of their perennially rainbow-chasing mother, Patsy, each sister's father had abandoned her when she was a toddler. That was Patsy's explanation. Vining suspected that Patsy had chased them away, but an abandonment story carried more drama. Vining was four years older than Steph and had dim memories of her sister's father, but none of her own. In a way, both sisters felt their lives were held together with duct tape, paper clips, and dreams of building better lives and sounder families.

They didn't much resemble each other physically. Steph was fair and petite, like their mother. Brunette, statuesque Vining had always been told she resembled her father.

As for their mother, Patsy Brightly, the sisters maintained a respectable level of contact, yet kept a reasonable distance, as one would do with a stingray, tiger, tarantula, or any other beautiful but potentially destructive creature.

Vining headed home, traveling west on Colorado Boulevard and going over Suicide Bridge. She reached Mt. Washington from the opposite direction she usually went, taking San Rafael up the hill, then going down the other side, turning left onto her cul-de-sac, Stella Place. The aroma of the pizza sitting on the passenger seat made her stomach rumble.

A car she didn't recognize, a brand-new white BMW convertible that still had the dealer plates, was parked in front of the house. She assumed it belonged to a guest of her new, unfriendly neighbors who had constructed a modern behemoth with a gated entrance after razing two boxy 1960s-era homes from the original housing development.

Vining drove up to *her* boxy 1960s home. It looked small from the street, as most of the house extended off the hillside, supported by cantilevers. Sure, she worried whenever there was a significant temblor or when El Niño came and the ensuing rains seemed as if the heavens had opened, but Mt. Washington's cliff-hanging houses had been secured into solid rock and built with care not given to the slapdash, newly constructed homes built too close together on unstable hillsides that seemed to be always slipping away. That's what she told herself when the earth shook like hell or the mountain seemed to be melting into mud. Brush fires had not presented a significant problem so far.

Granny's baby-blue Oldsmobile Delta '88 was parked in the driveway. The lights in the front of the house were off, although she could see the flickering of the television through the drapes. The darkness was Granny's doing; she had never shaken the WWII-era mentality of pinching pennies wherever she could, even if they were her granddaughter's pennies.

When Vining entered the driveway, a motion light turned on, illuminating the small front yard. The yard had a patch of grass that she or Emily occasionally mowed, hearty shrubs next to the house, and equally hearty old rosebushes planted by the previous owner, which bloomed defiantly with the smallest amount of care.

She always waited until she could see the garage before clicking the automatic opener, making sure no one sneaked in. She'd adapted her life in many ways since T. B. Mann had become a part of it. Her precautions had done little good, as he'd gotten inside her garage to deliver the bloody shirt, but the garage wasn't alarmed like the house. She and Em were fastidious about setting the alarm.

If he did get inside the house, Vining's weapons were close at hand. Emily was well trained on Vining's Glock .40 and her backup Walther PPK, as well as the arsenal in the locked gun case. Em knew that under pressure she should grab the Mossberg 500. She didn't need perfect aim, as it would stop anything within twenty feet of her.

Vining parked the Crown Vic next to her aging Jeep Cherokee in the two-car garage. She was counting the months, and there were not many, before Emily would get her driver's license. Her ex-husband Wes's tooyoung, too-thin, and too-involved wife, Kaitlyn, wanted to give Emily a new car for her sixteenth birthday. Vining thought that Kaitlyn had too much disposable income and time on her hands, even with two boys aged five and three—the distraction of which was mitigated by ample paid help—and was too concerned with appearances. They would need another car, as Vining took home one of the Crown Vics only when she was on call, but Em didn't need something brandnew.

Vining viewed this transition with both relief and trepidation. Emily being able to drive would simplify things, but would bring a new set of concerns. She had nurtured Emily's self-respect and sense of right and wrong and had imparted tools to navigate life's murky waters. She no longer knew, every minute of the day, where Emily was and what she was doing. She had to trust Em to do the right thing, while always reminding the girl that her mother was remaining ever-vigilant to insure that she did.

Emily was relishing this journey. Her new school had brought new challenges and friends. Watching Emily break out of the dark shell that had kept daughter and mother so tightly bound made Vining's heart soar. It was time for Emily to break from the past.

Vining felt the need as well. Her thoughts again trailed to Kissick. Her cheeks burned when she thought of the impulsive phone message she'd left him. Oh, well . . . She'd meant what she'd said. In spite of the recent prickly edges between them, she wanted him, and she wanted him here.

She threw her purse over her shoulder, grabbed her jacket, and hoisted the pizza with one hand. Beside the door into the house were the washer, dryer, and the laundry basket in which Emily had discovered the bloody shirt.

Vining opened the dryer door and saw that the clothes that Em had gone to retrieve that night were still inside. Vining decided that even though they were clean, she'd wash them. Maybe she'd throw away that laundry basket and buy a new one. The handle was cracked and about to break anyway.

Suddenly, Vining was overwhelmed with the desire to move on with her life. Lately, she'd often felt fed up and ready for a change, but now the yearning was almost physical, like a blow to her guts, or like someone compressing her heart between his hands.

Again, like all the times before, her helium balloon of hope grew a lead coat and dragged her crashing back to earth. She could not move on as long as *he* was still out there. T. B. Mann had broken her down and remade her. To get back her life, she had to repay the favor. She'd break him down, all right, and grind him into pulp.

TWENTY-SIX

Vining opened the door from the garage into the kitchen. The prealarm sounded. She was barely able to hear it over the blaring television. Granny still wasn't wearing her hearing aid.

She set her purse on the kitchen counter and dropped her jacket onto a dinette chair. Turning the oven on low, she shoved the pizza inside.

She heard the television in the next room broadcasting that Celine Dion song from the movie *Titanic*, but a woman other than Celine was singing. At the song's final note, a wave of whimsy hit Vining and she closed the oven door with a flourish, doing a half pirouette and posing with her hand in the air. The television audience applauded thunderously.

Walking from the kitchen into the adjacent television room, she saw Nanette Brown, her grandmother, reclined in the La-Z-Boy, covered with the chenille throw, dead asleep, snoring vigorously.

The television was broadcasting *Dancing with the Stars*. Vining picked up the remote control from Granny's lap, taking a moment to marvel at the indestructibility of the old woman's set-and-comb-out, which she had done once a week by the same hairstylist she'd gone to for decades, ever since she'd closed the beauty parlor that she had run out of her home. Vining and her sister had spent many an after-school afternoon there.

Vining looked at her grandmother's lank hand atop

the throw. Granny was wearing, as always, her diamond wedding set. Her husband, Wade, the foreman of a local machine shop, deceased for fifteen years, had added baguettes and round stones at each ten-year anniversary of their fifty-year marriage. Ever-present on Granny's arm were the heavy gold bangles Wade had given her over the years. Nanette and Wade had lived modestly, raising two girls and a boy in the Alhambra home where Nanette still lived. Vining's mother, Patsy, was the problematic middle child. Jewelry was Nanette's indulgence, and Wade loved spoiling her. A friend who worked in downtown L.A.'s jewelry district finagled discounts.

Other than her jewelry and perfectly coiffed hair, Nanette's indulgence was manicures, also a legacy from her beauty-shop days. She had her nails polished pink during spring, coral in summer, burgundy in fall, and red for the holidays. As it was early September, her nails were coral.

Vining shook her head at the expensive jewelry. She'd told Granny a million times not to wear it when she was going around town by herself. All Granny would say in response was "These old things?"

She clicked off the television.

Granny bolted upright, pushing down the recliner's footrest and snapping it into place, flinging off the throw, and was about to spring from the chair before she turned and saw Vining.

"Granny, it's me."

"Heavens to Betsy." Granny put a hand to her chest. "You scared me within an inch of my life."

"I'm sorry I startled you, but the television's so loud, you couldn't hear the prealarm."

"Say again?"

Vining repeated what she had said, almost yelling, ending with, "Where's your hearing aid?"

"The battery's dead."

Vining released an annoyed sigh.

"I'll get one tomorrow."

"I don't want you driving like that."

"Stop worrying about me." Granny grabbed Vining's hand and patted it, grinning broadly. Her false teeth looked oversize in her mouth. She was shrinking, but the teeth remained the same size.

"We'll go to the drugstore tonight after we eat. I picked up a pizza. I know it's late for dinner."

"I like pizza anytime. The crust is a little hard for me to chew, but I can eat the toppings." Granny scooted to the front of the chair seat, put both hands on the chair arms, and hoisted herself up, rejecting the hand that Vining offered. "I can get up by myself. I'm not that decrepit yet."

Vining thought she looked thinner. "Why can't you chew pizza crust?"

"My dentures are bothering me."

"Why don't you get them fixed?"

"I need to have new ones made."

"So . . . ?"

"My insurance only pays for part of it."

"Granny . . ."

She walked past Vining and through the doorway into the kitchen. "Don't worry about me so much. Your old grandmother can still take care of herself."

Vining wasn't so sure. Granny had been a mountain in Vining's life, a forceful, dependable, larger-than-life figure. While her mind was still sharp, over the past year, she'd become frail. Vining felt guilty. Had the stress of her attempted murder sucked up the last of her grandmother's vitality?

Granny leaned into the doorway off the kitchen that led to Emily's room downstairs. With her bejeweled hand against the side of her mouth, she shouted, "Emily, your mother's home."

Now that the television was off, Vining could hear hip-hop music emanating from downstairs.

Before Granny could yell again, Vining halted her with a hand on her arm. She unhooked her cell phone from her belt and pressed the speed-dial combination to call Emily's cell phone. "Hi, sweet pea. I'm home. I picked up a Tarantino's pizza."

Granny shook her head and went to the cupboard. "Kids today." She took out four plates and set them around the dinette table. Then she took out four place settings of flatware.

"Granny, there's just three of us."

Emily stepped from the staircase into the kitchen. Since Em had started her new school, she'd taken to wearing black. The outfit she wore now had to have been enabled by her stepmother, Kaitlyn, who loved to take Em shopping. Her black, skintight, cigarette-leg jeans were crumpled where the hems reached her black tennis shoes. On top, she wore a sheer black T-shirt with a lacy purple camisole beneath it. Both were lower-cut and tighter than anything Vining had seen Emily wear before. Emily had the figure for it. That was the problem. When Emily had started her new school, Vining had allowed her to start wearing a little makeup, but today Em was wearing copious black eyeliner and smoky eye shadow.

With her nearly black hair, which reached the middle of her back, and her alabaster skin, the dark clothing created a dramatic effect, but Vining didn't care for it at all. Emily insisted the shadowy garb wasn't a sign that she was into the Goth scene. Her motives ran deeper.

"Black is the absence of color, Mom," she'd testily explained, barely managing to keep her annoyance in check. It was an attitude that was new for Em, but that Vining knew well from her own adolescence. Mothers were totally clueless. "I don't know what my colors are going to be yet, and until I do, I will wear black."

Vining had looked at her daughter then as if a doppelgänger had taken her over. Right now, in spite of her grim attire, Em looked calm and happy. Today the gods of adolescent hormones were smiling.

Vining would talk to Em about the revealing clothing later. She walked with her arms outstretched to greet her daughter, but stopped short when she saw Lincoln Kennedy Zhang walk up the stairs behind Emily.

"Mom, this is my friend Ken from school."

"Hello, Detective Vining. Nice to see you again." He smiled and extended his hand. He was polite, but uncomfortable.

"Hello, Ken. This is a surprise." Vining quickly returned his handshake, smiling stiffly. She remembered the new BMW parked in front of the house.

"I told Emily how I saw you at the Hollenbeck Paper building," Ken said. "Have you found out who killed that guy?"

"We're working on it. When you said that Em was in your class, I didn't know you were such good friends."

Emily said, "We're doing a project together for our digital photography class. We're going to take panoramic shots from downtown L.A. Ken's mother is friends with the owner of the new Mandarin Palace Hotel. He'll let us on the roof to take pictures." She beamed.

"You're going to have some pizza with us, aren't you, young man?" Granny finished setting the table for four.

"Thank you very much, but I have to get home." Ken snagged the opportunity to escape. "Nice to see you again, Detective Vining. Or, should I call you Mrs. Vining?"

"Detective is fine."

"Oh, okay. So, I'll see you tomorrow, Em."

"I'll walk you to the door."

Ken stepped back to let Emily walk ahead of him.

Vining saw the look in her daughter's eyes and knew it well from her own experience. She and Wes had started sneaking around when she was not much older than Emily. Before long, they were having sex. Sometimes, they used condoms. Often, they didn't. She was damn lucky she hadn't gotten pregnant. When her mother discovered what was going on, she didn't tell Vining to stop. She took her to the doctor for oral contraceptives.

Vining had grown up too young. It was the last thing she wanted for her daughter. Emily had changed so much in the past year. Vining wondered if, like the changes in her grandmother, Emily would have experienced the same metamorphosis without T. B. Mann. Would her sweet girl still be spouting that she was the absence of color?

"He's a nice, polite young man." After making sure that the kids were out of earshot, Granny said, "We used to stay with our own kind, but I guess times have changed. He seems like a good boy."

"You don't know his family." Vining slipped into the entryway to try to hear them.

Emily was giggling, then there was silence.

Vining risked poking her head around the corner. They were kissing. This was no peck on the cheek, but a full-on soul kiss. Her heart dropped into her stomach.

Em lingered, hanging on to the open door, until Ken got inside his car, waving as he drove off. She floated down the entryway, where she saw Vining, who'd stepped from the shadows.

"You're spying on me."

"Yes, I am."

"Can't I have any privacy?"

"When you're an adult, supporting yourself, and living out of my house, you'll be free to do whatever you want."

Emily gaped at her.

"Em, you don't invite a boy into your bedroom."

"That happens to be where my computer is. We're working on a school project. And he's not a *boy*. He's a friend."

"A friend who you were kissing on the lips."

"So what? I'm not going to do anything stupid, Mom. I know better than that." She spun on her heel and stomped into the living room.

"Emily, I'm not finished."

Em wheeled to face her mother, her arms tightly crossed over her chest and her lower lip punched out.

"You're too young to be kissing a boy that way. Especially that boy."

Em shrieked, "*That* boy. What do you mean by *that boy*?"

"I know enough that I don't want you involved with him."

"You don't even know him. It wasn't his mother's fault that that guy got murdered on her property. She doesn't know anything about it."

"Emily, since you're talking to Ken about my investigation, why don't you ask him where his mother got the money to be smuggled out of China? How did she go from being penniless to constructing buildings? Who's his father?"

"His father is American and lives in Hong Kong. He does import/export. Why are you asking that? You don't know who your father is and you're not a criminal."

Touché, Vining thought.

"You don't like him because he's half Chinese. Is that it? I didn't take you for a racist, Mom."

Vining put a hand on her hip, aghast. "Emily, stop with that smart mouth right now. Ken's family has long ties to Chinese organized crime. His cousin is a convicted murderer. His mother withheld information pertinent to the homicide investigation."

"She was scared." Emily flung her arms and stomped away as if she was too frustrated to stand still. She spun around and nearly shouted, "And Ken's not in a gang. He would have told me."

The intimacy implicit in Emily's statements gave Vining pause. She took a second to compose herself, feeling dangerously close to losing control. Calmly, she asked, "Are you having sex with him?"

Emily widened her beautiful green-gray eyes, which, in Vining's view, she'd marred with the excessive makeup. Tears began to flow. "No!"

Granny found them and shouted, "Time for you two to sit down and eat. You can fight later." She retreated into the kitchen.

Emily turned to go, muttering, "She's really gotta get her hearing aid fixed."

Vining smiled and Em did, too. She gently took her daughter's arm. "Emily, you would tell me if you were becoming physical with Ken, wouldn't you? You know you can tell me anything."

She met her mother's eyes. "We're not having sex, okay?"

Vining wondered how she defined sex.

"Mom, can I eat now? I'm starving."

Arguing with her daughter was painful for Vining. She opened her arms and hugged her. After at first responding stiffly, Emily softened and returned her mother's hug with sincerity. Vining kissed Em's forehead, which was at lip height. Only yesterday, it seemed, she used to be able to kiss the top of her head.

"Mom, I can't breathe."

Vining released her a little, but still held on.

"Mom . . . Don't worry so much, okay? Please? It makes it hard all the time."

Vining felt tears well in the corners of her eyes but forced them back down, the way she forced many impulses back down. She stroked Em's hair. She prayed that they would never grow so far apart that they wouldn't be able to find each other again.

Emily struggled away. She wasn't as successful at fighting the tears as her mother. Eyeliner-blackened rivulets trailed from her eyes.

Vining reached into her slacks pocket. Beneath the pair of latex gloves that she always carried, she found tissues and a couple of lint-covered Altoids mints. She handed Em the tissues.

"Em, listen to me. You're only fourteen—"

"Almost fifteen."

"You're too young to be spending time alone with any boy. Do you understand me?"

Emily pouted and finally said, "Yes."

"Get some pizza," Vining said. "I was going to put out bagged salad, if you want any. I think there's a tomato and a cucumber."

"I threw out the cucumber," Emily said. "It was slimy."

"Eww . . . We seriously need to go to the market." They fell into an easy normality for which they were both desperate.

TWENTY-SEVEN

*A*fter *they'd* eaten, Vining and Emily followed Granny's car and went to look for a new hearing-aid battery at the twenty-four-hour pharmacy. They then followed Granny to her home. The old woman drove painstakingly slow, nipping a curb, and almost blowing through a red light.

Em voiced what Vining had been thinking. "Should she be driving?"

Vining reflected that one thing that Granny hadn't lost was her feistiness. "Taking her car is going to be a challenge."

"Who's gonna drive her around?"

Vining already knew the answer to that. Then she remembered, "You'll be driving soon."

"I don't want to drive that big gas guzzler."

Vining didn't respond, thinking that Granny wasn't the only one who was presenting a challenge.

They went to the market and stocked up on groceries, including raw meat and vegetables. Vining decided they needed to improve their diets. After Emily helped her put everything away, she went to bed.

Vining was exhausted, but still too wound up for sleep. She cleaned and chopped carrots, celery, onions, and potatoes, which she'd throw into the crock pot the next morning with beef stew meat, salt, pepper, a bay leaf, and thyme. She dragged out the crock pot from a corner in a low cabinet and washed off the dust and kitchen grime. If her life wasn't anything near a Betty Crocker dream, she could at least pretend. If she couldn't pretend, she and Em would at least have a hot, home-cooked meal in their bellies.

Even after the days of nonstop activity and her late-night Susie Homemaker efforts, she was still restless. She took the cure. She put on her favorite light cotton nightgown, made a mug of chamomile tea, grabbed a box of vanilla wafers, and curled up on the La-Z-Boy. It was too warm for the chenille throw, but she draped it over the chair arm, liking the cozy way it felt. The classic movie channel cooperated by broadcasting a crime movie, Hitchcock's *Vertigo*. Shortly after James Stewart rescued Kim Novak from the San Francisco Bay, Vining fell fast asleep.

She awakened in the middle of a dream. She couldn't quite grab the story thread, but someone was pelting her head with pebbles. When she opened her eyes, the classic movie channel was broadcasting one of the silent flicks they played in the dead of night. An actress's eyes were thickly lined with kohl, and it made her think of Emily.

She heard the sound of a pebble hitting glass. This was no dream. Someone was outside, throwing pebbles at the sliding glass door off the living room. She clicked off the television. Sending the box of vanilla wafers flying, she got to her feet. Barefoot and in her nightgown, she left the lights off as she slipped into the kitchen. She retrieved her service Glock from the empty box of Count Chocula and a magazine from a drawer behind the tea towels.

The sliding glass door was open a few inches, stopping where it hit the wooden dowel she kept inside the frame. The drapes were open the same amount as the glass door. She peeked around them into the darkness.

She heard the sound again but didn't see anyone and didn't know why the motion light hadn't turned on.

"Who's out there?" she demanded.

"It's me. Jim."

She pulled out the dowel, opened the sliding glass door, and stepped onto the terrace. She saw him standing in her ragged backyard in the moonlight.

He said, as loudly as he dared, "I drove straight back from Morro Bay."

She was wondering why when he added, "I got your message."

Now she remembered. "Right. My message." She sucked air through her teeth.

"You meant that you wanted me to come over, didn't you?"

"I did . . . I don't know. Emily's here."

"I take it the moment has passed."

She sonorously exhaled.

"Guess I should have called," he said.

"No, no . . . I'm glad you came. I'm happy to see you. Come up." She frowned at the darkened floodlight attached to the side of the house. "Why didn't my motion light go on?"

"It went on. I unscrewed it. I didn't want to alarm your neighbors. You need to move it higher up."

While he was making his way around the house, she turned to head back inside, only to stop at the sound of the wind chimes ringing in the still air. She recalled Auntie Wan's admonition, "The ghost is hungry. You don't take care of the ghost."

She looked at the chimes and silently commanded, *Stop.*

They didn't.

While he waited at the front door, she ran a brush through her hair, gargled mouthwash, sniffed her armpits, and smeared on deodorant. She put on a robe and slippers and ran to open the door, feeling her heart flutter.

His shirt was wrinkled, his tie askew, his hair mussed, and he needed a shave. He looked adorable to her. He stepped across the threshold and into her arms. The second soul kiss of the night occurred in that doorway.

Sitting at the kitchen table, he finished the leftover pizza with a Sierra Nevada Pale Ale that had been in the back of the fridge since he'd brought over a six-pack when they'd watched Fourth of July fireworks off her terrace.

Her small amount of sleep had energized her and she recounted the events of her day almost without taking a breath. She concluded with her arriving home to find Em with Ken Zhang and their subsequent argument. Simply describing it distressed her enough to bring tears to her eyes.

Washing down the now-chewy pizza crust with a swallow of beer, he slid his hand across the table to take hers. He pulled the backs of her fingers to his lips.

She told him of her concerns about Granny. He empathized and offered his help.

When it came time to talk about his day, he sketched the barest outline of his interviews with Zeke Denver and Marilu Feathers's mother.

"Did you ask them about the necklace? Did you show them mine?"

"Nan, I'm not prepared to go into details right now. Today I'm going to Colina Vista and meeting with Chief Betsy Gilroy. I'll call the lieutenant in Tucson about Johnna Alwin's murder to cover our bases. Then I'll prepare my report."

"Why do I have to wait for a report when you could just tell me?" She picked up his plate and glass and put them in the dishwasher.

"I need the freedom to work this thing my own way. To follow my nose."

"You think I'm going to get in your way. I won't."

"Nan, please. Honor my feelings about this. My instincts."

He got up from the dinette table and stretched. He half walked and half shuffled to the TV room, where he collapsed onto the La-Z-Boy with a groan. He reclined the chair and laced his fingers across his belly.

She stood over him. "You said that you'd tell me everything."

He closed his eyes. "No, I didn't."

"Yes, you did. Just this morning, after *I* opened my soul and told *you* everything."

"Is that why you lured me here, to needle me?"

"I'm not that conniving."

He had a small smile on his face.

"I'm glad you came, Jim. I like having you here."

He began breathing heavily. Shortly, his face went slack and he began snoring a little.

She sighed as she looked down at him. She picked up the chenille throw from the floor and draped it over him. He was still wearing his shoes, but she didn't want to risk waking him by taking them off.

She needed to get to bed herself. She always rose before Emily did, so she'd get him out of the house before Emily found out. Nothing had happened, but given her and Em's argument earlier that evening . . .

She stood, watching him sleep. She rubbed her hands over her arms in the thin cotton robe. The heat of the day had finally dissipated. While it was poised to rear up again in another couple of hours, it was cool right now. The sliding glass door was still open and she left it that way.

She went into the kitchen to finish cleaning up. She unloaded her Glock, stashing the magazine behind the tea towels and the gun in the empty cereal box in the cabinet. His jacket was askew on the back of a dinette chair. She picked up the shoulders to straighten it and spied the spiral binding of his notepad peeking from the breast pocket.

Resting her hands on the jacket's shoulders, she looked at the coiled silver wire. She knew she shouldn't.

His snoring in the next room grew more resonant. She could tell he was exhausted, because he didn't snore otherwise.

She argued to herself that she had a right to know everything he'd learned. If it wasn't for her hard work, sacrifice, and the risks she'd taken, he wouldn't have gotten as far as he had. She was peeved, and his notepad in which he always took meticulous notes, was right there.

She darted in her fingers and slipped it from the pocket. Standing beneath the overhead light, she flipped to his most recent notes. Sometimes struggling to make out his scrawled handwriting and to fill in the gaps in his shorthand comments, she was able to build a story about Marilu Feathers. She learned a critical name: Bud Lilly.

She reached the last page. He'd written: "Turquoise = December?" Then she reached the last line: "Mother has necklace."

The three short words were heavy with meaning, but there was no further information. She madly flipped through the remaining pages. Their blankness seemed to scream, "There's nothing for you here!"

Frustrated, she turned to the page where he'd written Marilu's mother's address and telephone number. She tore a sheet from the end of the pad and slipped her hand into the inside jacket pocket where he always kept a pen. When she did, she noticed that one of the outside pockets was bulging a little. She knew he had her pearls, so she kept her emotions in check when she reached inside that pocket and felt them in their satinette bag. But there was something else there. Her heart beating, she pulled out what she surmised was Marilu Feathers's necklace.

The gemstone in Marilu's was turquoise. Vining knew that Marilu had been murdered on Christmas Eve. Turquoise must be the birthstone for December. That's what Kissick's note had meant. Now there were three confirmed victims of T. B. Mann: her, Feathers, and Alwin. Nitro's four drawings had provided a map. There was only one left to confirm—Colina Vista police officer Cookie Silva.

She jotted down Marilu's mother's contact information and the information about the pedophile Bud Lilly. She put the necklaces and notepad back where she'd found them. She decided to make her betrayal complete and go through the rest of his jacket pockets.

In the other outside pocket, she found two small paper bags printed with *Susan Sells Seashells, Morro Bay, California*, and drawings of shells. Each held a pair of earrings with polished abalone shell. One pair was cute, with shell in a silver setting shaped like a daisy. The other was more sophisticated. The setting was also silver, but a dangling style.

He'd bought souvenirs for Emily and her. His girls. Now she really felt like a rat.

Vining woke up to bright sunlight streaming across her face through a crack in the blinds. Realizing the sun was too bright, she quickly rolled over to look at the clock on the nightstand. It was after seven. She'd slept later than she'd wanted. She let her head drop back onto the pillow and gathered the sheet around her neck.

She sniffed the air. The delicious aroma was unmistakable. Bacon. There was more. Coffee. She rose from the bed, as if the scents had wrapped around and were pulling her, like slithering tendrils in an old-fashioned cartoon. Possibly Emily was cooking bacon, but Vining didn't think she'd ever made coffee in her entire life. Course, she was learning new things about Em . . . Then she wondered . . . Jim wasn't still here, was he?

She put on her robe and slippers. She brushed her teeth and her hair, just in case. Halfway down the hall, she had an answer when she heard Jim and Em in the kitchen.

"Messenger representative," Emily said. "O, E, Y, V, N."

"Envoy," Kissick said.

"Right. Envoy. Okay . . . Normal. L, G, E, A, R . . ."

Vining stood in the doorway. Emily was standing, leaning on her elbows against the kitchen table, filling out the Jumble word puzzle in the newspaper with a pen. She was dressed for school, wearing the daisy earrings. The table was already set. A bowl of sliced cantaloupe was in the middle.

Kissick was next to the stove, breaking eggs into a bowl, his back to Vining. He was dressed for work. There was a gingham bow at the back of his waist. He was wearing Granny's apron that she kept here. An open carton of eggs was on the counter. He reached to start the toaster which he'd already loaded with four slices of wheat bread.

" . . . U, R. Regular," Em said.

"Excellent." Kissick turned to open the refrigerator and saw Vining. "Good morning, sleepyhead."

Vining sheepishly waved. "Look at the wonderful feast."

"Hi, Mom." Emily arched her neck. "See the earrings Jim bought me?"

Vining moved to get a closer look. "Aren't they pretty?" She was delighted to see that Emily had toned down her makeup. While the girl was wearing black cropped pants and black high-topped sneakers, she had chosen a light blue, short-sleeve vintage blouse with a Peter Pan collar that she'd proudly brought home from a thrift shop.

She smiled as Kissick handed her a mug of coffee. "That was sweet of you."

He let his fingers brush hers. "I'm just a sweet kinda guy."

"He bought you something too, Mom." Emily picked up a small bag from the kitchen table.

"It's just a little something." He poured milk into the eggs, added salt, and began beating them with a whisk.

She took out the earrings and tried to look surprised. "They're beautiful. Thank you."

Neither of them knew what to do, so they stood awkwardly.

Without looking up from the Jumble, Em let out an annoyed huff. "Kiss, *please*."

Vining shot a wary look at Em's back, but Kissick set down the bowl, slid his hands into her hair and pulled her toward him for a kiss that might have been several degrees hotter than brotherly, but was still appropriate for the situation.

Her back still to them, Emily said, "But we have to talk about this whole issue of having guys in the house." She tsked, shook her head, and said, "Seems like a double standard to me."

Kissick used the excuse of the toast popping up to disengage from the conversation. After he buttered it, he poured the eggs into the hot pan.

Vining went to her daughter, put her arms around her from behind, and gave her a wet smack on the cheek. She received a hint of a smile in return.

Leaning on her hand on the table, Vining looked over Emily's shoulder at the Jumble bonus question.

"Escape clause," Vining said.

Emily turned to look with exasperation at her mother. "Mom! I always do the clues first, then I do the bonus."

Vining shrugged. "It just came to me."

"Okay, you two. Breakfast is ready." Kissick began untying the apron. Looking at Vining's smile, he said, "What?"

She shook her head. "Nothing. It's just that this is nice."

TWENTY-EIGHT

The man whom Nan Vining called T. B. Mann took his normal route home from work. On the freeway, he drove his six-year-old Ford Focus sedan at sixty-five miles per hour, the precise speed limit. Faster drivers sped around him. Some even had the gall to tailgate him and flash their high beams, even though there was plenty of room to pass. Such foolish aggressiveness raised his blood pressure, but it wasn't worth getting too upset over it. He just licked his lips and made sure his foot on the accelerator didn't budge. Occasionally, some guy would tail him like that for miles. Didn't matter. Sixty-five *was* the speed limit.

He wasn't as concerned about adhering to the law as he was saving money. He'd run a test in the Focus. For a month, he drove like everyone else. Then for a month, he stuck to the speed limit and avoided jackrabbit accelerations. The latter strategy saved a lot of money each month, especially the way gas prices were these days.

He exited the 10 at Citrus and crossed into the city limits of Covina. After a few blocks, he made a turn and drove alongside the railroad tracks. He'd lived in lots of places. Many were much more scenic than the San Gabriel Valley bedroom community of Covina. But at this stage of his life, he found he liked the area's nondescript landscape, where the largest attraction was the mall, which wasn't even in Covina, but was next door in West Covina. He'd come to appreciate the even blocks of 1950s and 1960s housing developments of neat three-bedroom, one-bath homes, all identical except for small stylistic flourishes like crossed beams on the garages that made them look like barns or folksy cupolas with wind vanes on the roof. The streets were well organized, laid out in square grids. He liked the lonely whistle of the freight trains that rumbled down the Southern Pacific tracks. He liked the abundance of mobile-home parks.

He drove into his mobile-home park, Country Squire Estates, adhering to the twenty mile per hour speed limit beyond the gates. It was unlikely that children or anyone else would be in the park's narrow streets at this hour, but one never knew. It was still no reason for him to go tearing around, even though he felt that familiar yearning that egged him to go faster. That warm lure of the treat that awaited him.

At space Q-5, he pulled the Focus into the carport behind the thirteen-year-old pickup truck. It needed to be driven. He vowed to do it when he got up after sleeping. He had a long list of errands to run and he'd use the pickup.

He got out of the car and went around to the trunk from which he grabbed a couple of plastic shopping bags from the hardware store. He'd replenished his supply of duct tape, rope, green garbage bags, an awl, and other things he liked to have on hand at all times. He paid cash, as always. He'd pick up bleach and Microban disinfectant later.

Closing the trunk, he noticed a For Sale sign on a vehicle in his neighbor's carport that was adjacent to his. The 1962 Chevy Nova belonged to the son of the widow who lived there. The son's name was Enrique and he had shown up a few months ago to live with his mother. The Nova had been modified for street racing. The roaring engine and blubbering muffler often woke his neighbor who usually slept during the day.

He hadn't liked Enrique from the moment he'd set eyes on him. Enrique had been in jail for having run over an elderly man while street racing. Now free, he was unrepentant. He'd talked his mother into buying the Nova. He and his buddies wasted long afternoons working on it, playing their music loud, drinking beer, and smoking pot. This would go on until the wee hours of the morning, moving to the widow's porch or finally inside, if the neighbors complained.

While that behavior upset the tranquillity of T. B. Mann's evenly laid out, square grid life, it wasn't Enrique's worst offense. Enrique's worst transgression was mockery. He and his buddies loved to make fun of their neat, quiet, unassuming neighbor, calling him Egghead to his face, asking if he'd gotten laid lately, laughing like drunken hyenas.

He set his shopping bags on the Focus's closed trunk and stepped across the row of potted geraniums that separated his carport from the widow's. Walking to the Nova, its immaculate black finish glistening beneath the widow's porch light, he read the hand-printed details on the For Sale sign. He pulled back a corner of his mouth and sorrowfully clucked. She'd never get what she was asking for that car. Maybe she didn't really want to sell it. Maybe she couldn't accept that Enrique wasn't coming back.

He wasn't. That was for double damn sure. While Enrique and his buddies were laughing and farting and getting wasted on the porch, T. B. Mann was working on a home project on the other side of the slab. He'd removed part of his floor and had dug a hole beneath his mobile home. Enrique was buried there, in pieces eroding in lye.

The police had come around, of course, and conducted a lackluster investigation, in his view. Who could blame them? Why would they care about a loudmouthed, parole-violating ex-con who'd gone missing? Enrique didn't garner a scintilla of the investigative attention garnered by say, Johnna Alwin or Marilu Feathers.

He'd seen Enrique's mother crying, but she'd be better off in the long run. Sometimes, people needed to learn lessons the hard way. After all, she was the one who'd given birth to the asshole.

Retrieving his bags, he unlocked the several bolt locks on his reinforced door and entered his single-wide mobile home. It wasn't anything lavish, but it was more than sufficient for a man of modest needs.

It was pitch-black inside. He never left lights on when he was gone. It was a waste of money. He had sufficient money to cover his living expenses and to have some left over. Anything extra, he preferred to spend on his ladies. Lately, that hadn't amounted to much. He was socking away a lot of money. He found himself in a holding pattern not of his choosing. He was in a rut and couldn't seem to find his way out. He was stuck in Covina, saving money, and thinking about his next move.

He was a good, steady employee and had never had trouble holding on to a job. He didn't steal or lie and he was respectful to his superiors and coworkers. He had a life outside of work that some might find . . . exotic. But that was his business. As long as he showed up on time and put in a full day's work, who cared?

He entered the small kitchen, flipping on the switch for the fluorescent ceiling lights, and set the bags on the counter. He went into the hallway and switched on the central air conditioner. Heat built up inside the flat-roofed, thin-walled mobile home during the day, but the air conditioner cooled things off quickly.

From the refrigerator, he took out a bottle of Coors beer, twisted off the top, and drank half of it while he leaned against the sink and thought about his day. He had what he supposed were typical frustrations with his job. Probably less than most people because he chose to work in the middle of the night.

Still, when tensions threatened to spill over, he found a great deal of release by taking care of small problems like Enrique. It helped him maintain his equilibrium so he could focus on his larger goals.

From a cupboard, he took out a bag of Laura Scudder potato chips. He used to buy the Granny Smith brand, but started buying Laura Scudder when he learned that she was buried not far from where he lived. He had visited her grave. He was impressed with how it was marked. A stately granite stone was engraved simply: SCUDDER. Flat markers for the different family members interred there were beneath it.

The headstone was so elegant in its simplicity. T. B. Mann decided right then that he wanted a large granite stone like that, with just his family name on it. He was saving money for that, too. Death comes to everyone and if you don't make plans, who knows how you'll end up. Could end up like Enrique, who was disintegrating about six feet below where T. B. Mann was standing right at that moment.

The open bag was two-thirds empty. The top was

neatly folded down and held in place with a bright-pink plastic Chip Clip. He carried the bag of chips and the beer to the dinette set that was in the living room, but positioned close to the pass-through to the kitchen. The rest of the room was furnished with a leather swivel rocker-recliner, an end table on each side, and the largest flat-screen TV the room could accommodate. When it came to the few luxuries he enjoyed, he didn't scrimp.

There were no accommodations for guests, but he never had guests, except for Bob. For Bob, he had found a perfectly good easy chair that someone had left beside the Dumpster. The mobile-home park had also provided the old aluminum and Formica dinette set. An elderly woman had died and her daughter was selling her furniture.

The daughter was nothing more than a lumpy, frumpy hag herself. She impressed him as someone who hated life, and thus, everything in it. She poured her animosity into her negotiations about the price of the dinette set. He'd remained preternaturally calm, knowing his equanimity would further aggravate her. She finally gave him the price he'd originally offered, from which he wouldn't budge. She'd made a rude parting shot, "Now you and your boyfriend can have intimate dinners together."

It would have been so easy for him to have taught her a lesson. He could have grabbed her during one of her trips to the Dumpster and strangled her in the shadows. He would have enjoyed the paranoia the murder would have sent whipping through the park like a brushfire in love with the Santa Ana winds. But he realized he'd actually be doing her a favor. A more appropriate fate would be for her to live out the days of her miserable life, finally dying after years of suffering from a degenerative disease that, given her shabby physical condition and poor attitude, she was bound to contract.

Plus, he had bigger fish to fry. As rewarding as the immediate pleasure of watching the fear in the hag's bulging eyes as the blood vessels burst, hearing her final pathetic sounds, witnessing that wonderful, priceless, oh-so-rare moment when the life, the *life*, faded from her eyes, like a final dying ember that flashes brightly before it turns to ash, it would have been unwise to expose himself to such a risk right now. He needed to keep his eyes on the prize.

He sat at his table and thought of his prize, Nan Vining. Was there ever a moment anymore when he didn't think of her? Now he luxuriated in his thoughts of her. It was risky. There was danger in getting carried away. His thoughts weren't all happy. Still, they tempted him. Excited him. The combination of longing and fury, the sweet with the bitter, the idea of total *release* was enough to make him want to *explode*.

He felt the excitement and fury rising, his twin towers of passion and doom. They had come up suddenly and threatened to carry him away. He grabbed onto the dinette table as if it was a rickety raft in a turbulent sea. Too often lately, Officer Vining had driven him to these extremes. It was all he could do to keep from breaking up his furniture, running crazily into the street, driving his car onto a sidewalk crowded with pedestrians, or stabbing a total stranger to death in a frenzy.

He had to get ahold of himself. This was not good thinking.

But his mind was a runaway train, going faster and faster. The pressure moved up, up, and up, surging through his chest, out his arms and into his fingers until he could just . . .

He fumbled to get his keys out of his pants pocket, so frantic, he was whimpering. Keys in hand, he grappled with the tiny combination penknife and scissors on the key ring. He was sweating now. Trembling.

Control. Control.

It was too late for a pep talk. Pulling the knife blade open, he yanked up his shirt and exposed his soft belly. Without hesitation, he pierced his skin with the knife and made a shallow, two-inch incision. His belly was crosshatched with numerous cuts in various stages of recovery.

The red line hovered for a second, shimmering. Panting, watching, he held his breath, waiting for the release that would save him. Then it happened. The blood flowed. Gulping air, he tittered at the blood. He put his hand beneath it, to catch it, feeling its heat and silky texture. His mouth lolled open. He laughed with release as if he'd learned he'd been the victim of a practical joke.

He grabbed paper napkins from a holder on the table and stuck them to the bloody wound. Calmer now, feeling normal, he went into the kitchen and washed the blood off his hand, watching the red-tinged ribbons circle down the drain. Once his hand was clean, he took off his tie, unbuttoned his shirt, and took it off.

He peeled away the bloody tissue. From a kitchen cabinet, he took out mercurochrome, a box of gauze squares, and a roll of adhesive tape. Using the plastic wand in the bottle, he dotted the red disinfectant on the wound, wincing when it stung. He dressed it with the gauze and adhesive.

He returned to the dining room table where he removed the Chip Clip from the bag of potato chips and ate chips, now fully able to enjoy his beer.

When he was finished, he put the chips away in the cupboard and dusted his hands over the sink. He walked the empty bottle outside and put it in a garbage container that was dedicated to recyclables. Back inside, he triple-locked the front door. He was in for the remainder of his night.

He put away his supplies and put a single loose knot in the plastic bags before he stored them in another plastic grocery bag hanging from a nail inside his broom closet. The single knots made them easier to grab when he needed a bag for kitchen garbage or such.

Heading down the hallway, he opened the closed door of the small bedroom on the right. A lamp intended for a child's room was lit. A small motor made the shade turn, casting soothing blue, violet, and green images of stars, moons, and comets across the walls. Because he had sealed up the window, the lamp provided the only light in the room ever. A large standing, rotating fan churned the room's stale air that was benefiting from the air-conditioning.

The room was sparsely furnished with an inexpensive chest of drawers, an easy chair, a nightstand, and a bed. In the bed lay Bob.

"Evening, Bob." He bent over to pick up a plate from the nightstand.

"Why do you hate me?" Bob's voice was affectless.

"Was it cool enough in here for you today?" He examined the contents of the plate. "You didn't eat much."

"Why do you hate me?" Bob again asked in the same dull tone.

"I don't hate you, Bob. On the contrary."

"Oh."

He set the plate back down and picked up a steel bedpan from the bed next to where Bob was lying. He carried it toward the door.

Behind him, Bob asked, "Why do you hate me?"

He took the pail to the tiny bathroom, dumped the contents into the toilet, flushed it, and returned to Bob's room.

"Why do you hate me?"

"I don't hate you, Bob. If I hated you, would I look after you this way?"

"Oh."

He set the bedpan on the mattress within Bob's reach. He straightened the bedclothes, neatly squaring the edges of the sheet and folding it across Bob's chest. He pressed his palm against Bob's forehead. It was still too warm, but not as bad as it had been earlier. The aspirin he'd given Bob appeared to have brought his fever down.

"You hate me."

"I don't hate you, Bob. I had to punish you."

"Punish me."

"Yes, and you know why."

"Oh."

From the nightstand, he picked up a plastic cup from which a bent straw protruded from a screw-on lid. He shook the cup. "You're not drinking enough fluids. This is Gatorade. It'll replenish your electrolytes." He held up the cup and pressed the straw against Bob's lips.

Bob drank, smacking his lips afterward. "Why do you hate me?"

He set down the cup. "Okay, I'll see you after I get up."

"Why do you hate me?"

He closed the door. Now that he was done with his chores, he felt that other urge awakening in his pants.

He crossed the narrow hallway and opened the door of the second of the mobile home's three bedrooms. There was an overhead light fixture, but he didn't switch it on, finding the light it cast harsh. He crossed the room in the dark. Reaching out his hand, he found the fireplace and located the switch on the side of the unit. The fake flames jumped to life, casting a warm glow. He'd found the electric fireplace at a yard sale. On the weekends when he wasn't working, he loved to haunt neighborhood yard sales. You never knew what you might find.

By the light of the flames, he crossed to the long table against the opposite wall. He had draped it with shiny red satin that reached the floor. On top of the cloth were four white pedestals, two feet tall, fashioned from synthetic material to look like marble Corinthian columns. The pedestals had been bases for birdbaths that he'd found on sale in Target's garden shop. He'd bought all they'd had in stock, and had thrown away the bowls that attached to the top.

He moved along the first three pedestals, turning on the strands of tiny lights that he had woven around the large picture frames on top. The first frame held the official photograph of Officer Clarissa "Cookie" Silva. The second was Ranger Marilu Feathers. The third was Detective Johnna Alwin. All three women were in uniform and posed in front of a U.S. flag. Feathers's photo also had the state flag of California. He'd downloaded their official photos from the Internet.

The framed photo on top of the fourth pedestal was shrouded with a black cloth. It was his shrine to Nan Vining.

In front of the first three pedestals, a cherished trophy was displayed.

There was Cookie Silva's blouse. It had been on the ground when he'd cut her throat and had been drenched with her blood. Essence of Cookie.

There was the Ranger Stetson belonging to Marilu Feathers that he'd retrieved before it had been carried away by the surf. It had fallen from her head when her horse, with the mortally wounded Feathers astride, had madly galloped away. There was a small trail of blood splatter beneath the front of the brim. Essence of Marilu.

There was the green shirt from the uniform he'd stolen from the gardening service that maintained the grounds of the medical building where he'd stabbed Johnna Alwin. A patch above the left breast said "Hinojosa Gardening." He'd worn the uniform when he'd stabbed her seventeen times. He'd intended to triumph over Alwin via an elegant, single mortal wound, but she had made some remarks that he didn't care for and he'd lost his temper. It had gotten messy. Johnna, sweet Johnna. Essence of Johnna.

The space in front of Nan Vining's pedestal was empty. Only recently, the yellow Brooks Brothers polo shirt that was lavishly covered with her blood had been neatly folded there. He'd made a special trip to downtown L.A. to buy that shirt and had paid top dollar for it because he'd seen the man he was impersonating wearing the same style in that same daffodil-yellow color.

First, he'd covered up her photo, the image he'd worshipped all those long years, but now found too painful to gaze upon. Then, his beloved heirloom, the yellow shirt, began to feel as if a hex had been put on it. It lost its magic to enthrall and instead started to taunt him, to whisper his failure.

He'd once loved the shirt because it reminded him not only of the day he'd attacked Vining, but also of all the careful planning and anticipation. His mastery over his lethal ladies had taken months and sometimes years of methodical planning, but Vining in particular had been hard to nab. He'd set more than one trap, only for her to slip away. Then he had got her. Finally got her.

She should have died.

Her blood on the shirt, instead of thrilling him, had come to make him so, so sad. He still didn't understand how she had again slipped from his grasp. That day in the El Alisal house had gone perfectly. He had known what she was thinking before she did. She had played right into his hands. He had been so excited, it took all his powers of self-control to contain himself. Later, he'd found out that *she'd survived.*

This week, he had given her the bloody shirt. While the shirt had lost its allure for him, she was changing, too. She was fucking that detective, and he sure didn't like that. He'd taken a big risk delivering the shirt, but it had been worth it. Hiding in the darkness of the yard across the street, he'd heard her daughter screaming. Grinning, fists clenched in triumph, he'd witnessed the flurry of activity that had followed.

He was in psychic pain. She should be.

He didn't see himself as a bad man. He didn't go after weak or vulnerable women. The women he hunted had been trained to kill and, when tested, had proven their mettle. By taking them on, he had put himself in grave danger. They could have killed him. But none had, had they? They had submitted to his will. He had mastered them. Almost . . .

Because of Nan Vining, he had stayed in the area much longer than he ever thought he would. Other lethal ladies had attracted his attention. He had newspaper clippings in a filing cabinet. He thought he could love one or two of them. Yet he couldn't build any enthusiasm for a new pursuit. He told himself to move on, to acknowledge that the battle with Vining had ended in a draw, but he couldn't. He loved her too much to let her go.

He'd noticed a definite change in her since that day in the house on El Alisal Road. It had taken her a long time to get back on her feet. She was back at work, "picking up the pieces," as they say, of her life. It all looked normal from the outside, but he knew that she was different. He knew her so well. All it took was finding that bloody shirt to knock her down off that pedestal and send her spinning off again. See? He knew her better than anybody. She probably thought that detective she was fucking, Kissick, knew her, but he didn't. Not like *he* did.

He felt his rage rising, that familiar feeling that started deep inside his core. It radiated out, making his extremities tingle and burn as if his veins had been shot full of cayenne.

He forced himself to turn away from the shrouded, dark pedestal at the end of the table. Thinking of Vining would only dull his pleasure. No need to sacrifice more pleasure to her. She'd already stolen enough. This time was dedicated to his other three ladies. He dug his finger into the gauze that covered his fresh cutting. The sharp pain brought him around. Some tricks never lost their magic.

He moved to a couch across from his shrine. Sitting, he untied and removed his shoes. Standing, he took off his belt, then removed his pants, folding them over an arm of the couch. He took off his briefs and laid them atop the pants.

He plumped a throw pillow and reclined. The flickering orange and yellow flames of the electric fireplace cast his pallid skin in a warm glow. It helped to make him feel warm and cozy and safe and in control and . . . aroused.

With one foot on the floor, he began to stroke himself. As usual, he'd arrived home with a nice erection from thinking about his favorite after-work pastime.

Ignoring the darkness at the end of the table, he looked at his three dead ladies and conjured sweet memories of each one. Memories from when he had stalked them, learning everything about their daily routines, while they'd had no idea he was there. Memories from the magic moment when *the day* had arrived and they'd looked into his eyes, the last human eyes they would ever see. Memories from that flash of insight when they'd understood that he was going to kill them. Memories of when they'd died.

As his strokes grew faster and more urgent, his mind was drawn to Vining. He couldn't help it. Their last dance had been the most powerful and poignant yet. He'd squeezed her tightly, yet so gently, holding her pelvis pressed against his as he helped her to stay on her feet. All he'd needed was a few seconds more and he would have had his ultimate release. In his mind, he made it happen. It was happening. Happening now. The life fading from her eyes. Her breaths growing shallower as . . . as . . . as . . .

Suddenly, he was soft as dough.

Her death was make-believe. He was living a pathetic dream. He was pathetic. She was taking everything from him, even this small pleasure.

He bolted from the couch and stomped across the room. Yanking the scarf from her photo, he confronted her, screaming, "Do you ever see my face when you're fucking him? Do you? Well, do you?"

Swinging his arm, he knocked over her shrine.

Her photo sailed onto the carpeted floor. The pedestal toppled then rolled off the table onto it, breaking it. The firelight glinted off the spiderwebbed glass.

He dropped to his knees. Clawing with his fingers, he pulled an arrow-shaped fragment of glass free. Cutting himself would calm him and release his mind from this terrible place. Clutching the broken glass in his palm, he felt it press into, then slice his flesh. He opened his hand to see the blood. His thoughts cooperated and stopped swirling. He could see clearly now.

"No more blood spilled for you, my lady." Dropping the broken glass, he picked up the black cloth and wrapped it around his palm. "Not *my* blood."

He flipped over the photo and banged it against the

table leg, knocking much of the glass free. He turned it faceup and squared it on the floor, straddling it on the carpet, his fleshy knees bracing it. He again picked up the shard of glass that fate had formed.

"You owe me blood, Officer Vining."

He dug the glass into her image and made a long cut across her face.

"You *owe* me."

He sliced the photo diagonally in the other direction.

"You owe me. You owe me. You owe me . . ."

He cut and cut and cut.

TWENTY-NINE

*K*issick drove along Colina Vista Boulevard heading for the police station and his meeting with Chief Betsy Gilroy. The antique lampposts on the city's main thoroughfare were decorated with banners honoring the city's annual Trail Days celebration that took place each fall. Each Christmas the giant fir trees circling the civic center were decorated with thousands of lights. Springtime brought the Iris Festival. Nestled at the foot of the Angeles National Forest, the quaint hamlet had never lost its small-town feel. No freeways crossed it. It had no traffic signals. It was home to no industries. One had to make a special trip to go there.

There was little traffic. Drivers were polite. Crime rates were low. The last murder had been six years ago when two people sitting in a parked car had been shot. It turned out that neither the killer nor victims had any connection to the city. The largely affluent residents enjoyed exceptional quality of life yet were not the type to brag about their zip code, not that anyone would recognize it anyway, which suited them just fine. A few celebrities lived there, but they were not the attention-seeking type, and happily melded into the fabric of the community. Colina Vista was rarely in the news. Like many of the San Gabriel Valley's picturesque cities, outsiders had seen it often without knowing it, as it was a favorite Hollywood filming location.

Eight years ago, Colina Vista made the news when Betsy Gilroy was sworn in as the chief of police. She wasn't the first female city police chief in Los Angeles County—that honor belonged to the police chief of Sierra Madre, the neighbor of Colina Vista. But with Gilroy's promotion, she joined an exclusive but growing sorority of a dozen or so female police chiefs among the state's 335 city police departments.

Kissick arrived at the civic center and parked on the street. The police station was a single-story Mission-style building that shared its architectural design and a parking lot with City Hall. The police department consisted of eleven sworn officers, five nonsworn employees, and the chief.

Kissick waited in the small bright lobby for Betsy Gilroy to see him. Two civilian employees and a uniformed officer sat at steel desks behind a long, open counter that was not shielded by Plexiglas. The absence of this simple security measure made the station look friendly, homey, and decidedly old-fashioned. There was a wooden swinging door to the left of the counter. At the rear of the front office was a door with a window at the top.

The lobby was simply furnished with long wooden benches. Public announcements were posted on a cork bulletin board. Another wall displayed photographs of all the police department employees, both sworn and civilian. They were arranged in a pyramid, in order of department hierarchy. At the top was Betsy Gilroy.

Kissick knew her in passing as she had spent many years with the Pasadena P.D., starting fresh from the Academy and rising to lieutenant before she left for the opportunity to be deputy chief of the Colina Vista P.D. The city's then-chief was planning to retire. While there was no guarantee that Gilroy would be a shoo-in for the top job, she soon proved herself to the police department, mayor, city council, and citizens. She still had many friends in the Pasadena P.D., and enjoyed a close relationship with Chief Haglund.

Her official photo on the station wall showed a woman with a pleasant face that might be considered pretty in the right light and circumstances. Pretty was not an advantage here. She looked accessible in the photo, while hinting at toughness behind the bright eyes. She was in her early fifties.

Shortly, the woman herself came through the door into the front office and through the swinging gate into the lobby. She wore navy-blue slacks with a tailored blue-and-white striped shirt tucked into them, small, gold stud earrings, and a plain gold wedding band.

"Detective Kissick. So nice to see you again."

"Nice to see you, Chief." Kissick would have been surprised if she did remember him, but she seemed sincere.

"Nice of you to visit us here in Colina Vista. How is your boss, Sergeant Early?"

Her emerald-colored eyes stood out against her tanned skin. Her face was deeply lined, showing the brunt of years in the sun. Kissick could imagine her on a golf course. She was still lean and athletic-looking, although she had filled out a little since her PPD days. She wore her hair in a short yet feminine style with feathery layers. It was many shades of gold. If the color wasn't natural, it had been so artfully done, it was impossible to tell. She stood five feet, four inches, but was one of those people who possessed a natural gravitas: She seemed big and cut a commanding presence. One would have to be either naïve or foolish to mess with her.

"Sergeant Early is doing great and she told me to tell you hello."

"Please send her my best. Kendra and I go *way* back."

"I'll do that."

"Let's talk in my office."

She walked ahead of Kissick, holding open the swinging gate for him. She used a key to unlock the door at the rear of the front office. The neighborly Colina Vista P.D. was not completely immune to security issues. They entered a long plain corridor.

"Have you ever been to our police station before, Detective?"

"I have, but never past the lobby."

Gilroy pointed to a door with a reinforced glass window. A set of gun lockers was bolted to the wall outside it. "Our holding cells. I'm happy to say that they aren't used often."

She started walking down the corridor. "When I first came here from the Pasadena P.D., I thought, my gosh, this place is dead. I'll die of boredom."

Kissick smiled.

"But I've learned that it takes a lot of hard work to maintain the high quality of life and small-town atmosphere that we enjoy in Colina Vista."

"Keeping the wolves at bay."

"That's true in more ways than one, Detective. We often have more problems with wildlife than humans here."

He laughed and nodded.

There was a snap in her walk and in her speech, as if she possessed boundless vitality. Her persistent smile suggested perennial good humor, but Kissick knew that no one became police chief, even of a small city, without being able to bust heads as well as being politically savvy. He expected that the job was many times harder to be effective at for a woman.

She continued singing the praises of her city. "Colina Vista is consistently named one of the most desirable places to live in L.A. County. It's a testament to the residents' commitment to their community that the city has remained independent, even without a commercial tax base. We've thrived yet still manage to do things our own way. We feel we're pretty special. We're like Mayberry and we're just a short drive from L.A."

They passed offices with large reinforced glass windows in which a few uniformed officers, all men, sat at desks, writing reports on computers or filling out forms in longhand. The officers were trading wisecracks and laughing until they caught sight of Gilroy, when they whipped back to their work.

Kissick said, "When I first started with the Pasadena P.D. thirteen years ago, the department was smaller. Everyone knew everyone else. Now we're so much bigger and it's tough to have the same familiarity. I have to say I miss that." He was quick to add, "But Pasadena has one of the top mid-size police departments in the country. It's a great place to be."

"I loved my time there."

They passed large framed photographs tracing the history of Colina Vista, from its beginnings as a pioneer town and later, mountain resort, up through today. The corridor turned. In contrast with the utilitarian doors elsewhere, they reached an impressive edifice of rich dark wood. A brass plaque said EXECUTIVE OFFICES. Gilroy led the way inside. The plain linoleum floor changed to short-pile burgundy carpet. The walls here were not the practical beige of the rest of the station but were a warm caramel, the color of crème brûlée.

A secretary was sitting at a desk outside an office where a plaque beside the door said BETSY GILROY, CHIEF. She looked up as they went inside. "Chief, Kate Sanderson returned your call."

"Thanks, Anita."

Gilroy walked to her desk. "Please have a seat, Detective Kissick." She waved to a conversation area that was furnished with a small couch, two upholstered chairs, and a coffee table. "If you'll excuse me for two minutes. I need to return a phone call."

"Would you like me to wait outside?"

"No, no . . . This will just take a second. Would you like a cup of coffee?"

"No, thank you."

Her office was more expensively decorated than the executive offices of the Pasadena Police Department. The walls were a subtle shade of taupe that was complemented by the off-white ceiling and crown and base moldings. Gilroy's large desk and the bookcases that lined the walls were walnut and in a clean, understated design. Tobacco-brown, raw silk drapes dressed the large corner windows, which gave an expansive view of the nearby mountains. A landscape in a plein air style of those same mountains was on a wall.

Kissick knew that the affluent citizens of Colina Vista were fond of their police chief. He was getting an idea of just how fond they were.

On the phone, Gilroy was discussing arrangements for her acceptance of an award at a banquet to be held at the Beverly Hills Hotel. Near as Kissick could gather, the banquet was a fund-raising event for a nonprofit organization benefiting battered and at-risk women and children. Gilroy dropped the names of a couple of A-list actors who were apparently spokespeople for the organization and who were going to be there.

A credenza beneath the window displayed family photographs in silver frames. From what Kissick could see across the room, Gilroy and her husband had a couple of grown children. There were photos of babies and toddlers, likely grandchildren.

Framed photos and commendations lined the walls. Kissick saw photos of Gilroy with Mel Gibson, with Will Smith, with Angelina Jolie, with Governor Arnold Schwarzenegger, and numerous photos with less glamorous local celebrities and political figures.

Gilroy finished her call, walked to the door, and leaned out. "Anita, I would love a cup of coffee, if you have a second." She turned to Kissick. "Sure you wouldn't like anything, Detective. A soft drink . . . ?"

"A diet soda would be great. Anything you have. Thank you."

"Ice?"

"Sure. Thank you."

Gilroy asked Anita for the soft drink, then moved to sit in the chair beside Kissick. She casually crossed her legs. She was wearing low-heeled black pumps of smooth leather with patent-leather toes.

Before they could get started, Anita poked her head inside the office and said, "Lieutenant Johnson reports that Bessie's at it again."

"Oh, dear," Gilroy said.

"She's in the Peterson's avocado grove up on Leona Avenue. The lieutenant called Fish and Game and he's sent a patrol car out there. He just wanted you to know."

"Thanks, Anita." Gilroy said to Kissick, "Bessie is a brown bear with a taste for avocados during summer and persimmons during winter."

"I live in Altadena and we often have bears come

down from the foothills and get into people's garbage. A neighbor found a bear in her Jacuzzi."

She chuckled and shook her head.

"You're even farther up into the mountains."

"Yes, we are. We get bears, coyotes, and even mountain lions. We don't bother counting the skunks, raccoons, and possums. Hopefully, Fish and Game can chase Bessie back up into the hills. Last time, she ran up a fifty-foot pine tree. They blocked off a wide perimeter and it was hours before she came down. Welcome to a typical day for the Colina Vista P.D."

Gilroy's amused annoyance over Bessie the bear faded and she became somber. "You came here to talk about the murder of our poor Officer Cookie Silva. On the phone, you said that you think there might be a connection between Cookie's murder and that terrible attack on one of your female detectives last year. Cookie's murder was the most heinous crime in Colina Vista's history."

Kissick nodded. "I'm aware of that."

"Then you probably know that Cookie's murder has long been solved." The green hue of her eyes deepened.

Kissick felt he was staring into the depths of the ocean. "Yes, ma'am."

"The murderer is on San Quentin's death row." She folded her hands in her lap. "That being said, I certainly want to give any help I can in your unsolved attempted murder. Why do you feel it's related to our homicide?"

"Chief Gilroy, I appreciate your time. I know the Silva homicide is closed, but I have a curious lead that I need to follow through on. A couple of weeks ago in Old Pasadena, our officers took into custody a transient who had been behaving strangely. He had no ID and refused to speak. Our cops gave him the nickname Nitro." From his file folder, he took out the Polaroid photo of Nitro.

Gilroy scrutinized it and set it on the coffee table.

"We sent him to County General on a fifty-one fifty. He was treated and released, and that was the last we saw of him."

The secretary returned carrying a tray. Gilroy reached for coasters from a stack on an end table and put them on the coffee table. Anita set the beverages on top.

"Thank you so much, Anita," Gilroy said. "Would you mind closing the door on your way out?"

Kissick took a sip of cola before continuing. "Among Nitro's possessions was a drawing pad and drawing tools. The pad contained illustrations of flowers, trees, animals, and such. They were quite good."

Gilroy listened attentively. Her gaze was direct and unwavering.

"He also had four drawings that were not as . . . gentle." Kissick took out the photocopies of Nitro's drawings. He found the one of Vining and handed it to Gilroy. Her gaze darkened as she looked at it.

"That's our detective, Nan Vining. According to her, that drawing accurately depicts how she was attacked. Are you familiar with the circumstances?"

"I know she was stabbed while she was on patrol. I'd appreciate it if you'd fill in the details."

"Detective Vining was in uniform, picking up overtime, patrolling Madison Heights."

Still holding the drawing, Gilroy said, "Over by the Huntington Hotel and the Huntington Hospital."

"Correct. As you know, that's one of Pasadena's safest neighborhoods. It was early evening, near the end of her shift, when she was called out to investigate suspicious circumstances at a house on El Alisal Road. The house was for sale. The owners were absent, and the man who made the call identified himself as the house's realtor, Dale David. He said he'd arrived there to find a kitchen window open that he was certain he'd locked.

"Detective Vining arrived on-scene and followed this

individual into the kitchen. She found him odd. Thought he might be wearing a wig. Their conversation got strange. He didn't threaten her, but her instincts told her that something wasn't right. She radioed for backup. Soon after, the guy came at her with a knife. Vining drew her gun and got off a round even though he'd sliced the back of her gun hand. Then he stabbed her in the neck."

Gilroy frowned.

"He escaped using a route that he'd prepared in advance. Searching the house, we found a police scanner."

Kissick took out the police artist's rendering and handed it to her. "That was done based upon Detective Vining's recollection of the man who attacked her."

"I remember seeing this in the newspaper." Gilroy picked up the photo of Nitro and studied them side by side, her lips pressed together.

"Detective Vining said the man who attacked her was in his early thirties. White. She remembers his skin as pasty. Six feet. Medium build. Hair color unknown, because he was probably wearing a wig. Brown eyes, but Vining thought he might be wearing tinted contact lenses."

Gilroy set the sketch and photo on the coffee table. "How much information was reported by the media?"

"The call-out to the house by the alleged realtor and Detective Vining's knife wounds."

"Your Nitro could have drawn this based upon news reports."

"It's possible, but Detective Vining says that her assailant held her exactly as shown in this drawing. It's uncannily accurate."

Gilroy sucked in her cheeks. "It's a miracle that your detective survived. Thank God. How is she?"

Kissick flashed on the last time he'd seen Vining, laughing and chatting over breakfast earlier that morning.

"She's doing great." He detected his own hopefulness. "She's back on duty. We just broke that big double homicide in the Linda Vista neighborhood."

"I heard about that. Congratulations."

"Thank you."

Gilroy leaned forward to ape Kissick's posture. "So, Detective, you haven't told me what brings you here."

She wanted him to get on with it. He handed her another of Nitro's drawings. "That depicts the stabbing murder of Tucson Detective Johnna Alwin. It occurred in a storage closet in a Tucson medical building three years ago."

Keeping the last paper turned down on his lap, he handed Gilroy the drawing of Marilu Feathers. "That's California State Park Ranger Marilu Feathers. Eight years ago, she was shot while patrolling a state park near Morro Bay."

Gilroy nodded as she gravely looked at the drawing. "I remember when that happened." She set it on the table beside the other two.

"All three of these police officers had killed a man on duty in high-profile incidents that made them minor celebrities. Marilu killed a local pedophile. Johnna Alwin was working undercover when she killed a mafia associate. And Nan Vining—"

"Shot Lonny Velcro, the rock star, at his Pasadena mansion."

"That's right."

"Interesting. You think that the same man is responsible for all three."

"We have additional evidence linking the murders."

"You said your Nitro character had four such drawings." She pointed to the paper that was facedown on Kissick's lap. "I assume that last one shows Cookie."

He handed it to her.

Her reactions to the other materials had been appropriate and, Kissick felt, sincere but somehow measured, indicative of her nature as a political animal. Her reaction now was visceral. Tightly clutching the paper, she sadly sighed and said, "Poor Cookie."

After a minute, she set the drawing beside the others on the table, but slightly away from the other three. "This representation is correct. This is how we found her body. That's what he did to her. Still, whoever drew this could have based it upon news reports. A lot of information about Cookie's murder inadvertently got out. I had just started with the Colina Vista P.D. Our police department was not prepared to deal with a crime of that magnitude. The perimeter had not been adequately secured. Frankly, we messed up. A reporter was able to sneak onto the crime scene. We eliminated his photos, but he published a detailed description of what he'd seen.

"Detective, I understand your passion to get to the bottom of these crimes, to find a pattern that will lead you to your man, but Cookie doesn't fit the mold of these three others. She was certainly not a hero. She'd only been on the force for a year and a half. She'd just started patrolling solo. She'd never been in the news. I was very fond of her. I mentored her, but frankly, she was a challenge. I can't tell you the number of talks I had with her, trying to get her to straighten up and fly right. She'd promise to do better. We'd both end up laughing. Cookie could turn any situation around and make you laugh. She was wonderful with the public and was popular with the citizens. After I'd have one of my chats with her, she'd toe the line for a while, but she had a rebellious streak that was hard to tame. I was hopeful, though. Right up until the day they found her body."

Gilroy rose and walked to the large corner windows and looked out, her back to Kissick.

When she turned, he was surprised to see tears in her eyes.

Walking to her desk, she opened a drawer and took out a box of tissues. Grabbing a few, she tossed the box on her desk and blotted her eyes.

"Forgive me, Detective. I'm usually the one who makes people cry in this office, not the other way around."

She again moved to look out the window. "This brings back painful memories. You see, I took Cookie under my wing because she reminded me of myself at that age. Brash, with a head full of steam and a mouth to match. If I hadn't had a mentor at the Pasadena P.D., I'm sure I would have been bounced off the force. He saw my potential to be a good cop. I saw that with Cookie. I have two grown sons and four grandchildren. In many ways, she was like the daughter I never had.

"We both had tough childhoods. Cookie's mother was a crack addict. Her father was in and out of prison for drug dealing and robbery. Cookie was bumped around foster homes her entire childhood. She was a real tough girl. Petite. Barely five foot-two, but strong. She was like a terrier. She would grab hold and hang on. Cookie and I bonded from the start. She's buried in the Colina Vista cemetery. I still make sure there are fresh flowers on her grave. I'm the only real family she ever had.

"There's another reason that Cookie's murder can't be grouped with your others, Detective Kissick. We got our man. His name is Axel Holcomb. It was a good trial with a smart jury, a fair and honorable judge, and solid evidence. Holcomb's execution is coming up next year. He's run out of appeals. Can't come soon enough, if you ask me."

THIRTY

"A *xel Holcomb* was the live-in caretaker at the Foothill Museum," Kissick said. "I did some research. Cookie was murdered in an old barn on the museum property."

"The Foothill Museum is at the edge of Angeles National Forest," Gilroy explained. "It was once a diner called the Hiker's Hideout. It was in operation for eighty years until it closed in the sixties and was turned into a museum. Also on the property was a barn that was one of the original pack stations. Are you familiar with that little piece of Mount Wilson history, Detective?"

When he indicated he wasn't, she continued. "Starting in the eighteen sixties, pack trains of mules and burros began hauling supplies up to the residents who lived in the cabins in Colina Vista Canyon. People still live in those cabins. They're on U.S. Forest Service land. Very charming, made of logs and stones, but they have no running water, indoor plumbing, or electricity. No motor vehicles are allowed on the trail, so any supplies that the residents can't carry are hauled by the pack station. Sierra Madre also had a pack station. There's one still in operation, but it was moved farther into the forest."

Talking about the facts sobered Gilroy. Her unguarded moment had passed and the wall that separated and elevated the chief from everyone beneath her was again in place.

"At the time of Cookie's murder, Axel Holcomb lived in a small room in the back of the museum. Are you familiar with the circumstances of the murder?"

"Just the broad details." Kissick took out his spiral pad and pen. "I'd appreciate it if you could tell me everything."

She again sat. She picked up the cup of coffee and stared at it, not raising it to her lips. "Gosh, it must be ten years ago now." She set down the cup. "It happened early on a Tuesday morning in February. Cookie was taking her scheduled time off. She'd gone out with a couple of girlfriends to a bar in Arcadia. They left to go home around eleven that night. Cookie had parked her Nissan Sentra a block and a half away. She said good-bye to her friends, said she was going home, and that was the last they saw of her.

"When she didn't report for duty at eight the next morning, we started looking. Didn't find her until this older couple that runs the Foothill Museum went there around ten. They saw the Sentra in the parking lot. The log cabin was locked. Axel was supposed to open up the place. The old man went into the barn to get the spare key and found Cookie. She was nude, trussed like a deer, hanging by her ankles. Her throat was slit. Blood was everywhere." She grimaced. "Sergeant Mike Iverson was with me. We found Axel asleep in bed, covered with blood."

Her eyes took on a faraway gaze. "As soon as the trial was over, the city tore down the barn. The city council had wanted to get rid of it right away, but I told them it would be important for the jurors to see it, blood-soaked ground and all. The jurors did make a trip to see it. I think it helped make a compelling argument that Holcomb deserved the death penalty. Now it's up to the state to get off its behind and fulfill the will of the people."

"What's Holcomb's background?"

"He's a local man. Twenty-two years old at the time. He's a big man. Six-four. Two hundred fifty pounds. He was the town oddball. His family's lived here for generations."

"Were you surprised that he was responsible?"

"Everyone was stunned at first when it appeared that Axel had done it. But the evidence was irrefutable and he ultimately confessed. Later, people conceded that they weren't completely surprised."

"Did he have a history of violence?"

"Trouble seemed to follow Axel. Violence was often involved. For example, there was an incident when Axel was about sixteen. It was during summer and he was over at the public pool in the park. There were some local girls there, around his age. They were roughhousing in the pool and Axel held one of the girls' head under water until she nearly drowned. Axel's brother happened to be working as a lifeguard that day. The girl was blue by the time Axel's brother could get him to let go of her. She wasn't unconscious, but was close to it."

"Anyone press charges?"

"No. The families had known each other for years. You know how that goes in a small community. Our cops had picked up Axel a few times for fighting. They'd put him in the tank until he cooled off and his mother came and got him. He used to hang around with this group of about five guys who sort of adopted him as their pet. Because of his size, Axel really inflicted damage in a couple of the fights he was involved with. Folks around town knew to stay clear of Axel and to keep their kids away from him.

"Every community has a guy like Axel who just slips through the cracks until he does something really bad. Frankly, I had a hard time believing that Axel was capable of something so heinous. We questioned him, but the circumstantial evidence wasn't sufficient for an arrest.

A week after the murder, we brought him in again." She arched a sculpted eyebrow. "That time, he confessed."

Kissick raised his eyebrows.

"I asked one of our veteran sergeants, Ernie Bautista, to interview Axel with me. We put him through a long, tough interrogation. As you well know, you always hope your suspect will do the right thing, but how many times do we come away empty-handed?"

He nodded knowingly.

"Hours went by. Finally, Axel's conscience got the better of him."

"Well done."

She smiled modestly, her lips closed. "Thank you."

"Did Axel say why he murdered Cookie?"

"He had a crush on her. He was jealous of her and her boyfriend." Gilroy smiled ruefully. "We found out that she sometimes met her boyfriend, Philip Wondries, in the old barn. He was an officer with the Glendale P.D. I think he's still there. He lived in the San Fernando Valley. Cookie lived in La Verne, east of here. That barn was a convenient midway point for them to meet, especially when they both worked the graveyard shift. Phil said that they'd caught Axel watching them having sex in the barn. Cookie had told Phil that Axel had made comments to her about how good-looking she was and that she'd found Axel creepy."

"Had Cookie planned to meet Wondries there that night?"

"Not that night." Gilroy looked at him squarely. "We'll never know why Cookie went up there. Near as we can figure, she planned to meet someone other than her boyfriend. Axel said he was awakened by noises, went outside, and saw her there. Cookie, gutsy little thing that she was, had choice words for Axel, igniting that short-fuse temper of his."

Kissick nodded as he took notes. When he looked up,

she seemed agonizingly sad. "Everyone must have breathed a sigh of relief to have the murderer behind bars."

"Indeed, but no one in town was happy about any of it. Those were dark days in our little village. Looking back, I see how I made mistakes. I was in charge of the investigation. I was cocky to think that our little police department could handle it on our own. If it happened today, I would have been on the phone immediately to the Pasadena P.D. or the sheriff's, agencies with more experience in homicides. Still, we got our man. Our investigation might not have been the most elegant, but it was thorough and it was sound."

She scooted to the edge of her chair and reached to put her hand on Kissick's arm. "I'm sorry that Cookie's murder doesn't fit into your scheme. I wish you the best of luck in bringing to justice the man who attacked Detective Vining."

Kissick closed his notebook and slipped it inside his jacket breast pocket. He began gathering his materials from the coffee table. When he picked up the drawing of Cookie, he held it up.

"In this drawing, Cookie's wearing a necklace." He pointed at it. "The artist went to great pains to draw all these little circles that look like pearls. Was she found wearing a necklace?"

"No, she was not. Besides, pearls were not her style." Gilroy laughed bitterly.

"Did she mention someone having given her a pearl necklace? It would have been similar to this." From his pocket, he took out Vining's necklace and held it toward her.

Gilroy, still perched on the edge of the chair, was stock-still, her expression inscrutable.

When she didn't move to take the necklace, Kissick laid it on the coffee table. "Does this look familiar?"

"I've never seen anything like that before, during, or after the investigation." She pressed down the edges of her lips. "I'm sorry."

He returned the necklace to his pocket.

Gilroy pointedly looked at her watch. It was a Rolex. "If I've answered all your questions, Detective, I have an appointment."

He stood. "Thank you so much for your time, Chief Gilroy."

She stood as well and smoothed the folds from her slacks.

He extended his hand and she gave him a firm handshake. "You're more than welcome, Detective Kissick. I wish I could have been of more help. I know what it's like when evil strikes so close to home."

THIRTY-ONE

Vining went to the Terra Cosmetika building, across the street from where Scrappy had worked as a human directional. Behind it was the alley where the "Vining 187" tag had been painted on the back of the tire store wall.

She was the only one at the locked front door of the highly secured building. The employees entered from an underground garage via elevators. She pressed the button to announce her presence. Almost immediately, a buzzer sounded, and the lock disengaged. She entered a four-story atrium. Lush trees and plants were several stories tall, replicating a rain forest, complete with a waterfall and sounds of jungle wildlife. Peruvian folk music with Andean flutes played. Life-size toy monkeys, toucans, and a panther were tucked among the greenery. There was a bank of elevators and a small coffee and sandwich shop.

Vining walked to a semicircular reception desk where a pale woman on an Aeron chair wore a wireless headset. Her straight blond hair reached the middle of her ramrod straight back. On the wall behind her were banner ads touting the company's skin care products and cosmetics. The models were young, scrubbed, and vibrant, the sort of people who would still look great after a three-day bender, little needing cosmetic enhancements.

The receptionist was in her twenties and plainly dressed in an off-white shift in nubby raw cotton. She didn't appear to be wearing a smidgen of makeup on her flawless skin. She regarded Vining through eyes that were as blue as an Amazon morning. A shadow of disdain crept into those eyes when Vining displayed her shield.

Vining introduced herself and handed her a business card. "Who's in charge of your security?"

"Don Balch. Somebody else from the police already talked to him." She opened a drawer and found a PPD business card which she handed Vining.

It was Caspers's card. On the back, Vining saw that he had written his cell phone number. She reflected that the randy detective never let an opportunity slip by. When she put it in her pocket, the receptionist didn't protest.

"Is Don Balch here?"

"Yes. Are you here about Scrappy?"

"Did you know Scrappy?"

"Not really. I mean, I used to let him in to use the bathroom. That was terrible, what happened. I never knew anyone who'd been murdered before."

"Can you let Mr. Balch know I'm here, please?"

"Of course." She briskly made the call, as if to get rid of Vining.

Vining turned to look through the glass front door. She could clearly see the corner diagonally across the street where Scrappy had last stood with his arrow. There was someone wearing a gorilla costume there now. The full-head mask kept Vining from seeing who among Marvin Li's employees it was.

There was lots of traffic in and out of the coffee shop. While some of the people looked as if they worked for an organic cosmetics company, with free-flowing hair or shaved heads and just enough tattooed skin revealed beneath vegan clothing, most looked like office workers anywhere. It was a job and hopefully, a living.

When the receptionist had finished her call, she gave Vining a strained smile. "Don will be right down. Cute earrings. Is that abalone shell?"

"Yes, it is. Thank you. My, ahh . . . boyfriend gave them to me. He got them on a trip to Morro Bay."

"Nice boyfriend."

Vining smiled. "He is." She took out a note pad. "Can I get your name?"

"Matilda Jernigan. Matty for short."

"How long have you worked here?"

"About a year and a half."

"See that guy in the gorilla suit on the corner? How long have there been guys in costumes standing over there?"

She pursed her lips and drew them to one side. "Couple of weeks. Maybe a month or so."

"How many hours a day are they there?"

"From when I get to work to when I leave. Do you know who killed Scrappy?"

"We're working on it. Do you let anybody in off the street to use the bathroom?"

"*No.*" She was indignant. "He was wearing a clown

suit." She shrugged as if that made him harmless. "Look, I already got crap from my boss about that, okay? This is supposed to be such a holistic environment, but they're obsessed with people stealing stuff from them. Scrappy was nice. I was sad to hear what happened to him. You think about Pasadena and you don't think that people get murdered here, you know?"

"Did you ever see him talking to anybody?"

"On his cell phone."

"How much was he on his cell phone?"

"I don't know. Just like anybody, I guess." Matilda held up her index finger to interrupt the conversation and touched a button on her headset. "It's a beautiful day at Terra Cosmetika. One moment."

While she was on the phone, Vining picked up a product brochure from a display on the corner of the desk. A rainbow of wholesome-looking models of all ages hawked product.

After Matilda ended the call, she pulled open a drawer in her desk and handed a foil packet to Vining. "Would you like a sample of our new herbal revitalizing serum? It has jojoba, licorice extract, and Mediterranean brown seaweed and it's scented with ylang-ylang essential oil. It's wonderful. It'll bleach those brown spots on your face."

Vining accepted the small package. "Thank you." She self-consciously touched her cheek. She had noticed a couple of freckles that seemed to grow bigger each summer, but she hadn't thought they were *that* noticeable.

"Did you ever see Scrappy talking to anyone in person?"

Matilda looked out the glass door in the direction of Scrappy's former post. "People on the street would talk to him sometimes."

"Ever see this guy?" Vining showed her a surveillance photo of Marvin Li in his wheelchair.

Matilda frowned. "No. I would have remembered somebody in a wheelchair."

"He drives this van." Vining showed her a photo of Li's purple panel van with the ghost flames.

Matilda's blue eyes widened. "I've seen that van. I've seen it go down Newcastle Street." She broke to answer more phone calls.

"Do you know where the van went?"

"No, I've only seen it turn from Orange Grove onto Newcastle."

"How often did you see it?"

Matilda paused. "Sort of a lot, now that I think about it. At least a couple of times a day."

Vining knew it was reasonable for Li to check up on his employees, but that level of oversight seemed hovering.

A fiftyish man who stood out in a red jacket, crisp white shirt, sedate blue-and-red striped tie, and dark slacks exited an elevator and approached them. His brown hair was receding. He'd gelled what was left so that it stood up, the strands carefully mussed. A wire from an earphone in his ear trailed beneath his jacket. A name tag clipped to his pocket said: TERRA COSMETIKA SECURITY, D. BALCH.

He walked toward Vining with assured steps. She pegged him as former law enforcement or military.

"Hello, Detective." He gave her a firm handshake. "Don Balch. How can I help you?"

They exchanged business cards.

"Mr. Balch—"

"Don, please."

"Is there a place we can talk?"

"Sure. I already spoke with one of your detectives earlier this week about clown man across the street who got himself murdered. Is this about that or something else?"

"I have a couple of things I hope you can help me with."

"Let's go to my office."

Vining said, "Thank you, Matilda."

When she responded with the flippant "No problem," Vining mentally corrected her: *You're welcome*.

Balch held open an elevator door until Vining got in. He punched the button for the fourth floor.

"Don, I'm interested in the two CCTV cameras off your loading dock. There's fresh graffiti in the alley on the back of the tire store down the street. I'm hoping your cameras might have caught the guy."

"Think it has to do with clown man's murder?"

"Actually, it's a threat against me."

"I see. I'll get you everything you need. Always glad to help take a bad guy off the streets. I was with the L.A. County Sheriff's for twenty-five years."

"Yeah? Where did you work?"

"Fifteen years at the Temple City station. Norwalk before that. Retired as a sergeant five years ago. The first two years of retirement were great, playing golf every day. Never thought I'd get bored, but I did."

They exited the elevator. The walls were decorated with glossy framed photographs of rain forest flora and fauna interspersed with product shots that Vining recalled from the sales brochure.

"A friend told me the owner of this place, Mrs. Carranza, wanted her own security team. She'd contracted out and wasn't happy. I talked with her, checked out what she needed, and made her a deal. I set her up with the CCTV and smart-card systems. Hired a crew of watchmen who only carry two-way radios. She was paying for armed guards and didn't need to. Why have armed guards when the PPD response time is so great? She lets me run the show. I still play golf a couple of times a week."

"Sounds ideal," Vining said.

"It's worked out."

"The owner seems very security-conscious."

"She is. She started this company in her kitchen and she takes it personally when someone steals from her. Terra Cosmetika is a high-end product. Some of their face creams sell for five hundred bucks an ounce. Employee theft is a big problem, even with all the controls we have in place. We've had a couple of trucks boosted. Not here, thank God, but on the road."

"Is this building patrolled twenty-four hours?"

"Yes, one of my guys is always here. Most of the employees leave at five, but they have people on the customer service desk twenty-four/seven. Mrs. Carranza doesn't believe in outsourcing. She's very hands-on about how she runs her company."

Vining read between the lines and deduced that the owner was a control freak.

At the end of the hall, they reached a windowed door with SECURITY painted on it.

Balch took a smart card from his pocket and held it up to the electronic eye beside the door. The door unlocked and he pushed it open for Vining. She entered a large office that faced the corner of Orange Grove and Newcastle. Arrayed on a wall were framed photos of Balch and his six security officers with their names on plastic plaques beneath.

Vining looked them over. Some seemed familiar. She recognized one guy as a PPD officer applicant who had washed out.

A clean-cut young Latino who was dressed similarly to Balch looked up from where he sat behind a counter. His nametag said A. MONTOYA.

"Albert, this is Detective Vining from the Pasadena P.D."

Montoya stood to shake her hand.

"Here's the closed-circuit monitoring system." Balch

led her behind the counter where there was a row of television screens. Each had a label describing the areas being monitored and carried a split screen of broadcasts from at least two and as many as four cameras. The views changed continuously as feeds from different cameras were rotated.

Vining was impressed. "Is there any corner of this building that's not under surveillance?"

"The bathrooms. Mrs. Carranza wanted cameras there, but I talked her out of it," Balch said with a laugh.

He pointed to a monitor. "This one shows the feed from the two cameras you're interested in. They're set up to cover the loading dock, but they capture some of the alley, too."

"The tire store is two doors west of you. Can you enlarge the image from the camera facing that way?"

"Sure," Montoya said. He typed at a keyboard. The split screen disappeared. They watched as a large truck backed into the loading dock.

"The resolution's not great," Balch said. "You can't see the rear wall of the tire shop, but the camera would have caught anyone walking down the alley."

"Could I have the surveillance recording for the past week from this camera?"

"Can you do that, Albert?"

Montoya again typed commands. "I'll copy it onto a DVD for you."

"Thanks. Do your guards do foot patrols around the property?" Vining asked.

"Every hour or so, we'll take a stroll inside the building and around the perimeter outside," Balch said. "I'll ask our night-shift guys, Eduardo Gonzalez and Tanner Persons, whether they saw anything."

Vining scanned the CCTV monitors, taking a virtual tour of the building operations. Something on one of the monitors made her move in for a closer look. It was broadcasting a clear shot of the street in front of the building and the corner where Scrappy had last worked.

"Could I also get the feed from that camera for the past two weeks?"

"Sure thing."

While Vining was watching, a person in a wheelchair rolled down Newcastle to the corner of Orange Grove. She blinked and realized her eyes were playing tricks on her. It wasn't a wheelchair, but a bicycle. A man got off the bike and leaned it against the wall of the building there and approached the human directional in the gorilla suit.

"Albert, can you focus in on that corner?" Vining asked.

"Absolutely."

The camera zoomed in closer. They watched as the guy on the bicycle, who was in street clothes, took the large arrow from the guy in the gorilla suit, who then walked toward a car parked on Orange Grove.

"Must be relieving gorilla man for a break," Balch said. "Who knew that holding an arrow is so important, they can't leave that corner unmanned."

"You ever see anything funny with those guys?" Vining asked.

"You mean other than being there day and night? Nope. We've had our eye on them. I thought they were casing us. As time goes on and nothing happens, I'm thinking, maybe not. I've gone over there and talked to them. They all have the same story. 'I'm paid to stand here and twirl this sign. I don't ask questions.'"

"Did you report them to the police?"

"After the first two weeks, I did. Whoever I got in dispatch sounded like she'd had complaints about arrow guys before. She said there was nothing the police could do if all they were doing was standing on the street, not bothering anyone. I took things into my own hands. I make sure that my guys on each shift go over there to say hello, just so they know that we're watching. I've got a funny feeling that they're up to something, but I can't figure out what it is."

The guy on the corner was doing acrobatics with the arrow, twirling it over his head and around his back, dropping it, picking it up, and twirling it again.

Montoya held up his hand to indicate the television monitor. "I see these guys all over the city with those arrows. What kind of a job is that?"

"He's a human directional," Vining said. "It's a skilled profession."

"Looks like a skilled joke to me," Balch said.

THIRTY-TWO

A fter Vining left Terra Cosmetika, she drove across Orange Grove and turned onto Newcastle. She stopped near the guy with the arrow. She recognized him. He was George Holguin, an ex-con and a longtime member of Scrappy's gang, the NLK—Northwest Latin Kings. He had voluntarily come into the station along with Marvin Li's other employees, but he had spoken with someone other than Vining. He didn't know who she was, but Vining suspected he'd made the Crown Vic as a cop car.

She rolled down the window. "Where are the apartments that are for rent?"

He swung the arrow to indicate Newcastle Street. "Up there. You'll see them."

"Thanks." Don Balch was correct—the arrow guys' stories were consistent. She continued up Newcastle.

Small World War II–era stucco homes lined both sides of the street. The residential neighborhood was being squeezed by burgeoning development on Orange Grove and Mountain. The neighborhood was still reasonably well kept, with most of the lawns green and mowed, the houses well painted, and the roofs in good shape.

At the corner of Mountain, Vining saw Victor Chang standing with an arrow. He was wearing a red Aaron's Aarrows polo shirt and a plush toy dog on top of his head like a hat.

Something about Chang bothered Vining. All of Marvin Li's other employees were hard-core gangbangers and ex-cons. Li had given them the first honest job they'd ever had. Chang, however, had graduated from San Marino High School and completed a few courses at Cal State L.A., though he wasn't currently enrolled there. His criminal record was clean.

Marvin Li had explained that he'd taken eighteen-year-old Chang under his wing to save him from the gangbanger lifestyle. To Vining, that would entail Li keeping on top of Chang's activities, going out for meals or a baseball game, being a father figure, not having the young man stand on a street corner with a stuffed dog on his head and hanging around with a crew of criminals.

Vining spotted the PPD's surveillance vehicle on Newcastle south of Mountain. It was a Yukon Denali with tinted windows that the PPD had confiscated from drug dealers.

She pulled to the curb near Chang, grabbed her digital camera, and got out of the car. She had interviewed him at the PPD about Scrappy's murder. Like the rest of Li's employees, Chang said he didn't know anything about it and it had been a complete shock. Vining felt that he, and the others, had been telling the truth. Still, none of them would submit to polygraphs.

"Hi, Victor. What's going on?"

He shrugged. "Working." Holding the arrow by the two handles on the back, he passed it around his back, like a basketball.

"Isn't it humiliating, standing on a street corner, wearing a toy dog on your head?"

"Are you trying to humiliate me?"

"Mind if I take your picture?"

"Yes."

She'd already snapped him before he protested. In the next shot, she caught him flipping her off.

"I told you I didn't want you to take my picture."

She put the camera inside her pants pocket. "I heard you. Say, Victor . . . you're a smart guy. Why don't you get a real job?"

"Why are you jacking me up? I'm not bothering anybody."

"You're bothering me. Why are you standing here? You already told me you're working. Tell me something new."

He again twirled the arrow around his back, then grabbed both ends and jumped over it, like a jump rope.

"Where are those apartments you're advertising?"

"I don't have to talk to you."

"Victor, I'm just asking where the apartments are. Why are you so upset?"

"I'm not upset."

"You just flipped me off."

"I don't like talking to cops."

"Why? You been in trouble?"

He muttered something under his breath.

"What did you say?" She could see him struggling to keep his anger under control.

"Are you done?"

"No, I'm not done. I won't be done until I find out what you're up to out here, advertising apartments that don't exist."

He walked away from her and continued his acrobatics with the arrow.

Vining returned to her car. She called Sergeant Early to tell her what she'd learned at Terra Cosmetika and on Newcastle Street. "Any possibility of assigning a couple of cadets to go through the CCTV recordings?"

"I'll see what I can do," Early said. "Countless hours of tedious work will cure them of any notions about the glamour of police work."

Vining laughingly agreed. "Any updates from the surveillance team?"

"They haven't seen any unusual traffic patterns that would indicate criminal activity. No people coming and going at all hours. The street rolls up at eight o'clock at night. It's all normal."

"Except for the arrow guys in costume standing on each corner most of the night."

"If there was drug activity on that block, they've put a lid on it since Scrappy's murder. You'd think the arrow guys would have disappeared, too."

"I want to check out everyone who lives on that block of Newcastle," Vining said. "I don't know what Li's up to, but he's up to something."

"Where are you off to now?"

"Gonna meet with Sergeant John Velado, the San Gabriel Valley Asian gang specialist at the Temple City Sheriff's station. See if I can get information about Victor Chang. And I might pay Marvin Li another call."

"You taking Caspers?"

"I'd rather have him checking names on Newcastle Street." Vining remembered that Caspers had been more of a hindrance than a help the last time they'd interviewed Li.

"Keep me informed. Stay safe."

Vining drove off, taking a look around and glancing in her rearview mirror, ever watchful for a shadowy figure that could be T. B. Mann.

"Kicker Chang." Sergeant Velado laughed as he looked at the photo on Vining's camera. "What's he got on his head?"

"A stuffed toy dog."

"That surprises me, that Marvin Li can get those tough guys to wear costumes like that. Interesting that Kicker Chang is working for Li."

Vining was sitting in a rocky, rolling desk chair that Velado had pulled across the worn linoleum floor to his desk. Pairs of old Steelcase desks were bunkered together in a large open room that buzzed with activity.

Velado said, "We suspect Chang of being involved in a string of violent robberies of Chinese-owned businesses in Temple City and San Gabriel. The employees were pistol-whipped. Kicked after they were tied up. Word is, that's how Chang earned his moniker, kicking his victims."

He pulled a file from a holder on his desk and took out crime scene photos. "Chang's a junior psychopath."

"I didn't think he was a choir boy, but psychopath?" Vining rolled her chair to get a better look. The chair tipped slightly on its uneven wheels which made her jolt forward.

"A couple of months ago, we questioned Chang in the murder of a businessman and his girlfriend in a condo on Coolidge Street in Temple City. It was an incredibly violent incident. Six guys stormed the place and poured dozens of bullets into the victims. We had an anonymous tip about the IDs of the triggermen. They're associated with a set called Hell Side Wah Ching. Chang's name was mentioned. Again, we weren't able to get anyone to come forward. Gets very frustrating."

"I know," Vining agreed. "Who was the businessman?"

"Chinese from Hong Kong. Rumored to have been associated with the Fourteen K Triad there. They've had a long-standing dispute with Wah Ching over the control of prostitution in the San Gabriel Valley."

"So Chang does run with a gang."

"Suggests it, but doesn't confirm it. These Asian gangsters don't represent like the African American or Latino gangs. Victor Chang is a classic case of a guy who leads a double life."

"How so?"

"I'll show you." Velado stood.

As Vining moved to stand, the chair tipped back on one of its uneven wheels, almost toppling her.

"They need to get rid of this thing." Velado pushed the chair ahead of him as he walked, shoving it to roll into a group of disabled chairs in a corner. He walked to a tall bookcase that held a collection of yearbooks from local high schools. He ran his index finger down the titles until he found the one he wanted. It was from San Marino High School and was two years old.

Velado flipped through the pages. "Victor Chang was an honors student. On the gymnastics team and debate team. Here he is escorting the homecoming queen."

Vining looked at a photograph of a smiling Chang dressed in a tuxedo. An attractive young Asian girl wearing a strapless gown with a corsage, her hair done in an upsweep, was on his arm. There was also a photo of the homecoming queen giving a surprised-looking Victor a kiss on the cheek. The breezy caption said: "Go Girl."

Velado went on. "Victor's parents refuse to believe he's a criminal. Course, they're only here a few months out of the year. They spend most of their time in Taiwan where his father has a business. A housekeeper looks after Victor and his younger sister. That's not uncommon among affluent Chinese families. We call them the 'golden latchkey' kids.

"After we questioned Chang in relation to the double homicide, he went quiet. His name stopped coming up." Velado continued to flip through the yearbook. "He may have been told to lay low. It was news to me that he had a job holding arrows on street corners in Pasadena. Here's Chang with the photography club."

Vining glanced at the photo and was stunned by another face in the group. "Can I get a closer look?" She took the yearbook from him. Standing next to Chang, proudly displaying a camera with a giant lens, was Ken Zhang.

She flipped through the class portraits, finding Ken among the freshmen. He was also in a candid shot of a group of kids that was captioned "Friends Forever." Victor Chang was in it, too, with his arm draped over Ken's shoulders.

"You know anything about this boy?" Vining tapped the photo. "Full name is Lincoln Kennedy Zhang. Goes by Ken."

"Doesn't ring a bell. Is he still a juvenile?"

"Yes. I've already run him through JAI. He doesn't have a juvie record."

"Why are you interested in him?"

"He's a friend of my fourteen-year-old daughter."

"I see." Velado returned to his desk and typed commands onto a keyboard. "No LASD records on him. Does your daughter go to San Marino High?"

"She's at Coopersmith. It's a magnet school for the arts in Pasadena. Ken Zhang goes there now, too."

Velado turned to look at Vining. "Nothing comes up. You want me to ask around?"

"If you wouldn't mind."

"Be happy to."

Before Vining left, she made copies of the yearbook photos of Ken Zhang, Victor Chang, and the double homicide crime scene.

THIRTY-THREE

Vining parked across the street from Love Potion Bridal. Nearby was a van for a pest-extermination company that Vining knew held a team who was surveilling Marvin Li.

She dodged traffic as she darted across the street. When she reached Love Potion's extra-wide front door, it was pulled open by Marvin Li. Out came a lithe young Latina who was carrying a swollen garment bag draped across both arms.

"Bye, Marvin. Thank you." The young woman flicked a curtain of long hair over her shoulder with a joyful toss of her head. Her black hair shimmered with red highlights in the sun, looking as if she'd recently been to the hairdresser. She was wearing a sleeveless blouse tucked into white jeans that fit too loosely around her hips. She was getting married soon and had lost weight for the wedding. Spotting Vining, she beamed at her before floating down the street toward a compact car.

Li continued to hold open the door. "Detective Vining. What a nice surprise. Please come in." Today the ends of his braided Fu Manchu mustache were woven with metallic gold cord. He eyed Vining as she walked into the shop.

His tattoos were showcased in the sunlight coming through the front door, but they'd lost their allure for her. "So, Marvin, you actually sold a wedding dress. Did she give you twenty grand for a three hundred dollar gown?"

"Detective . . ." he said mournfully. "I'm helping out my aunt. This is a legitimate business. You still think I'm a bad guy. How can I prove to you that I'm reformed?"

He held up his hand to indicate the pest control van. "I'm not a suspicious man, but I have to wonder why that van has been parked across the street from my business since yesterday."

"Maybe there are a lot of rats in the neighborhood."

"I would hate to think that I'm under police surveillance."

"Why would you think that?"

"The Pasadena Police keep harassing me and my employees about Scrappy Espinoza's murder. I've told you everything I know and so have they."

"Where's your aunt?" Vining asked.

"She had an appointment. She'll be back soon." He coiled one of the tails of his mustache around his finger. "How are you minding that ghost, by the way?"

"Poorly."

"Come have a cup of my delicious Chinese tea. It makes everything better. I'll read your tea leaves. Tell your fortune. Don't worry. I only tell the good things."

"No, thanks. I came here to talk to you about something."

"You can talk while I'm having tea." He began rolling his chair toward the back room.

"I prefer talking out here."

He rolled his chair onto its back wheels and deftly

turned it to look at her. "Detective," he chided. "You really do have a bad opinion of me, thinking I might harm you in my aunt's store that she has kindly let me use out of the goodness of her heart. Come, have a cup of tea."

He turned the chair and went into the back room.

Vining followed. She opened the restroom door, then went to the garment rack that was crammed with gowns and costumes and searched through them.

Li didn't hide his amusement. He filled the electric kettle with bottled water and switched it on. He opened a foil-wrapped block, broke off a square of compressed black tea leaves, and put it inside the stoneware teapot. "Do you have any suspects in the murder of our poor friend Scrappy?"

"The investigation is moving along, but that's not what I came to talk to you about. Marvin, you have your human directionals working at each corner of Newcastle Street between Orange Grove and Mountain all day and most of the night. The managers of the only apartment building nearby didn't hire you. Your human directionals can't tell me where the apartments are that you're advertising. What are your guys up to on that street?"

After Li filled the teapot with boiling water, he took a wooden match from a box, flicked the end with his thumbnail to ignite it, and lit the candle in the stand beneath the teapot. "Who did you talk to in that apartment building?"

Vining took out her notepad and flipped through the pages. "A couple by the name of Shugart."

"That's not who hired us. Our building is farther north. I've posted the human directionals on those two corners because there's more traffic there."

"What's the address?"

He rolled behind the desk and opened a drawer.

Vining rounded the desk to watch him shuffle through file folders, keeping her eyes on his hands.

He closed the drawer. "Wait a minute . . . You're right. You said you spoke to the building managers. That's the problem. You need to talk to the owner."

"Who's the owner?"

"The name slips my mind and the bookkeeper has my records. Quarterly taxes are due. I'll get you the information."

Vining looked at Li dubiously. "You wouldn't lie to me, would you, Marvin?"

"Detective, I said I'd get you the information and I will."

"Why are your guys out on the street until midnight or later? There's nobody looking for apartments at that hour."

"This is not just a job for them. This is rehabilitation. I told you before, there should be a twelve-step program for gangbangers who want to leave the life. It's an addiction. I don't have meetings like at A.A. for them to go to at night, so I have to give them someplace else to spend their time. All I can do is keep them working."

"What about Kicker Chang?"

"Are you speaking of Victor Chang? I don't use my guys' street names. I don't let them use them around me."

Li picked up one of the straight-sided mugs that were facedown on a doily and poured tea into it. "You're sure you won't have some tea, Detective?"

"Yes, I'm sure."

"Would you care to sit down?"

"No." She remained standing where she could see his hands.

He made a face as if she was being painfully harsh.

"The head of the Sheriff's San Gabriel Valley Asian Gang Task Force has evidence linking Victor to a set called Hell Side Wah Ching. Victor's been implicated in a recent string of robberies of Chinese-owned businesses in San Gabriel and Temple City."

Li calmly sipped from the cup he held between both hands. "Implicated. Not arrested and charged. Could be mistaken identity. Maybe someone with a grudge named him."

She handed him the copy of the double homicide crime scene photo. "His name came up again in this Temple City shooting of a businessman who reportedly had ties with the Fourteen K Triad in Hong Kong. The businessman's girlfriend was also killed. Word is the Fourteen K Triad is at war with Wah Ching over the control of prostitution in the San Gabriel Valley. You were with a Wah Ching set."

"Yes, I was. Given everything you've learned about my life, I shouldn't have to explain myself again, Detective." He raised his voice slightly.

Vining was glad to see that she was finally making him lose his cool.

"Detective, don't judge me by the past, but by what I've done since. The people I've helped. Guns Gone. I can show you testimonials from local civic leaders. The mayor of L.A. The governor of California."

"Frankly, Marvin, I'm getting a confusing picture. On the one hand, you present this lifestyle that looks good on paper. Helping gangbangers get out of the life, guns off the street . . . Then I find out that one of your protégées, Victor Chang, is probably active in gang life in a big and bad way."

"Allegedly," Li was quick to add.

"I recognize that you're a pillar of society and all, but I can't make sense out of why you have guys standing on Newcastle most of the night. One of your employees was shot to death while tagging a death threat to you. Can you help me out, Marvin?"

While Li had been agitated before, now he seemed lost in thought as he stared into his cup. He slowly moved to set the cup beside the teapot. When he again turned his eyes to her, his demeanor had changed again. He seemed sad and resolute.

Vining had the impression that Li was doing a lot of thinking, and quickly.

"This is very distressing news about Victor. I didn't know he was implicated in two murders. Lately he's seemed distant and angry. I'd reached out to him, but he refused to open up to me. I, of all people, know that you can only help the ones who want to be helped, but Victor is a special case. I've known him since he was a little boy."

Li silently twirled an end of his mustache. "Now that I think about it, Victor and Scrappy had been having issues. There was bad blood. I broke up a fight between them. I got wind of others. My employees hide things like that from me because they know I'll send them back to jail. Victor has anger issues. I've seen him blow up."

"Why didn't you tell me this before?"

"I suppose I didn't want to admit it to myself."

Vining looked at him skeptically. Was he a savior of the streets, or an ordinary criminal, lying to protect himself?

"I need to get to the bottom of this," Li said. "I love Victor like a son. If he's in trouble, I need to find out. I feel responsible. I promised his mother I'd watch out for him. I don't take my promises lightly."

"Okay, Marvin. I want you to come with me to answer questions at the station."

He was suddenly jovial again. "I can't leave the store, Detective. I promised my aunt—"

"You're going to be leaving the store, Marvin."

Vining took her two-way from her pocket and keyed

it. She went to the shop's back door and opened the lock. PPD officers led by Sergeant Terrence Folke came through it. The front door buzzed when another pair of PPD officers and two San Gabriel P.D. officers entered.

"What's going on?" Li asked.

"We're arresting you on an outstanding bench warrant from last year," Vining said. "You did not appear at a scheduled hearing regarding late child-support payments."

An officer handcuffed Li while another searched him and recited his rights.

"I paid everything I owed," Li spat. "That court hearing was total bullshit."

"Judges don't like to be kept waiting, Marvin." Vining saw a new side of Li. She saw the angry punk who acted on an adverse comment in a crowded restaurant by opening fire. From her pocket, she took out folded papers and opened them in front of Li's face with a flick of her wrist.

"Search warrants for your computer and telephone records."

Folke picked up a BlackBerry from Li's desk. An officer was unplugging Li's laptop.

"Thanks, Terrence," Vining said to the sergeant as she headed toward the back door. "I'll talk to you at the station, Marvin."

Before she left, Folke told her, "We've got a car en route to pick up Victor Chang."

In the alley behind the shop, Vining saw Auntie Wan getting out of her car.

Vining gave her a quick wave and kept walking.

THIRTY-FOUR

Vining drove to San Marino and turned onto Huntington Drive, where many of the city's small businesses were located on a stretch lined with century-old magnolia trees. She found a parking spot in front of the two-story, midcentury building where Pearl Zhang maintained her office.

At the side of the building, she climbed an outside stairway of cement slabs connected by steel rails. For a city with sweeping mansions, the commercial buildings were modest, many homely enough so that only the locals loved them, and outsiders found little to entice them here. Vining walked a second-floor catwalk and found Zhang's suite. A plastic plaque beside the door said RED PEARL ENTERPRISES.

She entered a small lobby where a young Asian woman sitting at a disorganized desk was on the telephone. She was wearing a beige ribbed turtleneck sweater in spite of the warm weather. Her black hair had been hastily pulled back and fixed with a claw clip behind her head. Loose strands had broken free all over.

The desk was almost overflowing with file folders, scraps of paper, three-ring binders, and sales flyers. Perched precariously in each corner were glass vases of silk flowers, partially filled with clear plastic that resembled water, which at first glance made it appear that the clever fakes were fresh blooms. The area might have been organized at some point, but the order had eroded just as wind and water can reduce a mountain to a pitted shell.

A credenza behind the desk and a bookcase were similarly cluttered. A straggly potted philodendron on the bookcase struggled toward the light. Someone had draped its pale, almost bare vines around the edges of the bookcase and across a nail supporting a large calendar from the Quon Yick Noodle Factory. There were souvenirs commemorating the 2008 Olympics in Beijing.

Two new-looking leather chairs were against the wall on either side of a small table that had another dusty, ersatz vase of flowers and was strewn with brochures advertising Red Pearl's various property offerings.

Given Vining's brief encounters with Pearl Zhang, the office was not what she'd expected from someone who was so elegantly attired and polished. Vining had the feeling of visiting a stranger's fastidious home only to open the refrigerator and find it crammed with spoiled food.

The young woman acknowledged Vining with a quick wave while she continued her telephone conversation in Chinese.

The suite was small. A short hallway led from the lobby with a few doors on either side.

When the secretary showed no indication that she was close to ending her phone call, Vining pulled back her jacket to make sure the woman saw the badge on her belt. She also took a business card from her pocket and set it on the desk.

The secretary quickly ended her call. "Sorry, sorry. Can I help you?"

"Is Pearl Zhang here?"

The secretary again picked up the phone receiver and punched buttons on the keypad while watching Vining.

She spoke urgently into the phone in Chinese, keeping her voice low. Almost before the secretary had ended the call, a door opened and Zhang stepped out.

"Detective Vining. How nice to see you. Please come into my office."

Zhang's appearance was as picture-perfect as the night Vining had first seen her tromping across the rubble of the Hollenbeck Paper building construction site. Her skirt suit was understated, but the cut and fabric weren't anything that could be procured off-the-rack. She held out her hand as Vining approached. Rainbows cast from the sparkling diamonds that adorned her watch, rings, necklace, and earrings drew Vining's attention in spite of herself. The glint was enough to put one's eye out. Her bloodred nail polish again matched the color on her precisely outlined lips.

Shaking Zhang's fine-boned, smooth hand made Vining feel as if hers was a weathered baseball mitt. Zhang had the same aura of composure and steely resolve as when she'd seen Scrappy's body, suggesting that she was a woman who handled whatever life threw in front of her, and then stepped over it in her designer stilettos.

Zhang led the way into a small office. The décor was minimalist in comparison to the lobby. It was furnished with a blond-wood desk in a simple Danish design with two matching chairs in front. A credenza was against a wall. Other than Zhang's pale pink leather desk chair, there was no other furniture. The desk was empty except for an open laptop computer, a multi-line telephone, an iPhone, and a round, cut crystal paperweight. The top of the credenza held photographs of her son Ken in crystal frames.

Vining privately observed that the woman liked cut glass. She pushily walked to the photos and began picking them up.

"What a cute baby Ken was. Look how chubby."

Zhang peered around Vining. "That was his first birthday."

Zhang was in a couple of the photos with Ken as a baby and young child. She seemed ageless, but her financial situation had matured. In one photo, Ken was four or five years old, looking adorable in a suit with a bow tie and short pants. Zhang was standing beside him, holding his hand. She was also decked out, looking slightly trashy in a snug sheath dress in glossy purple fabric. Gardenias were pinned to her slicked-back hair. Dramatic eye makeup and bold lipstick fought each other for dominance on her face. Vining wondered about the path that had taken Zhang from Ross "dress for less" to Armani and diamonds.

"And here's Ken all grown up," Vining said.

Most prominent among the photos was a large recent shot of Ken wearing a tuxedo with a boutonnière. He was leaning against a tree with arms folded, lips barely turned up at the corners. His gaze was steady, expression confident. He looked much older than seventeen and ready to take on the world. Vining imagined him plowing through a string of girls like Emily before he was finished. As polite as Ken was in person, Vining was certain she detected in his eyes an arrogance that said, "Life is a game."

Maybe so, Vining thought, *but my daughter's not going to be one of your pawns.*

Zhang pointedly took the photo from Vining's hands and returned it to the credenza. As she was straightening the frames, she said, "Detective Vining, I assume you're here with news about who committed that murder on my property."

"The investigation is still under way. I'm here on another matter." Vining took out her digital camera, turned it on, and showed Zhang the photo she'd taken of Victor Chang in his dog hat, flipping off the camera. "Do you know this man?"

The edges of Zhang's red lips tightened slightly. She took a perfunctory glance and moved to sit behind her desk. "I do not."

Vining didn't sit, but stood over the desk. "No? Take another look." She turned the display toward Zhang.

"I don't need another look."

"His name is Victor Chang. His street name is Kicker. Your son Ken knows him." Vining handed her copies of the yearbook photos of the San Marino High School photography club and the group of friends in which Victor had his arm thrown over Ken's shoulders.

Zhang's eyes brightened as she looked at the images. "My son is popular with his schoolmates. He has many friends. Perhaps, Detective, you can get to your point. I don't have a lot of time."

"The point is that while Victor Chang was a high school honor student, he was also associated with a very violent criminal gang called Hell Side Wah Ching. He's implicated in a string of violent robberies of local Asian-owned businesses and the shooting death of a Hong Kong businessman and his girlfriend."

She set the gruesome crime scene photo on her desk.

Zhang's red lips trembled and two fine, vertical lines appeared in her forehead. She flipped the photo face-down and glared at Vining. "The purpose of your visit is still unknown to me, Detective."

"I want to know whether Ken has any involvement with a gang or criminal activity."

"My son is not in a gang."

"How do you know?"

"Because I know my son. How dare you come here and ask these questions and show me this horrible picture." Zhang shoved the photo with her index finger, sliding it toward Vining. "My son is a good boy. He's an honor student. He's an accomplished pianist. He tutors disadvantaged children in his spare time."

She darted her finger toward Vining. "If he was white, you wouldn't be here. That's what this is about, isn't it? The inscrutable Chinese people. Outwardly respectable, putting on a proper face, while behind the scenes, we're criminals, taking advantage of anyone, especially our own people. How racist."

She stood. Her voice was even yet seethed anger. "You're looking for any reason to keep my son away from your daughter. I know the questions you've asked about me and my background. Your insinuations that I have done something illegal and dirty to get where I am in life. Ken told me he doesn't feel welcome in your home. Don't worry about my son and your daughter. I will forbid him to go near her or any daughter of a police officer. Good-bye, Detective."

Vining didn't know if Zhang was being truthful about her son's involvement in criminal activity or even if she was aware of it, but she'd gotten what she wanted.

THIRTY-FIVE

Vining returned to her cubicle on the second floor of the PPD and picked up a voice mail message from Azusa P.D. homicide detective Gary Blanco, returning her call.

Azusa was about a dozen miles east of Pasadena and was where Sandra Lynde had been murdered during a convenience-store robbery over twenty years ago. Sandra was the mother of murdered LAPD vice officer Frances "Frankie" Lynde, whose battered body had been dumped beneath Pasadena's Colorado Street Bridge. Vining and Kissick had solved that sordid case.

Auntie Wan had admonished Vining to appease the ghost that follows her. Vining thought that Frankie's spirit should have been appeased. Vining had seen to it that Frankie's killer had paid for her murder, big time, yet Frankie's ghost would not leave her in peace. Maybe, Vining thought, she was overlooking the obvious. Justice for Frankie was not complete. Her mother's murder remained unsolved. Maybe that was why Frankie's spirit was still restless. Or maybe not, but it was worth a try.

Detective Blanco had left the response for which Vining had hoped. He would look into the long-cold Sandra Lynde homicide.

Vining called Dispatch and asked them to get in touch with Officer Frank Lynde, Frankie's father, a twenty-five-year veteran with the PPD. He was a mountain of a man, rotund and florid-faced, and a steady cop, even and predictable. The only time anyone had seen Frank lose control was when they'd found Frankie's body. He quickly got back to her.

Vining kept her explanation simple. "Sandra's murder has been on my mind. Blanco said the lead detective on the case moved out of state twelve years ago and no one's looked at it since. Fresh eyes and all."

Frank's voice was gruff, fitting his size and appearance. "In the early years, I used to check in on it, but time has a way of getting past you. Now with Frankie dead, too . . ."

"I understand, Frank. I just wanted to let you know."

Vining ended the call. She felt the same hollow sadness she'd experienced after her other recent interactions with Frank Lynde. Talk about a dead man walking . . .

Before she had a chance to move on to the next thing,

she got a call from Sergeant Terrence Folke whose officers were going to pick up Victor Chang.

"Nan, Chang is in the wind."

"What happened?"

"The guys surveilling Newcastle say that an hour ago, Chang leaned his arrow against a lamppost and walked away. We're looking for him, but no luck yet."

"Nobody followed him?"

"The mission of the surveillance was to watch who came and went on that block, not to keep tabs on anyone in particular. I've pulled four patrol units in and they're going door-to-door, chasing through backyards. I put out an APB—"

"Crap." She loudly exhaled.

"I'm sorry, Nan. But I do have new information about what's going on in that block. After the guys in costumes go home around midnight, fresh teams arrive. They sit in their cars all night at each of those two corners of Newcastle. We've also discovered some interesting characters living on that block. There's Drew Huebner, age thirty-eight. He was a mortgage banker with that big bank in town that the feds took over during the home loan crisis. Got laid off. Was arrested for soliciting prostitution in Hollywood. Runs an Internet porno site out of his home."

"Nice."

"We've also got a Mrs. Elena Irani, sixty-three, who has a habit of shoplifting."

"Uh-huh."

"There's a mother and daughter who are especially interesting. Grace Shipley, age forty-two, and Meghan, age twenty. They live at twenty-five-eighteen Newcastle, right in the middle of that stretch that's being guarded."

"Why do we like them?"

"The mother's had a couple of DUI arrests and did time for drug possession. The daughter has no criminal record. The surveillance team has photos of Li going into the Shipley house and of Grace and Meghan at the Love Potion Bridal Salon. Li and the Shipley women are cozy. Hugging. Kissing. Possibly a romance between one of the women and Marvin Li."

"Too much of a coincidence for me. Can you get me those photos?"

"I'll bring them right over."

Carrying the photos of the Shipley women with Li, Vining found Sergeant Early in her office and brought her up to date.

Vining said, "We've got probable cause to get warrants for the Shipleys' telephone records and computers."

"Absolutely, we've got the P.C. I hear that Li's memory improved after you tightened the noose."

"He suddenly recalled Victor Chang having had words with Scrappy."

"Remarkable," Early joked.

"Did you know that Li is not a citizen? He's a permanent resident."

"I didn't know that."

Vining's cell phone rang. She plucked it from her belt and looked at the display. She told Early, "It's the deputy D.A.," and then answered, "Hi, Mireya." Listening for a moment, she snapped into the phone, "I want Li to tell me what's happening on that block of Newcastle. No deal for anything less. I'm tired of his B.S. An accessory to murder conviction will be his third strike. At minimum, I'll have him deported."

She angrily clasped the cell phone closed. "Mireya just talked with Sammy Leung, Marvin Li's attorney. Li is still claiming that his arrow guys are advertising apartments. Now, he's saying the apartments are actually on La Pomelo Road, one block east of Newcastle. There probably are apartments on La Pomelo, and Li's attorney has someone there right now, paying off the manager to say he hired Aaron's Aarrows."

Early added, "While another guy is busy making up a backdated sales contract."

"I've had about all I can take of that smooth-talking, inked-up jerk."

"What inked-up jerk? Our friend Marvin?" Kissick said as he came through the door.

"Hello, stranger," Early said.

Vining smiled. "Hey, Jim. See all the fun you've been missing?"

"What's going on?"

Vining summarized the developments with Marvin Li, Victor Chang, and Grace and Meghan Shipley.

"Looks like you're close to breaking this thing."

Vining saw him give an admiring look at the earrings he'd given her. "I'm hopeful."

Early asked him, "What's going on in your world?"

When he went to sit down, Vining started to leave.

Early said, "Nan, stay. You're part of this."

Kissick went over what he'd learned about Marilu Feathers from his trip to Montaña de Oro and Cambria.

Vining pretended it was all news to her, even though she'd sneakily read his field notes. She showed surprise when he revealed Feathers's pearl-and-turquoise necklace that she'd already handled after searching his jacket pockets. She hoped she hadn't overdone her acting job.

Kissick went on to describe a telephone conversation he'd had with Lieutenant Owen Donahue, the lead investigator in the Johnna Alwin homicide in Tucson. "He said that Alwin had been wearing a pearl necklace when she was murdered. It had a garnet stone in it."

The information that Johnna Alwin had owned a pearl necklace matching the others was now out there,

Vining thought. Kissick had kept her secret that she'd traveled to meet with Donahue and had somehow "acquired" Alwin's necklace. She'd withheld from him the details of how she'd gotten her hands on it. He hadn't pressed, showing that he didn't want to know.

Kissick left his visit with Colina Vista Police chief Betsy Gilroy for last. Before he got to it, he took out the satinette bag that held Vining's pearl-on-pearl necklace and handed it to Early.

There it is, Vining thought. *Out in the open.* Judging from Early's nonchalant response, Vining suspected that Kissick had already spoken to Sarge about it.

While Early took out and read the handwritten note on the panel card, Vining explained how it had shown up in her mailbox after the Lonny Veltwandter shooting.

Early didn't question Vining about why she hadn't come forward when she'd received the necklace and the note. She said only, "The three necklaces suggest a link between Feathers's and Alwin's murders and Nan's murder attempt."

"There's a fourth necklace," Kissick said. "The beat-up one that Nitro was wearing when we apprehended him."

"That's right." Early put Vining's necklace and the panel card inside the satinette bag. "Wonder if and how that plays into all this."

Vining doubted she'd ever get her necklace back. She had to get used to the idea that the evidence, her evidence, and research was now out in the open for everyone to poke and prod. It was all good. So, why did she feel empty?

Kissick moved on to his meeting with Betsy Gilroy.

Sergeant Early brightened. "How is my buddy Betsy?"

"She's great," Kissick said with admiration. "It's true, what everybody says. She's the queen of Colina Vista."

Early laughed. "Yes, she is, but she earned every

accolade she receives. Jim, I hope you gave her my
regards."

"I did, and she sends hers."

Early added, "I couldn't be prouder of her."

Vining had known Gilroy slightly when she'd been
with the PPD. She'd heard gossip about how ambitious
the then-lieutenant was. Vining was in no position to
judge, as she had been the topic of similar gossip. While
she didn't think that being political or ambitious was a
negative trait, it did make one wonder, like with any
politician, when push came to shove, on what side
would the political animal's loyalties ultimately lie?

As Kissick and Early chatted about Gilroy, even
Bessie the bear came up. Vining was anxious to get on
with it and hear what Kissick had learned. She stood
with her back against the large windows that overlooked Garfield Avenue, her arms stretched along the
window sill. Looking into the suite through the windows on the facing wall, she saw Caspers poke his head
over the top of his cubicle to share something funny
with another young male detective a few cubicles away.

"About Cookie Silva . . ." Kissick leaned forward in
his chair.

Vining leaned forward as well.

"The Silva murder has been long closed," Kissick
said. "A man named Axel Holcomb, a caretaker at the
Foothill Museum where Cookie was murdered, is on
death row in San Quentin. Physical evidence and Holcomb's confession put him there."

"He confessed?" Vining repeated with surprise.

Kissick described what Gilroy had told him about
Holcomb's reputation as the town bully, including the
incident as a teenager in which he'd nearly drowned a
girl at the public pool. He mentioned the unwanted
attention Holcomb had paid to Cookie and his jealousy
about her boyfriend.

"There's no doubt in Gilroy's mind that they got their man," he said. "Holcomb's circumstances couldn't be more different than those that implicated Jesse Cuba in the murder of Johnna Alwin. Cuba was found dead of a drug overdose. The police pegged him for Alwin's murder based on circumstantial evidence. Holcomb was convicted after a jury trial and has already gone through a couple of appeals.

"Cookie's murder doesn't fit the profile of our other three victims in a couple of ways. Unlike Feathers, Alwin, and you, Nan, Cookie hadn't done anything heroic that landed her in the news and that would have drawn our bad guy's attention. She wasn't as solid a cop as the other three victims. Gilroy described Cookie as headstrong. She said that Cookie reminded her of herself when she was just starting out. She and Cookie were very close."

Early nodded knowingly but said only, "Cookie's murder must have hit her hard."

Kissick remembered Gilroy's tears. "It did."

Vining tapped her fingernails against the window frame and thought about Axel Holcomb on death row. She couldn't fathom why he'd confess to a murder he hadn't committed. Still, history has shown that there are innocent people on death row. She found it merely interesting that Cookie didn't fit the profile of T. B. Mann's other victims. She didn't enjoy Kissick's and Early's lauding of Gilroy. That would only make it harder to convince them that even after the police and judicial system had followed all the rules, a mistake could have still been made. She saw T. B. Mann's grubby fingerprints all over Cookie's murder. The link was there. They just couldn't see it yet.

The more they talked, the more annoyed Vining became. They were not taking a step back from the official version of Cookie Silva's murder case. Sure, it all looked thorough and complete, and it probably was, but they needed to question everything. It was precisely because of a similar unwillingness to look deeper that T. B. Mann had gotten away with Johnna Alwin's murder in Tucson. Their discussion now brought back to Vining her wisdom in having investigated T. B. Mann surreptitiously. She knew her theories about him went beyond standard thinking, maybe even too much, treading into the realm of irrationality. She knew her peers and higher-ups would have just patted her on the head and told her to relax, while exchanging knowing looks behind her back. They would gently caution her to look at the *facts*. Well, she had facts right here—long scars on the back of her hand and down her neck.

"What did the chief have to say about Nitro's drawing of Cookie's body?" Her private musings had gotten Vining worked up. Drumming her nails, she asked questions in rapid succession. "Was it accurate? Did it reveal inside information?"

When Kissick again spoke, his voice was lower than it had been before, trying to calm her down.

"Chief Gilroy said the drawing accurately depicted the crime. The Colina Vista P.D. wasn't sophisticated about handling a high-profile murder and hadn't adequately secured the scene. A reporter got inside and took photos of Cookie's body. The police got rid of the pictures, but that didn't stop the reporter from writing what he'd seen. I confirmed that by doing an Internet search on the Cookie Silva murder. Several articles accurately described the disposition of Cookie's body in that barn."

Vining pushed away from the wall and nervously strode across the office, rattling off more staccato questions. "Did you ask Gilroy about whether Cookie was found wearing a pearl necklace? Had Cookie been given one?"

"I asked all those things, Nan. Chief Gilroy said she'd never seen a necklace like that."

Vining pressed. "Did you show her my necklace?"

He responded softly. "I did, Nan. She didn't recognize it."

Vining bit her lip, thinking. "Did you *specifically* ask her if there was a necklace on the body?"

Early watched their exchange, her head resting atop the steeple she'd made of her hands.

"There was no necklace, Nan."

Vining continued to pace, gesturing with her hands. "The crime scene photos would show that. Did you ask to see them?"

"I didn't, but maybe you can come with me and we'll have a look."

"I'm curious about Holcomb's confession. Why did he confess?"

"Gilroy and a sergeant did a good job at interrogating and Holcomb's conscience finally got to him." Kissick held up both hands, palms tilted down, trying to calm her. "Nan, I realize this is emotional for you, but see no need to second-guess Chief Gilroy."

Vining's voice was strident. "I'm not second-guessing Chief Gilroy. I've been tracking this guy long enough to know that nothing is ever the way it seems at first. Back then, Gilroy didn't know what we know now. Doesn't it make sense to take another look through different lenses?"

Kissick was beginning to get annoyed. "Nan, Axel Holcomb is on death row."

"You know darn well that juries sometimes set murderers free to walk the streets while innocent people spend the rest of their lives in prison." Vining again moved to the wall and leaned against the window. "Here's the thing, we can't disregard Nitro's four drawings. They're a set. Cookie Silva's murder was ten years ago. Marilu

Feathers's was eight years ago. Johnna Alwin's was three and the attack on me was fifteen months ago. With each one, his setup and execution became more complex and daring. I can make an argument that Cookie's murder doesn't fit the mold because it was his first."

Kissick and Early watched her with more than simple interest.

Vining went on. "It took him a while to refine his craft, so to speak. We can't forget how cagey this guy is. He stalked me for *years*. He planned and waited and waited until just the right . . ."

Vining's cell phone rang again. She looked at the display. "It's my daughter. I apologize. I have to take this."

"None necessary," Early said.

When Vining answered the phone, Early and Kissick could hear Emily raging. They were surprised when Vining barked, "Em, get ahold of yourself."

She left Early's office and went into the conference room to have a brief and unpleasant conversation with her daughter. Emily had gotten wind of her mother's meeting with Pearl Zhang and their mutual decision to forbid their children to see each other.

When Vining left the conference room, she saw Kissick and Early still in her office, heads bowed toward each other, as if engaged in a serious and confidential conversation. Vining knew they were talking about her and that she wasn't being paranoid.

She took a deep breath and went back inside Early's office, sitting in a chair beside Kissick. She demurely crossed her ankles, tucked her feet beneath the chair, and rested her hands in her lap.

"Everything okay at home?" Early asked.

Vining shrugged lightheartedly. "Emily's definitely a teenager. We're having a rift. It'll blow over."

"Having raised girls myself, I know what you're going through." Early looked at Vining with concern.

"Nan, I fully appreciate that you have a lot of emotions tied into the investigation of the man who attacked you. Still, we can't forget that we're trying to make sense out of four drawings we found on a mentally disturbed transient. We don't even know if Nitro drew them. Two of those murder cases are closed. Granted, there are a lot of holes in the Tucson P.D. hanging Johnna Alwin's murder on her informant. But Cookie Silva's case is good and closed. Finding those necklaces is interesting, but they're not leading us anywhere. As it stands now, you and Jim have gone as far as you can with this. We've exhausted all our leads. We have to conclude that the case is no longer active."

Vining knew that Early was trying to soften the blow by not calling the case "cold."

"This is hard for me to say, Nan, and I hate saying it, but unless your guy kills again, or makes a barroom or jail-cell confession, or does something else stupid, or a witness comes forward, we might not ever get him. Those are the cruel facts of our profession. Sometimes the bad guy gets away."

Vining nodded as if she agreed, but she did not. Intellectually, she saw the logic of Early's argument, but her bond with T. B. Mann went beyond logic. It was something she felt beneath her flesh and even beneath her bones. It lived in the marrow of her bones and the cells of her blood. Sometimes she felt it had burrowed even deeper than that, that it had infiltrated and mutated her DNA. It had certainly infiltrated her soul. It surpassed all attempts at reason.

Sergeant Early's eyes were careworn yet sympathetic when she looked at Vining. "Now that Jim's back, he can work the Scrappy Espinoza—"

Early was distracted by the appearance of one of the PPD cadets, Allison Moricz, hesitantly hovering outside her door. She was carrying a portable DVD player.

"Yes, Allison," Early said.

"I'm sorry to interrupt, Sergeant, but I found the video showing the guy who spray-painted the Vining one-eight-seven tag."

THIRTY-SIX

Allison Moricz followed Early's instructions to set the DVD player on a bookcase so they could watch it at eye level. Moricz was nineteen years old and a student at Pasadena City College, like most of the PPD's cadets. Her thick, naturally curly blond hair was pulled back from her face and pinned into a tight bun. Her pretty face was marred by a struggle with acne but she was cute and had a wholesomeness about her that Vining found rarer than perfect skin.

The DVD was on pause, but in the image on the screen, Vining recognized the plank fence surrounding the backyard of the house across the alley. She recalled the children's toys she'd seen in the yard when she'd looked through a hole formed by a missing plank.

She turned when Caspers entered the office.

Sergeant Early gave him a questioning look. "I don't need a team for this job, Caspers."

"I know, Sarge." He grinned winningly. The tactic occasionally worked with Sarge. "I'd like to see this tagger. Maybe I know him."

Early muttered a dubious "Uh-huh," and looked at Caspers glancing at Allison, which she suspected was the real reason he had found an excuse to be there. She didn't order him to leave.

"I backed it up to just before he enters the scene." Allison pressed Play.

A date and time display in white at the bottom of the screen counted the passing seconds as nothing changed in the dimly lit alley. Then someone entered the frame, walking down the alley in the direction of the camera. The figure was dark and fuzzy. Taggers were nearly always men, but this individual's sex, race, and age were impossible to determine. His pace and slender physique suggested a young man. He appeared to be wearing a black, short-sleeved T-shirt.

An attribute of the tagger that could be determined was his height. "He's tall," Early said. "His head tops that fence, which I assume is six feet."

"We could have it enhanced," Kissick said, "but I don't know if it would do us any good."

Vining couldn't tear her eyes from the shadowy figure. Something about him spoke to her. Something was familiar.

"Okay, Bozo," Caspers said. "Show us what you got. Get busy."

He disappeared from view for a while, probably walking toward the tire store wall, and then moved back into the frame.

"What's he doing?" Kissick asked. "Is he holding a can of spray paint?"

"He's doing a sketch of the tag before he starts painting," Vining said. "I saw pencil marks on the wall."

"I've never known a tagger to be so fastidious," Caspers said.

"He does this for about fifteen minutes," Allison said. "I can fast forward it."

She did, returning to normal speed when the tagger

began jerking his arm back and forth beside his head. His arm looked spindly, matching his legs.

"Shaking the spray paint," Kissick said.

Holding up the can of paint, he moved toward the wall. After a minute, they glimpsed him briefly when he stepped back, his right hand holding the paint, before moving forward again.

"Allison, fast-forward," Early said.

They watched the jerky, speeded-up images on the screen as the DVD player raced through the tagger's art project. The others grew restless. Vining, however, was transfixed. She couldn't shake that disorienting feeling of déjà vu. There was almost a tinkling feeling in her head, as if her thoughts were steel shavings, pinging and scraping as they drifted into each other. She was waiting for a moment, a sign that would confirm what she felt in her gut.

At one point, the tagger stepped back and appeared to be admiring his work.

There was a flash of car headlights coming from the opposite end of the alley. They grew brighter.

Flailing his arms, the tagger scampered away, looking like a daddy longlegs spider. Reaching the fence, he dropped to the ground where he remained huddled until the car had passed.

Vining felt as if a flare had been fired inside her head. "It's Nitro."

"Nitro?" Kissick said with disbelief.

"The guy who ran naked through Old Town and wouldn't talk?" Caspers asked.

Vining ignored them. "Allison, could you play that again, please, from before the car passes through?"

Allison complied and they studied it once more.

Vining turned to confront their dubious faces. "It's Nitro. I'm certain of it. That's his body language. I've never known another person who moved like that."

Early dispatched the cadet. "Allison, thank you very much. Good job. Leave the DVD player, please."

Caspers chided, "Nan, you're seeing these guys everywhere. You thought the guy who attacked you had been at Scrappy's murder scene and now you think this joker is Nitro."

"Caspers," Early snapped. "Don't you have work to do?"

"Yes, ma'am." Caspers slinked from the office.

Early closed the door.

Kissick raised an eyebrow. "Nan, I'm not saying it's not Nitro, but I don't see how you can be so sure from that dark video. I was with Nitro, too. I saw him."

"Not like I saw him." Vining felt them studying her. Not wanting to be insubordinate, she directed her venom toward Kissick. "Jim, you're looking at me like I'm nuts and I'm not. There is no doubt in my mind that that tagger is Nitro."

One of the detective sergeants who shared the office with Early came to the closed door. Through the window, Early signaled that she needed five minutes.

Vining replayed the sequence with the tagger while Kissick and Early watched. "This explains why that tag doesn't look like any we've seen before. Think about it. The style of that tag is similar to the artwork in the drawing book we found on Nitro. He painted that tag, so he must have made those drawings, too."

"Why did he turn into a tagger?"

"Why did he run naked through the streets of Pasadena with drawings of four murdered policewomen in his backpack?"

"Three," Kissick said. "Three murdered policewomen. You're still with us, Nan."

"Right," Vining conceded. She looked at Sergeant Early who was quietly watching the exchange. Vining sensed she was waiting to say something, so she fell silent.

"Nan, you've been juggling a lot of balls lately and doing a great job at it. It was your instinct to follow the Asian gang thread in the Espinoza case, and it looks like it's going to pay off."

Vining waited for the other shoe to drop.

"But all those long hours are taking a toll on you. Frankly, you look exhausted. I wonder how you do it, with that guy who attacked you still out there, playing sick games, and that Nitro character on the loose. It would get under anyone's skin. Jim can take the Espinoza case from here. Your scheduled days off start tomorrow, anyway. Take the rest of this afternoon off and get a good rest. Spend time on your family situation."

Vining wasn't planning on taking any days off until she broke the Espinoza murder. She felt it would happen soon. She smiled without amusement. "Do I look that bad?"

Early responded without hesitation. "Frankly, Nan, you do. You look worn out. I can't have an overtired cop out there."

Kissick, to his credit, didn't chime in.

"You're taking the Espinoza case away from me? What about Marvin Li sitting in a cell downstairs?"

"I'm not taking the case from you," Early said. "You're taking your scheduled days off. We'll see what next week brings."

Vining knew better than to argue. "Thanks, Sarge."

As she was gathering her things into her leather case and straightening her desk, Kissick came by.

"Are you okay?" he asked.

Getting her purse from her desk drawer, she said, "I'm fine." She tugged one of her earlobes, showing the earrings he'd given her. She said softly, "I love them. Thanks."

At the In/Out board, she picked up a magnetic tab that said "EOW" for End of Watch, and put it beside her name.

After the initial wave of vanity and ego had passed, she felt relieved to dump the whole Scrappy Espinoza mess into Kissick's lap. She had other work to do.

THIRTY-SEVEN

After walking out the front entrance of the PPD, Vining jaywalked across Garfield. Navigating the lunchtime crowd on the sidewalk in front of the Superior Courthouse, she crossed Walnut with the light. She jogged up the steps of the main branch of the Pasadena Library. Beyond the lacy iron scrollwork screen was a courtyard with a fountain in the middle and stone benches. She heard jazz music coming from the café on the right where people were sitting at small tables, reading and drinking coffee beneath market umbrellas. Normal people, she thought, although she of all people should know that appearances were deceiving.

This pretty spot was across the street from the PPD, but she never came here. Even today, she didn't linger, but kept moving past three-story-tall palm trees, opening one of the library's tall doors, and entering the soaring lobby.

She crossed the fired-tile lobby floor and asked a young man at the information desk where she would find archived newspapers. He directed her to the lower level reference area. She walked through the periodicals room where rows of leather, Mission-style easy chairs were occupied as was each computer workstation tucked into partitioned desks. Some of the people finding respite there looked homeless and some were asleep.

Vining descended a wide staircase with dark wood banisters. The reference area was more austere, filled with microfilm scanners, photocopy machines, and steel cabinets with short drawers that held spools of microfilm. Only one other person was there, a young woman who looked like a student.

Colina Vista did not have its own newspaper, so Vining looked for editions of the *Pasadena Star News* from September, ten years ago. She also grabbed boxes of microfilm of the *Los Angeles Times* from the same period. She sat down at a reader and began to go through them.

Cookie's murder had briefly caught the attention of the *Los Angeles Times*. It was initially front-page news and then got bumped to the second section that covered local news, but interest quickly faded. In contrast, the *Star News* obsessively followed the investigation, arrest, and trial with feature articles on the front page. Photos of then-deputy chief Betsy Gilroy were second only to those of Cookie Silva. The grisly murder of a police officer was sufficient to propel the story into the papers, but perky Cookie, tough yet cute, was the reason it stayed there.

Axel Holcomb was taken into custody the morning the murder was discovered. Photos showed him handcuffed in plaid pajamas on which bloodstains were visible as he was led by Gilroy and Sergeant Mike Iverson from the rustic Foothill Museum. Holcomb was a big man, head-and-shoulders taller and twice as broad as Betsy Gilroy.

In Holcomb's mug shot, his long hair was rumpled, as if he'd been asleep. He was wearing the same plaid pajamas and looked as sleepy, confused, and dull as in the photos from when he'd been pulled out of bed. The more notorious among his various scrapes with the law were recounted. Unnamed "friends and neighbors" were quoted.

After Holcomb was questioned by the police, he was released. Betsy Gilroy issued a statement saying there was insufficient evidence to arrest him. A week later, he was questioned again. That time, he confessed and was put away for good.

As Vining reviewed the articles, she learned a surprising fact that made her sit upright from where she'd been leaning toward the screen. Holcomb's I.Q. was 78, indicating well-below-average intelligence.

Why hadn't Kissick mentioned that Holcomb was mentally slow? She felt certain he would have mentioned it if Gilroy had brought it up. Gilroy had found it important to describe to Kissick an old incident about Holcomb roughhousing at a public pool, but had neglected to reveal a detail as germane as his mental capacity. A mentally slow person confessing to murder can't help but raise suspicions that the suspect was railroaded by cagey police and prosecutors. Maybe Gilroy had taken enough heat because of the confession and simply wanted to let sleeping dogs lie.

A public defender had represented Holcomb. Vining didn't recognize the attorney's name. While she knew many fine public defenders, many were too overworked to do a thorough job. There were bad apples, as in any profession.

Vining was familiar with the prosecutor. She was tough and had sent lots of people to prison, but she had integrity. Vining didn't believe that she'd have knowingly sent an innocent man to death row. Yet, the prosecutor had since moved up the ranks in the D.A.'s office. Having won big trials had helped her career, just as having snapped the cuffs on a monster had helped Betsy Gilroy's.

Both the prosecution and defense had agreed on certain details. Around eleven o'clock on a September night, Cookie Silva had left her friends on the street in front of the bar in Arcadia, had driven up the lonely road to the Foothill Museum, and had parked her Nissan Sentra in the gravel parking lot.

Axel Holcomb was asleep in the back room of the log cabin that housed the museum. He was awakened by noises. He got out of bed, looked out the window in his room, and saw a dim light coming through the openings between the slats of the old barn that was near the cabin. The big barn door was ajar. He put on his slippers and crept to the barn in the moonlight. He recognized Cookie's personal car. It wasn't the first time that he'd happened upon this situation. Cookie often arranged for trysts with her boyfriend during the middle of the night. Holcomb had often slipped out of bed and into the shadows of the barn to watch. He liked to watch.

The barn was lined with old corrals. The hull of a Model T Ford was just inside the barn door. Holcomb dashed the few feet from the door to the safety of the old car—his normal hiding place. He saw Cookie in the barn.

The middle of the tale is where the two versions diverge.

Both sides agreed upon the end. After Cookie was dead, a blood-splattered Holcomb ran from the barn, leaving bloody footprints, and returned to his bed. He pulled the covers over his head and huddled there, eventually falling asleep. At ten the next morning, the couple who runs the museum arrived to find the log cabin locked. The husband went into the barn where a spare key was hidden and came upon Cookie's body, tied by her ankles, dangling from the rafters. The police arrived in minutes. They roused the still-sleeping Holcomb and took him in.

When Holcomb confessed a week after the murder, he said that he had come upon Cookie, who was in the barn alone. She had lit a Coleman lantern that was usually kept there and was sitting on an old quilt spread out on the ground. She appeared to be waiting for someone. She saw Holcomb enter the barn and hide behind the Model T. Cookie became outraged. She was known for her in-your-face personality and began yelling at Holcomb, taunting him, insulting him, accusing him of stalking her. Holcomb became enraged and ran from the shadows, wielding a knife he'd taken from the kitchenette in his room.

Holcomb slugged Cookie, knocking her out. He took off her clothes. He found a length of cord that was kept in the barn and tied her wrists. He then tied her ankles and hoisted her into the air. She had awakened by then and began screaming and yelling. He silenced her by putting duct tape from the cabin over her mouth. While she was hanging upside down, he slit her throat.

In closing statements, Holcomb's defense presented a different chain of events.

Awakened by noises, Holcomb had slipped into the barn and hid behind the old car. A fully clothed man whom Holcomb had never seen before was leaning over Cookie, tying her wrists behind her back. She was limp on the ground, lying on a patchwork quilt. The Coleman lantern was lit. The man tied her ankles with a cord. His back was to the Model T and to Holcomb.

Cookie awakened then and began hurling insults, though not at Holcomb, at the man, calling him a freak and a psycho. He threw the cord over a rafter, hoisting Cookie up by her ankles. He cut a length of duct tape from a roll and put it over her mouth. He then grabbed her from behind and slit her throat.

Holcomb screamed and jumped up from behind the

Model T. The man turned and saw him. He ran, the knife in his hand. The knife was not found.

Holcomb rushed to Cookie, seeking to help her.

She was thrashing wildly. He couldn't find anything to use to cut her down. Blood flew everywhere, including onto Holcomb. Soon, it was over and Cookie was still. Terrified, Holcomb ran back to his room.

The defense claimed that Betsy Gilroy and Colina Vista P.D. sergeant Ernie Bautista, who was also in the interview room, intimidated Holcomb into signing a confession that they wrote for him. An attorney was not present. Gilroy said that Holcomb didn't request one.

The *Pasadena Star News* printed the composite sketch of the man Holcomb said he'd seen fleeing the barn. Holcomb described him as about six feet tall, medium build, twenty to twenty-five years old, with light brown hair. The composite sketch showed an apple-cheeked man with narrow eyes and a thin upper lip. It was a miserable piece of work, minimalist to the point of absurdity, yet Vining saw the essence of T. B. Mann.

Was Caspers correct? Was she so obsessed with T. B. Mann that she was seeing him everywhere?

She needed more information. She wanted the details that had never made it into the newspapers. She wanted to talk to Betsy Gilroy, but not yet. Right now, she would search out Mike Iverson and Ernie Bautista, the Colina Vista P.D. sergeants involved in the case. She had many questions, but one in particular dogged her. Why did Holcomb confess?

THIRTY-EIGHT

*C*olina Vista P.D. Sergeant Mike Iverson wasn't hard for Vining to track down. The Pasadena P.D. had close ties to the Colina Vista P.D. Vining found a veteran PPD officer who told her that Iverson had retired and was living in Montrose, a small city near Pasadena. She didn't have the same luck finding Sergeant Ernie Bautista. She'd had to call the CVPD for information about him. She learned he'd also retired but had moved to New Mexico. The staff assistant she spoke with wouldn't reveal his phone number. Vining would track him down later.

Shortly, she was on the 210 freeway heading west, making the quick trip to Iverson's house in Montrose. He was home and willing to see her now.

Montrose was another bedroom community of Los Angeles that was desperately trying to hang on to its small-town flavor, fighting off chain restaurants and big-box stores. Vining exited the 210 at Ocean View and headed south. She finally found Florencita Court. She spotted Iverson's house by the pickup truck parked on the curb in front that had his business name painted on the door: Waterscapes. Custom ponds. Fountains. Water features. The PPD officer had told her that Iverson had started the Waterscapes business after retiring.

The Iversons lived in a well-maintained 1970s ranch-style house on a spacious corner lot surrounded by a white picket fence. At one time, the large front yard had probably been a lush grass lawn. Today, the grass was restricted to a small corner and the rest of the ground was planted with drought-resistant native plants in large amoeba-shaped beds. A natural-looking stream flowed beneath a willow tree, burbling around rocks and boulders before spilling into a pond. It was an excellent advertisement for Iverson's water feature business.

Vining admired the rambling stream as she walked up the flagstone path to the front door. Upon a closer look, she saw that the rocks and boulders were cleverly constructed fakes.

She rang the doorbell and Mike Iverson answered, greeting her with a hearty handshake.

"Detective Vining. Nice to meet you. Come in."

"Thanks for seeing me on such short notice."

"Don't mention it. Would you like a cup of coffee? I just made some."

"I would, thank you."

"Come inside."

Iverson had lost most of his hair, making his face appear even rounder. His remaining hair was sprinkled with gray and cropped short. He had a broad, rectangular smile that seemed to take up the lower half of his face, and animated blue eyes, the bright whites exuding vigor. He was about five-eight and was trim in clean Dickies dungarees, blue-and-yellow windowpane-print Oxford cloth shirt, and heavy work boots. He radiated good humor.

To Vining, he seemed to be one of those people possessed of preternatural good spirits. She'd come across a few such souls in her life. She wondered how they did it. Everyone had their share of hard knocks in life—some more than others—but certain people seemed to take them in stride and to keep smiling. Vining didn't consider herself a morose person, although she'd had her moments over the past two years. Still, she was a bit in awe of the happy people. What was their secret? Perhaps it was just a different form of neurosis.

She followed Iverson into the kitchen. The house was neat and well appointed, but neither fancy nor fussy.

He grinned as he poured coffee into mismatched mugs—one from the New York New York hotel in Vegas and the other decorated with an infant's photo and "I Love Grandpa."

"How long have you been retired, Mike?"

"About seven years now."

"Do you ever miss police work?"

"Sure, there are parts about it I miss. Cream or sugar?"

"Black."

"Me, too. Well, you have a ways to go until you turn in your badge."

Vining knew that one day she would retire and that also one day she might feel differently about this job she loved, but right now, she couldn't imagine doing anything other than what she was doing—good crime fighting.

Grinning, he handed her the "I Love Grandpa" mug without thought. "Let's go out back. I'll show you my garden. Do you like peaches and plums? I'll pick you some. My wife used to make jam, but ran out of time this year and the fruit's falling on the ground." He grabbed a paper grocery bag and led the way from the kitchen through the dining room and out sliding doors to the patio.

The large lot had an old-fashioned kidney-shaped swimming pool that had been updated with colorful tile and a dark gray lining. It was surrounded by a child-protective fence. There were fruit trees on one side of the long yard: peaches, apricots, plums, and lemons. Tomatoes, summer squash, chilies, cucumbers, and Japanese eggplant grew in raised beds. The rest of the yard was planted with California natives and a small patch of grass.

Vining sipped coffee and followed Iverson as he picked the last fruit of the season and talked about Axel Holcomb.

"I grew up in Colina Vista and knew Axel and his brother from when we were little kids. I was in the same class as his brother, who was on the high school football team with me. Axel was three years younger." He handed her a ripe, black-skinned plum. "That's a Santa Rosa. Delicious."

Vining took the fruit and held it to her nose. "This smells like an actual, bona fide plum. Not like the ones you find in the supermarket."

"Wait until you have one of these peaches."

Vining handed the plum to Iverson and said, "Newspaper articles around the time of Cookie's murder had stories about Axel getting into trouble and the locals being afraid of him."

Iverson laughed dismissively. "Axel was a child in a big man's body. He used to get into trouble because he didn't realize how strong he was. He thought he was one of the kids, but he was a grown man. He had a temper, but only when provoked. Some of the local jerks—teenagers, college kids—would bait him. Make fun of him. Play mean jokes. Over the years, I pulled Axel off some guy or another on numerous occasions."

Vining had thought the newspaper stories had been hard on Axel. "There's a story about Axel as a teenager having almost drowned a girl at a public pool."

Iverson shook his head. "He didn't almost drown her. Axel was horsing around with some girls at the pool and he held a girl's head under water a little bit. Axel's brother, who was working as a lifeguard, got him to let her go. Axel wasn't trying to hurt her. He just didn't know when to stop. The part that no one remembers is that after Axel realized what he'd done, he sobbed like a baby and couldn't stop apologizing to the girl. She was fine. It was over in a minute.

"Because of things like that, he got an unfair reputation in town. He was a sweet guy at heart. Not a sicko. What was done to Cookie, that was a whole other kind of sick. Hanging her upside down, slitting her throat, and letting her bleed out—that's evil."

Vining observed, "It does take a certain kind of bad man to pull that off."

"Axel wasn't like that," Iverson said. "The couple who run the Foothill Museum gave Axel that job as a favor to his family. It worked out great for a couple of years. Axel took care of the place. Opened and closed it. No problems until Cookie decided the barn was a good place to meet her boyfriend."

Vining said, "When the murder was discovered, Axel was brought in for questioning. He was released for lack of evidence. A week later, Betsy Gilroy hauled him in again. That time, he confessed. What happened?"

Iverson twisted a plump peach so ripe it easily released its grip from the branch. He held the fruit in his palm and studied it, his mind seeming to travel as he gently ran his thumb across the fuzzy skin. He let out a long sigh.

Vining realized that in spite of his cheerful demeanor, the ghosts still haunted. Every cop who'd been around the block a few times had them, the one or two cases that stood out from the thousands he or she'd been involved with, the ones that didn't sit right and that never would. Justice had not been done. The bad guy had gotten away.

Iverson gently placed the peach inside the bag on top of the others. He looked at Vining. His eyes were still bright blue, but darkness had crept in behind them, a darkness that hadn't dimmed the hue, but had dimmed his spirit.

"When we first interviewed Axel, the day we found the body, both Betsy and I believed Axel was telling the truth about having seen an unidentified man kill Cookie. Given the evidence, we could paint a picture of Axel having done it, but . . ." Iverson's voice trailed off.

Vining said, "So Gilroy agreed that Axel didn't have it in him to do something like that."

"She told me so. Killing someone accidentally in a fight, maybe, but not that. Betsy and I agonized over it. Plus, Axel liked Cookie. Everyone liked Cookie. You wanted to wring her neck sometimes, but she was a very engaging, lovable girl." He made a quick movement with his hand and modified his comment. "Woman."

"Did anyone other than Axel know that Cookie met her boyfriend in that barn?"

"It came out later that one of the younger officers who used to go out drinking with Cookie knew. He got into trouble for not having said anything."

"I've heard Cookie described as headstrong," Vining said. "Gilroy mentored her to help straighten her out. She secretly met her boyfriend in that barn, but she must have done things that people knew about."

Iverson smirked. "Yes, she did. Cookie was a lot of fun and generally was a good cop, but her mouth got her into trouble. She liked to pretend that she was a rebel. She had a couple of adverse comments in her files for conduct unbecoming. Once she was smart-mouthed with a man after she'd pulled him over for rolling through a stop sign and he got testy with her. Another time, she made a crack about another officer in front of a citizen. I'd heard that she'd talked herself out of a DUI in Pasadena once."

Vining rolled her eyes.

"Cookie probably would have washed out if it hadn't have been for Betsy. Their relationship went beyond the professional. Betsy said that Cookie reminded her of herself when she was young. I'd heard stories from PPD guys who knew Betsy back in the day, about how wild she was. I don't know what kept Betsy going during those first days after we found Cookie. She was . . . crushed."

"Gilroy was the deputy chief then. Didn't the chief give her any heat for shielding a problematic officer?"

Iverson made a face like the notion was ridiculous. "Watching out for your friends was the status quo under Ben Stevens, who was the chief then. Stevens was an old-school small-town police chief. He fixed parking tickets. Got friends and friends of friends out of scrapes. He was thick with the movers and shakers in town, playing golf, going fishing, and drinking at the country club. Rumors were that they greased his palms. I never saw it. That said, Stevens lived in a very nice house and he and his wife had a brand-new Cadillac every year. One of his buddies owned a Cadillac dealership. Chief Stevens was not into rocking the boat and he didn't like being bothered with day-to-day police business. He'd been talking about retiring for years. When the then-deputy chief retired before he did, he was annoyed that he had to actually work and recruit someone.

"So in comes Betsy Gilroy, bright-eyed, bushy-tailed, and ambitious. She took over. Chief Stevens couldn't have been happier. She'd only been on the job a few months when Cookie was murdered."

"Were you interested in being deputy chief?"

Iverson winced and shrugged at the same time in a gesture that Vining interpreted as a yes.

"I already had a foot out the door," Iverson said. "I'd

already started the water feature business in my spare time."

Vining nodded as she thought. "So the day Axel confessed, why had Gilroy brought him in for questioning again?"

"I don't know. I was off that day. She grabbed a sergeant, Ernie Bautista, and picked up Axel. Next thing I hear, Axel's in jail."

"How did the confession come about?"

Iverson picked one last peach and moved to the lemon tree. "Only Betsy, Bautista, and Axel Holcomb know what went on in that interview room."

"Doesn't the Colina Vista P.D. videotape interviews?"

"Bautista said they couldn't get the equipment to work."

"Not even an audio recording?"

"Nope."

"That's odd," Vining said. "Gilroy came up through the ranks of the PPD where making recordings is the norm. Even our patrol officers carry cheap digital audio recorders."

"All Bautista and Betsy would say is that they'd put Axel through a tough interrogation and finally broke him down. They said that the D.A. forbid them to discuss it."

"Did Axel ask for an attorney?"

"Apparently not."

Vining frowned as she followed him into the vegetable garden. "What's Bautista's history?"

"He was a twenty-five-year veteran on the force. One of Chief Stevens's hires. He retired shortly after Axel was convicted."

"What about Axel's family? Didn't they protest?"

"His mother did, but she didn't have the money to hire a big-gun defense attorney."

"What about his brother, your old football team-mate?"

"He'd been dead for a couple of years. He was an insurance salesman. Had a little agency in town. Had a cerebral aneurysm at his desk."

"The community?"

"Everyone was glad to have someone in jail for the murder. The city council and the mayor were delighted to put it behind them and to let Colina Vista slip into obscurity again. Few people were sorry to see Axel gone. Like I said, people were leery of him. After Betsy and the chief paraded Axel as their man, the citizens lined up behind them."

"Chief Stevens was on board?"

"Almost everyone was on board. Let's be honest. The evidence put Axel at the scene. The circumstances of the confession weren't ideal, but it had been witnessed by two veteran police officers who had spotless records. Chief Stevens could care less about a couple of folks' misgivings. He was happy to have the pressure off. Closing that case didn't hurt Betsy any. It made her career. When the chief retired, Betsy was a shoo-in for his job."

"You told me earlier that you didn't think Axel was capable of something so evil. Do you still feel that way?"

"Axel was found guilty."

"But you have doubts."

He straightened, holding three zucchinis. He placed them inside the paper bag that he'd set on the ground. "Axel said something about that night that I can't get out of my mind. You won't read it in any news report, because Betsy and I never spoke of it publicly, and for some reason the defense didn't bring it up during the trial. Axel told us that when Cookie was hanging by her ankles from the rafters, before the killer slit her throat, he'd unzipped his pants and started masturbating. Axel said that as the guy masturbated, he kept saying, 'Do you see this, Officer Silva? Look at this.' "

A chill went down Vining's spine. She flashed back to the kitchen in the house at 835 El Alisal Road. T. B. Mann had peeled a tiny magnet from a set of poetry magnets on the refrigerator, had placed it in his palm, and held it out for her. "Officer Vining, I want you to see this. Do you see this?" Soon after, he'd grabbed the knife from a set in a wood block on the kitchen island and plunged it into her neck, the bullet she fired at him having gone haywire.

Iverson's story confirmed something about T. B. Mann that she'd suspected. *That's the only way you can get off, isn't it, asshole?*

Iverson gritted his teeth. "Then he went over to Cookie, with his penis still hanging out of his pants. He took a folding knife from his pocket and slit her throat. Apparently, he intended to finish masturbating while watching Cookie die, her blood flying everywhere, probably onto him, too. He didn't get the chance because Axel said that's when he screamed and jumped up from his hiding place. The killer went running from the barn with his dick in his hand. Forgive the crass description.

"That whole scenario always stuck in my mind. I never thought that Axel had the smarts or the imagination to make something like that up, especially in such detail. Axel is black or white. There are no shades of gray. So, yes, I have my doubts."

"Did you find the murder weapon?"

"Never did."

"What about other suspects, like the Glendale police officer Cookie was dating?"

"Philip Wondries. Cookie had been dating him for about six months. He was working that night and was able to account for all his time. As far as Axel's story of the stranger, he provided enough of a description to do a decent artist's sketch. We ran it in all the newspapers and on television, but no solid leads came of it.

"We tracked down a couple of guys Cookie had dated during the prior year. One guy in particular interested me. A girlfriend of Cookie's told us about him. Cookie had gone out with him just once, for drinks. She told her girlfriend that he was a creep. Then he started showing up at places where Cookie was."

"Stalking her?"

"Sounded like that. The friend said that Cookie was more annoyed by him than afraid. Cookie wasn't shy. She told him to back off."

"What was his name?"

Iverson sucked in air through his teeth and gazed off, trying to remember. "Teddy something? Teddy Pierce, maybe. It would be in the case files. He worked as a security guard at a shopping center in Pasadena. The Rose City Center, by the freeway. He was the kind of guy who had all the right answers, but it seemed phony to me, and I can't tell you why. He had these intense eyes. Not crazy, like Charles Manson, but cold and calculating. Ice cold. In fact, they were light blue, just like ice. No alibi, but that doesn't mean anything. How many people have alibis for every minute of their day?"

"What did Betsy Gilroy think of him?"

"She didn't talk to him. By the time Cookie's girlfriend had called me to say that she remembered one more guy Cookie had known, Axel had already confessed. No one was interested in hearing about some weirdo Cookie had gone drinking with."

"No one asked Axel if the security guard was the man he'd seen that night with Cookie?"

"Look, they had their killer. They had physical

evidence and Axel's confession. Betsy was the heir apparent to the chief's office. Who was I to go against her?"

Vining knew what that felt like. "Was this the man?" She handed him the photo of Nitro cowering on the floor of a PPD jail cell.

After studying it for a minute, Iverson shook his head, then frowned dubiously. "That's not the guy, but he has those same ice-blue eyes. That's uncanny."

"How about this man?" She took out the artist's rendering of T. B. Mann.

Iverson took a long time looking at the drawing. "Again, we're going back ten years, but I can't say that this *doesn't* look like him. Who is this?"

"That's the man who stabbed me and left me for dead."

"Damn." He took a closer look at the drawing. "He's still loose?"

"Yes."

He gave her the drawing back. "You should have them pull the case files over at the Colina Vista P.D. All the names and photos of everyone we interviewed would be there. But keep in mind that Betsy Gilroy didn't want to hear about this guy then, and I'm sure she doesn't want to hear about him now."

"Any way to go around her?"

"Call and ask for Joanne Temple. She's handled records there for thirty years. Tell her I told you to call. She'll want someone to approve the request. Suggest she ask the watch commander."

"Thanks, Mike."

"I hope you get your guy." He hoisted the grocery bag, testing its weight. "Is this too much? I can't give any more away to our friends and neighbors. They're maxed out."

"That's very generous. Thank you."

"You can make a terrific marinara sauce for dinner with those tomatoes."

She looked at her watch. "Speaking of that, I have to scoot to pick up my daughter from school."

She took the heavy grocery bag that he handed her and gave him the empty "I Love Grandpa" mug. "Thanks, Mike, for everything."

"It was my pleasure."

They headed toward the house.

"Mike, one last thing. Did Cookie ever talk about receiving a pearl necklace as a gift? Did you ever see her wearing a pearl necklace? It would have come down to about here and would have had a little pendant on it, maybe with a dark blue stone."

He let her enter the house ahead of him. "I don't recall such. Her girlfriend might, if you can track her down. Betsy might."

"Was there a necklace on her body?"

He opened the front door and paused with his hand on the doorknob.

She again detected the darkness that lurked behind his sunny disposition. He never mentally returned to that barn, not voluntarily. She recognized his sacrifice. He was doing it for her, because of her own spilled blood and the pursuit of her own madman.

He closed his eyes and pinched the bridge of his nose. He opened his eyes, gratefully returning here, but she detected a shudder. "I remember Cookie's body, the expression on her face and in her eyes, and blood. I remember blood everywhere. I can't tell you whether or not she was wearing a necklace."

Vining shifted the heavy paper bag to shake his hand. She left.

THIRTY-NINE

In the Detectives Section conference room, Jim Kissick passed around photos of Marvin Li, Grace Shipley, and her daughter Meghan that were taken by the surveillance team. Present at the briefing were Sergeant Kendra Early, and Detectives Alex Caspers, Louis Jones, and Doug Sproul.

The women were slender and wearing tight jeans, low-cut snug tops, and high-heeled sandals. Meghan, a college student, had straight hair that fell past her shoulders. It was severely streaked blond. In one photo, she'd been snapped through Love Potion's windows trying on a bridal veil. In another, she held a wedding gown against herself, admiring it in a mirror. Her mother still had a great figure, but her face looked hard. Her shoulder-length hair was as blindingly blond as her daughter's.

There was a shot taken in the driveway of the Shipley home on Newcastle Street. Li was in his wheelchair. Grace was bent over with both arms around his shoulders and was kissing the top of his shaved head.

Kissick passed information gleaned from the PPD's records search.

Caspers lingered over Meghan's photos, especially one in which she was on the sidewalk, wearing tight jeans, her back to the camera.

"I sent the Shipleys' photos and information to Sergeant John Velado of the Sheriff's Asian Gang Task Force,"

Kissick said. "Marvin Li's attorney, Sammy Leung, says that Li and Grace Shipley are having a romantic relationship. Leung tells us that the manager of an apartment building on La Pomelo Road, one block east of Newcastle, is the guy who hired the Aaron's Aarrows human directionals. We talked to the manager. He was nervous, but he insists that he hired Li's arrow guys. Leung says that Li has no knowledge of the guys who arrive after the human directionals leave at midnight and who stay parked on Newcastle until morning. So far, the search of Li's phone records and computer haven't turned up anything suspicious."

"The top guys keep themselves insulated," Early said.

Just then, one of the staff assistants knocked on the open conference room door. "Sorry to interrupt. Detective Kissick, Sammy Leung says he and Marvin Li want to speak with you."

The Coopersmith School sat on a ridge above the junction of the 210 and the short stretch of the 710 that had been constructed in Pasadena. The grassy, tree-shaded property and its stained-wood buildings surrounded by a tall chain-link fence, were a bucolic sip of water for drivers barreling down Pasadena Avenue toward the freeway entrances past the mammoth Huntington Hospital compound.

The two-acre Coopersmith School campus and its woodsy buildings were all that remained standing after a historic church was razed in the 1970s in preparation for the completion of the final six-mile stretch of the 710 freeway. Back then, Cal Trans had bought many homes and properties along the proposed route. Decades later, many of the homes still remained empty and the lots where structures had been razed were still bare as a virulent city-against-city fight raged on in the battle over traffic flow versus preservation of thousands of trees and hundreds of historic homes.

Vining had gone home and switched cars to her Jeep Cherokee as she was no longer on-call. She had to circle the block to get in the queue of SUVs driven by parents waiting to pick up their kids. A school employee stood at the parking lot entrance and directed traffic.

As Vining inched forward, she looked at the Rose City Center across Pasadena Avenue. Mike Iverson said that was where the guy who had piqued his interest in Cookie's murder investigation had worked as a security guard. She would check it out after she picked up Emily.

T. B. Mann working as a security guard made perfect sense to Vining. His M.O. suggested familiarity with police procedures and access to buildings and property. He also had knowledge of officers' work schedules. That wasn't hard to figure out. Gangbangers used cheap police scanners to find out which officers were on the street. T. B. Mann also could have developed contacts within the local police.

As she waited in the queue of cars, she called Joanne Temple at the Colina Vista P.D., as Iverson had instructed. After introducing herself and catching her up on what Iverson was doing, she got to the purpose of her call.

"I chatted with Mike because I'm investigating an assault against a Pasadena police officer that has similarities with the Cookie Silva murder. Mike was very helpful, but he couldn't remember a lot of the details of Cookie's murder, and said I should contact you to see the case files."

Temple's voice was slightly raspy, suggesting that she was an older woman and a longtime smoker. Vining soon learned that the passing years had not affected her fortitude.

"Of course, Detective, but such requests have to be approved by Chief Gilroy."

"I hate bothering the chief with a case that's been closed for years. Perhaps the watch commander could approve it. All I'd need is a half hour at most."

Joanne Temple would not be budged. Vining got the message 'loud and clear. If she was going to get anywhere with the Colina Vista P.D., she had to go through Gilroy. Kissick was right. Gilroy was the queen of Colina Vista.

She thanked Temple for her time and said she'd contact the chief directly. Vining might not find the answers to her questions about Cookie Silva's murder investigation in the case files anyway. She would have to meet with Gilroy face-to-face.

She thought about Iverson's statements about Axel Holcomb not being capable of such a murder and the strange circumstances of Axel's confession. Iverson didn't say anything overtly condemning about Gilroy, but he left ample room for reading between the lines. He also hinted that he was passed over for the deputy chief job that went to the shining outsider, Betsy Gilroy. Vining could see that there was much about Gilroy for longtime CVPD officers to dislike. Iverson didn't seem like a guy who would have a problem with a female boss, but who knows?

The school's traffic monitor finally waved Vining into the parking lot. Among the cluster of teenagers waiting beneath a slatted-wood porch covering was Emily sitting on the edge of a cement block planter. She was animatedly talking to Ken Zhang, who was standing in front of her, his body between her knees. They were holding hands. Emily didn't let go even after she'd spotted Vining. Her demeanor was chilly.

Ken did release Emily's hand and greeted Vining with a quick wave that was not accompanied with a smile.

Pearl Zhang had probably called her son on his cell phone before Vining had exited the front door of her office suite.

Emily picked up her backpack from the planter and slid to the ground. She pointedly kissed Ken on the lips before heading to the car.

Ken turned toward the parking lot.

Vining struggled to keep her anger in check. She said through the open driver's window, "Hi, sweet pea."

Emily uttered a disconsolate "Hi," opened the Jeep's rear door, tossed her pack on the backseat, and stopped just short of slamming the door closed. She flopped onto the front seat, staring straight ahead. Her silence was deafening.

Vining didn't attempt to remedy it. She circled around the parking lot, still in the caravan of cars.

Emily looked longingly at Ken, who was getting into his BMW.

Vining looked at her watching him. She then took a closer look at her daughter. "Where did you get that T-shirt?"

The white, short-sleeved top was printed with a diagonal pattern of multicolored butterflies. The tight, stretchy cotton knit revealed Em's blossoming figure.

Vining frowned at the artwork. It jarringly reminded her of the tattooed butterflies on Marvin Li's torso.

Emily responded without looking at her. "Ken made it in his silk-screen class."

"Where's the blouse you were wearing this morning?"

"In my backpack. I changed in the girls' bathroom. What's the big deal?"

"Put your blouse on over it."

"Why?"

"That T-shirt is too tight."

Emily sneered, "You don't want me to wear it

because Ken gave it to me. I know everything you told Ken's mother." She yelled, "Mom, how can you think that Ken's in a gang?"

The car in front of Vining pulled into the street. It was finally her turn. She took advantage of a small break in the traffic and gunned the Jeep, cutting across three lanes barely in front of the oncoming, speeding cars. A horn blared.

Emily complained, "Do you *have* to do that?"

"I need to make a quick stop here."

"So you drive like you're in hot pursuit? Are you ever *not* a cop? Can't you just be a normal person sometimes?"

Vining found a parking space in front of the supermarket and cut the ignition. She faced her daughter. "One, I've had it with this snippy attitude of yours. Knock it off, right now. Two, I have good reasons for thinking that Ken could be involved with a Chinese gang."

"Good reasons? Because he's Chinese? Because he went to school with a guy who's in a gang? Because his cousin used to be in a gang? Because he doesn't know who his father is?" Emily's voice grew shriller with each question.

"All those reasons, yes. Furthermore, you're too young to be holding hands, kissing, and riding around in a car with a seventeen-year-old boy. I don't care who he is."

"I'm almost fifteen."

"So you keep reminding me. I don't care. I don't want you seeing that boy."

"How can I not see him when we go to the same school? Coopersmith only has two hundred students."

"Emily, don't be smart. You know what I mean. Quit while you're ahead."

Tears started down her face. In spite of the tears, the

girl gave Vining a look so full of loathing that it shocked her.

"Not everyone is a criminal until proven innocent, Mom. I'm not like *you*. I don't go around looking for the worst in people."

Vining raised her index finger. "That does it. You're grounded for a week." She was so angry, she'd bared her teeth. It was more than anger. She felt a wave of helplessness.

"Grounded?" The tears streamed down Emily's face. "Like how?"

It was the first time Vining had been compelled to punish Emily like that. She knew what being grounded meant when she'd been a teenager, but had to think fast to translate it for today's world. She didn't even know if the term was still used. "You're coming straight home after school. No going to the mall or to movies or walking around Old Town." She paused as she thought. "No cell phone other than to call me or your dad or in case of emergency."

"*What?* I can't use my cell phone?"

"Only to call me or your dad or in case of emergency."

"What about text messages?"

"*I said no cell phone.*" Vining didn't think she'd ever been this exasperated. Her fourteen-year-old daughter had gotten to her in a way that hardened criminals hadn't managed to do.

"For a *week*?"

"Emily, this conversation is over. I have to go into the market."

"Why? We shopped yesterday."

"I have to do something."

Emily wiped tears with her hands. She found a small box of tissues in the glove compartment. "Dad's picking me up. I'm staying with him and Kaitlyn until Sunday."

She added defensively, "It's his weekend with me, anyway. I didn't go last time at all, so . . . Kaitlyn will take me to school and pick me up."

Vining had called Wes to discuss the Ken Zhang situation. He said he'd talk it over with Emily the next time they were together, but she didn't know they'd already spoken. "You might have shared this with me sooner. I made all that stew that's been cooking in the crock pot all day."

"When did I have time to tell you? You've been on my case since I got in the car."

"Emily, I don't know where you learned this habit of talking back, but stop it. And by the way, your father and I agree about the Ken Zhang issue."

Vining had told her ex-husband, "We have to stand together on this, Wes."

He said that he agreed, but was worried about their actions having the result of pushing Em into Ken's arms. "You know how we were."

"That's what I'm worried about."

"I think you and Emily could use some space."

Vining realized, for the first time ever, that it was true. Ever since Wes had walked out on them when Emily was two, mother and daughter had been exceptionally close. Vining had fretted that their "two against the world" stance had put an undue burden on her daughter. She knew she depended upon Em too much. Ken Zhang was perhaps merely a catalyst, bringing to light fissures between her and her daughter that had already been there. She wondered when the fracture had started. There came a point when girls tried to differentiate themselves from their mothers and pulled away. That was natural and expected. But something about what was happening between her and Emily felt unnatural. Had her obsession with T. B. Mann polluted even this, her most precious relationship?

She couldn't blame everything that was wrong in her life on T. B. Mann. Like a skilled predator, he'd taken advantage of her weakness, but the weakness had been hers before he'd dug in his talons.

She indulged in a guilty pleasure. Having Emily out of the house for a few days would be a relief. She had a lot on her mind and much to do.

"Ken's not an *issue*. He's a boy."

"Okay, fine. Emily, I asked you to get the blouse you had on this morning and put it on over that T-shirt."

Emily huffed with the melodrama that only a teenage girl could muster. She said sarcastically, "Yes, *ma'am*."

"You just earned another week of being grounded."

"But there's a dance—"

"Emily, keep it up and you'll be grounded until you're eighteen."

Vining got out of the car. She was deeply disturbed about their confrontation. She had spent most of her life trying not to be like her mother. Patsy had gone through men as quickly as she went through bottles of drug-store cologne. She'd generally ignored her two daughters unless there was an opportunity to display them like cute accessories.

Vining swore that Em's life would be different. She'd made sure that Emily had a good relationship with her father. Wes had his faults. More than most men, in Vining's humble opinion. But he deserved credit for being there for his daughter, providing emotional and financial support—after he'd abandoned her, of course.

Vining's focus during Emily's life had been to give her a steady, calm, and secure home. She'd held tightly to the effort not to mimic her life with Patsy. Had the force of her viselike grip led to the same result, another daughter alienated from her mother?

FORTY

The grocery-store manager gave Vining the name and phone number of the security firm the shopping center's property-management company had used for the last fifteen years.

When she returned to the car, Emily had followed her instructions and was wearing the short-sleeved blue blouse she'd been wearing when she'd left the house that morning. Listening to her iPod, she slid her eyes to acknowledge her mother's return.

Vining winked and received a tiny, but welcome quiver of a smile back. She reflected that maybe her bond with Emily was not hopelessly ruptured. Maybe it never could be. Perhaps that was the eternal saga of mother and daughter. As much as Patsy often infuriated her, Vining still made an effort to see her and to honor her birthday and Mother's Day.

Vining turned left onto California Boulevard, heading for Arroyo Parkway and the 110 freeway to head home to Mt. Washington. While Vining was stopped at the light at Fair Oaks, Emily surprised her.

She yanked out one of her ear buds and asked, "When's the last time you saw that house?"

Vining knew without asking that "that" house was the one where T. B. Mann had ambushed her, where the first strand of yarn had been pulled, where her life had started to unravel—the house at 835 El Alisal Road.

Vining had also been thinking of the house. She always did when she was in that neighborhood.

"It's been a while," she replied.

"Have you ever gone back inside?"

"Never."

Just parking across the street from the house was sufficient to take her breath away. Once, she'd tried to walk up the brick path to the front door, just as she had done that Sunday in uniform, responding alone to a simple suspicious-circumstances call in a safe neighborhood that saw little crime. She was only able to make it a few feet down the path before her devil of fear came to call, draining the blood from her extremities, making her hot and chilled at the same time, filling her head with metal shavings that pinged and abraded, leaving room only for a single, compelling thought: *Flee!*

"Let's go," Emily said.

Vining continued on California, past Arroyo Parkway. After a few blocks, she turned right on El Alisal Road, entering a well-kept neighborhood of mostly two-story Colonial Revival or Spanish Revival homes built in the early years of the last century on spacious lots. The streets were lined with trees as old as the homes, with a different type on each block: magnolia, cyprus, elm, and camphor. The camphor trees' expansive branches created a green canopy over those streets. The gentle Midwestern style of the neighborhood was an anomaly in Southern California and thus was a favorite filming location for movies, television, and commercials.

It seemed as if nothing bad could ever happen in this neighborhood. Of course, that made it all the more salacious when something did.

Vining parked at the curb in front of 835 El Alisal Road. The sight of the house alone was enough to incite uneasy feelings. Today, the feeling was enhanced by a For Sale sign that said OFFERED BY DALE DAVID REALTY.

An identical sign had been on the lawn the day Vining had responded to that suspicious circumstances call. T. B. Mann had worn a dark wig and the Brooks Brothers polo shirt to match the realtor's photo on bus benches around town.

Emily stated the obvious. "It's for sale again."

"What happened to the people who just bought it?" Vining asked. "They'd moved in and remodeled."

She had learned that much from Kissick. He'd found out that the new owners had gutted and redone the kitchen. Maybe they'd had plans to do so anyway or maybe they'd tried to remove traces of the crime that had happened there. She wondered if a molecule of her blood remained, having seeped through the grout of the tile floor, missed when the subfloor had been routed, even though the construction crew had likely been given specific instructions to get rid of every speck of blood.

If only it was that easy to eradicate bad karma. Vining wasn't able to get rid of hers. If a clipping of her hair were analyzed, she imagined it being detected there, like traces of arsenic.

She wondered if, while their children had babbled happily at breakfast over bowls of cereal and glasses of juice, the parents had been aware that a ghost shared their table. Along with that molecule of blood that Vining was certain still remained, the ghost of her and T. B. Mann's unfinished business haunted that kitchen.

Probably, they had never thought of her, unless a rude dinner guest had made a comment along the lines of "Wasn't a cop stabbed here?" Not wanting their lovely home to seem tainted, they would brush off the question, perhaps even with a joke, "Her body's still in the broom closet," pour more wine, and change the subject.

"You know, Mom, you could probably get the realtor to let you in."

Vining had considered that. Marvin Li's aunt was right about a ghost following her, but there was more than one. It was time she finally confronted the ghost of her former self that resided at 835 El Alisal Road. "Maybe I will. But not today."

She glanced at Emily, who was looking at the house with sorrow. Em could have been sad simply because she was forbidden to text-message her friends. Still, Vining was suddenly sad herself.

While Vining was looking at her daughter, Em shifted her gaze to meet her mother's. The girl's tears started anew. Vining was aware that Em's emotions were rubbed raw, but suspected that these tears had their genesis in a different tragedy.

She took Emily's hand between both of hers. She found the strength to say to Emily what her mother, Patsy, had never said to her.

"Emily, I'm sorry. I'm sorry for all the pain and distress you've gone through since I last walked inside that house. You had to grow up too fast and shoulder burdens that never should have been placed on you. Part of your childhood was stolen. I'm sorry."

Tears again rolled down Emily's face.

"I don't always show it, Em, but you are the most important thing in my life. You are the best thing in my life."

Emily released a massive sob and threw herself on her mother. Vining stroked her hair and let her cry, her tears soaking into Vining's blouse.

"It's okay, Mom." The girl's face was mashed against Vining's chest and she could barely make out what Emily was saying. "None of it happened on purpose."

Vining said, "I know," without sincerity. It had all happened on purpose, according to T. B. Mann's evil plan. A taunting childhood rhyme entered her mind. *All the king's horses and all the king's men . . .*

She ignored it. "I will fix this. By hook or by crook, I will make things right again."

Emily pushed herself up and grabbed more of the tissues. "By what?"

"By hook or by crook . . . It's an old saying of Granny's." Vining smiled. "I don't know what it really means other than 'in spite of any obstacle.' "

"Mom, maybe things can't be the way they were, but we can still be all right."

Vining smiled at her daughter who was wise beyond her years. "That's a good thought, Em, and you're right." She started the car. "But you're still grounded."

Emily groaned.

FORTY-ONE

At home, Vining had a cup of the stew and packed the rest into the refrigerator. Wes came to pick up Emily and Vining was able to offload some of Iverson's homegrown fruits and vegetables. After Em had left with her dad, Vining freshened up and headed for Colina Vista.

She took surface streets to Colina Vista Boulevard and drove through the center of town toward Angeles National Forest. After passing the civic center and small commercial district in the flatlands, the boulevard started going up. She drove through a residential neighborhood of nice homes on big lots. Farther into the foothills, the road became curvy and pine trees appeared. The homes varied between cozy wood-and-stone cottages and large, woodsy new homes. She passed traces of scorched earth and skeletons of trees and other vegetation, reminders of a brush fire that had recently licked across the hills and valleys. Hundreds of homes had been threatened, but none were lost, as the firefighters and weather worked in tandem. Homemade signs thanking the firefighters and police were affixed to fence posts and tree trunks.

A sign announced that the elevation was 3,000 feet, the next services were fifty miles away, and chains were required in snowy weather. Another sign said that it was fifteen miles to the Mount Wilson Observatory.

The road narrowed and the houses disappeared. An easy-to-miss sign on the road said FOOTHILL MUSEUM and offered an arrow. Just beyond, another sign marked the boundary of the Angeles National Forest.

Vining turned onto a gravel road through scruffy pine trees and sprawling sycamores. The road was barely wide enough for two compact cars to pass. At the end was a cabin of logs and river rock. A gravel parking area was in front. The cabin was on one side of a clearing, suggesting the absence of a building that had previously been there: the barn where Cookie Silva had been murdered.

A carved wooden sign attached beneath the eaves of the front porch said FOOTHILL MUSEUM. FORMER SITE OF THE HIKER'S HIDEAWAY. The posted hours indicated that the museum was hardly ever open. She was lucky to find it open now, but it was just about to close.

She got out of the car and took a deep breath of the pine-scented air. The temperature was cooler. The silence was broken only by the songs of birds in the trees. It was a beautiful spot—remote, quiet, and serene. An ideal location for a madman to take his time torturing and murdering a young female cop.

She walked up steps of split pine trunks that had hollows worn into them. She crossed the porch and opened an old screen door that had a wooden frame. A cowbell attached to it jangled. A thick wooden door painted forest green was held open by an iron doorstop shaped like a squirrel.

It was at least ten degrees cooler inside. The ceiling was wooden with exposed beams of round pine boughs and so low that Vining could touch it with outstretched fingers. Small, deep windows were set into the thick walls. Many windows had their original glass that was marked with bubbles and ripples. A large bar where presumably alcohol was once served took up an entire wall. It was of gray river rock with a lacquered wooden slab on top. Now the ancient cash register in the corner was only used to ring up the few souvenirs for sale: stuffed brown bears, fake Indian arrowheads, trail maps, and slender books by local historians.

Cases displayed antique tools, household implements, and toys from the pioneer era. Mannequins behind glass were dressed in period costumes: a pioneer husband and wife; a trapper in a beaver coat with a shotgun over his shoulder, holding a string of pelts.

Vining saw a low doorway off the back and figured it led to the room where Axel Holcomb had lived. Through that doorway now passed an elderly man and woman. The man was stooped and shuffled when he walked. The woman was straight-backed and petite. The passing years had made them the same height. Her silver hair was neatly coiffed. She was wearing a cardigan sweater over a floral-print shirt tucked into a slim skirt. He had on a plaid flannel shirt tucked into khaki pants. His wide leather belt had a large, oval silver buckle imprinted with a complicated pattern that Vining couldn't make out.

The couple reminded Vining of a set of vintage salt and pepper shakers that her grandmother had.

The man spoke first, in a wavering voice, having already seen the badge on Vining's belt. "Hello. What can we do for you?"

She handed him her card. "Hello. I'm Detective Nan Vining from the Pasadena Police. Who do I have the pleasure of speaking with?"

"I'm Norton Van Allen and this is my wife, Tressa."

"Very nice to meet you. I'm hoping to get some background information on the Cookie—"

Mrs. Van Allen interrupted with, "Oh, dear," and a hand to her cheek. She wore rings with large diamonds and other gemstones. A diamond and ruby cross was around her neck.

The lavish jewelry reminded Vining of her grandmother.

Mr. Van Allen shuffled forward. His voice was unsteady but his gaze was not. "Now, why would you want to open that can of worms?"

"It might help with a case I'm working on in Pasadena. There's a grieving family who would like closure." Vining claimed that she didn't believe in closure. She didn't believe that crime victims and families could, one fine, bright day in the future, permanently deposit what had happened into the past, but most people did. Yet she continued to chase it. She was not immune to the idea that her motives might be based in the less noble arena of vengeance.

"I won't take more than ten minutes," she added. "Were either of you around at that time?"

The old guy wasn't buying it. "Does Chief Gilroy know you're here?"

"Absolutely." Vining guessed that the chief would know in short order. "Did you and your wife live in Colina Vista at the time of the murder?"

"We've lived here for sixty years," Mr. Van Allen said.

Mrs. Van Allen shook her head. "Who could ever forget what happened to that girl? She was such a sweet, pretty thing. It was very hard on everyone in our little village."

"Did you work at the Foothill Museum then?"

"Oh, yes," Mrs. Van Allen said. "We've run the museum ever since it opened. I used to come here by myself and was never afraid. There was a period of time when *he* was here, too."

Her husband glowered, not happy with his wife being forthcoming.

"You're speaking of Axel Holcomb?" Vining asked.

"It was a long time before I came back," Mrs. Van Allen said. "But there was no one else to take care of the museum and keep it open for the schoolchildren. I don't come here by myself anymore. Norton comes with me now."

She looked around the area as if it were evaporating before her eyes. "I don't know what will happen to this place when we're gone. The people who own the land are getting up in years, too. Their children . . . No one cares about tradition anymore."

Mr. Van Allen patted his wife's arm.

Vining smiled and said, "The two of you don't look like you're going anywhere anytime soon. You're the picture of health."

"Well, we're here today," Mr. Van Allen said. "We'll give you a little tour, since Chief Betsy said it was okay."

Mrs. Van Allen said, "We just love our police chief. She's one of the best things to happen to Colina Vista."

Mr. Van Allen raised his hands. "This is pretty much the whole museum, right here. Guess you're more interested in where he lived. That's in the back."

They walked through the low doorway and entered a short hallway. At the end was a door that led outside. On the right was the door to a restroom. A sign on it indicated it was unisex. A door on the left was closed.

Mrs. Van Allen opened it, gesturing for Vining to enter while she stayed in the hallway. Mr. Van Allen followed Vining inside.

The small room was now a storeroom. There was a sink, a mirror, and a desk. Shelves were bracketed to the wall. Boxes of office supplies and the souvenirs for sale in the museum were on the shelves. Mops, brooms, a bucket, and a plastic carrier with cleaning supplies stood in a corner. It was a corner room, and there were windows on both outside walls.

Mrs. Van Allen leaned into the doorway and pointed. "That's where his bed used to be." She added, through clenched teeth, "It was covered in blood."

Vining asked, "Mrs. Van Allen, were you ever afraid of Axel when you were with him by yourself?"

She blinked as she thought. Her eyelids were adorned with pearled blue shadow. "No, I can't say that I was ever afraid. Axel was always nice and polite to me. I heard the stories that went around town about the trouble and fights he got into, but I never had a lick of a problem with him."

Vining peered out one of the windows. "When he confessed to that terrible murder, what did you think about that?"

"We were shocked," Mr. Van Allen said. "Everyone was."

Vining stepped from the room and walked to the back door. The bolt lock was engaged. "Is this the door that Axel went out that night?"

"Yes." Mrs. Van Allen pointed. "He went right through there."

Vining unlocked the door, crossed a small porch, and went down steps to the bare ground.

The Van Allens followed.

Joining Vining on the packed dirt at the bottom of the steps, Mrs. Van Allen seemed eager to share lurid details. She pointed. "There was a bloody footprint right there. Cookie's blood was on the doorknob."

Several yards away was a clearing covered with dry grass. Vining walked to stand in the middle of it. "Is this where the barn was?"

The Van Allens moved closer but stayed on the clearing's edge.

"Yes, ma'am," Mr. Van Allen said. "The city tore it down."

"Did either of you ever think that maybe Axel didn't do it?"

The couple exchanged a surprised glance. He responded, "What kind of a ridiculous question is that? Of course he did it. He confessed."

Vining said, "Sometimes people confess to crimes they haven't committed."

Mr. Van Allen said, "Maybe so, but that's not the situation here."

Mrs. Van Allen said, "I have to say that Axel did a good job. Did everything he was told. He kept this place spic-and-span. It hasn't looked that good since."

FORTY-TWO

Jim Kissick and Deputy D.A. Mireya Dunn met with Marvin Li and his attorney Sammy Leung in the PPD interview room.

Leung was in his sixties, with salt-and-pepper hair that was expensively cut, and an Italian suit that was also expensively cut, but he had craggy, pitted skin that made him look like a tough guy.

Marvin Li wore a dark blue, long-sleeved shirt that covered his tattoos except for a small triangle that peeked above the top shirt button. The braided tails of his mustache were tied up with dark rubber bands and not dangling with sparkly ribbons. He wore black slacks. While he'd removed the steel drums from his ears, the lobes had been so stretched, light was visible through the empty holes. He was deferential and subdued. His attorney did the talking.

"Mr. Li would like immunity from prosecution," Leung began.

"Immunity." Deputy D.A. Dunn repeated the word with a hint of derision. She was in her late thirties and was originally from Venezuela. Standing not quite five feet tall and with a round figure, she wore her black hair in a bob with bangs that reached the middle of her forehead. Her nickname was "the Fireplug," although "firecracker" would have been a more apt description of her personality and passion for justice. She stood with her arms crossed over her chest. Her head was nearly even with Kissick's, who was sitting.

"Immunity's a big request," Dunn said. "What does Marvin have for us that merits immunity?"

"Mr. Li knows where Victor Chang is hiding," Leung said. "He's confident he can convince Victor to turn himself in and to confess to murdering Scrappy Espinoza."

"Tell us where Chang is," Kissick said. "We'll go pick him up."

Li shook his head. "It's not that simple. I'm the only one he'll talk to."

"You'll wear a wire," Dunn said.

Li again shook his head. "No wire. That won't fly with

Victor. He'll know. Let me go where he's staying and talk to him alone. He'll come with me. I guarantee it."

"How can you guarantee that?" Kissick asked.

"I know Victor. He'll listen to me."

"You need to meet him someplace public, where we can protect you," Kissick said.

"Can't do that," Li said.

Kissick looked at Dunn who threw up hands that were as small as a child's. "Marvin . . . Sammy . . . You haven't given us anything here. You want immunity, but for what? Give me something I can work with."

"How about you tell us something about this." Kissick showed them the surveillance photos of Grace Shipley and her daughter Meghan being affectionate with Li in front of the Love Potion. "Marvin, what's your relationship with Grace Shipley and why do you have guys posted on her street twenty-four/seven? They're not there to advertise apartments. Don't even bother telling us that lie again."

Li was stone-faced.

Leung said, "Mr. Li and Mrs. Shipley are having a romantic relationship, as Mr. Li has already explained to you, Detective. Meghan has been having problems with a young man with whom she terminated a relationship. He's been bothering her. Mr. Li sent his employees to Newcastle Street to watch out for Meghan's safety."

"Did Meghan file a police report or request a restraining order?" Dunn asked.

"Not yet," Leung said. "She'll be doing so soon. Today."

Dunn balled her fists at her sides. "Marvin, this is bullshit. Stop wasting our time. Are you going to give us something to bargain with or not?"

Marvin hooked his fingers for Leung to move closer. They spoke quietly in Chinese. Leung sat back and nodded at Li, who said, "I'll show you the house where Victor is."

"That's progress," Kissick said, leaving the room. "Let's go."

FORTY-THREE

*W*hen *Vining* showed up at the Colina Vista police station, she was immediately ushered into Chief Gilroy's office, as if the chief had been expecting her.

Anita, the chief's secretary, closed Gilroy's door after Vining had entered. Gilroy was busy signing letters at her desk and did not look up when she commanded, "Detective Vining, please sit down."

Vining took one of the chairs facing her desk.

The chief continued to work as if Vining wasn't there. She was in uniform. Vining guessed she had an official function that day.

Several minutes passed during which Vining listened to Gilroy's pen scrape across sheets of stationery. The chief finally gathered the pages, tapped the edges together, and walked them to her secretary.

Again closing the door, she returned to sit behind her desk, back straight, hands on the chair arms, expression somber. She wasted no time in getting to the point.

"Detective Vining, I've already had a lengthy conversation about the Cookie Silva murder with your colleague, Detective Kissick. He reached the conclusion that Cookie's murder is in no way related to those other attacks on policewomen. I realize that you have a lot personally invested in tracking down the man who stabbed you. I'm sensitive to the pain you've gone through and that you're still going through. However, you must understand that there is nothing in Colina Vista that will help you in your quest."

She paused. Vining was about to speak when Gilroy went on. "Detective, little goes on in this city that I don't know about. I don't appreciate you going behind my back and upsetting our citizens by opening old wounds. Mr. Van Allen called me, troubled about your visit to the Foothill Museum. Then our lady who's in charge of records tells me you tried to gain access to the Cookie Silva case files without going through me."

"I know how busy you—"

Gilroy silenced her with a raised hand. "I am busy, but I do make appointments. I also know you met with Mike Iverson. I know what he told you without having to ask. I sidelined him in Cookie's murder investigation for good reason and he still carries a grudge. Frankly, I'm somewhat miffed that you felt it necessary to go around me. I am more than happy to tell you and show you everything you need to know about Cookie's murder, but I'm extremely busy right now and honestly, I don't know what else I can tell you that I haven't already gone over with Detective Kissick."

Vining was briefly cowed by the chief's diatribe and didn't know how to begin. Still, she was determined not to leave until she'd asked Gilroy the questions that nagged her.

In the silence, Gilroy softened. "Detective Vining, I can't imagine how horrible it must have been to have gone through what you did. I wish I had more for you here. I've admitted that my investigation into Cookie's murder was not perfect. When it happened, I was new and arrogant and I was in over my head. That being said, we got our man."

Vining nodded. She looked out the windows behind the chief's desk at the foothills that were turning deep blue and violet as twilight descended. She wondered if Sergeant Early and Kissick were right. Was it pointless for her to study drawings found in a mute transient's backpack as if they were the Dead Sea Scrolls? Her mind was swirling with so many thoughts that she couldn't separate logic from her gut feelings. She needed time and quiet to sort things out. Still, she knew she'd never rest until she at least asked Gilroy her few questions. The chief certainly couldn't begrudge her that.

"Chief, thank you for your time and your candor. I realize I'm digging up painful memories for this community and police department."

Gilroy gave her a small regal nod.

"If I can steal a few more minutes. There are a couple of issues that Detective Kissick didn't raise. If I could explore them with you, it would help me reconcile matters in my mind."

Gilroy didn't stop her, so she continued.

"This is the artist's rendering done based upon Axel Holcomb's description of the man he said he saw slit Cookie's throat." She set the crude drawing on Gilroy's desk. "This is a sketch of the man who attacked me." She set the sketch done based upon her recollections of T. B. Mann beside it.

Gilroy gave them a perfunctory glance, her expression enigmatic.

"Mike Iverson told me that there was another person of interest in Cookie's murder. This guy had seen Cookie socially and had been bothering her with unwanted attention. He was working as a security guard at a shopping center in Pasadena. Iverson thought his name was Teddy Pierce. I will find out his name once the security firm goes through their records. Instead of waiting, if you'd let me examine Cookie Silva's case files, I can find out who he is right now. There might be a photo of him in your files. Maybe he's the man depicted in these two drawings."

Vining thought she saw Gilroy's posture stiffen. "I can get that information for you, Detective."

Vining didn't want to press her luck by asking for a timeframe. "Thank you, Chief."

Gilroy pushed back her chair, as if concluding the meeting.

"Chief, may I ask one more thing?"

The fine lines around Gilroy's mouth deepened. "Certainly."

"In your conversation with Detective Kissick, I'm curious about why you never mentioned that Axel Holcomb has a subnormal I.Q."

Gilroy raised her eyebrows. "I didn't mention it? I guess it didn't occur to me." She smiled and shook her head as if she couldn't offer any further explanation.

"Everyone I spoke to who knew Axel and a lot of the newspaper articles said that no one could believe he was capable of such a terrible murder. Mike Iverson said that you and he agreed that Axel hadn't done it. Then, you decided to question him again and somehow, he confessed."

"What's your point, Detective?" Gilroy's eyes bored into her.

"I wonder what motivated you to change your opinion about Axel. And Axel's confession . . . I'm certain there were questions raised—"

Gilroy's hand came up and she pointed at Vining. "Are you that desperate to build a serial killer theory around what happened to you? You're so possessed by this crazy idea of yours that you come into *my* police station and question not just *my* integrity, but the integrity of my police officers, our city government, our citizens, the prosecutor, the judge, and the jury?

"You should know something, Detective Vining. I have plenty of contacts in the Pasadena P.D. They talk about you plenty. They speculate that when you died, maybe you brought some of the dark side back with you. They think you're a scary person, Detective. There are questions about whether you're fit for duty. Your visit here makes me wonder whether there's truth to the gossip. You come in here with your sad history and your gruesome scars that you don't even try to hide and make these scurrilous accusations. I'm the chief of police in this town and I say that this conversation is over."

Vining silently picked up the two artists' sketches and returned them to her leather folder. Reaching inside her jacket pocket, she took out Nitro's battered and scratched pearl necklace. The one she'd stolen from him. She flung it onto Gilroy's desk where it clattered like dried bones.

Vining had surmised that *this* was the iconic necklace. *This* was where T. B. Mann's murderous journey had started. It was a guess on her part, based upon gut instincts that were perhaps refined when she took that two-minute journey to the other side. The gossipers were right. She was a scary person.

It was satisfying to see Gilroy, in her pressed navy-blue uniform, draped with brass and ribbons, jump as if confronted by a rattlesnake. She recovered quickly, a professional to the core, but Vining had seen her blink.

"Have you ever seen that necklace before, Chief?"

Gilroy didn't move to touch it. "What's this about?"

Vining headed toward the door. "Chief, everything you've said about Cookie's murder and Axel Holcomb makes perfectly good sense. Everyone involved made good decisions with the information they had at the time. But I have new information and I know it's not welcome, but it has to be examined. I think that necklace belonged to Cookie. I think the man who murdered her gave it to her. I think that man murdered two other women and almost murdered me. Chief, have you ever seen that necklace before?"

Gilroy didn't answer.

"I'll leave it with you so you can think about it."

"I don't want it," Gilroy snapped.

"There's an innocent man who doesn't want to be on death row." Vining left without looking back.

FORTY-FOUR

V ictor Chang's in that house." Marvin Li pointed to a small Craftsman-style bungalow that had peeling dark blue paint and needed a new roof. A manual sprinkler attached to a hose was in the middle of the un-fenced yard. Spots of bare dirt peeked through the patchy grass. The sprinkler wasn't running. No cars were parked on a cracked-cement driveway that led to a detached garage behind the house.

Li was handcuffed in the backseat of a Mercury Mountaineer, a plain-wrap SUV that Kissick had taken from the pool of undercover vehicles. Caspers was driving and Kissick was in the front passenger seat. They had pulled to the curb across the street from the house.

A few doors down, a Chevy Caprice sidled next to the curb and cut its lights. In it were Corporal Cameron Lam and Detectives Louis Jones and Doug Sproul.

Li had taken them to the historic neighborhood in Northeast Pasadena known as Bungalow Heaven. Its modest homes were built early in the last century when middle-class families moved into the area already populated with wealthy Midwestern transplants. Many of the homes in this cozy neighborhood had been painstakingly restored while others were barely hanging on.

Kissick used his cell phone to call in their location and request information about the house where Li had led them. He was leery about using his two-way radio, as their broadcasts could be monitored by anyone with a scanner. "How do you know Victor's there, Marvin?"

The car engine was running, but Caspers had cut the headlights. It was dark outside, but this neighborhood came to life once the sun had set. People were in the street, walking dogs, pushing babies in strollers, jogging, or waving at neighbors who were sitting on gliders on wide front porches.

The house that Li had pointed out appeared shuttered and forlorn. Thin drapes were closed over the front windows. A light that appeared to be from a table lamp glowed dimly inside. They could see a flickering television through the drapes. While most of the other houses on the street had their front doors open behind their screen doors to take advantage of the cool night air, the front door of this house was closed. An old window air conditioner at the side was cranking for all it was worth, dripping condensation onto the ground.

"Victor's grandfather lives there," Li said.

"That doesn't answer my question about how you know Victor is there." Kissick was getting tired of Marvin Li. In spite of all of Li's and his attorney's promises, he had yet to give them anything useful.

He thought of Nan and wondered what she was up to. He hadn't heard from her since she'd left the station earlier that afternoon when Sergeant Early had told her to go home. He was concerned about what had happened between her and Emily that had prompted Em to rage at her mother over the phone. He recalled how edgy she'd been in Sergeant Early's office earlier that day. He'd never seen her like that before. He was worried.

"I don't know *absolutely* that he's there right now," Li said. "This is where he usually goes when he wants to hide out."

"What does he need to hide out from?" Caspers asked. "What made him run? One minute, he's holding his sign on Newcastle Street, the next, he's gone. What happened from one minute to the next, Marvin?"

Kissick took out his cell phone and began typing a text message to Vining. He was going to keep it a simple "How R U?" but his fingers got carried away with him and he added, "Im w Ac and tats." He told her he was with Alex Caspers and Marvin Li. "M/B found chang. Call U L8r." He pressed Send and hoped she had her cell phone turned on.

"I guess he got scared," Li said. "If you let me go to the door, I can talk to him."

"Did someone tip him off that you were arrested?" Kissick returned his cell phone to the holder on his belt.

"I don't know," Li said. "I'm telling you that if you just let me talk to him, I can convince him to turn himself in."

"How are you going to convince him to do that, Marvin?" Caspers turned to look at Li in the backseat.

Li was looking almost forlornly at the bungalow across the street. The confrontational persona that he'd wielded in his earlier interactions with the detectives was gone. Kissick thought he looked shaken and afraid.

"What's troubling you, Marvin?" Kissick hooked his arm around the headrest of his seat and turned toward Li. "Talk to us. We can help you."

Li's cuffed wrists behind his back made his muscle-bound upper body stretch the seams of his shirt. "I'm troubled because Victor needs to do the right thing. Let me call him at least."

"So you can tell him we're here?" Kissick's cell phone pinged, indicating he had a text message. He looked at the display that said: Message from Nan Cell. He clicked to read it.

"Good luck w Chang. Im home. All quiet. Stay safe. Love."

"No, so I can convince him to do the right thing," Li replied.

Kissick smiled as he slipped his phone back onto his belt. Motion at the house across the street drew his attention. "Suspect on the move."

He picked up the two-way radio and raised Lam while he watched Victor Chang exit a door at the side of the house, walk down two steps to the driveway, and head toward the garage.

Li lurched toward the car door and wrenched his body around, yanking the handle with his hands that were cuffed behind him. The door locks and window controls in the backseat were disabled. From the driver's seat, Caspers turned and grabbed Li, pulling him away from the window while Li pleaded, "Let me talk to him! I need to talk to him."

"Stay here. Get backup," Kissick ordered Caspers. Bolting from the car, he began running across the street.

Everything happened at once.

When the Mountaineer's door opened, Li started yelling in Chinese.

The Chevy Caprice roared toward the driveway.

Chang rabbited.

At the wheel of the Caprice, Lam dodged dog walkers and people ambling after dinner as he drove across the lawn and came to a skidding stop across the driveway, nearly plowing into the house. The detectives spilled from the vehicle.

"Halt! Police! Freeze!"

Some people on the street stood as if stunned while others ran with their dogs and kids toward the safety of their homes.

Chang dashed across the backyard, ignoring the detectives' commands.

Kissick reached the backyard in time to see Chang scamper over a wooden back fence. Lam, the youngest and the fastest of the cops, was quickly over the fence behind him.

Kissick ordered Jones and Sproul to drive the Caprice around the block. Kissick clambered over the fence. He heard sirens in the distance and the pop of gunfire. Dropping to the ground and rolling, he was grateful there weren't rosebushes on the other side. He spotted Lam crouched behind a tree, returning fire, as Chang ran along a side yard. Kissick drew his gun and remembered he wasn't wearing his Kevlar vest. He hadn't even brought it. They had been going to look at the house and get the exact address, not get out of the car. He felt stupid not to have taken this simple precaution.

"Stay inside!" Kissick shouted when he saw faces appear in the windows of the house. "Get down!"

Kissick followed Lam through the side yard. Kissick saw Chang cross the front yard and run into the street as Jones in the Caprice pulled across it, blocking it. Citizens scattered, yelling and crying as they ran into homes and locked doors. PPD black-and-whites filled the street in both directions. A field sergeant shouted to the citizens to stay inside and away from the windows.

Younger, faster officers pursued Chang in his crazy effort to escape as he vaulted over hedges and fences, going from yard to yard.

Kissick kept up, buoyed by adrenaline, hating to lose a fight.

Above, a PPD helicopter was making a tremendous

racket, bathing Chang in white light. Still, he ran, splashing through a child's plastic wading pool.

A large mongrel dog joined in the chase, grabbing onto Chang's pant leg and slowing him down as he scaled a chain-link fence. Officers moved in, cutting off his escape route, dropping into firing position beside the house and behind trees in the yard where he had intended to run. Other officers blocked his return through the yard he had just traversed. Kissick and Lam were in position there.

Chang was stuck on top of the chain-link fence, his gun in his hand, illuminated by the spotlight from the helicopter churning the air above. He might have been on stage as he considered the most important decision of his life.

A voice amplified by a bullhorn came from the shadows. "Drop your weapon. You are surrounded. You cannot escape."

Kissick was crouched behind a steel storage shed. He was talking to the field sergeant on the two-way, holding it in his left hand while he held his gun up in his right. He explained to the sergeant that they might try getting Marvin Li to see if he could talk Chang into surrendering.

While the sergeant sent someone to retrieve Li, Kissick moved slightly forward from the flimsy protection of the storage shed and shouted, "Victor, this is Detective Kissick. Move very slowly and drop the gun. You have your whole life ahead of you. We're bringing Marvin Li to talk to you."

Literally on the fence, Chang wavered, looking disoriented as he blinked in the bright light from the helicopter. At Kissick's last words, he defiantly drew himself straight, shoulders back, chest out. "I'm not taking the fall for China Dog."

Kissick moved a little farther out to get a better look at Chang. "Victor, there's no way to escape."

"Yes there is." Chang took a shot at Kissick, sending his radio flying from his hand and sending him backward into rotting leaves piled behind the shed.

By the time the gunfire had stopped, Victor Chang was no longer on the fence.

Lam flew to the side of his fallen comrade. "Jim, you all right? You hit?"

"I'm okay. I don't think I'm hit." Kissick was bent backward over the hill of leaves. He tried to get traction to stand.

Lam offered his hand.

Kissick took it and got to his feet. "Is Chang dead?"

"Oh yeah."

Kissick felt something on his left hand. Looking at it, he saw blood.

"You're hit," Lam said.

Kissick worked his fingers. He stepped from behind the shed to get better light. He saw Chang's bullet-ridden body on the far side of the fence with scads of cops surrounding it. The police helicopter spotlighted the gore. Farther up in the sky was a TV news copter.

"The bullet just grazed me. I was holding my radio. I wonder if it took the hit. I just need a Band-Aid."

"You were lucky."

He heard the two-way radio scratch to life, broadcasting Sergeant Early's voice. He followed the sound in the darkness and found the radio against a fence behind the shed. He brought her up-to-date.

"Sarge, it's nothing. It's just a scratch. I don't want to take the time to go to the E.R." He knew he was going to lose that battle. He reflexively felt for his cell phone and discovered it was not in the holder on his belt.

"Okay, I'll have it checked out." He signed off. He drew his hand through his hair as he looked around. "Where the hell is my cell phone? Oh, *man* . . ."

FORTY-FIVE

Vining went home after her meeting with Betsy Gilroy. Alone and too rattled to sit still, she cleaned the house, dusting and vacuuming the remotest nooks and crannies. It was after eleven and she was still going. When she'd arrived home, she'd intended to put on her pajamas and robe, curl up in the La-Z-Boy with the TV remote, and take it easy, like everyone was admonishing her to do. Problem was, she couldn't do it.

The office of the security firm where the creepy guard had worked wouldn't be open until nine o'clock in the morning. So Vining cleaned, hoping she'd exhaust herself and be able to collapse into bed and succumb to deep, dreamless sleep. She thought of Kissick. Since she hadn't heard from him again, she wondered if he'd successfully apprehended Victor Chang and was busy interrogating him.

She picked up her cell phone from the dinette table where she'd left it and sent him a text message: "All Ok? Good here. Restless! Love."

She smiled as she pressed Send. She got a kick out of signing off with "Love." It made her feel as giddy as a teenager.

Realizing she was hungry, she foraged in the refrigerator. There was a lot of leftover Crock-Pot beef stew, but she'd already had some when she was home earlier before Em's dad had picked her up. She felt like having something more indulgent. In the freezer she found a pint of Ben and Jerry's Cherry Garcia ice cream. Em had thrown it into the shopping cart. Among other changes in Em, adolescence had brought on a sweet tooth.

She grabbed the ice-cream container. It felt light. She took off the lid and saw a few spoonfuls left.

Walking into the TV room, she picked up the remote control and turned on the television. Seeking something lively and distracting, she found *The Tonight Show*. Jay Leno was interviewing a lithesome young actress whom Vining had never heard of. They were laughing. Vining had wanted something lively, but found their too-animated laughter grating, so she turned off the television.

Feeling the air in the house was stuffy, she undid the locks on the sliding glass door and walked onto the terrace. She half expected to see the ghost of Frankie Lynde standing there, which would pretty much make her trying day complete. Happily, she saw no other-worldly being and the wind chimes were silent. She was grateful. She had enough ghosts to deal with right now. Other dead women would not let her rest: Marilu Feathers, Johnna Alwin, and Cookie Silva.

Her meeting with Betsy Gilroy gnawed at her, especially the chief's cutting comments, which had hit their mark. Vining knew that no investigator likes to have how she's handled a case questioned, especially a closed case and especially by an outsider. Still, she felt that Gilroy's attack had been particularly venomous and shockingly personal, especially coming from the chief.

Vining had to admit that in her worst moments, she felt much as Gilroy had portrayed her. She sometimes felt that she hadn't fully returned from that place—the other side. She wondered if the different pieces of herself would ever be rejoined. She feared she would forever remain fractured.

Did she have to wait until she was dead before she would feel complete?

She dragged the spoon around the melting edges of the ice cream and ate it as she leaned against the railing and looked at her forgotten corner of the city. Across the night sky, a TV news helicopter tore past, heading in the direction of Pasadena.

She heard her cell phone ringing. Her heart skipped a beat as she bolted into the house to answer the phone that she'd left in the kitchen. It had to be Jim.

She frowned as she looked at the display. The area code was local, but she didn't recognize the number.

She answered, "Nan Vining."

"Detective Vining, this is Chief Betsy Gilroy. I apologize for calling so late."

Disappointed the call wasn't from Kissick, Vining was bewildered: Gilroy was the last person she expected to hear from. "No problem, Chief. I'm up. What can I do for you?"

She heard Gilroy take a long breath before speaking. "Look, Detective, I wasn't completely up-front with you today."

From Vining's brief exposure to Gilroy and what she'd heard about her, she thought the chief sounded uncharacteristically hesitant.

The chief explained. "I . . . ahh . . . want to come clean with you. You deserve that. I have information about that other person of interest you spoke of. The . . . um . . . security guard."

"That's fantastic."

"The thing is, Detective, given the delicate nature of what I'm going to tell you, I don't want to meet in my office."

"Okay. Whatever works for you, Chief."

"I want you to come to the Foothill Museum, uh, now."

"Right now?"

"Yes, and come alone."

"I can come now, but why alone?" Vining asked this even though there wasn't anyone she could bring with her. The only one she'd want with her was Kissick and he was tied up. Plus, she wasn't supposed to be pursuing T. B. Mann leads. Sergeant Early would have her hide if she found out she'd gone to see Chief Gilroy. Vining had no reason to doubt what Gilroy was telling her, but it was strange.

Gilroy sensed her hesitancy. "There's something at the Foothill Museum that will help you understand what happened the night of Cookie's murder. This is for your eyes only. I was rude to you today and I'd like to make it up to you. I'll also tell you about the pearl necklace with the blue stone."

"I'll be there in half an hour."

"Will you be driving your department Crown Vic?"

Her question brought Vining up short. Why would she care?

"It's very dark up here," Gilroy said. "The spotlights will come in handy for you."

That was a good point, Vining thought. Plus her Jeep Cherokee was almost out of gas. "I'll be in the Crown Vic."

"Good. Then I'll know it's you. You'll see my white Escalade in the parking lot."

Cadillac Escalade, Vining thought. The citizens of Colina Vista did like their police chief. "Okay, great. I'll see you shortly."

"Ah . . . Detective . . . I want you to know that the museum is nine-point-eighteen miles from the freeway. At the Angeles National Forest sign, you take the V. Don't forget."

Vining winced as she tried to understand the chief's instructions, which didn't make any sense.

"Detective, remember what I told you so you don't get lost."

"I'll do that. See you soon."

Vining thought about Gilroy's last cryptic instructions. The Foothill Museum wasn't more than five miles from the freeway. Plus vehicle odometers didn't display hundredths of a mile. She shrugged and hurried to change her clothes.

FORTY-SIX

While Vining drove to meet Betsy Gilroy in Colina Vista, she called Kissick's cell phone. Someone should know where she was going. She got his voice mail. He was definitely busy with Marvin Li and Victor Chang. That was good. Hopefully, he was needling confessions out of them.

She left a voice message. "Hi Jim. I know you're tied up, but I want you to know that I'm headed to the Foothill Museum. Chief Gilroy called and asked me to meet her there. She says she has something to show me about Cookie's murder. Don't get mad, but I drove up and met with Chief Gilroy earlier today. She got kinda ticked off. Now she says she wants to make it up to me.

I'll have my phone with me, so call or text when you get this. Bye. Love you."

She got off the freeway. Remembering Gilroy's mileage information, she punched the distance gauge, returning it to zero, thinking, no way was it nine miles to the Foothill Museum and the point one eight mile made no sense at all.

Her car windows were down and the wind rustled her hair. The night air grew cooler as the elevation rose. She would have expected her mind to be racing, but instead, it was surprisingly clear, as if she'd been meditating. She recalled something that someone had once told her. You have to make space in your life in order for something new to come in. Who had told her that? She couldn't remember, but the advice made sense. Something new was coming in. Or was what she was experiencing only the calm before the storm?

She drove up the dark, winding road. Her headlights caught the small sign pointing to the narrow lane that led to the Foothill Museum. Recalling Gilroy's mysterious instructions, she saw that it wasn't a V intersection, like Gilroy had said, but was a hard left. She looked at the distance gauge. She'd traveled just over five miles, not nine. Was the chief coming unglued?

The woods seemed to encroach on the lane in the darkness, nearly overwhelming her headlights. She was grateful for the full moon that was hanging low and large in the September sky.

She soon saw the log cabin. The porch light was on and the two front windows were lit. A dusting of snow, and it would have been a perfect scene for a Thomas Kincaid Christmas card. A new, white Cadillac Escalade was parked in the gravel lot.

Vining cut her headlights and stopped her car while she was still at the edge of the clearing, out of sight of anyone in the cabin or the car. She took her binoculars from the glove compartment and looked around.

Gilroy's nonsensical parting message about the nine-point-eighteen miles bugged her. It contributed to the one percent doubt she felt. That one percent was more than enough to kill her.

She put down the binoculars and blew out a stream of air. She took out her cell phone and looked at it. Who could she call? Kissick was busy. If they had apprehended Chang, she assumed everyone on the team—Caspers, Sproul, Jones, Lam—would be busy, too. As far as calling the one person she *should*—Sergeant Early—fuggeddaboutit.

Vining thought about it logically. She was meeting the *police chief*, for goodness' sakes. Still, her cop gut instincts warned her that something was hinky.

She called Kissick again. Again, his voice mail picked up. "Hey, Jim. I've arrived at the Foothill Museum. Gilroy's white Cadillac Escalade is here. No other cars. Don't see anyone. Lights are on in the building. I'm going inside. Call me." Before she hung up, she gave him the Escalade's plate number.

She drove the Crown Vic with the headlights off far enough into the clearing so she could turn around and point it heading out. Leaving the keys in the ignition, she exited the car. She pulled her Glock from its holster and darted into the woods surrounding the log cabin. She ran through the woods, looking around and behind her, until she was even with the side of the cabin. Her rubber-soled work shoes crunched against the gravel as she sprinted to a small window and looked inside.

There was no one in the front of the cabin. She dashed to the back corner where Axel Holcomb had lived. She peered through a window there. The light was on, but she didn't see anybody.

She tried the doorknob on the back door. Unlocked. She pushed it open and leaned in, gun ahead of her, calling, "Chief Gilroy."

As she took a step inside, motion behind her caused her to whirl around. She caught a glimpse of a shadowy figure before two darts from a Taser reached their mark and were embedded into her back, sending 50,000 volts of electricity through her. She yelled. She felt as if she were being deep-fried. She flew face-first onto the ground across the open doorway, losing her grip on her gun. She was aware of nothing but blinding, incapacitating pain. She struggled to keep her eyes open.

She was aware of someone kicking her gun away. Finally, the Taser's trigger was released, killing the electric surge. The pain stopped. The small amount of breath she had left was knocked out when her assailant dropped on top of her, straddling her back. A handcuff was snapped onto her right wrist. Sucking in air, she began thrashing her body, flailing her left hand and managing to pull her right hand free with the cuff attached. She tried to shake off whoever was astride her and to loosen the darts' contact with her skin. If she could knock out just one dart, she'd break the circuit. The jackass had gotten a solid shot with the Taser gun and the darts were well embedded into her back.

Her assailant again squeezed the Taser's trigger.

She yelled and was again clawing the floor.

"Officer Vining, the more you fight me, the more I'll have to hurt you."

Officer Vining. Those were the words and that was the voice that had infiltrated her nightmares and haunted her waking moments for over a year. She'd always felt she'd hear them again, but in her fantasies, their roles were reversed. How had this happened? How was she again being victimized by T. B. Mann?

He released the Taser's trigger and repeated what he'd said, knowing she'd been unable to absorb it the first time. "Officer Vining, the more you fight me, the more I'll have to hurt you."

She gasped for breath. He had her pinned with his knees on either side of her back. He retrieved her right wrist, grabbed her left, pulled it behind her, and snapped on the other handcuff, saying, "I knew you'd walk around the cabin first."

Now that she was handcuffed, he patted her down, remaining astride her.

She bowed and arched her back, working her shoulders, trying to dislodge the darts. She grabbed her jacket and yanked the fabric. She felt the dart that was over her right shoulder blade move. Her skin where it had pierced her and delivered its voltage was so sore, she couldn't tell if she'd knocked it out or not.

He found her backup Walther. She felt him remove it from her ankle holster.

The pang of losing her Walther was nearly as severe to Vining as being Tased. That gun had saved her life.

"I've just gotta love you, Officer Vining. So by the book right up until the moment you're not. But that's been happening a lot lately, hasn't it?"

She raised her head and craned her neck as far as she could. Out of the corners of her eyes, she caught his glance. This was the first time since he'd stabbed her that she'd faced those eyes again in person. In her nightmares, they had been dark brown. That's the color they were that day at 835 El Alisal Road. She'd wondered whether he'd been wearing tinted lenses. Now she saw why he would have.

His eyes were remarkable. Deep-set and ice blue, as chilly as the soul behind them. His scalp had been recently shaved clean as not a speck of hair was visible. His eyebrows were light brown. His face, lengthened by his bald dome, was a perfect oval. His ears were compact and neat. His nose was slightly broad, but suited his face. His upper lip was thin, the bottom lip full. He was as ordinary as she'd remembered. But for his striking eyes, he could walk through life without attracting a second glance.

He took his time searching her, which felt more like an adolescent's awkward petting than an attempt to find weapons. After what he'd done to her in the kitchen at 835 El Alisal Road, his timid touch felt innocent.

She continued looking him over. He was dressed up, wearing a white dress shirt and a blue-and-red-striped tie. The shirt was tucked into navy-blue slacks with a plain leather belt. He had on black dress shoes with black socks. A nylon holster for the Taser was attached to the belt with Velcro. A small nylon pouch next to it probably held Taser cartridges.

He was beefier than in her memory. A belly protruded over his belt. His cheeks were fuller and he had the beginning of a double chin. She guessed he'd gained forty pounds. She took delight in the thought of him drowning his troubles in cookies, ice cream, and potato chips. She, however, was more physically fit than ever, and wiser.

Who was she kidding? She was the one prone on the floor, handcuffed, with Taser darts embedded in her back. Still, she remained calm. He would take his time setting the scene. That was his M.O.

She saw that while he'd stuck her small Walther into his already snug waistband, he'd set her Glock on the floor near him. There wasn't enough room beneath that belt for two guns.

He finished patting her down and sat erect astride her. He seemed to recognize the momentousness of this moment because he took a few seconds to sit quietly, taking it all in.

They were together again. At long last. All her precautions and planning, all her vicious thoughts of revenge, had been undone by a single trusting act. Had Betsy Gilroy set her up or had she been forced to tell her to come here? Gilroy had sounded under duress when she'd made the phone call. Her car was here. Where was she?

Vining twisted to look at him again. His gaze was like a lover's. She remembered that from before. More than adoring, his gaze was all-consuming. Hungry. Looking at her was not sufficient. Touching her was not sufficient. He wanted it all. He wanted *everything*.

Straddling her, he could have easily made a sexual move. While she felt obsession in his stare, she didn't feel a sexual charge. She thought about the story Axel Holcomb had told former Colina Vista Police sergeant Mike Iverson about watching Cookie Silva's murderer masturbate while torturing and killing her. Intercourse didn't get him off. Terror and murder did. Now he was engaged in housekeeping. He was saving the good stuff for later.

He kept those ice blue eyes locked on hers. His eyes were familiar to her. They were the same light blue as Nitro's.

"Asshole," she said. "The proper way to address me is either Corporal or Detective Vining."

He depressed the Taser's trigger with no effect. He looked at the gun with surprise.

She'd broken the contact of one of the darts. She took advantage of the moment to retract her elbows, ball her fists, and shoot them down her back into his groin.

He inhaled wretchedly and rolled to the side, pulling his knees to his chest. He struggled to breathe.

She shoved herself away, digging her feet against the

linoleum. On her knees, she scampered toward the Glock that he'd foolishly left on the floor nearby.

Still bent over, in a ball on the floor, he managed to throw out his hand and snag her left leg.

She kicked violently at him with her right foot, smacking him in the face, slamming his nose. She kept at it, landing solid blows. He let go.

As she scrambled toward her gun on the floor, not sure how she would fire it with her hands cuffed, he jammed the Taser directly against her buttock and fired. The "drive-stun" had the same effect as a cattle prod.

She yelled and dropped face-first, grimacing, against the linoleum. Grit from the floor adhered to her lips.

He bolted out of range of her feet, stood, and picked up the Glock.

"I know your rank is corporal and that you're a detective," he said with annoyance. He touched his nose, bloody from her kicking.

She was sorry that she hadn't broken it.

He studied the blood on his fingers, almost with a look of wonder. "But you were Officer Vining when I first saw you on television after you'd rid the world of a rat—that has-been rock star. A television reporter and a cameraman were after you and the idiot reporter kept saying, 'Officer Vining, Officer Vining, a word please.' You just kept walking. You didn't run. You didn't turn around. You kept walking to your car, got in, and drove away without even looking at them." He touched his nose again and his eyes grew hazy as he looked at the blood. "For me, you will always be Officer Vining. Guess I'm sentimental that way. Get up."

She unsteadily climbed to her feet. She tried not to stagger and cursed herself for having to take a single sideways step to keep her balance.

He grabbed the second Taser dart from her back and

gathered up the cartridge he'd ejected. He shoved her toward the log cabin's main room.

She walked until he ordered her to stop. She still didn't see any sign of Betsy Gilroy.

He took a wooden chair from behind the bar where the museum docents rang up sales of souvenirs on the old cash register. On top of the bar was a black nylon duffel bag like the ones PPD officers used to carry their gear.

He set the chair in the middle of the floor. "Sit there. Wait." He snatched her badge off her belt. He looked at it with satisfaction, tossing it in his hand, feeling the weight.

She wasn't completely surprised when he returned it to the same spot on her belt. He could have taken her badge at the El Alisal house and hadn't. She guessed that it gave him a charge to see her wearing it. She had so many questions, but she didn't want to tip her hand. She didn't want him to know how much she'd found out, how much she cared, how obsessed she was. Information was power and her power was in short supply right now.

"Now sit."

Her legs were shaky, but she was careful to lower herself onto the seat without plopping down. She was committed not to show weakness or fear. She refused to give him that satisfaction. She refused to feed that wolf.

He had a satisfied smile on his stupid bland face. She thought about how much she'd like to wipe off that smile. No. *Tear* it off.

His translucent blue eyes glittered. "You . . . You're really something, you know that?"

He extended his fingers toward her and gently pulled her hair away from the left side of her neck, smoothing it over her shoulder. She maintained her sangfroid, coolly keeping her eyes on his face, as he drew his index finger down the entire length of her scar, starting from behind her ear and disappearing beneath her shirt collar. His finger felt moist and clammy. She did not recoil. She didn't move a muscle, even when a sadistic grin toyed with the corners of his lips.

Having his fill, he pulled his hand away from her skin and moved it to her hair, drawing it between his fingers from the roots to the tips. A single strand came free. Caught on his hand, the hair reflected the light as he waved it in the beam from the overhead lamp. He playfully tossed the strand toward her. It landed on her slacks.

He told her, "You weren't supposed to live, you know. You messed things up for me."

She remained motionless.

"What's it like, a pretty woman like you going through life with a big scar on your neck?"

"What's it like for you, a young guy who can only get off when he's killing policewomen? Get many dates?"

He punched her in the jaw with his fist, pitching her sideways. The chair tipped and almost fell. Stars burst before her eyes.

He smiled fully for the first time that night, revealing small, even teeth and low gums, like a rodent's.

In spite of herself, she inhaled a shuddering breath. She worked her jaw to make sure it wasn't broken.

He went to the duffel bag. From inside, he took out a blue-and-white printed kerchief. He tied it around her eyes.

"Stay there," he told her.

Not being able to see scared her more than anything else he'd done to her that night. She closed her eyes, finding that being blindfolded wasn't as terrifying that way, and focused on staying calm. It was the hardest work she'd ever done.

She heard him moving about the cabin. She dared to

open her eyes and realized that she could see a little beneath the bottom of the kerchief. He was turning off lights. She heard him securing the back door. There was the rip of Velcro and the sound of something mechanical clicking into place. He'd replaced the cartridge in the Taser.

"Where's Chief Gilroy?" she asked.

"Chief Gilroy," he repeated, slathering the name with as much honey as when he said "Officer Vining." He sighed. "Yes . . . Good Chief Gilroy."

"What did you do to her?"

He clicked his tongue against his teeth, suggesting a sad situation that couldn't be helped. "Nothing that she hasn't earned."

FORTY-SEVEN

Vining felt a pain in the pit of her stomach. "What does that mean?"

"Don't ask so many questions. Especially when you might not want to know the answers."

Behind her closed eyes, she envisioned his face. Not the face she recalled from 835 El Alisal Road with the dark wig and brown contact lenses, but *this* face, the chubby version with the shaved head, double chin, and plump cheeks. She'd seen this face before, and recently.

She thought she heard him rummaging inside the duffel bag. "I have a question I would like the answer to. What's your name?"

"My name . . . You don't even know my name and

here I know so much about you. You don't know where I live or what I do or even something as simple as my name."

The pride in his voice sickened her.

"You must have called me something, all this time. You cops love to give guys like me nicknames. Do you have a nickname for me?"

Now he sounded hopeful, in a pathetic way, like the wallflower waiting to be asked to dance.

"What do you want me to call you?" she asked, refusing to give him the pleasure of knowing what a large role he'd played in her life. How she and Emily had given him a powerful, awe-inspiring name: The Bad Man. Thinking of him now, she thought, *What a dweeb. He doesn't deserve the name T. B. Mann.* She wasn't about to elevate him by revealing it.

"Don't you and your colleagues have a name for me around the police station? You have to refer to me somehow, right? You know, guys like the Night Stalker and the Hillside Strangler."

She didn't respond.

She felt him move beside her. His hand brushed the hair over her ear.

A chill went down her spine.

"You don't think I'm in the big league, like those other guys."

He continued stroking her hair in a wispy, tentative way that tingled and annoyed her, yet sent icy shivers through her body.

"Officer Vining, I think you know that I'm better than those guys. What sort of planning did they do? Throw a half-assed murder kit into the trunk of the car? Drive around looking for some girl to lure with a fake badge or for an open bedroom window? For that, they get nicknames and everyone in the city is afraid of them?"

He continued stroking her hair.

She focused on shutting herself off from his touch, on withdrawing and separating from her skin. It was working. She could almost not feel him, but it had the effect of making his voice more resonant, as if it was the only sound in a sealed room, vibrating through her ears and tickling the gray matter of her brain.

"You know I'm better than those guys, Officer Vining."

"Don't flatter yourself."

"Oh, Officer Vining. I have it on good authority that you are very familiar with the caliber of my work."

How could he know that? She thought of Betsy Gilroy. Had he tortured her? Forced her to tell him what she knew about Nitro's drawings, the necklaces, and the other victims?

She heard a metallic "snick" noise. She thought it sounded like a retractable knife blade being ejected. She was right. He pressed the tip against her neck, against the scar that told the story of how he'd stabbed her.

"Your resistance makes me think that you do have a nickname for me. I want to know what it is."

She gritted her teeth, waiting for him to cut her. She felt hot tears in the corners of her eyes.

"What's the matter, Officer Vining? Cat got your tongue?"

Seconds passed like hours. She again tried to remove herself from her body, but the sharp pain against that most vulnerable part of her kept drawing her back inside her skin. It stung brutally. Had he cut her? He must have broken the skin. She grappled for control over her emotions. She could not give in to him or she'd be lost for sure.

There was a second part to his show. Whatever he had planned, it wasn't going to happen here. He had been closing up, preparing to move out. Opportunities to get away would present themselves. Just hold on. Hold on . . .

Her cell phone rang.

She heard him close the knife, pressing the blade back until it locked.

He grabbed the phone from her belt. "Kissick is calling. He must be wondering where you are. He must be so worried about you." He added with a sneer, "Isn't that special?" After another two rings, it stopped. He did not return the phone to her belt.

She heard him walk a few steps and then heard a rip, like tape being yanked from a roll. He returned to her and she felt him press a wide piece of tape across her mouth. He walked away.

She was glad it was just a piece of what felt like duct tape. He hadn't stuffed something inside her mouth or wrapped the tape around her head.

She heard another ripping noise. The zipper on the duffel bag? She thought she heard him slide the heavy bag off the bar. He was again beside her, grabbing her by the arm. "Get up."

They were entering the second phase of his plan. She recalled personal safety talks she'd given to women's groups. Her own words came back to her. If you're abducted, the harm won't occur at the site of the abduction, but at the place the bad guy will take you to—the remote country road, the cheap motel room. Do not go to the second place. Do whatever you can to avoid being taken to the second place.

When she didn't budge, he moved in front of her and tried to raise her with his hands beneath her armpits. She drove her head into his belly. He was already unbalanced by the weight of the duffel bag and she knocked him off his feet. Tilting her head back to see beneath the kerchief, she saw him on his back. She kicked his head, stunning him. She was about to stomp on it when, through animal instinct, he grabbed her raised foot and rolled, pulling her standing leg out from under her. She landed on top of him, partially knocking off the blindfold. Her hands handcuffed behind her, she spread her legs, pinning him.

He reached for her hair, but she was still able to rear her head back and deliver a resounding head butt.

It stunned her, but stunned him more. He lay back, blinking.

Getting to her knees, she again reared back her head, intending to cram his nose into his skull. When she heard the snick of the switchblade and felt the tip of the knife pierce her neck in the same spot he'd cut before, she froze.

"That's a good girl."

He pushed himself up from the floor, still holding the knife against its mark. On his knees, he crept close to her. She felt his hot breath on her face. It was mint-scented, just like before.

Her breaths through her nose grew short. She felt that familiar combination of being ice cold yet sweating. Her head began to fill with metal shavings that scraped and rattled. The last thing she needed was to have a panic attack.

As he kneeled beside her, the knife still against her skin, his lips brushed her cheek. She felt the heat rise from him. She knew he smelled her fear. This is what did it for him. Her terror. She heard his breathing quicken. He was becoming sexually aroused.

There was nowhere to flee. Nowhere to go. She was terrified to move, lest he stab her. She was trapped. She began seizing air. Her nostrils burned. She tried to force the hobgoblin back into its box, focusing on mentally reciting the phonetic alphabet.

Adam, Boy, Charles, David, Edward . . .

The kerchief had partially come off in the struggle.

Through her slit eyes, past the spots that clouded them, she glimpsed him watching her.

Breathing through his open mouth, he took the knife away from her neck and pushed the blade back inside the hilt.

Her breath slowly returned, although she still felt ice cold and her thoughts ricocheted around her brain.

He got to his feet and helped her to hers.

She felt that he would kill her there if he had to, if she gave him no other alternative. She had little choice but to go to the dreaded second place. She was too beaten down to muster a defiant gaze. He had won this battle.

Somewhere, maybe from inside the duffel bag, she heard her cell phone emit the tone that indicated she'd received a voice mail message. Kissick had stolen a few minutes to call and leave a message. Maybe he'd been worried when she hadn't answered and would drive up here. Certainly, he'd at least call again. He was the only one who knew where she'd gone. Emily was at her dad's house. Vining wasn't expected at the station. How much time would pass before anyone realized she was missing?

He again tied the kerchief over her eyes. Pulling her by the arm, she heard him open the cabin's front door. He led her outside. She could see a sliver of the porch light beneath the edge of the blindfold. The light went off and she heard him close the front door.

He guided her a few feet and began tying her hand-cuffed hands to something. She felt the broad porch railing with her fingers.

"Where are your car keys?" he asked as he peeled the duct tape away so that she could speak.

"In the ignition."

"Be right back," he said, again pressing the tape against her mouth.

She heard his footsteps go down the steps and fade as

he walked across the gravel. She leaned back her head to look beneath the edge of the kerchief. The light of the full moon helped. A short time later, she heard a car engine and caught sight of the Crown Vic approaching. She heard him unlocking the trunk. He returned and untied her from the railing. He guided her down the steps and to the car.

Chief Gilroy had wanted her to drive the Crown Vic. Now she knew that he had ordered Gilroy to tell her that.

"Step up," he commanded.

She rammed her legs against the car's rear bumper before she was able to climb inside the trunk and lay down. She was relieved when she didn't feel anyone else in the trunk. She was hoping he wouldn't tie her legs, but he did better than that. He hog-tied her, binding her ankles together then tying them to her wrists behind her. He was no amateur.

He slammed down the trunk lid.

While the car was bumping down the lane, the most recent time she'd seen his face came back to her. The necktie he was wearing had tipped her off. It was the same tie worn by the security team at Terra Cosmetika. The company occupied the building across the street from where Scrappy had last worked. She recalled her conversation with Security Chief Don Balch. Photos of his security officers had been on the wall of the suite. She thought that a few of the faces had looked familiar. She now knew that one was definitely familiar. Fatter, balder, and familiar.

Balch had mentioned the names of the watchmen who worked the graveyard shift.

Mike Iverson, formerly of the Colina Vista P.D., thought the name of the creepy security guard whom Cookie had dated was Teddy Pierce. That wasn't a bad guess, as Vining suddenly remembered the names of Balch's two night watchmen: Eduardo Gonzalez and Tanner Persons. In her mind, she saw the photos with the name placards. She finally had a real name, after all this time. She said it in her head, trying to get used to it.

Tanner Persons.

As the car rolled along, Chief Gilroy's bizarre driving tip came back to her.

The museum is nine-point-eighteen miles from the freeway. Take the V.

Vining interpreted the meaning anew. *918V.* That's what Gilroy was trying to tell her. It had been a warning. The code 918V was an informational radio code. It communicated the presence of a violent insane person. A psycho.

FORTY-EIGHT

*V*ining judged from the street noises that he had not headed farther into the foothills but had turned back toward town. He made a couple of brief stops, which would have been the stop signs along Colina Vista Boulevard heading from the forest.

While traveling the quiet lane that led from the log cabin, she'd strained to detect the sound of another car engine. She heard only the uneven rumbling of the Crown Vic that was in need of a tune-up and was unpleasantly permeating the trunk with exhaust fumes.

After a while, she heard the sounds and felt the speed of traveling on the freeway. He didn't appear to be taking her to a remote mountain cabin. The closer to civilization, the better for her to find the means to escape or to kill him. While self-preservation was primarily on her mind, bloody and primal vengeance competed as a close second. If she didn't have Emily, she felt that she wouldn't care if she had to go down with him in order to take him out.

Given what she knew of him, she guessed he would take her to a place of significance for him or her. He'd confessed what she already knew: He was sentimental. He also enjoyed taking risks, skirting the line of getting caught. Whatever plans he'd hatched to dispatch her, they wouldn't be executed quickly. The murder of his select women was like a seduction for him, prolonged foreplay leading to the final release. She hoped to parlay this knowledge of his timeline into an opportunity. Once she saw where the final confrontation was going to take place, she could better formulate a plan. Even though she was in dire circumstances, her moment of disabling panic had passed. The hobgoblin was back inside his cave for now.

He turned on the car radio. She had left it tuned to a station that broadcast a "mellow mix" of Top 40 and oldies. At night, they played love songs with sappy listener dedications read by a woman whose voice always sounded on the verge of cracking with emotion. Vining sometimes listened to that show with voyeuristic fascination. She wondered if T. B. Mann—or Tanner Persons, as she knew him now, happy to strip him of the awe-inspiring nickname—hadn't turned the channel because he had been in love before. Perhaps he was using it as a blueprint to understand the typical human heart.

She rubbed her face against the carpeted trunk floor, struggling to loosen the blindfold. She felt it slide. She might be able to push it off, but then, he'd only tie it tighter. She thought she could see a bit more, but it was too dark to tell.

She tried to search the trunk, scooting backward, extending her fingers from where her wrists were bound to her ankles. It seemed empty. He had taken out her duty bag and car supplies. In one corner, she found a plastic container. Exploring further, she felt a handle and a screw cap. She rapped it with her fingers and it felt full. Her nostrils were full of exhaust fumes, but she thought she detected the odor of gasoline. Why would he need extra gas? Was he taking her someplace remote after all?

She could do nothing more until he opened the trunk. She lay down her head and closed her eyes. After a second, she again raised her head to hear better. Gad, he was singing. She listened to him warbling tunelessly along with a song playing on the radio. It was the Sheryl Crow version of "The First Cut Is the Deepest."

It used to be one of Vining's favorites. She cringed behind the blindfold as she listened to him mangle it. Now like many other things in her life, he'd ruined it for her forever.

While she waited until they got to the next place, she took stock of herself. She was physically uncomfortable, tied up, bouncing along in a car trunk, breathing exhaust. Her back burned at the two spots where the Taser darts had delivered their voltage. Her butt burned where he'd drive-stunned her. Her jaw ached where he'd slugged her with his fist. She probably had a lump on her forehead from head-butting him. She felt stinging pain on her neck. The jackass had actually cut her there.

She evaluated her mental state. While she might need her fists and feet to get out of this situation, most likely her survival hinged on her mental dexterity. Recalling his hot, excited, minty breath on her face made her stomach turn. Realizing she was now having an involuntary physical reaction to a memory brought tears to her eyes and made her angry. Why couldn't she control her mind?

She'd lost the mental game to him in the kitchen at 835 El Alisal Road and it had nearly cost her her life. An image of her funeral flashed into her mind. There were her mother, grandmother, and her sister Stephanie and her family. There were Wes, Kaitlyn, and their boys. There were Kissick, Early, and many others in blue uniforms with black bands across their shields. And there was Emily, all standing as her coffin was lowered into the ground.

Her stomach clenched tighter. The kerchief over her eyes absorbed her tears. Bile singed her esophagus.

This is not helpful, Vining.

She gave herself a pep talk. *Okay, lady, a couple of months ago, you stood on your balcony and issued a challenge to that asshole driving this car. "Game on." The game is on now. What's it gonna be, Vining? You or him?*

The nausea in her belly turned into fire. Her tears stopped. She issued a new challenge to Tanner Persons, aka T. B. Mann, aka the Asshole Who's About to Meet His Maker.

You want a fight? You're gonna get one.

FORTY-NINE

They exited the freeway and were again traveling surface streets. Vining heard other cars on the road.
After he made a right turn, the traffic sounds faded.

She heard a dog barking from about a block away. A
second dog answered from a different direction. They
were big dogs. She guessed they were in a residential
neighborhood of single-family homes.

He slowed and made another right turn, this one
sharper. Maybe they were going up a driveway. He
stopped the car, cut the ignition, and got out. The
Crown Vic's trunk opened.

Vining saw stars—real ones in the night sky. That was
all she saw before his body blocked her view and he
reached toward her. She'd shoved the kerchief almost
all the way off, but hadn't realized it in the darkness of
the trunk.

"Let me fix this," he said. He went about undoing the
kerchief and retying it without rancor, with the attitude
of a parent tying a child's shoelaces for the umpteenth
time. "You're probably wondering why I've blindfolded
you. Maybe we'll play Pin the Tail on the Donkey or
maybe we'll play another game."

She let his words drip off her. Water off a duck's back.
She was no longer going to be intimidated or creeped
out by his words. Sticks and stones.

He leaned into the trunk and began untying the cord
binding her ankles to her handcuffed wrists.

She heard crickets singing in the night air. Crickets meant he'd parked someplace where there were bushes and green space.

"Oh fudge," he cursed mildly when he had trouble untying the knots.

Her feet now free, he said, "Let's go." He helped her from the trunk, guiding her with his hand on her forearm. Once she was standing, he ordered, "Stay there."

She heard his footfalls in his dress shoes as he walked around the car and opened and closed the doors. She thought she heard items being placed on the pavement. He slammed the trunk closed. She was certain of one thing. Wherever they were, this was the second place. Where it ended.

She felt him brush past, then the sound of a key being inserted into a lock, followed by a bolt lock being disengaged. A door opened. His footsteps disappeared. A door banged closed.

She back-stepped until she felt the car trunk. She then started walking forward as quickly as she dared. He had driven up a driveway. If she followed it back down, it would lead to a street. If he found her before somebody else did, she'd drop to the ground and force him to carry dead weight. She would kick him and cause a commotion. There had to be neighbors around. He'd tied the blindfold tighter this time and she couldn't see anything beneath the bottom edge when she leaned her head back.

Stumbling blindly, her legs felt disjointed, as if she couldn't control them well without her vision. She thought she was putting one foot in front of the other, but then grunted when she plowed face-first into something leafy and dusty—a tall shrub. It was sticky and wispy, too. Spiderwebs. She madly rubbed her head against the woody branches, which maliciously scratched her as she tried to peel off the blindfold.

The door opened and she heard footsteps quickly approaching.

She kept moving, going faster, running as fast as she had the courage to, her elbow brushing the hedge to guide her. She breathed madly through her nose, the duct tape still over her mouth.

She heard a car go by. She must be close to the street. Then that all-too-familiar pain incapacitated her. He'd again fired the Taser. She was on her knees, then face-down on the ground. When the electric surge stopped, she knew she'd lost this battle. She let him help her to her feet and lead her where he wanted her to go.

After taking a few steps, they stopped. He tilted her head with his fingers beneath her chin.

"You ninny. You've scratched your face. You're bleeding."

She cringed when she felt something warm and wet trail up her cheek.

"Mmm . . ." he purred. "Tastes like cherry pie."

A shiver again surged through her when she felt his breath against her ear. He cooed, "Officer Vining, the more foolishly you behave, the more you're going to get hurt."

He led her by the arm. "There are three steps and then you'll go through a doorway."

He nudged her in front of him. "Step up. One, two, and three. That's a good girl. Up again over the threshold." He led her several feet across what sounded like a hardwood floor, before restraining her by the arm and saying, "Stop."

She heard him walk back and close the door. The bolt lock slid into place.

He again took her forearm and turned her around.

"There's a chair behind you. Sit down."

She moved until she felt the chair against her legs. She sat. The seat was cushioned and the back was not.

He was again tying her feet, this time to the chair legs. Then, thankfully, he was removing the blindfold, pulling it off her head, tearing a few strands of her hair with it.

The first thing she saw was him standing in front of her, a silly grin on his face. She looked around. She was in a well-appointed kitchen. It wasn't just any kitchen. It had been remodeled. The paint, counters, and floor were different, but she still recognized it. She thought she'd recognize it even if the place burned to the ground. He'd brought her back to the house at 835 El Alisal Road.

Over his shoulder, she saw the door where she had stood that late Sunday afternoon, just about to leave, when he'd rushed her, grabbing a knife from the wooden block on the island. The island was still there, with a new countertop. His black duffel bag was on it. The pantry was still there, where she'd crawled through her own blood after he'd stabbed her.

After the long months of having nightmares about what had happened here, again and again seeing this room and his face, after reliving the tragedy a zillion times, after many failed attempts to return to face her demons, she was finally *here*. She was surprised that she now felt oddly detached from this place and that other time. In some strange way, those events had finally been transfigured into "the past." They no longer held power over her. She'd broken free of their sticky clutches and was now free to engage this new drama.

Tanner Persons's face, on the other hand, while he loomed in front of her, still seemed mired in "what was." He looked like a tentative suitor who'd just handed his beloved a carefully selected Valentine's Day card with words that beautifully captured all that he felt and more. He was now anxiously watching and waiting for her response as she read it. Only this greeting wasn't about delivering love, it was about inciting fear.

She looked at him with as much fake apathy as she could muster. She sought to rob him of his wish to make her afraid. Her indifference didn't faze him. He continued to smile with his lips closed and slightly trembling, like an excited puppy.

"Officer Vining." He took a big step to his left, revealing what he had been hiding behind him.

Sitting tied to a chair facing Vining, duct tape over her mouth, was Chief Betsy Gilroy.

Vining couldn't disguise her shock, giving Persons the response he clearly desired as he broke into a full smile, revealing his sharp little rat's teeth.

He walked behind Gilroy and rested his hands on top of her shoulders. She stiffened at his touch and slit her eyes with disgust.

"Officer Vining," Tanner Persons said again. "I believe you've met my mother."

FIFTY

Vining looked wildly from Gilroy to Persons. MOTHER?

Persons stroked Gilroy's hair with its expensive color weaving job.

Gilroy endured the attention, wincing slightly, her eyebrows wavering. Around her neck, on top of her blouse, was the beat-up pearl-and-sapphire necklace that Vining had thrown at her earlier that day.

Vining saw the familial relationship in their facial
shape, jawline, and deep-set eyes. Their noses were identical. His face was chubby and hers was lean, but there was
no doubt. Betsy Gilroy had given birth to this monster.

A flurry of possibilities flew through Vining's mind.
Gilroy found out that her son had murdered Cookie.
She framed the slow-witted caretaker Axel, saving her
son from prison and herself embarrassment and loss of
status in the community and police department. She
had sent an innocent man to death row to protect her
own ambitions. But if Gilroy had rescued Tanner Persons's sorry behind, what was she doing here?

Gilroy hadn't taken her eyes off Vining's. Vining was
sure the chief had guessed what she was thinking. Vining, though, couldn't read Gilroy's thoughts. There was
fear, certainly, but there was something else. Shame?

"Yep. This is my dear old ma." Persons clasped
Gilroy's head between both hands and gave it a playful
side-to-side shake.

The vertical creases on Gilroy's forehead deepened.

Persons was delighted. "You know what they say.
You can pick your friends, but you can't pick your family." He laughed uproariously, making a ridiculous
high-pitched hiccupping noise.

While Persons was standing behind her, touching her,
Gilroy winked at Vining.

Vining understood. As much as she found Gilroy
despicable, they had to work together to bring him
down.

"And you, *Mother*, already know Officer Vining. The
Pasadena P.D.'s little worker bee. Into everything. No
stone unturned. Kudos to you, Officer Vining. Because
of your inability to stop picking the scab, you've made
this little reunion possible. I'd longed for such a day,
but didn't know how to pull it off. When Officer Vining
visited the sweet hamlet of Colina Vista, a plan took

shape for me. What I had thought would never happen now seemed possible."

Vining realized that she indeed had been the catalyst for this. Again, she had orchestrated her own destruction.

Still standing behind Gilroy, Persons ran his hands over her hair and neck. The gestures moved beyond friendly and playful into suggestive as his caresses turned intense. His face became serious, his breathing shallow, and his voice raspy. "This is a dream come true. Mother, I've dreamed of this moment."

Gilroy looked down with what looked to Vining like pure sadness.

He stepped away from Gilroy, slowly drawing his fingers across her neck, savoring the sensation of skin against skin until the final touch.

Vining realized she was holding her breath.

He put his hand on his pants and adjusted himself. Making a small sound of pleasure, he almost skipped to the kitchen island.

Vining exhaled. She saw Gilroy's shoulders relax as she also exhaled, free of her son's fearsome yet cloying touch. Vining met her eyes and arched an eyebrow, as if to say, *Now what?*

Gilroy arched an eyebrow in response and narrowed her eyes.

Vining nodded, but who were they kidding? It was ballsy posturing on their part, an effort to keep up their fighting spirits. If he chose to dispatch them while they were tied to chairs and handcuffed, they didn't have a chance. He had to cut at least one of them loose if they were to have a prayer of fighting back. Vining knew he loved the cat-and-mouse game. He'd played it with her in this same kitchen. Such risk excited him, but this time, was there too much at stake for him to take that chance, as delicious as he might find it?

Persons unzipped his duffel bag.

Vining checked out her surroundings. The honeycomb shades over the kitchen windows were closed. A few decorative items had been set around by the realtor to make the house look inviting: a crystal vase with a fading bouquet of seasonal flowers, a large, brightly painted ceramic rooster, and a wire basket full of lemons. On the island stood a bottle of Veuve Clicquot champagne and four crystal flute glasses. On the floor beside the island was a five-gallon, red plastic jug of gasoline, perhaps the one that had been in the Crown Vic's trunk.

"I'm sure you have many questions, Officer Vining. My mother has the answers, but she's a little tied up right now." He laughed at his lame joke, sounding a drumroll with his fingers against the island's granite countertop. "Yes, Mother's tied up right now," he repeated, enjoying saying it.

He methodically began taking items from the duffel, holding each one up, making sure the two women saw them, before setting them on the island. First out was the roll of duct tape followed by a tied length of cord.

He began a monologue. "I found out a lot about Betsy Gilroy and my birth father. The man who contributed a single orgasm that delivered the single sperm that combined with a single egg inside my mother's womb to create *the miracle of life*." His words dripped sarcasm.

He removed the Taser from its holster on his belt. He'd already ejected the spent cartridge he'd used to subdue Vining when she'd run down the driveway. He opened the Velcro case on his belt, took out a cartridge, reloaded the Taser, and returned it to the holster.

"See, Officer Vining, my mother gave me up for adoption. Once I was out of her womb, she couldn't wait to get rid of me. Mother, did you even bother to look at your bouncing baby boy?"

Gilroy sat immobile.

He pulled a Glock .40 from the duffel and held it up while he waited for Gilroy's response. Vining thought the Glock might be her own service revolver.

"Mother . . ." He ejected the magazine, checked the remaining bullets, and reloaded the gun. "Answer me and don't lie. I have a finely tuned bullshit monitor. I probably got that from you. That's a good asset for a cop." He leveled the Glock at Gilroy. "Mother, did you look at your bouncing baby boy?"

She almost imperceptibly shook her head.

"No. Of course you didn't want to see me." Persons set the Glock on the island. "I was living proof of the biggest mistake you'd ever made. You probably promised yourself that you would never again be so stupid, right? Falling for the seductive words of a handsome, rich, sweet-talking doctor who'd promised the world to little Betsy Gilroy from the wrong side of the tracks who'd had to bust her behind for every crumb she'd ever had."

Vining saw how he was savoring this, a sumptuous meal that would never be repeated. He was holding court at his banquet; standing at the head of the table he'd lovingly set with his best tableware, the courses chosen with care to provoke the precise oohs and aahhs from his guests. He was the host with the most.

"The private detective I hired to find my birth parents pointed me in the right direction. I did a lot of research on my own to fill in the blanks. Just so you know, Mother, if you've ever had the tiniest bit of guilt, I was adopted by a very nice couple. The Personses loved me as much as they could. They tried to do the right thing. It wasn't easy for them, let me tell ya."

He seemed wistful as he looked up toward the drawn shades over the kitchen windows. "When I was ten, they told me I was adopted. They were afraid of how I would react, but actually, I was relieved. My life finally made sense, because I always knew I didn't belong to them. I never felt . . . connected. As much as I've learned about you, Mother, and Dr. Daddy, I still have unanswered questions. Tonight, at last, all will be revealed."

He took out a small pistol, a Walther PPK. Vining recognized her much-beloved backup weapon. She cringed as he played with it, aiming it TV-cop-style between both hands, then gangbanger-style, one arm out, hand turned sideways.

He set the Walther on the island and took a rag from the duffel bag. He walked around to the jug of gasoline, unscrewed the top, and tipped the jug to moisten the rag. He used it to wipe down the Walther and the Glock. Holding the guns with the rag, he set them on the island.

Vining knew he was removing fingerprints. Whose was he concerned with? His?

"Officer Vining, here's what I know about the story of Betsy Gilroy and Dr. John Nickerson. Betsy was a young police officer with the Pasadena Police Department. She was an up-and-comer, landing key assignments, making friends and making lots of enemies. Then Betsy met Dr. Daddy, who was a fancy heart surgeon in Pasadena. How did you meet him, Mother?"

Gilroy had been staring at the floor. She looked up.

Walking over to her, he grabbed the edge of the duct tape and yanked it off.

Gilroy grimaced with the pain.

"How did you meet him?" Persons repeated.

Gilroy stared straight ahead, not looking at him or Vining. "He'd reported a burglary in his office. Some drugs were stolen. I took the report."

"And you started fucking him."

"It wasn't so sudden."

"No, of course not. There had to be seduction

involved. Romance. Nickerson was married. He and his wife ran with the Pasadena social set. Tell me how he seduced you."

Gilroy swallowed. "Can I have some water, please?"

He took one of the champagne flutes, washed out the dust at the sink inside the island, and filled it with water. He held it to her lips as she drank, wiping the dribble from her chin.

"Thank you," she said obsequiously. "I later saw him at a city event. He asked me to coffee, saying he wanted to ask my advice about something, and . . . one thing led to another."

"One thing led to another." Persons gave her a closed-lipped smile. "That covers a lot of ground, Mother. Where was the first time you and the good doctor had sex?"

She asked with annoyance, "Why does this matter?"

"Because it does," he yelled. "Because I need to know the story of my life. Every kid wants to know where he came from. It's human nature. Yet you denied me this simple request, forcing me to take these extreme measures. Mother, the time has come for you to tell me everything."

She looked at him. In that moment, Vining could see her change her strategy. The longer he wanted her to talk, the longer she'd stay alive. "Dr. Nickerson and I had relations in his office, after hours."

Persons sagely nodded, as if all was clear. "How long did your affair last?"

"A couple of months."

"Did he buy you pretty things?"

"Sometimes."

"And you loved them. You who came from nothing. He got a charge out of his blue-collar, tough lover who carried a gun and a badge. Who was so different from his society wife. And you saw a different path for yourself."

"I was young and naïve," Gilroy conceded.

"Did he say he was going to leave his wife for you?"

"He said they were unhappy."

"Is that why you got pregnant? To force his hand?"

"The pregnancy was an accident."

"An accident, you say. Bull, I say. You knew exactly what you were doing. You were naïve, all right. Naïve to think he'd leave his socially prominent wife and her old Pasadena money for you, a street cop. Nickerson didn't care that you were a rising star in the police department. He was more concerned about being shunned by his social set. He worried that no one would sit with him over lunch at the Valley Hunt Club. How did he react to the news that you were pregnant? I'm sure you couldn't wait to tell him."

"After the shock wore off, he was happy. His wife wasn't able to have children. They'd tried everything. He thought that maybe they'd adopt you."

"Was he going to pay you?"

"He had talked about a price."

"How much was I worth?"

Gilroy shrugged. "They'd spent a lot of money on fertility treatments. They really wanted a baby."

He put his hand inside the duffel bag and held it there. "But that didn't happen. You took a leave of absence from the police department. Near as I can find out, no one there knew you were pregnant."

Persons pulled out a narrow, rectangular wooden box from the duffel.

Vining had been focused on Gilroy, but the box drew her attention. It looked jarringly familiar.

He opened the box and held it up to reveal a set of knives with polished horn handles, nestled in old and fragile royal-blue satin. The cutlery ranged in size from an eight-inch chef's knife to a three-inch paring knife. It included a honing steel, also with a horn handle.

Vining gaped at the knives. Her grandmother had a set just like it. Granny had received it as a wedding present and had used them at every holiday gathering. Could these be Granny's knives?

When he turned the box, she saw an "S" carved on the bottom. This *was* Granny's set. Her sister Stephanie had carved her initial there one Thanksgiving years ago on a dare from Vining. She felt a wave of panic. Had he harmed her grandmother?

Persons gave Vining a smug look, guessing precisely where her mind had gone. He didn't explain the cutlery, but took out the smallest of the set, the paring knife. He tested the blade with his thumb.

"Dull," he pronounced. "Your grandmother should take better care of such a fine set of knives."

"Grandmother?" Gilroy said with alarm.

"Shut up!" he shouted, thrusting the blade in her direction. "You will speak only when spoken to."

Achieving silence, he took the hone from the box and ran the blade against it, methodically drawing it down one side and up the other.

The metal-on-metal noise further unnerved Vining. He might have been honing the knife against her spine.

Persons again tested the blade of the paring knife against his thumb. "Why did you give birth to me in secrecy, Mother? Why did you change your mind about letting the Nickersons take me?"

Gilroy said, "I just did."

Persons pouted. "I never got to meet my father. By the time I tracked him down, he'd been dead for years. I have gotten to know Dr. Daddy's and his skeleton wife's spawn—my half brother, Robert. We both have Daddy's unusual blue eyes. Bob tells me he also inherited Daddy's tendency to be . . . for lack of a better word, high-strung. The little fucker was okay as long as he stayed on his meds. But then he decided he didn't like experiencing life in soft-focus. Wanted a little postgraduate education after art school. That didn't last too long at my house."

While Persons drew his thumb across the knife blade, his gaze grew dreamy as he indulged in a recollection. He was chasing his brother Bob through the mobile home. He cornered him. Bob cowered on the ground as Persons got closer. "You've been a bad boy, Bob . . ."

Vining had been barely listening to Persons's soliloquy, sick with worry about her grandmother, but this last part drew her in. He had a blue-eyed, disturbed half brother who had gone to art school? He must be speaking of the nutcase she knew as Nitro.

"It sounds like a good family adopted you," Gilroy said. "Money isn't everything."

"Maybe not, but it would have been nice to be like Bob and have the option of saying, 'I'm sick of living in this big house in this ritzy neighborhood. I want to live on the edge.' " He continued to draw his thumb across the knife blade. He smiled, still transfixed by the blade. "I showed Bob the edge all right."

He looked at Gilroy. "But Mother, the point is, while I didn't want for material goods with the Persons, if Nickerson and his wife had raised me, I would have been with my own flesh and blood. I would have felt like I belonged somewhere. You took all that from me."

"I thought it was best for you."

"That is such tripe. Tell me the truth."

"I did it to get back at him, for all his empty promises."

"Maybe that's part of it, Mother, but that's not the whole story. I think revenge was the smallest part of your decision not to let my father keep me. Tell me the real reason you hid your pregnancy, gave birth to me in secret, and gave me away."

"That *is* the real reason. You were better off raised by a married couple, but not John Nickerson and his wife. He was a manic-depressive drunk and an adulterer who possibly killed himself. His boat was found drifting off Marina Del Rey. His death was reported as an accidental drowning. I think it was suicide, staged to look like an accident. Cleaner and better in terms of the insurance. His wife was a shallow woman who was addicted to prescription pills."

Persons listened thoughtfully, nodding, pressing the corners of his lips down as if it all made sense. He stepped quickly toward Gilroy, the paring knife clutched in his fist, and shouted, "Wrong!"

She was doing a good job at keeping her composure, but she reared back when he came at her with the knife.

He kneeled beside her and pressed the tip of the knife into her cheek.

She angled her eyes at the knife, her forehead furrowed.

"Why are you doing this, Tanner? Don't do this!"

He shouted into her face. "Don't you dare say my name." He picked up the piece of duct tape from the ground and pressed it over her mouth. Without hesitation, he again raised the knife and drew the blade down her cheek, making a long cut.

Gilroy let out a muffled scream behind the duct tape. She began panting, furiously seizing air through her nose. Her eyes were wild.

Persons hypnotically watched the blood beading along the wound before flowing, dripping down her chin and onto her white blouse. His breaths grew short. A pink flush bloomed on his cheeks. He licked the fresh blood from the blade.

FIFTY-ONE

Vining's stomach churned. Behind her horror, she still wondered what her role was in this drama. Had he brought her to be a witness?

"Here's the truth, Mother," he panted, again holding the knife against her bleeding face. "You decided to have the baby. Maybe you thought you'd keep it and make Dr. Daddy pay for everything. You'd have the satisfaction of knowing how the tongues in his social set would wag. But then, something wonderful happened. Your long-sought-after promotion to corporal was finally coming through. You'd tried to get promoted before, but your reputation as a hell-raiser kept you back. Finally, all your hard work and sacrifice was paying off. You thought they'd rescind the promotion if your secret came out. They'd have second thoughts because of the bad judgment and lack of character you'd shown by getting knocked up by the well-respected husband of one of Pasadena's most prominent women. Of course, the brass would never say that to you. You'd just be shunted to the side for the rest of your career. You have so much invested in that insignia on your uniform and how people see you, throwing it away would be like throwing yourself away.

"You were at a crossroads. Baby or career? It was too late for an abortion, so you made up a story about having to care for a sick grandmother out-of-state and took a leave of absence. The baby problem gone, the illicit affair buried, you went on to a stellar career."

Vining saw him tremble as his excitement fed off Gilroy's fear. His fluffy cheeks were steadily flushed now and he was breathing through his mouth.

"You became a real hero, Mother. An inspiration to women everywhere. Look at Betsy Gilroy! See what she accomplished! Look at the heights we women can reach!"

He waved the knife in front of Gilroy, like an artist facing his canvas, waiting for the muse to direct him where he should apply the paintbrush next.

"You had all the time in the world for polishing the brass stars on your collar, but you couldn't give the time of day to your first-born son. I spent a lot of time and money to find you. Remember the gift I'd bought just for you? Pearls and your birthstone. It was a simulated sapphire, but it was all I could afford then."

He darted the knife toward Gilroy, who jerked back. He picked up the pearl necklace with the knife blade.

"When you finally agreed to meet me, you at first looked at me like I was the abortion you wished you'd had. I was the last person you wanted to see in your little village where you were hot stuff. The heir apparent to the top cop. I was your dirty little secret incarnate. Then you came around and were polite and pleasant and said all the right things, political animal that you are. You looked thrilled to receive my little gift.

"For a time, I deluded myself into thinking that you were being motherly toward me. You even helped get me a security job at the Rose City shopping center. You found me a place to stay in the Joseph's guest cottage. For my part, I honored your wish to keep our true relationship a secret. I honored your wish until *you* betrayed *me*. It was a small betrayal, but aren't they always the most cutting?

"You gave my humble gift—the pearl necklace with the sapphire—to your beloved Cookie. I had no choice but to respond. To hurt you like you'd hurt me. Cookie probably confessed to you that she'd lost the necklace."

He put on a falsetto voice. "Silly me. How could I have been so careless? Can you forgive me, Betsy?"

His voice returned to normal. "I'm sure you told her not to worry, while secretly you were glad to be rid of it. How could you have known that I had stolen it from Cookie's apartment, and I forced her to put it on before—" He lunged his face menacingly close to Gilroy's. "I slit her throat."

Vining saw spray from his mouth fly onto Gilroy, who flinched and pressed her eyes closed.

"I destroyed her, your sweet, little Cookie-Ookie." He picked up the necklace from Gilroy's chest and drew his fingers along it as he spoke.

"She'd gone out with her girlfriends. They were drinking and laughing. Cookie had parked away from the others, down a dark street. 'Don't worry about me, girls. I'm a cop.' They'd all had a big laugh and Cookie walked away, almost right into my arms. Imagine her surprise when I grabbed her from behind and put my hand over her mouth. 'Hello, Cookie. Remember me?' She thought she was a tiger, but . . ." He shrugged.

The fire and fight that Gilroy had shown earlier was slipping away. She seemed resigned to her fate.

As absorbed as Vining was by this perverted family tale, one question above all others nagged her. *Why was she here?*

Persons stroked Gilroy's necklace as he continued to talk. His voice had a chilling, affectless monotone that hinted at the churning passions beneath. "I put her into her own car and drove it to the Foothill Museum, where she always met *him*. That night, though, she had a date with *me*."

His plan had been to rape Cookie and to disappear. To leave town and the mother who didn't want him, never to return. He'd left his truck where he'd abducted Cookie, planning to walk back to get it later. At the barn, he'd set the scene with the Coleman lantern and the patchwork quilt Cookie had used during her trysts with her boyfriend. He'd had her strip off her clothes and then he'd tied her wrists and ankles. Completing the scene, he'd slipped the pearl necklace over her head. Cookie had seemed passive as she lay on the quilt. Everything was ready. Everything except . . . him. He was a limp noodle.

His impotent fumbling roused Cookie from her stupor. Her notorious sharp tongue unleashed a barrage of insults to his manhood. She wouldn't stop, even when he strung her up by her ankles, thinking he'd show her a thing or two. Surprisingly, *that* got him going. The more afraid she was, the more excited he became. Her talking now got in the way, so he took duct tape from the duffel he'd thrown into her car and used it to silence her. He gave her a good shove and watched her swing upside down as he stroked himself, her terrified eyes sending him to new heights of excitement. Then he had a wicked idea. It excited him even more. He took out the folding knife that he'd used to cut the rope and slowly moved toward Cookie, savoring every second of her horror.

But Tanner's fun had been interrupted by that idiot caretaker who'd jumped screaming from his hiding place. Tanner had fled into the woods, covered in blood. After the handyman had gone back inside the cabin, Tanner had again crept into the barn. He'd finally achieved release at Cookie's expense, but the victory was Pyrrhic. As he picked up Cookie's blood-splattered blouse to keep as a souvenir he vowed that next time, he would get it right. Still, he'd learned an important lesson: Murder was an aphrodisiac.

He let out a small moan and bit his lower lip as he replayed Cookie's murder in his mind. "Until I killed Cookie, I didn't realize how pleasurable—how satisfying—the act would be. It went beyond my wildest dreams. It set my life on a new path. It touched a part of me that I thought might exist, but had never experienced. It was a deity of delight."

He cackled and looked at Vining for approval of his attempt to be cute.

She gave him a weak smile and nod.

His eyes had brightened while recounting his moment of epiphany, but they darkened again. "You knew I murdered Cookie, didn't you, Mother?"

She shook her head and made muffled protestations.

"Yes, you did."

She continued to express denial.

"Then why did you take the necklace off Cookie's body? I made Cookie wear it as a message to you. When you took it, you were telling me, 'I understand.' "

Gilroy shook her head, frowning gravely.

"When you and that lame-brained sergeant were the first to arrive and he had to run outside to puke, that gave you just enough time to take the necklace. You threw it into the woods. You probably thought it was simple luck that it was never found. But I was still there, hiding. I wasn't going to miss any of the fun. I picked up the necklace that you threw away and it's served as my inspiration ever since. I wore it during the whole walk back to my truck, covered in Cookie's blood, laughing and laughing. See, Mother, that was the night you became my accomplice. Didn't you?"

Gilroy persisted in shaking her head and protesting from behind her duct-taped lips.

"You've been my accomplice ever since. By railroading Axel Holcomb, you showed me how a pro covers up a murder." He shouted, "Admit it!"

He was blocking Vining's view when she heard Gilroy's muffled protests turn into a muffled scream.

When he moved away, Vining saw a Z carved into Gilroy's other cheek. Blood dripped onto the other side of her blouse. She was breathing hard through her nose. Her forehead glistened with perspiration.

Persons admired this new wound, the tip of his pink tongue poking between his lips. He touched the cut and put his finger into his mouth, wrapping his lips around it as he pulled it out. The bulge in his pants was undeniable.

"Didn't it happen just like that, Mother?"

Gilroy still feebly protested while staring at his hand that still held the knife, wondering where it would land next.

Without warning, he slammed the knife onto the counter and began half unbuttoning and half tearing at his shirt buttons. He yanked off his tie and threw it to the ground, followed by the shirt.

Vining and Gilroy both looked in horror at the many small wounds, both fresh and scarred-over, that covered his pasty-white, overhanging belly. There was a tuft of hair on his chest between his flabby pectorals and pink nipples. He grabbed the knife and cut his abdomen.

Vining was so startled, she rocked the chair backward, the legs scuttling against the wood-plank floor, almost toppling over.

Persons looked down at the damage he'd inflicted, and then closed his eyes with obvious relief. Surprisingly, his skin color improved. His face wasn't as bright red as it had been before. Blood ran down his belly onto his pants and dripped onto the floor. He touched the blood and held up his hand as if to admire it.

Reaching his bloody hand into the duffel bag, he took

out a roll of paper towels. He tore off a sheet, folded it into a square, and slapped it against the wound, making it look like a perverse shaving nick.

Taking one of the champagne flutes from the island, he filled it with water from the sink there and drank it down. He seemed eerily calmer and had recovered the disturbing boyishness he'd shown earlier.

He reached inside his black bag of tricks and took out another handgun—a .45. He stuck it beneath his belt, where it made an indentation against his flabby, blood-streaked belly.

He held his hand over the open box of knives, as if trying to decide upon a bonbon from an assortment. He reached in and pulled out the butcher knife. He ran his thumb over the blade. Again, he found the edge wanting and began to hone it against the steel. He took no notice that the blood-soaked paper towel had fallen off and blood was dribbling everywhere.

He again rounded the island, but this time, he went to Vining.

The knife blade flashed as he twisted and turned it in front of her face. "This is such a fine instrument." Picking up the rag, he moistened it with more gasoline and cleaned the knife before setting it down.

"Officer Vining, I'm going to untie you, but you have to promise to be a good girl. Bad girls get punished. Just ask Mother." He shot a mischievous glance at Gilroy.

He loosened the cords that bound Vining's feet to the chair. He began to peel the duct tape from her mouth, using more care than he'd shown with Gilroy.

"Stand up," he ordered. He unlocked her handcuffs.

She brought her hands front and rubbed her wrists.

Using the rag to pick up the freshly sharpened butcher knife, he presented it to her and said, "Kill her. Kill Betsy Gilroy."

FIFTY-TWO

Vining's role was now clear. Every policewoman he'd murdered or had attempted to murder had stood in for the one he couldn't bring himself to kill—his mother.

He sat in the chair she'd vacated, holding the .45 aimed at her. He slid his fingers beneath the butt of the Taser in the holster that painfully dug into the mound of fat that billowed over the top of his belt. He stood, took out the Taser, and set it on the island. Using the paring knife, he periodically made more small cuts in his abdomen. He stuck folded squares of paper towels on them from the roll by his feet. The paper towels weren't doing the job.

Vining wondered, the way he was bleeding, if he would lose enough blood to pass out or even die. She tentatively held her grandmother's butcher knife, without conviction.

"Go ahead, Officer Vining," he goaded.

Vining looked at Gilroy, who seemed unaffected by this development. Vining decided she was either shell-shocked or didn't fear she'd actually do what Persons wanted.

He raised his eyebrows as if something had just become clear. "A knife's not your style? Then pick another weapon. Pick another room in the house. Remember that old board game called Clue? We'll make our own game of Clue. Officer Vining killed Betsy Gilroy in the study with the candlestick."

He again laughed like a castrated hyena.

Vining toyed with the butcher knife. "What did you do to my grandmother?"

He pressed his lips together, making his cheeks puff out. "Nothing. She was snoring like a locomotive in bed when I left."

She was inclined to believe him, thinking he would have bragged about killing the old lady. She hoped.

"Your plan is to make it look like I killed Chief Gilroy and you weren't even here."

"Exactamundo."

"But your blood is getting all over."

He laughed, "Yeah," as he looked down at himself. "I'm a mess. Doesn't matter. They're going to find a murder committed by a cop with emotional problems who spilled gasoline all over and set the house on fire before she shot herself. They're not going to analyze buckets of blood."

"Why do you cut yourself like that?" She knew about cutters, but thought it was the domain of disturbed teenaged girls.

"You mean, like this?" He flicked the paring knife against his arm the same way he might flick off a fly. He shuddered as he observed the fresh wound. "It hurts, but it feels good, too. It relaxes me."

As revolting as she found this behavior, she egged him on. If he cut himself enough and she waited long enough . . .

"Tanner . . . May I call you Tanner?"

"Please do."

"Tanner, you say cutting calms you, but I think it excites you too, maybe a little."

"It's not about the blood. The blood's a by-product. It's about the metal against flesh. It's the opening up. It opens up and you see something new. You release something bad. It's like the chaff that comes away from the wheat." He pulled off a soaked paper towel and gingerly probed a fresh wound, making it bleed anew. "See. Look how much is there beneath the skin. I don't really like guns. There's no art in firing a gun. You can't control a bullet like you can a knife. I'm talking about for the finer work I do."

She leaned against the island and set the butcher knife on top. Guns were her weapons of choice in all situations. Her two guns were inches from her fingers. Could she reach them before he could shoot her? She doubted it.

"I'm confused, Tanner, because you used a gun to kill Scrappy." She'd sensed his hand in Scrappy's murder since she'd first seen the China Dog 187 tag. She was fishing now and hoped he'd bite. He did.

His expression changed to disdain. "Scrappy. That wasn't art. That was extermination."

"Why did you kill him?"

"He tried to blackmail me."

"Over what?"

He turned his ice-blue eyes on her and said matter-of-factly, "You. Those arrow guys started showing up across the street from where I work. Scrappy was the one there at night. My boss told us security guards to keep an eye on them. To go over there and chat them up. See if we could find out what they were up to. He thought they were planning on robbing the company. Steal all their organic face cream, or something.

"So, each night I went over and me and Scrappy had a chat. We got kinda friendly. He talked about how much he hated this Chinese guy he worked for and how much he hated cops. Somehow your name came up. He talked about how you used to pay him for information. He had the hots for you. Your name came up a couple of times. Maybe I brought it up. One night, he had that drawing of me that was in the papers and demanded money."

He made a rude noise. "Stupid beaner junkie. I told him I'd give him money. Drugs, too. Whatever he wanted. I gave him a place and a time and told him to come alone." He beamed, showing those small teeth. "Easy as pie."

Vining nodded. "And you painted the China Dog tag to make it look like it involved his boss, Marvin Li."

"Precisely. It worked, didn't it? The cops landed on that slope gimp like flies on manure."

"You sent us in the wrong direction, that's for sure." She grinned.

He grinned back. The blood from the wound on his arm that he hadn't bothered to blot dripped onto the floor.

Vining thought it looked like the deepest one yet. "Tanner, I'm so glad we have this chance to talk. There's so much I want to ask you."

"We have time." He sat back down.

"Tell me something. You didn't use a knife to kill Marilu Feathers. You used a gun."

He turned up his lips, dwelling on the memory. "Marilu. If I had it to do over again, I would have chosen a knife."

"You didn't have the chance to touch her like you did Cookie and Johnna Alwin, and certainly weren't able to hold her like you held me." Out of the corner of her eye, she saw Gilroy maneuvering her feet. The chief was wearing slip-on shoes. If she could get her feet out of them, she might be able to slide from the cord that bound her ankles.

"Remember how tightly you held me, Tanner?" Vining moved to stand in front of him, blocking his view. "How excited you were? *I* remember."

He gave her a look that was so replete with sexual longing, it was all she could do to keep from gagging.

He squirmed in the chair. He had a goofy expression

on his face that she interpreted as a perverted come-hither look.

She went on, giving Gilroy time to keep working her feet free. "Remember my blood gushing all over your yellow shirt? Flowing from my neck and down your chest onto that pretty yellow shirt. And you kept that shirt. Did you touch yourself while playing with it? I bet you did. Tell me about it. Don't leave out any details."

He inhaled a wavering breath and lost his aim with the .45 when his wrist dropped as he became distracted. "You'd better slow down."

"Why, Tanner? Why should I slow down?"

"Because I told you to."

"But why? All that blood. . . ." Vining lowered her voice seductively. "You held me *so* tight. I knew what you wanted. I felt you, so hard against me." She wondered if this was how it felt to be a phone-sex operator.

He made another quick cut on his arm. It was also deep, and bled furiously. His tone of voice changed. "I don't want to talk about that." He stood, covered in blood, and again aimed the .45 at her. "I'm in charge here. Not you."

She inched away from him along the kitchen island.

"Pick up the knife and get busy." He staggered.

Betsy Gilroy, in her stockings, her shoes left behind on the floor, hands handcuffed behind her back, flung herself off the chair at Persons, barreling her head directly into his groin. They flew backward, knocking over his chair and toppling the jug of gasoline, which spilled across the wooden floor.

He aimlessly fired the .45, weakened by blood loss and tangled up in the chair.

Gilroy grappled to get away from him and his bullets, trying to get traction on the gasoline-slick floor, not having her hands to help her.

Persons shot wildly as he tried to get to his feet.

As soon as Gilroy made her move, Vining spun around and grabbed a gun from the island. She thought she'd grabbed one of her weapons, but ended up with the Taser. She didn't dare spend the time to trade it for something more lethal. She fired at Persons.

She got off a good shot. The two darts hit Persons in the upper chest. She kept her finger on the trigger, sending a steady stream of 50,000 volts into him.

He dropped the gun and fell back onto the floor, frenetically jerking from the electric jolt.

Gilroy got her feet against the island and was able to push away from the convulsing man. She managed to get around to the other side of the island and away from the gasoline.

She was so covered in blood from the wounds that Persons had inflicted, Vining didn't know whether she'd been shot.

Suddenly, there was a whoosh as the gasoline ignited, set off by sparks from the electric charge. While thrashing on the floor, Persons had become drenched in gasoline. Now he was engulfed in flames.

Vining threw down the Taser and jumped out of the way of the growing blaze.

Screaming in agony, Persons rolled on the floor, only further spreading the flaming gasoline. He got to his feet and lumbered around, as if amazed at what was happening. His naked chest was charred black in places and seeping pink and red in others as his flesh seemed to melt from him. As he staggered, flames leaped from him onto the window shades. They were consumed in a heartbeat. The crown molding, made of synthetic material, also caught, and fire raced around the ceiling.

Vining was frozen, astonished at seeing him being incinerated before her eyes.

He wavered on his feet, as if about to finally go down, when he saw her across the kitchen. His face was a blackened, oozing mess. His lips were burned away. Still, he smiled as if somewhere in his dark diseased brain, he was happy. He took rickety steps toward her, arms outstretched as if seeking a final embrace. While still a few feet away from her, he crumpled like a house of cards onto the floor.

Vining roused from her trance. Dodging the encroaching flames, she opened cabinets, searching for a fire extinguisher. She opened the door of the pantry and had plunged inside before she realized where she was. For a few precious seconds that she couldn't afford to spend, she was stunned to find herself there, the place where she had crawled over a year before, the knife that T. B. Mann had stabbed her with still jutting from her neck, the wound that she would die from, gushing blood. The place where she had met her doom. Dazed, she ran back into the kitchen.

Someone nudged her back to the here and now. She turned to see Betsy Gilroy, duct tape still over her mouth, hands cuffed behind her back, and her feet in stockings. She still wore the costume pearl-and-sapphire necklace that her son had given her on top of her blood-soaked blouse. She gestured with her head, urging Vining to get out.

Vining pulled the neck of her shirt up over her mouth and nose and followed Gilroy out of the kitchen, keeping low, beneath the flames that had nearly engulfed the area. She remembered to grab her Glock and her beloved Walther PPK from the kitchen island before she ran through the doorway into the butler's pantry. She passed through the dining room and then made a left turn into the foyer with its Oriental carpet runner. She had to open the front door for the handcuffed Gilroy. When she had crossed the threshold onto the front porch, she'd completely retraced the steps she'd made that fateful day when she'd first entered that house at 835 El Alisal Road. Now she was out. She had fled it and its spell over her.

Gilroy kept running until she reached the grassy parkway, where she collapsed.

Vining dropped to the ground beside her. She peeled the duct tape from the chief's mouth and asked, "Are you all right?"

"I'm okay. How about you?"

"I'm fine. I don't have a key for those cuffs."

Gilroy shrugged and watched the flames leaping into the dark, early-morning sky.

There were sirens in the distance.

Vining said, "Chief, even if I could unlock those cuffs, I wouldn't. I'm arresting you as an accessory to the Cookie Silva murder."

Gilroy's steely gaze returned. "Do what you need to do but you need to know something. I did not frame Axel Holcomb. I did not coerce a confession from him. Decisions were made based upon evidence."

"Did you take that necklace off Cookie's corpse?"

Gilroy looked unblinkingly at Vining, seemingly oblivious to her own sliced face. "I'm not discussing this with you further."

Vining dropped it for now, while thinking that poor Axel Holcomb was in for a pleasant surprise.

As neighbors stepped from their homes in robes and slippers, fire trucks and emergency vehicles poured into the street. In the midst of them was a dark Crown Victoria that swerved erratically to the curb and stopped. The door flew open and out ran Jim Kissick.

Vining leaped to her feet when she saw him.

He was out of breath as he rushed to her. "I was on my way to the Foothill Museum when I heard a broadcast about a fire at Eight-three-five El Alisal. I just had a feeling."

They embraced in the middle of the street.

After breaking from their kiss, he examined her all over, looking for injuries. "Are you okay?"

"I'm fine." She spotted his bandage. "What happened to your hand?"

"A bullet grazed me during the Victor Chang shoot-out. Lost my cell phone and it took me a while to find it. That's why I didn't answer your calls right away."

"Shoot-out?"

"Yeah, we located Chang in Bungalow Heaven and . . ." He saw Betsy Gilroy standing a few yards away. "What's Chief Gilroy doing here? Why is she bloody?"

"Tanner Persons—T. B. Mann—cut her."

"*What?* He was here?"

"He's dead." She recalled her last moments in the kitchen when she'd taken a final look at Persons's charred body. "He . . . I . . ."

She suddenly started shivering uncontrollably and could barely stand.

He put his arm around her shoulders and walked her to the opposite side of the street where they sat on the curb.

She turned her head into his chest and began to weep. Her teeth chattered so much, she could barely get out her words. "All these months, I dreamed of doing terrible things to him. I wanted to give him the most horrible, painful death possible." She sobbed. "Now, I've done it, and it *was* horrible."

"I know. I know . . ." He held her and stroked her hair. "But hey, it was him or you, right?"

FIFTY-THREE

*B*efore daybreak, Kissick, Caspers, and a fleet of Pasadena and Covina police officers swarmed Tanner Persons's trailer in the Country Squire Estates mobile-home park. They nearly shot a pale, spindly man whom they found wandering about looking dazed. He cowered when confronted with the bright flashlight beams and weapons, fleeing to crouch against the wall like a cornered spider. It was the same behavior that Vining had observed in the tagger who had painted the threatening message on the alley wall.

Kissick recognized the disturbed man as Nitro, yet something was amiss—more amiss than usual. Kissick held off the officers and their guns as he moved toward the terrified man for a closer look. When he was finally able to move Nitro's hands from his head and see his face, he was jolted by the presence of an awl jutting from the corner of his eye beside his nose.

A search of the trailer revealed the satin-draped shrine with fake marble columns in honor of Cookie Silva, Marilu Feathers, and Johnna Alwin. Nan Vining's slashed photo and pedestal were on the floor, still there from when Persons had knocked them over in a fit of rage. A filing cabinet held massive amounts of exacting research on these four women and others too. The file on Vining was by far the largest and most current, including recent photos of Emily at home and school.

More surprises were in store for the police in the little

single-wide of horrors. Persons's bedroom at the end of the narrow hallway provided its own unique charms. Persons, having generally ascetic habits, slept on a tidy army cot against a wall. A king-size bed took up most of the rest of the small room. It was a grand affair, four-poster with a lace canopy and a richly embroidered, satin bedspread. Laid side by side on top of the bed-spread, dressed in frilly peignoirs, were two mummified corpses. An urn full of cremated remains took the place of a head above a third peignoir.

DNA analysis would later prove that he'd robbed the graves of Cookie and Marilu.

The remains in the urn turned out to be not human but canine. Johnna Alwin's body had been cremated and her ashes scattered in the Saguaro National Park in Tucson, as per her wishes. The pooch in the urn was never identified.

Tanner Persons's neighbors weren't completely sur-prised at the news that the neat man who was generally polite and kept to himself, but who could be quite prickly and unpleasant, was a serial killer.

Further investigation revealed not only his neighbor Enrique's grave beneath the trailer, but several other dis-membered bodies as well.

Vining declined to go with Kissick to Persons's trailer. The old Nan would have pored over Tanner Persons's possessions with perverse glee. The fire that had consumed Persons had also brought the beginnings of a transformation in Nan. She admitted to a morbid curiosity about the bric-a-brac of Tanner Persons's life, but knew it wasn't healthy for her to go to his home. It was a small step toward a different way of life for her.

As soon as the police had arrived on-scene at 835 El Alisal Road, Vining sent a car to check on her grand-mother. The officers soon reported that the old woman had been fast asleep in bed. Granny was delighted when they revealed the news that Nan's attacker was dead. Tanner Persons had easily accessed her house through the front door, which Granny had forgotten to lock.

After seeing the televised news reports about the drama on El Alisal Road, Vining's ex-husband Wes had driven Emily to the PPD to wait for her mother.

When Vining had finished giving her statement, she briefly met with the chief. Afterward, Emily was waiting and ran into her mother's arms.

"Is it over?" the girl asked.

Vining replied, "It's *so* over."

FIFTY-FOUR

Medical specialists who assessed the case of twenty-five-year-old Robert Nickerson, aka Nitro, agreed that he had been the victim of a home lobotomy. In spite of Robert's limited ability to describe what had happened to him, the doctors were able to determine that his half brother, Tanner Persons, had administered the lobotomy via the precise insertion of an awl into the brain after Robert had "been bad."

While Robert had not participated in Persons's murders, he had assisted him in robbing the graves, which was a recent inspiration. Robert had been an avid audience for Persons's tales about his lethal conquests. He identified the drawings in the spiral pad as his work. He'd made the accurate renderings of the attacks on the four policewomen based upon Persons's lovingly detailed recountings of the events.

Robert's mother, Diana Nickerson, hadn't heard from her son in some time. She knew he had been staying with his half brother in Covina. He normally checked in with his mother every few days when he was away. He had been living with her, splitting their time between homes in Vail, Colorado, and Sarasota, Florida. They had moved from Pasadena after Dr. John Nickerson's death, which the already mentally fragile Robert had taken hard. After Robert had earned his bachelor of fine arts, his mother was pleased when he'd landed some freelance work for an ad agency.

When Tanner Persons had tracked down Robert and his mother with the help of a private investigator over ten years ago, Robert fell in thrall to his older half brother, telling his mother that he'd lost his father, but at least he'd found a brother. Tanner and Robert got tight fast, with Robert tailing Tanner to the places he lived—Tucson, Morro Bay, and the Pasadena area, among others. This last visit, to Tanner's Covina home, had been the longest. Robert had been there for nearly two months and had spoken of moving in permanently with Tanner.

This was not welcome news for Diana Nickerson. She hadn't cared for Persons. While there was nothing specific she could put her finger on, she had found his presence unsettling.

The police made educated guesses about the blanks in Robert's story. Inventorying the pills in his prescription containers showed that Robert had gone off his meds shortly after arriving at Persons's Country Squire mobile home. As Robert's mind traveled off the reservation, the already significant influence of his brother grew. This may have been when Persons revealed his secret life to his half brother. Trouble started when

Robert did some freelancing of his own, streaking nude through Pasadena with his drawing pad and the pearl-and-sapphire necklace. Robert's spray-painting the "Vining 187" tag on the building near where Persons worked was presumably another of his own initiatives.

Robert had become a liability for Persons. Persons couldn't bring himself to murder his half brother and cherished blood relative, so he neutralized him with a home lobotomy.

Tanner Persons's desire to connect with family had led to his downfall.

FIFTY-FIVE

As Marvin "China Dog" Li sat in a jail cell, weighing his options, and Victor "Kicker" Chang's corpse cooled at the county morgue, the Pasadena Police detectives met in the Detectives Section conference room to sort out what had happened.

"As you can see, Nan is not here," Kissick said. "She's . . . um . . . been suspended for three weeks."

Caspers had been tapping the eraser end of a pencil on the table and stopped, to Kissick's relief, at the statement about Vining. "*Three weeks?* Nan? What did she do to earn three weeks' suspension?"

Louis Jones and Doug Sproul were less overt, but their faces betrayed their surprise.

Sergeant Early exchanged a glance with Lieutenant Beltran, who inclined his head in her direction, signaling her to explain. Early leaned forward in her chair.

"The details of Detective Vining's infractions are confidential, but I can make a general statement and say that she was guilty of conduct unbecoming a sworn officer of this police department."

Kissick privately recalled the scene that night when he'd arrived at the burning house at 835 El Alisal Road and found Vining and Chief Gilroy on the parkway in front. Betsy Gilroy was wearing the pearl-and-sapphire necklace. When patrol cars descended, Sergeant Terrence Folke, who had been involved with the Nitro escapade in Old Pasadena, recognized Nitro's necklace. When he asked Gilroy about it, she readily said that Vining had given it to her. More accurately, had thrown it at her.

Vining, instead of fabricating another lie, came clean about how she had confiscated the necklace from Nitro's personal possessions when he'd been incarcerated in County General's psych ward. Kissick knew that no one had yet found out that she had also absconded with Johnna Alwin's pearl necklace from the Tucson P.D. She'd likely be terminated if that ever came out. He'd be in big trouble as well for having kept her secret.

Early said, "Nan's discipline could have been much worse, but the chief took into consideration all she's been through over the past year and a half." She added, "I'm disappointed that someone under my command would tarnish the reputation of this department."

Kissick found Early's last shot unnecessary, especially since Nan wasn't there to defend herself. He knew that Sarge was hard on officers who violated their sworn oaths. So was he, but if Nan hadn't pressed the envelope, they wouldn't be here reviewing a slew of closed cases. He wondered if Sarge's harshness toward Nan was residual emotion over the downfall of her once-revered friend, Betsy Gilroy.

"Sarge, I can't condone Nan's act that caused the suspension," Kissick began, "but she had the guts to stand up to criticism and question the official investigations into the murders of Officer Cookie Silva and Detective Johnna Alwin. Ranger Marilu Feathers's loved ones now know who was responsible for her murder. Also, Nan asked the Azusa P.D. to reopen the Sandra Lynde murder case. Sandra is the mother of LAPD vice officer Frankie Lynde, a homicide we worked a few months ago. Azusa P.D. got a cold hit on old DNA evidence. Their guy's in Folsom for a different robbery and was about to be released."

Early turned tired eyes on him.

Kissick thought it best to drop it. He was about to move on when Caspers asked, "So what's going to happen to Chief Gilroy?"

When it appeared that Sergeant Early wasn't going to take the question, Lieutenant Beltran leaned forward, folding his hands on the table. He tapped his thumbs together. "The State Attorney General's office will be doing the investigation into the charges against Chief Gilroy. Due to the chief's long relationship with local law enforcement agencies and the L.A. County District Attorney's office, there were conflicts of interest preventing the situation from being investigated locally."

Beltran said nothing further. Most in the room privately thought: *Chief Gilroy's going away.*

Breaking the weighty silence, Kissick said, "Alex, please present your overview of what we've learned about the goings-on at Newcastle Street."

Caspers became lively, happy with his moment in the spotlight. "Grace Shipley, who lives on that block of Newcastle Street being guarded by Marvin Li's felons, is the longtime girlfriend of this guy, Sun Kao. He goes by the moniker Weasel."

He held up a mug shot of an Asian man with a thick neck and piercing cold eyes.

"He's forty-five years old and is the longtime head of Hell Side Wah Ching. He's serving life-without-the-possibility-of-parole at Corcoran State Prison. Our friend Marvin Li was also incarcerated at Corcoran. The Sheriff's San Gabriel Valley Gang Task Force suspected that Kao was calling the shots on the street from behind bars but didn't know how his orders were getting through.

"This other gang, Black Dragon, controls the drug tax in Temple City, making drug dealers pay to do business on their turf. Black Dragon and Hell Side Wah Ching are bitter rivals. Black Dragon's head guys were recently rounded up on federal racketeering charges, putting their leadership in turmoil. Last month, a Black Dragon member was shot to death outside a Temple City bar. The Sheriff's Task Force suspected that Hell Side was taking advantage of Black Dragon's weakness and making a grab for power. But a murder like that is usually green-lighted by someone high up. The sheriff's naturally thought of Sun Kao, but how to prove it?

"Ironically, our surveillance of Marvin Li and his guys because of the totally unrelated murder of Scrappy Espinoza handed the sheriff's a big break and caused them to look again at Grace Shipley. She'd been on their radar, but they'd turned their focus from her because she's hardly had any contact with Kao since he went up. Turns out that Grace's daughter Meghan visits Weasel Kao at least three times a month. So what's up with that, right?"

"Kites," Jones said, speaking of the tiny coded notes that prisoners cleverly pass to visitors.

"Exactly." Caspers flashed a smile. "Yesterday, before the Victor Chang shoot-out, sheriff's investigators apprehended Meghan as she was leaving Corcoran and confiscated a kite. In it, Kao had green-lighted a murder of another Black Dragon associate."

Sproul bobbed his head. "When the men are in prison, the women run the show on the streets."

Early's focus was so deep, she hadn't moved a muscle until now. "So Marvin Li, whose Guns Gone organization had been awarded grants from the state and many cities to reform gang members, remained a faithful captain and active member of Hell Side Wah Ching. His job was to protect the acting head, Grace Shipley. So he deployed teams of criminals under the auspices of Aaron's Aarrows to serve as lookouts."

"Thanks for your report, Alex," Kissick said. "Li probably told Chang that his number was up, that if Chang falsely confessed to Scrappy's murder, we'd stop sniffing around and Li would be able to protect what was really going on—a gang war between Hell Side Wah Ching and their rivals, Black Dragon. He'd set it up to make it look like he was delivering Chang to us, but Chang wasn't about to go down for a murder he didn't commit."

Lieutenant Beltran stroked his upper lip. He'd shaved his mustache weeks ago, but still subconsciously smoothed it. "So Scrappy Espinoza, a two-bit snitch, is murdered in Old Pasadena, which leads to Marvin Li, which leads to Grace and Meghan Shipley, which leads to Sun Kao, which leads to breaking open a violent territorial war between two rival Asian gangs."

Kissick concluded. "All discovered because Scrappy Espinoza had recognized Tanner Persons as the man who'd attacked Nan Vining and tried to blackmail him."

They sat in silence for a while.

Kissick caught Early's eye and said, "Word is Axel Holcomb will be released from prison soon."

With that last piece of news, he ended the meeting.

FIFTY-SIX

At home that evening, at dusk, Vining stood on her terrace and enjoyed her view of the hindquarters of L.A. and the tips of the downtown skyscrapers that she could glimpse above the hilltops. She'd stopped by the market and bought groceries for favorite treats of hers and Em's that she hadn't cooked in a long time: lasagna, stuffed bell peppers, enchiladas, and Toll House cookies. She had time on her hands.

On impulse, because she rarely drank, she bought a margarita in a flip-top can. She'd poured it into a glass over ice and stood on the terrace sipping it.

For the first time in a year and a half, she hadn't felt T. B. Mann out there, watching her. Now he had a face, he had a name, and he wouldn't bother her anymore.

Vining let an ice cube slip into her mouth and chewed it. She put down the glass and walked to the wind chimes. They were silent. She didn't even sense a vibration from them as she had in the past right before they had been set ringing by Frankie Lynde's ghostly hand. Vining hoped she had finally appeased the ghost who followed her.

She took the clapper between her fingers and hit it against one of the larger steel tubes, emitting a somber, resonant tone. She sounded it for Frankie Lynde, then once again, for each of the others: Cookie Silva, Marilu Feathers, and Johnna Alwin.

After the last tone faded, she rang it one more time. This was for the Nan Vining that T. B. Mann had made. She was no longer a reflection in his twisted eyes. She and Em were finally free of his dark shadow. Vining was her own Nan now.

FIFTY-SEVEN

That weekend, Vining released Emily from being grounded and let her go to the school dance with a group of friends, including Lincoln Kennedy Zhang.

Vining conned Kissick into helping her serve as a chaperone. She was wearing a late-summer dress she'd bought and strappy high-heeled sandals she'd found in the back of her closet. Her grandmother, the former hairstylist, had done her hair in an upsweep.

They stood in the shadows of the school's multipurpose room, watching Emily slow dance with Ken.

Vining told Kissick, "I apologized to Pearl Zhang for accusing Ken of being in a gang."

"How did that go over?"

"Better than I expected. She apologized to me, too, for her cousin Marvin."

He nodded.

They stood listening to the music, their fingertips interlaced. After a while, he asked, "Would you like to dance?"

"I would, except I think that Emily would be embarrassed."

"She's not paying attention."

They both looked to see Emily and Ken gazing into each other's eyes as they danced.

"Oh-oh," Vining said.

"Oh-oh is right. Come here, you." He pulled her onto the dance floor. As they swayed to the music, he said, "Did I tell you that you look fantastic?"

"Yes," she grinned.

"It's worth saying again. You look fantastic."

"Thank you."

He nuzzled her neck.

She squealed a little when it tickled. "Watch yourself, Detective. There are minor children present."

He held her close. "Nan, promise me one thing. No more lies?" He said it as a question.

"Never again," she replied, and at that moment, she meant it. She leaned her head against his shoulder and closed her eyes. She saw no nightmarish scenarios playing on the backs of her eyelids. Instead, she glimpsed a happier future for her, Emily, and Jim.

There were more words to say, many more, but they could wait. They had time. The song ended. The dancers clapped. One couple was not quite finished. Kissick tipped Nan backward into a dramatic dip. She arched her neck and pointed her toe.

Emily watched the whole thing. While she expressed to her friends that she was mortified, secretly she was delighted.

Read on for an excerpt from

LOVE KILLS

by Dianne Emley

Published by Ballantine Books

TWO

"T hanks, honey, but I'm just going to relax at home. I've cracked a bottle of Veuve and I'm going to enjoy some peace and quiet."

Catherine "Tink" Engleford strolled around the swimming pool in the backyard of her estate in Pasadena's San Rafael hills while talking on her BlackBerry to her girlfriend and waving a glass of champagne.

"Cheyenne didn't call you?" Tink pursed her lips. The Juvederm treatments she'd had in the lines around her mouth allowed the fifty-year-old skin to crinkle slightly. "I agree. She's not the best personal assistant." She laughed.

"Well, she's had a hard life and I'm trying to give her a leg up. We can all use help now and then, right? But yes, it's time for another talk with her when she gets back. She's in Ventura for the weekend and I'm enjoying the peace and quiet."

She changed the subject. The less certain of her friends knew about her life, the better. "Kingsley's out of town, too, on a business trip to Dubai. He's great. It's too soon for us to be spending holidays together anyway. Honey, don't worry about me. I'm fine being alone on Easter. I haven't been alone until just now. I went to the nine a.m. service at Church of the Angels and then I had brunch at

Annandale with golfing friends. I'm looking forward to curling up with a good book."

Tink let out a yelp when her stiletto heel teetered on an uneven piece of flagstone. "Dammit! Spilled champagne on my new St. John." She brushed her bright pink jacket with her fingers and walked across the patio to the open bottle of Veuve Clicquot in an ice bucket. She refilled her glass.

"Darling, I only had one tiny mimosa at brunch. Three of my four friends didn't touch a drop. Everyone was going on about how old they are. They can't touch a drop in the middle of the day, they can't wear heels anymore, blah, blah . . . It's like they're in their eighties, not their fifties. When did medical procedures become cocktail party conversation? I couldn't wait to escape and get home."

In truth, Tink couldn't tolerate the flashes of pity in her friends' eyes. The caring hand on her arm, the probing gaze, and the inevitable question, "How are you *doing*?"

She'd lost her twenty-three-year-old son, Derek, and her husband, Stan, in the space of two years. Her son, the product of her first marriage and her only child, had been killed in a motorcycle accident three years ago. Her husband of five years, the love of her life whom she'd felt blessed to meet in middle age, had dropped dead at the Annandale golf course just over a year ago. She felt like telling the concerned souls, "How the hell do you think I'm doing?"

All things considered, she was all right. Every day she got out of bed. Every day she did something to improve her mind, body, and spirit. She sought solace in traditional sources: her Anglican faith, good diet, Pilates, and yoga. She'd also dabbled at the fringes, into alternative philosophies and practices. She'd flirted with the occult. The pendulum was swinging back from the fringes. Lately, she'd been doing some spiritual housecleaning. Severing ties that she'd come to learn were more than simply not *nurturing*, but were downright *parasitic*.

She looked at the spot the champagne had left on her jacket. "I can't believe it's already Easter. Can you believe it? I haven't even started on my New Year's resolutions. How can you not make New Year's resolutions? Mine are the same as last year's. Lose weight. Fall in love. Meet my astral shadow."

The last one was a joke.

She paused. "Wait a second, honey." She pressed the phone against her chest and said to her guest, "This is a surprise. What are you doing here?"

Tink moved the phone back to her ear. "Honey, I've got to run. Everything's fine. Have a wonderful time tonight. I'll call later. Bye."

She walked around to the other side of the pool, still holding the phone. "Let's go inside. Looks like it's going to rain again." She started to walk past the chaise longues lined up side by side. "Want something to drink?"

Before she knew what hit her, Tink stumbled backward and fell into the pool. What had hit her was a long cushion from one of the chaises. Her champagne glass flew into the water. Disoriented, Tink found her bearings and started swimming for the surface. Her wool knit suit grew heavy and one of her shoes fell off.

Just as her right hand broke through the water's surface, she was again submerged. The cushion was over her torso, her assailant now in the pool and on top of her, keeping her from raising her arms. In shock, she opened her mouth and swallowed water. She began to panic.

Stay calm, Tink. Then she thought, *I didn't do anything to deserve this.*

She'd always been athletic and wasn't going down without a fight. She wrenched her body and kicked viciously, touching the side of the pool with her feet. Retracting her legs, she propelled off it, moving the two of them and the freaking cushion toward the shallow end. Her toes touched bottom. Then her feet did, too.

She clawed at the cushion and felt her acrylic fingernails tearing. Her long blond hair became tangled as she thrashed. Using her hard-earned flexibility and strength, she hooked a leg around her assailant's, shifting the balance. The side of her face broke the surface of the water. She opened her mouth against the cushion and was able to take in a strangled breath. It wasn't much, but enough to keep her going. She got her other leg around, encasing her would-be murderer's other leg in a viselike grip. They were now both sinking beneath the surface.

You're going down, too, asshole.

She knew it was false bravado as she felt herself growing weaker. Every cell in her body cried for oxygen. Then she felt herself floating off, observing from someplace that had nothing to do with water, earth, or air. The fight didn't so much leave her as it seemed silly to struggle any longer. Her legs released their grip. Her hands opened against the cushion. She was floating. She'd always loved the water. It will support you if you only let go. She was being moved along with the current. Everything except her lungs felt light and free. They burned. They were all that was holding her back. They would feel free, too, if she only released that last part. She saw her dead husband and son, smiling, like the last time she'd seen them together. There was something else, lurking at the edges. Was that her astral shadow? She finally let go.